I0646885

the Dream Merchant Saga

BOOK TWO
the Silver Sword

Written by
L.T. Suzuki
in collaboration with
Nia Suzuki-White

Book Cover, graphic design and layout:
Scott White
Shinobi Creative Services
www.shinobicreativeservices.com

Note for Librarians:
A cataloguing record for this book is available from the Library and Archives Canada at: www.collectionscanada.ca/amicus/index-e.html

ISBN 978-0-9867240-7-7

Acknowledgements

A special thank you to my husband, Scott for helping make this book a reality.

Dedications

*This book is dedicated to
all the 'Imago' fans
that have returned to share in
an all new adventure!
With much gratitude, Lorna.*

*To my sisters and brother,
Joanne, Kristina & David!
I hope one day that we can share
an adventure together!
Love, Nia.*

Contents

1

As You Wish

"Damn these bloody branches!"

This solitary voice was quickly overwhelmed by the boisterous *'caws'* as a murder of crows jostled for position atop the broken fir tree.

Gazing to the south, the palace in Fleetwood had shrunk to an indiscernible shape on the distant hill. The knights and soldiers that had poured into the courtyard armed with bows and arrows to down him as he took flight were now nothing more than insignificant specks.

Unwilling to break formation while still within the mortals' sight, Loken waited until he was confident no one in pursuit would be able to single him out from the crows in his company.

In a few more hours, darkness would fall. He'd be free to assume his usual form, unbeknownst to all with the exception of these ebony scavengers.

"It will take a miracle for the Princess to reclaim it now!" gloated the shape-shifting Sprite, as he struggled to keep the dreamstone in his grasp.

He ruffled his black feathers, heaving a weary sigh of relief as he settled high above the ground. His head bobbed, ducking to avoid getting smacked by the swaying boughs as the agitated crows squabbled and flapped about, vying for the choicest branch to perch on.

Loken's need to blend in, to become one with this flock was no longer possible as several crows nearest to him suddenly spied upon the golden chain and the bead of crystal clutched in his clawed feet. The fine links and smooth stone sparkled, reflecting the sun's light high overhead.

One especially brazen crow greedily eyed this shiny object. Its head cocked from side to side as it hopped along the branch for a closer look.

"Back off!" snapped Loken. In the form of a crow with honey-amber eyes, he tugged at the chain that had tangled around a twig. Yanking the strand of gold free, he fluttered to the branch below just as the bird's beak lunged to snatch up the crystal.

Fixated on the allure of the glittering gold and its luminous orb, the thieving crow moved swiftly before the others tried to steal away with this newfound treasure. It either ignored or didn't care that the amber-eyed one possessing this shiny bauble was *speaking* rather than *cawing* in protest.

"Bloody hell!" cursed Loken, his beak jabbing at the crow's head as it made another attempt to snatch the necklace away from him. "Back off or I'll kill you!"

Wishing to avoid another nasty assault, the crow hopped to a lower branch, its dark, beady eyes still fixed on Loken's prized possession. Thinking its flock mate was merely good at mimicking human voices, the bird remained undaunted, thinking of another way to acquire this treasure before another crow did.

Before Loken could issue another useless warning, the crow attempted to snatch the necklace again. It missed its mark when a larger bird wishing to make its own daring move landed on the branch Loken was perched on.

"Enough!" snapped the Sprite, transforming under a great show of light. This brilliance momentarily startled the crows nearest to him. Forced to take to the air, these birds landed on neighbouring boughs a safe distance away. Instead of flying off in fear of Loken's new form, the crows became agitated, cawing long and loud as they regrouped.

"Be gone, all of you!" demanded the Sprite. He unfolded his magnificent wings in a threatening gesture. As a much larger red-tailed hawk, Loken was sure to strike fear, if not respect, in their hearts! To his surprise, his ebony antagonists did quite the opposite. His transformation into a great bird of prey only caused these scavengers to act instinctively.

The crows summoned more of their kind, inviting them to help mob their winged nemesis. They began an aerial assault with two or more crows at a time diving at Loken. Those with enough courage or too stupid to anticipate the true level of threat from this raptor came in dangerously close; landing a well placed peck or raking his feathered back with their claws.

Loken swore beneath his breath, cursing his own stupidity for forgetting the number of times he had witnessed crows in flight, boldly harassing eagles much larger than the hawk form he now assumed.

Greatly outnumbered and confronted by multiple attackers, the Sprite knew he'd become even more of a target if he took to the air.

"I'll show you!" snarled Loken. In a flash of white light, he transmogrified into a deadly predator feared by all.

In an explosion of ebony feathers, the frightened crows erupted into flight as a large mountain lion abruptly appeared where the hawk once perched. Balanced on this branch, Loken lashed out. His curved claws slashed the air, batting two crows from mid-flight. His amber eyes shone with cruelty as he watched his wounded assailants spiral to the forest floor.

"Now that gives a whole new meaning to the expression *a murder of crows!*" mocked the Sprite, waiting for another bird to come within striking distance. Instead, the flock dispersed, heading off in different directions to escape this vicious creature.

"That's right! Fly away before I eat you!" hissed Loken's feline form. His fur bristled, standing on end to make him appear larger, while his tail twitched nervously, flicking to and fro.

He watched, waiting for another chance to kill. Struggling to keep the necklace trapped under his paw as the branch began to bend, Loken roared in fright as it snapped under his weight. He gasped in surprise as the crystal fell from his grasp, and he followed.

Lacking the grace and agility of a true cat, boughs and branches slapped at his body. Before he was able to assume his normal form, the Sprite smacked his furry head, striking it hard against the tree trunk. It would be the last thing he'd remember as his mountain lion form tumbled to earth, bouncing, banging and crashing through the branches and foliage until the Pooka's limp body landed atop the crows he had downed.

"Hurry up, will you?"

Rose unleashed a disgruntled sigh upon hearing Tag's demand. Her response was curt: "If you were to guarantee I will have fun on this mission, perhaps I would."

"Excitement, adventure and the uncertainty of success are the only things I can guarantee," promised Tag, as he paced the length of the room while the Princess prepared for their ongoing quest.

"Fine, but why must you be so impatient? The morning is barely done, and already, you want to leave the palace, traipsing on to who-knows-where, for God-only-knows how long," grumbled Rose.

Concealed behind the oak framed screen of silk as she dressed, Tag could still detect the sharp edge to her tone, even though her words were slightly muffled as her attendants helped her don a new gown befitting one of her royal status.

"My father once told me it is important for one to complete a task, if one had the nerve or was foolish enough to begin it in the first place," reminded Tag.

"You only say that because you want to see me suffer," responded Rose, squeezing out the last bit of air from her lungs.

"Believe what you want, but you know it's the right thing to do, Princess. And a little suffering can help build one's character."

"I will have you know I have plenty of character, more than you can shake a stick at! And no disrespect to your father, but need I remind you, he is long dead?" grunted Rose.

She exhaled completely, and then held her breath as Mildred, the oldest and heaviest of her attendants, braced the Princess by her shoulders. Alice cinched the back of the gown together as young Evelyn worked quickly to feed the ends of the satin ribbon through the eyelets, weaving it in a criss-cross pattern before tying it off.

"No need to remind me of that," sighed Tag, fondling the brass pommel of his father's sword he now proudly wore. Sheathed in a scabbard carved of oak and wrapped in a fine strip of black leather; it was suspended from a baldric that draped over his right shoulder to rest across his chest. This weapon was constantly at his left hip or never far from reach. "And even though it's true, that does not mean his words have lessened in importance over time."

"If the words of your deceased father still have that much sway over your actions, then I do believe Captain Yairet would tell you differently. Had he been here, he would recommend leaving me in the safety of Pepperton Palace, while you and Cankles venture forth to reclaim the *stone* on my behalf from that deranged, little Poobah."

"*Pooka*," corrected Tag, rolling his eyes in frustration.

"Whatever!" snapped Rose. "You know I am speaking of that devious, shape-shifting Sprite; the instigator of all this grief."

"I believe my father would have said that I should be responsible for keeping *you* safe, while the *three of us* venture forth to reclaim what you lost, especially since you were the real instigator of this grief from the very beginning. And this being so, how much longer are you going to take? We should have left by now."

"Endure a little longer, young Master Yairet!" Mildred scolded him from behind the dressing screen as she steadied Rose, while Evelyn gave one final tug on the ribbon before knotting it into a perfect, dainty bow. "Remember what your father used to say to all young men considering the knighthood?"

"Chivalry and justice are the hallmarks by which all knights should uphold for the greater good," responded Tag.

"Yes, but Captain Yairet also said: Patience is a fine virtue," reminded Mildred. "It is one that must be mastered to truly appreciate the meaning of chivalry. So be patient, young sir."

"I shall keep these words of wisdom in mind, Millie, but I am merely a squire well behind in my training to become a knight, no thanks to your royal charge," explained Tag, his words matter-of-fact.

"Never mind that," grunted Rose, "you cannot rush beauty. I will be done when I am done!"

"I'm not rushing *beauty*; I'm trying to rush *you* along."

"Har, har!" sniffed Rose, in mock laughter. "Court jester or not, sadly, you are still not funny."

"Well then, it's a bloody good thing you kept your promise to relinquish me of that role," teased Tag, a smug smile curling his lips. "Had it continued, eventually, I'd end up slaying you with my wit."

"And with a wit as sharp as yours, I am sure it would have been a lingering, painful death," muttered Rose, finally inhaling as she adjusted the bodice of her gown, "probably more agonizing than if I were to carve out my heart with a rusted spoon."

"You mean a *sharp knife*," corrected Tag. He resumed pacing the length of Rose's bedchamber as he waited for her.

"No, I do mean a spoon; a very dull, rusted one. That is how sharp I believe your wit to be."

"Oh, my! You're the one who should have been the court jester," decided Tag, not even glancing up at Rose as she and her attendants finally stepped out from behind the screen. "You were actually funny for once in your privileged life!"

"Who said I was being funny?" grumbled Rose; hands resting on her hips as she struck a pose in her new outfit. "So, what do you think? Lovely, yes?"

Tag stopped his pacing to stare over at Rose as Mildred, Alice and Evelyn framed the Princess.

"Beautiful!" declared the young man, nodding in approval.

"Well, thank you!" responded Rose.

"I was speaking of Evelyn. She looks absolutely beautiful this morning!" corrected Tag.

"Master Yairet, mind your words!" gasped the handmaiden. Evelyn's cheeks blushed with modesty. She was flattered to be the recipient of this unexpected compliment, but embarrassed for the Princess that she was not.

"You insolent knave!" snarled Rose. Feeling the cruel sting of humiliation, she snatched the sandal from her foot.

Tag dove for the door, slamming it shut behind him just as the heel of her shoe struck, biting into the wood to add to the grouping of indentations marring the door.

She could hear him chuckling as he shouted from the other side, "Cankles has readied our horses. I'll meet you in the courtyard, Princess!"

🍂🍂🍂

"Don't quite know how we're gonna manage with all this," said Cankles. He scratched his head in thought, barely glancing up at Tag as the young man skipped down the stairs of the keep, two steps at a time, to meet him in the courtyard.

"What is all this?" questioned Tag. He stared at three, large cedar trunks crammed so full the lids were straining against the locks and hinges, waiting to explode open.

"My clothes, of course!" Rose called out from the top of the stairs. She held up the hem of her gown, taking dainty steps as she followed behind her father and mother, King William and Queen Beatrice.

"I figured out that much, but what are they doing here? Are you thinking of donating them to goodwill?" asked Tag.

"Now, *you* are being silly," admonished Rose.

"Seriously, are you planning to take all this with you?" gasped Tag, his brows arching up in dismay.

"For the sake of practicality, yes, I am."

"How can travelling with your entire wardrobe be practical?" snorted Tag, giving his head an incredulous shake.

"Since I am not in possession of the *you-know-what*, it is not as though I can just wish for a new outfit each day. And if you must know, this is only a fraction of my wardrobe!"

"If you don't mind me sayin', Princess, and I don't mean to be takin' sides," chirped up Cankles, "but the young master's right. That'd be an awful lot of clothes you're packin'. Looks to be one for each day that you think we'll be away."

"Oh, no, no! You silly goose, of course not! Some I can wear several times by mixing and matching pieces, accessorizing to give the *illusion* of a new outfit each day."

"And just how do you intend to transport three trunks?" questioned Tag. "Our horses are not designed to carry these big, bulky containers."

"I know," replied Rose, pointing to four steeds hitched and ready to go, "however, those beauties are designed for *pulling*, hence the need for a sturdy horse-drawn carriage."

"I mean no disrespect to my liege and the good Queen, for they are your parents, but give your head a shake, Princess! Clear out those cobwebs messing up your mind," urged Tag. "In our last little adventure, how practical was a carriage? Do you not recall there were no roads suitable to maneuver a carriage through much of the lands we travelled?"

"Oh…" was all Rose could manage to squeak out.

"I suggest you get very practical and rethink what you plan to bring," recommended Tag, his hand patting the pack secured onto the back of his saddle. "Take only what you can fit into one of these and do so quickly."

"Are you daft? That is ludicrous! And impossible! gasped Rose. "It is impossibly ludicrous!"

"Excuse me, my lady," peeped timid Evelyn. "Seeing how light Masters Mayron and Yairet were travelling, I thought you'd be doing the same. I took the liberty of packing this for you… just in case."

Rose heaved a disgruntled sigh, and then she spoke: "I suppose a thank you is in order, Gwendo-"

Tag's scowl of reproach was enough to cut the Princess off.

"I mean, thank you *Evelyn*," said Rose, accepting the pack from her handmaiden. "I shall secure it to my saddle."

"You are welcome, Princess Rose." Evelyn responded with a polite curtsy as she smiled inwardly, knowing that after all this time, her royal charge finally got her name right, plus, she received a 'thank-you' no matter how forced it was.

"Cankles, secure this to my saddle," ordered Rose, thrusting the pack into her comrade's hands. "Tie it well, so it does not fall off."

"As you wish!" said Cankles, taking it from her without question. "Now, you best say your farewells, m'lady."

"Quite right!" agreed Rose, turning to face her parents.

"My dear, brave child," said the King. With a wistful sigh, he lifted her chin so he could gaze into her violet eyes, "no sooner do you return to our palace that you venture forth once again to face the cruel world beyond the safety of these mighty walls."

"Oh, father, I am no longer a child," assured Rose, speaking with confidence as she stood a little taller.

"I suppose that is very true with the approach of your sixteenth birthday."

"More important than your years is your maturity," added the

Queen. "Your conduct and how well you accept responsibilities are far more telling as to whether you truly are an adult and deserve to be treated as one."

"I do believe my willingness to embark on this quest speaks for itself," reminded Rose.

Tag said nothing to contest her words. He merely cringed inwardly, knowing full well just earlier this very day he had to goad the Princess on to right a wrong by assuming this task.

"I must say, I was more than a little surprised," admitted her mother.

"In a good way?" queried Rose.

"A very good way," confirmed the Queen, nodding in approval as her staff looked on. "I am proud my daughter is willing to undertake this mission to reclaim the *you-know-what* before something irrevocably tragic befalls this realm."

"So you better make haste, daughter," urged William. "Be on your way!"

"Alas, I do not know when I will return," lamented Rose. "Perhaps, if my luck holds, I shall be back in time for my birthday celebration."

"Take as much time as necessary," responded the King. "A day, a month, a year; it makes no difference."

"You jest?" gasped Rose.

"Well, you must admit, it would be irresponsible of us to intervene on your behalf," added her mother. "You did bring this grief unto yourself, after all."

"And if I do not return in time for my birthday gala, then what?"

"Though I am a powerful ruler, it is not as though I have the power to keep time at bay," responded her father.

"Worry not, my dear," said the Queen. "If you miss the grand occasion, in your absence, we shall make merry in grand style; celebrating in your honour."

"But what is *my* birthday party without *me?*" gasped the Princess, shaking her head in disbelief.

"When you return, should it happen after the appointed date, we shall have a simple, but elegant gathering to celebrate with a few worthy friends and acquaintances," answered her mother.

"But it should be a grand affair, being my sixteenth birthday and all!"

"Aah, but think of our subjects," urged King William. "I hardly feel they will be pleased if the monies we gather in taxes are used to orchestrate another gala. It is monies that can be used to fund other more worthy causes than another extravagant event only those of high society will be invited to."

"You will not just postpone it for now?"

"Oh no! The invitations went out long ago! It will be frowned upon in the worst way possible if we cancelled the gala at such short notice. Our esteemed guests have made plans to attend long before you chose to go gallivanting off after your ill fated encounter with Pancecelia Feldspar," explained the King.

"But I was duped by that Tooth Fairy!" insisted Rose.

"For some reason, your father and I remember differently, my dear," responded the Queen. "In any event, it is too late and in poor form to postpone the birthday gala now. Just make haste; do what you must and pray you make it back in time."

"I suppose," sighed Rose.

"You know we are right, but think of it as motivation to get the deed done," added her father. "If you meet with success and return home in time, you will be honoured in grand fashion."

"Then I will leave now," decided the Princess.

"A brilliant idea!" Her parents responded in unison, nodding their heads in agreement.

"I promise you, Your Highness, I will do everything in my power to keep Princess Rose safe," pledged Tag, as he bowed in respect.

"I know you will, Tagius," agreed King William. "You have always treated her like she was your own sister, so we know you will protect her from harm."

"I only wished there was a way we can send the three of you off with a contingent of knights for added protection," said Queen Beatrice. "An armed escort would guarantee the safety of all."

"True," said the King, "however, we discussed this matter at length. You know to do so will only draw attention that they are on some kind of mission. And, as this involves the magic *you-know-what*, the last thing they will need is utter chaos if word should get out it is what they set off to reclaim."

"Yes, I do suppose secrecy will be paramount in order to succeed on this quest," decided the Queen.

"Absolutely, Your Majesty," averred Tag. "The few who do know is already too many, especially in light of who is in possession of the item in question."

"True enough," agreed the King. "No point in raising suspicion."

"Then what shall I tell those questioning my presence as we search the lands for the nefarious Sprite?" asked Rose.

"If you are queried, you, my dear daughter, will merely disclose that you are visiting neighbouring countries in search of a suitable royal or nobleman to court you," answered her father.

"It sounds plausible," decided Rose. "However, I am not yet sixteen."

"That is why you will merely reveal that your father and I had already proposed potential suitors, none of which you were satisfied with," offered her mother. "To resolve this matter, we had asked that you find a suitor to your liking by your sixteenth birthday or we shall choose a future husband for you," offered Queen Beatrice. "And to add credibility to this tale, you can add that the young man will be presented during your birthday gala, if you return in time."

"Of course, there is no real rush to find a suitable candidate for betrothal," added the King, not relishing the idea of spending an exorbitant amount on a wedding anytime in the near future, especially so close to the planned birthday gala.

"I mean no disrespect, Your Majesty, but as plausible as all this sounds, perhaps there is another excuse we can use," suggested Tag, turning to the Queen.

"For what reason?" she asked.

For a brief moment, Tag was clearly flustered.

"What say you, young man?" probed King William.

"I am merely thinking of the political ramifications," explained Tag. "After all, you do not want to lead some poor fellow astray with hopes of marrying the Princess, when she has no intentions of doing so. False representation in this matter can potentially lead to a misunderstanding with grave, diplomatic consequences."

"I appreciate your misgivings and concerns, young man," responded Queen Beatrice. "But I do believe Princess Rose will be preoccupied with matters of reclaiming that certain little *bauble* to truly consider a young man for potential matrimony. Remember, it will merely be a ruse to disguise your true intentions as you conduct this search."

"Plus, I get the final say to any suitor my daughter wishes to present for this purpose, if this event should arise," reminded Rose's father.

"Still… if you can avoid raising the ire of neighbouring kingdoms or members of aristocracy hoping to take advantage of the benefits of an alliance through this type of *partnership*, you may want to consider another reason," urged Tag.

"You are so much like your father, God rest Captain Yairet's soul! I can understand your concern for diplomacy," said King William, nodding in appreciation to Tag. "However, love, arranged or otherwise, is fickle; as fickle as Princess Rose is. Any young man wishing to win her heart will discover soon enough he will be as welcome as an out-of-style frock and a pair of mismatched shoes, where my daughter is concerned. Such is the way of young love."

"Unless there is something truly outstanding about him, enough to sway my heart," chirped Rose.

"True enough, I suppose," responded Tag, ignoring the Princess' comment. "However, do you not think it's rather undignified to parade your own daughter before these potential suitors if our hand is indeed forced?"

"I am touched you are concerned of the possible diplomatic woes and for wanting to protect my daughter's dignity, but keep in mind, it is only a ruse that shall be called upon if there is a need for it," explained the King.

"Mind you, should she find a suitable nobleman or prince along the way, no harm in that," said the Queen.

"Oh, you are quite right, Mother!" exclaimed Rose, her hands clapping together in glee. "At the very least, he should be a handsome, wealthy land baron with a title no less than that of an earl."

"If this is so, then how will she choose without your wisdom to guide her in the selection process?" queried Tag, looking to her parents.

"You worry all for naught, young man," assured the King. "Throughout your childhood, you have always watched out for our Rose-alyn, separating wheat from chaff when it came to those wanting to befriend our daughter for all the wrong reasons. You have your father's good sense to help you discern those of good character from those sorely lacking in the finer qualities we value. If the opportunity arises, you can be of great service to her."

"Me?" groaned Tag. "Why me?"

"Why not you?" responded King William. "After all, you are of sound character and wise beyond your years. And of all the people in my royal court, you know Princess Rose better than any of her friends."

"I know we can trust you to select wisely if Princess Rose becomes too enthralled by a young man's handsome face to see what is truly in his heart," added Queen Beatrice.

"It is kind of you to have such faith in my abilities," said Tag. "But I hardly think I'm qualified in selecting a proper suitor for the Princess."

"Nonsense! Why would you say such a thing?" responded the King.

"Yes… why would you?" questioned Rose, staring at Tag through narrowed, suspicious eyes. "Not that I would even need your help to begin with."

"Because I would feel…" Tag's eyes fell to the ground as he

searched for the proper words.

"*Jealous?*" offered Cankles, scratching his head in thought as he pondered his comrade's reluctance.

All eyes glanced at Cankles, and then to Tag. His cheeks burned a fierce red as embarrassment threatened to swallow him up whole. The ensuing silence was broken as Rose burst out in a fit of giggles.

"I was going to say it was not my place to choose whom the Princess would like to find herself betrothed to," explained Tag, his eyes flashing in annoyance at Cankles for suggesting such a preposterous thing, then toward Rose as she chortled in ridicule.

"Oh poppycock, young man!" dismissed King William. "You have a good head on your shoulders, enough to warn you if an unsavoury character should come calling on my daughter."

"Yes... takes one to know one," Rose muttered beneath her breath as she gave Tag a cynical smile. Her grin quickly dissolved as she watched Tag's eyes. At first, they were narrowed in resentment, and then they were replaced by a mischievous glint as he reconsidered the King's words.

"Come to think of it, my liege, I do believe I have discerning taste, enough to know a fitting suitor for the Princess when I see one," decided Tag, as he gave Rose a wicked smile.

"Where our daughter is susceptible to words of flattery and can be easily swayed by a young man exuding a plentitude of charm and good looks, we are confident you will see beneath this polished veneer to know what lies beneath a handsome exterior," stated Queen Beatrice.

"Yes, I am not easily fooled like some," agreed Tag.

"Should that time come, I have no doubt about it, young man," acknowledged King William. "But for the time being, you will see to it that my daughter maintains her good character and virtue. If she is made to call upon this ruse, you will see to it that any potential suitor remains on his best behaviour."

"You mean I am to act as a chaperone?" questioned Tag, a mischievous grin spreading across his face as he pondered the possibilities. "To accompany the pair if she is invited to a social function with the bloke?"

"Especially if the young man wishes to see her alone," cautioned King William. "After all, we do not need to send the people's tongues a-wagging!"

"That will not happen! But a *bloke?* Only an ordinary fellow of average or below standing in life falls in the 'bloke' category. Hardly a serious contender worthy of my hand in marriage, where I am concerned!" grunted Rose. "I do have taste, after all!"

"A taste that tends to lean toward the superficial," added her mother. "You need a young man with substance, something I am confident young Master Yairet will be more than capable of helping you to discern."

"Oooh, how excitin'! I feel like the village matchmaker!" giggled Cankles, delighting at the prospects of pairing the Princess up with a suitable gentleman of proper lineage and adequate wealth.

"You are many things to the village, but you are certainly not the village matchmaker," grunted Rose, shooting a baleful glance at this simpleton of a man.

"Just use your good wisdom and common sense, Tagius," urged the King. "It will never steer you wrong."

"Worry not, Your Highness. I will do exactly that," promised Tag. "I will keep Princess Rose's best interest in mind at all times."

2
A Strange Twist of Fate

A painful groan drifted through the twilight forest as day prepared to surrender to the night.

Loken stirred from this unnatural sleep, his tortured body still aching from the treetop tumble. The same boughs and branches that thrashed his mountain lion form to cause him such pain now were the same ones to break what was sure to have been a fatal fall.

A low growl rumbled in Loken's ears, forcing him fully awake. His eyes flashed open as a pointed snout and a wide, heavily clawed forepaw shoved aside the Sprite's large, feline body to get to the second crow still trapped beneath him.

Loken roared in surprise, springing to all fours as an old badger jumped back with a start, surprised this cat was suddenly wide awake and completely lucid. Though momentarily startled, the badger stood its ground, unwilling to pass up on such an easy meal. The coarse hairs on its back bristled, making the animal look larger before his mountain lion adversary.

Rather than limping off, the adrenaline coursed through Loken's body. It fuelled his muscles and mind, making him unnaturally alert and coordinated as he prepared to square off against the badger.

A low, guttural growl rumbled forth from the badger as his stout legs braced for an attack. Its beady eyes darted between the dead crow he wanted to eat and the large cat steeling itself for a confrontation.

"You want this stupid crow? You can have it!" snarled Loken. Just as his paw was about to bat the dead bird to the badger so it would take it and run off, the animal attacked.

Thinking its opponent was about to claim its meal, the much smaller predator charged at Loken. Its loping gait propelled its stocky, low-slung body with unexpected speed.

"You crazy beast!" cursed Loken. He leapt back, but too late.

The badger's claws grazed his muzzle, tearing off several whiskers in the process. Loken swore under his breath as the badger made another attempt to run him off, away from its intended meal, if not out of its hunting territory.

Dodging the badger's powerful paw, Loken growled, retaliating with a swipe to its forefoot. The badger snarled; flailing about as it landed on its back. Realizing the threat this fully conscious predator now posed, it scrambled to upright itself. With a snap of its drooling jaws, the badger snatched up the dead bird, scampering back to its den. Dragging the crow along in its mouth, it left behind a trail of ebony feathers and droplets of blood.

Seeing that the badger no longer posed a threat, Loken decided he had enough of this feline body. In a flash of light, he willed himself back into his original form.

For a moment, he stood amongst a scattering of feathers, a black beak devoid of the skull and a pair of clawed feet now frozen as though perched on an invisible branch. These objects littered the blood stained earth. It was obvious the badger had consumed the first crow before he came to, and now, this was all that remained.

Loken rubbed his stiff neck and aching back, his translucent wings rattling with indignation for having to endure the badger's assault. His back suddenly straightened. His eyes darted about, searching the forest floor as he wondered, '*What happened to the dreamstone?*'

"Did you hear that?" whispered Rose, squinting into the shadows of the forest as dusk prepared to dissolve into darkness.

"I hear many things," answered Tag, listening to the ambient sounds of the impending night as a velvety shroud settled on this hinterland. "Crickets, tree frogs, the rumble of Cankles' stomach…"

"Do admit I'm feelin' a wee bit peckish," said Cankles, his hand rubbing his belly.

"No, not those sounds," responded Rose. Her eyes darted about, nervously searching the forest looming before them. "Listen…"

"Hmph," grunted Tag, hearing the distant cry of two animals engaged in a hostile encounter. "Sounds like a mountain lion is on the hunt."

"Or perhaps it's the one being hunted," offered Cankles.

"I was not speaking of *that* sound," said Rose. "I am talking of the one much closer to us. Listen…"

"Who, who, whoo… who, who whoo!"

"There it is again!" said Rose, reining her mare in as she motioned the others to do the same. "Did you hear it this time?"

"Of course I did. It's called an owl!" scoffed Tag, urging his steed on.

"No…" argued Rose. She listened above the steady plod of their horses' hooves and the chorus of crickets and tree frogs chirping in symphony. "It cannot be."

Again, this mournful call echoed through the forest before them: *"Who, who, whoo…"*

"It's an owl," insisted Tag.

"No, it is not!"

"And just why not?" questioned Tag.

"It's too perfect… like a man trying to *sound* like an owl," decided the Princess, nodding judiciously. "Yes… an *owl-man!*"

"Trust me, it's an owl. In fact, it sounds just like a male great-horned owl, calling to defend its territory from the other owls in the area," countered Tag.

"I think you are being fooled," responded Rose. "What owl sounds just like a human being saying *'Who, who, who?'* It is an owl-man… or that Poopa thingy pretending to be an owl."

"Methinks you're either tired, loopy, or both," chuckled Tag, shaking his head in dismay.

"Do not mock me! It sounded too human to be an owl!"

Once more, this call sounded, reverberating through the impending night.

"What say you, Cankles? Is it an owl or is it what the Princess says, an *owl-man?*" Tag asked while trying not to laugh in Rose's face.

"Most definitely, it's an owl," confirmed Cankles, speaking with conviction.

"You are both fools! It is not an owl! It is saying *'who'* too perfectly to be an owl."

"What do you expect an owl to say? *'Wha – what, what?'*" teased Tag.

"Or how about *why? W-hy, why,* for that matter," hooted Cankles, chortling at his own joke.

In utter frustration, Rose rolled her eyes to the heavens. "You are both idiots! Think again. Since when does an owl sound like a man asking *who?*"

"I hate to say this, but you're the one sounding like an idiot," retorted Tag. "That *is* an owl! It's just that you so rarely hear them as you don't venture out of the palace as often as you should."

"Quite right, my friend," agreed Cankles. "You really haven't been exposed to the great outdoors as you should, Princess, so you're just not used to hearing the sounds of nature."

"What's so great about being out here?" grumbled Rose, swatting at a cloud of black flies hovering before her. "Just mark my words! That was no owl! It was probably some crazy person stalking us or that Poodo thing pretending to be an owl."

"It's called a *Pooka*, for pity's sake!" corrected Tag. "And why would that Sprite be here? He's got no reason to follow us now that he has the dreamstone."

"Who can say?" answered Rose. "All I know for sure is that he assumed the form of an owl before, he can do it again."

"Which begs the question: why would he do it again?" grunted Tag. "He'd have to be out of his mind to show up anywhere near you after you picked him out of the tree with your sling."

"I believe evil and demented go hand-in-hand," reasoned the Princess, her hand reaching back to pat the bag containing her weapon and the suede pouch carrying the never-ending supply of steel balls. "He probably figures those as gullible as you two are would assume exactly that, so he would be safe to take this form to keep watch over us!"

"As I said before, that Pooka has no reason to remain anywhere near Fleetwood, now that he has the crystal," argued Tag. "In fact, if I were a betting man, I'd say he has every intention of delivering it to the Sorcerer."

"Well, you don't bet, nor are you a man, so I would say you're wrong on your assumption!" snorted Rose, her tone mocking.

"Oh, my!" gasped Cankles. "Those are harsh words, m'lady."

"Worry not, my friend," said Tag, heaving a disgruntled sigh. "I'm used to her harsh words and cynical attitude. I've developed somewhat of a thick skin having endured her for all these years."

"More like a thick head, if you cannot see the reasoning behind my words," grumbled Rose.

"Oooh, I'd say your tongue is sharp enough to fillet a fish!" exclaimed Cankles, his brows arching up in surprise.

"Too bad she didn't have the wit to match her sharp tongue," teased Tag.

"Well, this is just lovely! I now have two fools to contend with on this quest," groaned Rose.

"I'm the fool," reminded Cankles. He was proud of his new appointment, should he return, as Pepperton Palace's latest court jester with Tag's release from this posting. "He's the knight, or perhaps it's better to say a knight-in-the-making.

"Never mind! Enough of this foolish chatter," scolded Rose. She abruptly dismounted from her horse.

"What do you think you're doing?" asked Tag, glancing down at the Princess as she stretched her weary back.

"We are going to stop for the night – set up camp here in this meadow, and then in the morning, we'll venture on into this forest," answered Rose.

"I thought you were in a hurry to catch up to the Pooka and your dreamstone," grumbled Tag.

"Hush! Not so loud! There may be unwanted eyes and ears near to us," cautioned Rose. "Refer to the you-know-what as the *you-know-what,* if you please."

"Oooh, can't be too careful where the *you-know-what* is concerned, especially if the *you-know-whom* is lurkin' about," agreed Cankles, hopping off his mount's back.

"The Poobah?" questioned Rose.

"How many times must we say it? It's called a *Pooka!* If that's too hard to remember, just call it a Sprite," said Tag.

"Aah, but it is no ordinary Sprite. Because of its ability to magically adopt other forms, it is referred to as a Puka," explained Rose.

"I already know that," grumbled Tag, dismounting from his steed. "And I do believe you're trying to drive me to the edge of madness."

"At times, I believe you are already there, and it would not take much of a nudge to push you over that edge," scoffed Rose.

"Methinks it's gonna be a long journey," sighed Cankles, sensing the rising tide of animosity between Tag and the Princess.

"It'll be that much shorter if we push through the night, continue on to where the *Poo-Kah* and his feathered friends were last seen," insisted Tag, making sure to enunciate each syllable of the word Rose either deliberately mispronounced or could not be bothered to remember.

"True, however, this time we shall cover far more distance in less time as we have our horses from the onset of this quest," argued Rose. "And what is the point of travelling through the dark of night when there is the potential of getting hurt or missing clues that demented little creature may have left behind in his wake?"

"Though you should be commended for undertakin' this quest with such determination, young master, I'm thinkin' the Princess is quite right," stated Cankles.

"Good God! Appointing you to court jester has only served to bolster your intelligence!" praised Rose, nodding in approval. "You have become the voice of reason."

"Thank you, but I can't rightly say I am… just seemed to make sense to me, that's all," said Cankles, his shoulders rolling in a modest shrug.

"Well then, if anything, *you* sir, have more sense than *he* does," grunted Rose, her eyes narrowing as she glared at Tag.

"Fine! We'll rest for the night, but we move on at first light," conceded Tag.

"I am amenable to that," said Rose. "Can we build a fire?"

"Sure you can."

"*Me?*" questioned the Princess, her delicate brows arching up in surprise.

"We don't need one on this night, but if you want a fire, I won't stop you from making one," responded Tag, as he untied his pack from the saddle.

For a moment, she mulled over his words. The first and last time she built a fire, it was in a contest against Tag. She won, even out-hunting him for grouse. However, it was at the cost of singeing her hair and almost burning her eyebrows off when she tried to coax the sparks into a flame.

"You will not be building it for me?" she asked hopefully.

"Why should I?"

"What happened to being chivalrous?"

"I'm not yet a knight, so it's a quality I'm still working on."

"That is just a poor excuse for avoiding a little work," countered Rose.

"You have two hands and I know you're capable of making your own fire, if you really wanted to," reminded Tag. "And if it's that *little work* required to build a fire, then you're just being lazy."

"Excuse me, but it is called being a *princess!*"

"Then I suppose *princess* and *lazy* means the same thing," teased Tag.

"It means; I do not partake in such menial tasks. It is below my station! You would never see me doing such things in and about the palace."

"At this moment, you are far from the palace." Tag rolled his eyes in frustration. "And you're the one making excuses just so you can be lazy and avoid the work."

"If you're concerned that Tag or I might speak of this to others, no worries!" promised Cankles. "We won't breathe a word of this to those back home, if you be wantin' to do this."

"I am *not* lazy! But tell me this: Since when does anyone of royal blood stoop down to the level of a commoner to undertake such labour intensive, menial tasks?"

"What happened to wanting to pull your weight and doing your share?" countered Tag, even though deep down, he was not surprised she'd revert to her old ways. "I seem to recall we got much more accomplished when we all shared in the duties."

"But that was before everybody, my parents included, mistook me for an old peasant woman. I am a princess in every respect; therefore, I shall be treated accordingly now."

"You are a princess who got far more than she bargained for," teased Tag. "It's like before; you want *and* need our help, but it'll require cooperation on your part, princess or not."

"You will not waver on this, will you?" questioned Rose, heaving a disgruntled sigh.

"And rightfully so!" announced Tag.

"I gotta admit the young sir is right, m'lady. It's only fair after all," chirped up Cankles.

"So much for being the voice of reason," muttered Rose, shaking her head in woe as she glared at the man for siding with Tag.

"I'll meet you half way," offered Tag, digging about his pack for a piece of flint. "If you help gather firewood, I'll get a fire going for you."

Rose was about to sulk once more until Cankles spoke up: "I'll give you a hand with collectin' wood, Princess."

"That sounds fair, especially as I was going to share the fire with you two anyway," decided Rose.

"I'll clear out a safe place to build a fire; gather some sticks and twigs for kindling as I already have some dry bulrush down to use as tinder," offered Tag.

"Good plan," said Rose, as she turned to point at Cankles. "You, come with me. I shall pick, you will carry; being that you're so much stronger than I am."

It was not so much this gangly stick of a man was all that much stronger than her, but Rose just did not relish the idea of lugging an armload of wood in the dark, especially when it's too hard to see what assortment of slugs, spiders and other creepy crawlers made their home on or under these pieces of wood. In her way of thinking, she could use just her finger and thumb to carefully pick up firewood, thereby reducing possible contact with these creatures. Any living thing clinging to the wood would be Cankles' concern, not hers, if he was the one appointed to carry the stack.

"Sounds like a good plan to me," praised Cankles. "Quickly now, before we lose the last of the sun's light.

Loken forced down the lump catching in his throat as panic gripped his heart. His anxious eyes scanned the dimming forest floor for the precious dreamstone. Wiping away the beads of sweat from his forehead, he rifled through a pile of leaves littering the base of the tree, hoping against hope it had fallen with him.

Nothing... Not even the broken links from the gold chain.

"Where can it be?" Loken wondered aloud.

Trying to recount the last time he saw the dreamstone, he contemplated how he came to be on the forest floor. The thought suddenly occurred to him the magic crystal was still somewhere in the tree, perhaps snagged on a branch.

Pushing off the ground, the Sprite fluttered to the boughs overhead. Glancing up, he could see the trail of bent and broken branches that marked his abrupt descent. It promised to be a long, exhaustive search if this hunt took him all the way up to the treetop again. And judging from the fall, he was confident had he remained conscious, it would have been a terrifying tumble punctuated by words of high profanity each time he bounced off a sturdy branch with little give.

Alighting upon the lowest bough, Loken commenced his search. Scrutinizing every branch and twig in the wake of his fall, he desperately flew and scrambled, traversing in a back and forth pattern, higher and higher. He raced against the impending darkness, hoping the sun's waning light would be enough to guide him to his missing treasure as he hunted about for that telltale golden glint of the necklace or the shine of the crystal orb.

Half flying, half scrambling, the Sprite ventured ever higher into the tree, his anxious eyes searching each branch for his lost prize. Already halfway up, Loken panted from the exertion as he journeyed on. Dogged by frustration, he slammed his tiny, balled fist against the tree trunk. By a strange twist of fate, the dreamstone he worked so hard to steal away with was nowhere to be seen.

"Curse those bloody crows!" Loken muttered beneath his breath as he shook the pain from his hand. His frustration mounted as he raced against the setting sun. It seemed that fate indeed was conspiring against him as every twig and gust of wind, no matter how small, caused him grief as he ascended.

Between being battered by the boughs and jabbed by the fir needles as the branches swayed at the mercy of the wind, his disheveled head of hair kept snagging on overhead twigs or blew across his face. These strands would obstruct his vision as his wings thrummed, fighting against the evening breeze whispering through the tree.

Raising his hand to swipe the hair out of his face, he winced in pain as strands clotted with drying tree sap were plucked from his scalp. Tangling onto fir needles, his hair would stay as a reminder of his passing and on-going struggle.

If indeed one of the crows had made off with the dreamstone, his chance of recovering the crystal was slim to none. Considering he didn't see which bird made off with his prize, nor was he conscious to see in which direction the culprit flew, Loken's chances were fading as quickly as the light of the sun.

Before launching his body off yet another branch, the Sprite bit off a small chunk of pitch. This sticky tree sap oozing from a crack in the deeply fissured bark had dried into a gummy, sweet substance. It would provide Loken with some badly needed energy as he resumed his search. He let it slowly melt on his tongue, rather than to chew on it, getting it stuck to his teeth like warm, soft taffy. This bit of sustenance was enough to settle his rumbling stomach as he resumed his search.

Ignoring his muscles that ached in protest from the previous fall, Loken glanced about, scrutinizing the nearby twigs. For a fleeting instant, the thought of abandoning this search entered his mind. He knew if he were to be extra cautious, it would be easy enough to avoid the Sorcerer's wrath for failing to deliver the dreamstone. His ability to take on other living forms would make it terribly difficult, if not impossible, for Parru St. Mime Dragonite to locate him. Contemplating this idea, Loken decided that failure to return with the dreamstone would mean an abrupt termination of their agreement with potential for deadly consequences.

Loken was forced to resume his search in the impending darkness.

"See? Is this not better?" asked Rose, using her mare's saddle on the ground as a made-shift stool as they settled down for the night after a simple meal of smoked meats, cheese and bread.

"I'd say," agreed Cankles. Flopping back, his head rested on a soft tussock of grass so he could stare up to the heavens in relative comfort.

"More so because we all worked together," added Tag, tossing a log onto the fire.

"So now what?" asked the Princess.

"We sleep, for tomorrow will be an early day," answered Tag, lying back on his bedroll to join Cankles for some stargazing before drifting off.

"The stars have barely appeared in the sky. It is much too early for sleep," argued Rose.

"What do you suggest we do? It's not as though we have a lot of options," responded Tag.

"I can sing," offered Cankles.

"Do you know any songs?" asked the Princess.

"No, but I'm sure I can make something up."

"Never mind…" groaned Rose.

"*Sleeeep…*" snored Tag, attempting to plant a subliminal message in her mind to persuade her to drift off than to prattle on.

"We can talk," suggested Rose.

Fearing the conversation would centre around her, and only her, Tag closed his eyes. Inhaling deeply, he pretended to snore long and loud.

Snatching up a stick from the dwindling wood pile, Rose put it to good use. Taking this make-shift weapon, she gave Tag a sharp jab in his ribcage.

Tag coughed and sputtered; his eyes snapping wide open as he bolted upright.

"We can talk, but it need not be for long," reasoned Rose.

"Talk about what?" asked Tag, his eyes narrowing in suspicion as he glanced at her.

"I'm willing! I'll talk about anything, as long as it's not about girlie stuff," offered Cankles.

"What would you know about *girlie stuff*?" questioned Rose, staring with raised eyebrows at her comrade.

"Not much, that's why it's not a good topic of conversation for me," answered Cankles. "I'm not up on the latest fashion or what goes on in the female mind."

"Especially in *that* female mind," teased Tag, pointing at the Princess.

"That is because I am complicated; too complicated for a simpleton like you to ever understand!" insisted Rose, turning her nose up at Tag.

"Call it what you will," responded Tag, "But it is a subject I'd rather not broach. Now, if you want to talk about this quest and discuss possible strategies, then I'm all ears, and then some."

"Fine!" pouted Rose. Her arms wrapped around her legs as she rested her forehead on bended knees. "Then I shall keep my thoughts to myself."

As she sulked in silence, Tag counted aloud, "Ten… nine… eight… seven… six…"

"Why you countin'?" asked Cankles, scratching his head in bewilderment.

"Wait for it," urged Tag, as he continued his count down. "Five… four…"

"I do not understand," whined Rose, peering up at her comrades.

"I knew you wouldn't even make it through ten seconds before you started yakking away," grunted Tag.

"I had something thought-provoking to share," argued Rose. "It hardly qualifies as 'yakking'!"

"Believe me; admitting you 'do not understand' is far from thought-provoking. You merely stated the obvious," scoffed Tag.

"Now, now, my young friend, allow the Princess to speak," recommended Cankles, wishing for nothing more than to maintain peace. "Obviously, she has something on her mind that weighs heavily on her conscience."

"Yes, I do," declared Rose.

"Go on then," coaxed Tag.

"As I was saying, before I was so rudely interrupted; I do not understand."

"I know," responded Tag, nodding in agreement.

"You do not even know what I am speaking of."

"I'm just agreeing that you do not understand, and coming from you, that is really not much of a revelation. In your privileged, but stifled life, there is not much of the real world that you *do* understand."

"You are not funny," grumbled Rose.

"Ah, but I *am* speaking the truth," countered Tag.

"If it makes you feel any better, you're in good company, Princess. There's not much that I understand either!" admitted Cankles.

"Coming from you, I do not take comfort in your words! Not in the least," snorted Rose. "What I was referring to was why those in the palace no longer viewed me as the wrinkled old prune of a peasant, and yet, their treatment of me had been less than proper. Even my parents, though relieved to see me again, seemed rather eager to see me off on this quest than to have me remain in the safety of the palace."

"Well, just be grateful they even bothered to acknowledge you as their daughter this time," said Tag.

"Methinks the deal you made with the Dream Merchant in order to claim the magic crystal to begin with may still be workin' on them," decided Cankles.

"But I no longer possess the dreamstone," reminded Rose.

"In my way of thinking, though what you say is true, you made a binding agreement in order to take possession of the crystal," reasoned Tag. "For now, I think it's a blessing the Wizard's magic still has some hold over your parents, even though the Pooka now holds the dreamstone."

"How can it be a blessing?" questioned Rose.

"Well, if they ignored you as they did with the onset of this deal you struck up with Silas Agincor, they'd either lock you up in your bedchamber just so they wouldn't have to deal with your attitude and ineptitude or they'd wash their hands of you, ousting you from the palace altogether."

"I suppose you have a point," sighed the Princess.

"If anything, their current state of mind where you are concerned is what allows them to so willingly let you venture off with us," determined Tag, as he glanced over at Cankles.

"So, all their good wishes as they saw me off was an act?" asked Rose.

"I'd say so. Look at it this way, Princess, they have to put on a good show before their staff and subjects that they are loving, doting parents," said Tag.

"Really?" gasped Rose.

"Why do you think they were so eager to see you off in the first place?" snorted Tag.

"But they were so convincing... like they truly cared."

"It's called putting on a convincing show," explained Tag.

"I suppose it was better than when they ignored me completely," decided Rose.

"Their indifference has at least evolved that they can pretend to genuinely care about you, than all out ignore you as you had claimed this was the deal you made with the Dream Merchant."

"But what about my attendants? They treated me with respect, like they truly cared about me."

"I hate to say this, but it is their *job* to act respectful and to care for, if not about, you," reminded Tag, "at least to your face."

"I'd say the power of the Dream Merchant's curse, for lack of a better explanation, is at half-strength just by the sheer fact you no longer have the *you-know-what* on your person," reasoned Cankles.

"You think?" asked Rose.

"Sometimes I do," admitted Cankles, nodding proudly.

"It makes perfect sense to me," said Tag. "I only pray that evil little Sprite doesn't figure out how to access the crystal's powers."

3
Rotten Luck

"Stupid! Stupid! Stupid!" Loken grumbled beneath his breath. With grim resolve, the Sprite continued his search for the dreamstone with nothing more than the cold, silvery light of the moon and the stars to guide him through the high branches. "If I could, I'd just wish for it to miraculously reappear in my hands."

His weary wings rattled in the night air as he bounced off a flimsy bough to launch himself higher. Peering between the multitude of twigs, his hands pushed aside the stiff needles to search about for a glint or glimmer of light that would betray the whereabouts of the precious crystal.

Loken drew another weary breath as his stared into more darkness. "I'll go blind at the rate I'm going."

In a swell of golden light that pushed against the darkness, Loken transformed, shrinking down in size to become a firefly. In this new beetle form, he raised the smooth, hard shell protecting his wings folded beneath. Spreading them open, he fanned them several times, working out the creases until he was ready for flight. The warm glow emanating from his new firefly posterior provided enough ambient light to show the way and to illuminate the immediate area.

Leaning into the light breeze, he took to the air, circling the tree as he checked every branch as he ascended. The light glowing from his insect abdomen was just bright enough for Loken to see the branches as well as the glint of the crystal or chain, if it was near to him.

Following the path of broken branches along the trunk, Loken was nearly at the top and losing hope quickly. It was just as he feared. Either one of the crows stole away with the dreamstone or it had landed on the forest floor with his fall, only to be stolen by a human or an animal drawn to such shiny objects.

"Damn it all!" cursed Loken, his compound firefly eyes seeing all around him. "Why me? Why does misfortune always hound me?" A sudden glimmer of light reflecting off his bioluminescence caused his tiny heart to swell with renewed hope. Hovering closer for a better look, just as he alighted upon the twig, this glint of light abruptly vanished as the gold chain slipped from the fir needles it had snagged on.

Loken's wings buzzed as he dove down to grab the necklace, all the while hoping the dreamstone remained attached and intact. His six legs latched onto the last gold links before they fell from his reach, but the weight was too much. He lurched forward, his wings fluttering madly as he pulled, frantically trying to hoist up the crystal. Instead, he fell, plunging down once more. Before Loken could transform into a creature strong enough to hang onto the chain, but light enough for the tree branch to support his weight, his fall came to an abrupt halt. The dreamstone landed below, coming to rest on the fork of a twig.

"Thank goodness!" gasped Loken. In a flash of light, he assumed his regular form. His ragged wings shuddered as he released a sigh of relief. For once, his luck had changed for the better. He pushed aside the sharp needles, scrambling down to perch on the bough's twig that snagged the dreamstone.

For the longest moment, Loken stared at the profound blandness of this magic crystal. For something that was imbued with such great powers, it was underwhelming in magnificence. Though absolutely flawless and polished to smooth perfection, it lacked the dazzling brilliance of a fine, multi-faceted diamond. In fact, it looked quite unremarkable.

"So much pain and suffering for a stone that looks so very ordinary," grumbled Loken, heaving a weary sigh. He peered into the orb that was as big as his head, searching for a sign that this crystal was indeed magical.

"Perhaps, looks are deceiving," hoped the Sprite. "In your case, I certainly hope it is, for you have caused me so much grief."

Loken paused, waiting for the dreamstone to explain itself. Instead, he was met with utter silence.

"I suppose you are a magic crystal, not a *talking* one," decided the Sprite. With a puff of his breath, he used the condensation fogging up its smooth surface to wipe away the many smudges.

"Hmmm… I wonder how this works?" whispered Loken, staring at the perfect sphere. "And if I knew, I wonder what I'd even wish for?"

A blur of ideas flashed through his mind as he considered the possibilities, if this were to be his magic crystal for the keeping. *'Mind you… I was the one to find it. By rights, it should be mine. Why should*

I just hand it over to that demented, old coot? Knowing Dragonite, he probably has no intention of keeping his end of the bargain to begin with.'

These troubling thoughts permeated his senses. Why could he not just claim this dreamstone as his own? He would be free of the Sorcerer, once and for all. And if this crystal can truly grant him anything he could dream of, he would merely wish the Sorcerer never struck up a deal with him in the first place. Either that, or he'd simply erase the very thought from his corrupt, festering mind that this magic crystal even exists. The possibilities were endless! Loken's heart began to race with excitement.

"This *should* be mine," decided Loken, his words spoken with conviction. His arms wrapped around the sphere like it was a long lost love. "After all, I'm the one who went through all the trouble of stealing it from that foolish mortal girl, not him."

If the thought of betraying Dragonite caused the Sprite to feel even an ounce of guilt, it was yet to show, as Loken continued to convince himself this was the right thing to do. And if anything, where the Sorcerer was concerned, it would not be guilt to plague him for crossing Dragonite; it would be the fear of retribution.

"It would be a grand thing to be free of that necromancer... and grander still to get whatever I want, without having to grovel before him – to be at his constant beck and call."

Lifting the crystal by the bead cap, Loken inspected it, searching for any instructions that would reveal how to use the dreamstone.

"Nothing..." muttered the Sprite, thinking himself foolish for even bothering to look. "Of course the Dream Merchant would not be so careless as to leave instructions on how to employ its magic, but still... there must be a way of making it work."

Loken gave the crystal a sharp poke with his index finger, and then he stood back, waiting for something miraculous to happen.

The orb did not respond to this prodding.

The Sprite then slapped the sphere, thinking the assault would prompt it to glow with light as an indication it was functioning.

Again, the crystal remained unresponsive, not even casting a dim light from deep within.

"Stupid dreamstone!" cursed Loken. This time, instead of slapping it with a single hand, he smacked at it repeatedly. His impatience played out in a haphazard tune like the crystal was a cheap drum to beat upon.

After venting his frustration, Loken stopped this exercise in futility. He stared for signs of life, or magic, to appear within the bead.

"Maybe a gentler hand will do the trick," decided the Sprite. The palms of his hands were red and smarting after assaulting the sphere with unabashed abandon. Shaking off the stinging pain, Loken began to rub the smooth, cold surface, as though the growing friction would somehow activate the magic within.

As he set to work, a jumble of thoughts tumbled through his mind as to what he'd wish for, if this dreamstone truly did work as the Sorcerer insisted it would. The first thought to enter his tumultuous mind was to wish for his former life back, but it was so long ago it was hard to imagine himself as anything but what he had become; a shape-shifting Sprite with a notorious reputation for creating havoc. This thought was quickly replaced by another wish as his stomach rumbled with hunger. If he could wish for food, he'd conjure up a big helping of tiny fly maggots, lightly toasted on a hot rock to bring out their nutty, sweet flavour.

But as his mouth watered at the mere thought of indulging in this delicacy, the idea of having new wings, or at least the wings he had prior to all the ordeals he had endured, suddenly entered his mind. The hardships of life left them frayed and tattered. Loken often struggled just to fly in a straight line in even the lightest breeze.

For that one moment, he recalled how much easier it was to maneuver through the air when his wings were in pristine condition. In his mind's eye, he envisioned the translucent, gauzy wings that would rattle and hum in the air, like a dragonfly in flight.

"Oh, dragonfly wings would be lovely."

He longed to be able to fly with such speed and grace once more, to effortlessly glide, hover and dart about without constantly compensating for the tears and ragged edges that now hampered his every aerial move.

'It would be such a simple wish, to fly with ease again,' thought Loken. If it were possible, he'd wish for a set of wings more durable than the tatty ones he had now. His hand absentmindedly rubbed against the crystal as he imagined how he'd look with a handsome pair of new wings, unmarred by the abuse of daily living; a beautiful set that would impress the one he loved.

Loken yelped in surprise as a strange 'popping' sensation high on his back between his shoulder blades sent a shiver down his spine. His eyes widened in wonder as he gazed upon the reflection on the surface of the crystal orb.

"Wings! A beautiful, perfect set of dragonfly wings!" gasped Loken, launching off the branch as the dreamstone lived up to its reputation. "Unbelievable!"

The Sprite took flight, moving with incredible dexterity between the swaying branches as his wings shimmered in the moonlight.

"Woo-hooo!" shouted Loken, his clenched fists pumping the air as he spiraled about, only to dive down, weaving between the tree branches. No longer hindered by ragged edges that compromised his speed and agility, for the first time in longer than he could remember, he was as nimble as a hummingbird and almost as swift.

Effortlessly darting between the boughs swaying in this restless breeze, a breathless Loken alighted upon the branch where he left the dreamstone. He threw his arms around his precious find, embracing it as he kissed its polished surface.

"I love you! I so *looove* you!" declared Loken, planting another kiss on the crystal as his heart raced. "You're the best thing to ever happen in my life in a very long time!"

The Sprite rolled about on the branch, his feet kicking in the air in gleeful abandon. He broke out in a fit of giggles as his mind reeled with all the endless possibilities.

"Oooh! What to do? What to do?" gasped Loken. Drawing in a deep breath, he tried to contain his excitement. Now that he knew the dreamstone was indeed capable of making his wishes come true, Loken was now faced with deciding which of his dreams he'd like to make a reality come true next. He exhaled slowly, allowing his jumbled thoughts to clear.

"But how did I do that?" Loken scratched his head in thought as he tried to recall how he made this wish for a new set of wings come true.

"No… it cannot be as easy as that. Can it?"

He peered into the sphere, searching for traces of magic, but all he saw was his reflection highlighted by his beautiful, new wings.

Was it possible to have this dream come true by simply wishing for it? By imagining it to be real? It was the only thing Loken could think of that worked, for poking, prodding and slapping it did nothing.

"That must be it! I just have to imagine whatever I dream up by seeing it clearly in my mind while rubbing the crystal."

The idea of making Parru St. Mime Dragonite forget about the existence of the dreamstone was perfect, however, he'd have no way of knowing the wish worked until he was able to engage the Sorcerer himself to see if he did indeed forget about it. It was a move that could prove deadly to him, if it failed. He needed to test out this magic more just to make sure. It had to be a wish that he could see the results immediately to gauge its effectiveness.

As the moon continued to journey across the cobalt sky, the Sprite set to work. Loken closed his eyes, cleared his mind and as he rubbed the dreamstone, he pictured his body free of the many old scars and fresh abrasions. As vain as this wish seemed, it was a sure way to test the crystal. He imagined how he looked before he was cursed.

Once he had a clear image in his mind's eye, giving the sphere one more vigorous rub, he announced, "Make it so!"

Unlike the sensation he experienced when his new wings materialized, there was nothing, not even a mild tingling sensation to indicate something magical had just transpired.

"What the…" Loken gasped as he opened his eyes.

He examined an old scar on the back of his right hand; a permanent reminder of his nasty altercation with an angry squirrel attempting to evict him from its tree hollow. Instead of vanishing as he had wished for, this mark remained, as were the newest abrasions and scratches he acquired scrambling through this tree in search of the dreamstone.

"Why did it not work?"

The Sprite began rubbing the crystal as he pictured in his mind having a body totally free of all these imperfections to better match his handsome set of wings. As soon as he imagined how he would look, he declared: "Dreamstone, make it so!"

Loken heaved a weary sigh of disappointment as he opened his eyes. His simple wish remained unrealized as he stared at his reflection.

"Perhaps I cannot wish for two wishes that involve improvements to my person."

This time, Loken closed his eyes, cleared his mind with a deep, cleansing breath and proceeded to imagine a heaping platter of freshly toasted fruit fly maggots – crispy on the outside, sweet and juicy on the inside. With mouth salivating at the very thought of dining on this delicacy, the Sprite even imagined how it would taste.

"Grant me this wish!" demanded Loken. His eyes snapped open to discover the magic crystal denied him once again. Slapping his hand in frustration against its cold surface, his face reddened with anger.

"What the bloody hell is wrong with you? Are you broken or something?"

The Sprite glared at the dreamstone and his angry reflection. "Why am I even speaking to you?"

Loken plopped down next to the sphere; trying to recall what he had done differently that was preventing him from tapping into the crystal's powers.

After several more failed attempts, Loken came to this conclusion, "The dreamstone must be damaged… broken during the fall. That wish was the last one it was able to grant."

Lifting the crystal, he gave it a shake to see if something had broken loose with his vigorous rubbing. Holding it up to the light of the moon, his inspection found nothing, not even a hairline crack. "What rotten luck…"

As the midnight hour came and went, he digested this troubling bit of news and how best to take action, if there was any action to be taken at all.

'To pretend I never had it to break in the first place would be easy enough, but with my turn of ill fortune of late that crazy Sorcerer will only set me on another quest to reclaim it,' thought Loken.

The Sprite's chin rested on tented fingers as he considered his limited options. *'Mind you, if I delivered this dreamstone to Dragonite, telling him I did not test it out beforehand, therefore, not knowing it was damaged to begin with it, it might be just enough to get the potion he promised. I can be free of him before he can discover this magic crystal is magic no more.'*

Playing over in his mind exactly how he planned to let this act of deception unfold, Loken made his decision. *'That is exactly what I'll do. Deliver this dreamstone as Dragonite insisted, trade it for the potion, and then flee before he can figure out it is damaged and useless.'*

"It must be midnight by now," whispered Rose, staring at the ghostly pale orb shining against the velvety dark sky.

"By my reckoning, it's well after that," determined Tag, wanting nothing more than for the Princess to stop talking so he could fall asleep. "So why don't you just get some rest?"

"I am trying, but I keep thinking about the…" Rose glanced about, searching for an invisible foe before whispering, "the dreamstone. I had one wish left before day's end and now, if it were in my hands at this moment, I would have three more at my disposal."

"And had this been so, I'd have you wish us home and this travesty of a quest over with," stated Tag, rolling over to his side so his back was to her. "In fact, if it were possible, I'd have you wish that I was a full-fledged knight rather than a squire scrambling to catch up with the other boys my age well on their way to joining this brotherhood."

"What is it with you and becoming a knight?" snapped Rose. "There is more to life than that you know?"

"Not in mine. That is what I *should* be; what I was meant to be until – "

"Heard it all before," interjected the Princess, raising her hand for silence.

Before Tag could remind her how it was her fault he had fallen far behind on his formal training, Rose changed the subject. "Never mind that! What about me?"

"What about you?" grumbled Tag. "It's not as though you can wish for that dreamstone to be back in your hands. You should just accept the simple fact that the only way to get it back now is to hunt the Pooka down. Steal it back from him."

"I guess…"

"Well, I *know*," stated Tag, flopping onto his back as Cankles snorted, exhaling loudly as he drifted off to settle back into a sound sleep. "There is no other way around this little problem you created."

"I did not create it on purpose."

"You wanted that damned crystal! You just didn't expect things to end so badly for you."

The Princess knew there was no point in arguing with Tag, but she had no intention of admitting to him that he was correct.

"Do you think that cursed little Spritie thing has used the dreamstone yet," asked Rose.

"Try not to think about it," urged Tag.

"I cannot help it."

"You don't even know if it can be used by another. If it can, maybe the Pooka won't be able to figure out how it works," said Tag.

"But if he did…"

"Then I'm sure his demented little mind would wish for something that would spell certain doom for us, considering he knows if anyone was going to try to reclaim the dreamstone, it would be us."

For a moment, Rose cogitated on Tag's words before nodding in agreement. "I suppose you are right. In no uncertain terms, he would wish for our demise."

"Well, so far, we're alive. The world is still as we know it," said Tag, glancing at their surroundings to note that everything remained unchanged.

"And what will happen if the dreamstone does work for another? After all, the Dream Merchant did warn me of the dangers if it should fall into the wrong hands."

"That is why we must make every effort to reclaim the crystal," explained Tag. "Whether the Pooka finds a way to use it or not, we must get it back."

"I suppose the one good thing is that the dreamstone is not in the hands of the Sorcerer."

"True enough," agreed Tag. "And we must make sure it stays that way – keep that Sprite from delivering it to him."

"But what if we fail?"

"Do not even entertain the thought," urged Tag, as he shook his head. "It will be hard enough trying to locate that little thief. We need not add to our woes."

"Do you truly believe he has yet to manipulate the dreamstone's powers?" asked Rose, looking for reassurance.

"As I said before, we'd be dead if he had. All we can do is to search out the crystal and pray it does not come to that."

"Well, I shall pray that we reclaim the dreamstone before misfortune befalls us," said Rose.

"You do that," Tag responded through a great yawn as he rolled over in his bedroll to fall asleep.

"I just hope it is not an exercise in futility. Praying is like making a wish without the aid of a dreamstone; just hoping that luck will be on my side. Do you think it is a waste of my time, Tag?"

Thinking he was deep in thought before giving her an answer, Rose waited for his response. Instead, all she got was a heavy exhalation of spent air as Tag snored, embraced in a deep slumber.

"Good answer," Rose grumbled in sarcasm, rolling her eyes in frustration. She released a loud, dreary sigh, hoping it would rouse Tag.

The Princess was rewarded with another of Tag's long, low snores, joining Cankles in a nasal symphony that droned in the night air. It was evident there would be no more intelligible conversation with him on this eve.

To wake Tag with a poke or a prod of a stick would be tantamount to rousing an irritable, old bear from its hibernation well before the coming of spring. Rose decided it was time for her to go to sleep than to invite trouble.

For the longest moment, she lay on her back; eyes squeezed shut as she tried to convince herself to sleep. With the hard ground poking through the bedroll to accost her delicate shoulder blades, Rose flopped onto her side, and then onto the other side. She tried to block out the incessant chorus of crickets and tree frogs, clamping her hands over her ears to smother these nocturnal sounds.

Finally wriggling about in a position that was somewhat comfortable, Rose attempted to fall asleep, but sleep proved to be elusive.

"I know, I shall count sheep," she whispered to herself.

Closing her eyes, a flock of fleecy white sheep waited to bounce effortlessly over a split-rail fence, one-by-one. As each woolly beast leapt over, the Princess kept count, but just as the monotony of this was causing her to drift off, a sheep cleared the hurdle as it bleated: "*Baaad* girl."

The next sheep bounded over the fence, this time bleating: "*Naaaghty*", but just as it cleared this obstacle, it glanced back at her. Rose gasped! Her eyes snapped wide open as the sheep staring back at her bore a man's head. It had an uncanny resemblance to Silas Agincor, the Wizard better known as the Dream Merchant.

"For pity's sake… how am I to get any rest when my mind is already being accosted by nightmarish visions? I will never fall asleep at this rate."

Flopping onto her back, she stared up to the dusting of stars glittering across this dark canvas.

'If not sheep, then I will count the stars,' thought Rose. *'Beautiful, diamond stars are better to count than a smelly flock of sheep, especially ones resembling a crafty Wizard.'*

Studying the night sky, the abundance of celestial bodies made it difficult for Rose to begin her count. As her weary eyes scrutinized the constellations, the Princess unleashed a groan as one of them took the form of the evil, shape-shifting Sprite.

Rose squeezed her eyes shut. Why was this happening to her now? She never had problems falling asleep before. But then again, never was she faced with the ramifications of her ill-conceived ideas. She glanced over at Tag and Cankles. Releasing a dreary sigh, Rose realized the voice of reason and her conscience in the form of her two comrades were the ones to blame for her restless mind. A guilty conscience was still rather new to the Princess. Though it pleased Tag to see her accepting that her actions could have severe repercussions, especially for others, it was something she was still becoming used to.

Tag had told her if she did not have a guilty conscience for all the times she had caused grief to those around her, then it would make her something less of a human being.

In her own mind, being a genuine princess superseded all else in the natural order of things, but if being *human* and accepting all that it entails had greater bearing over her royal title as Tag insisted it did, perhaps being a princess with human and humane qualities was not such a bad thing. But at this moment, being human and dealing with the guilt that comes with it was costing her valuable time in lost beauty sleep.

If the dreamstone was in her possession now, Rose knew exactly what she'd wish for; to drift off into a peaceful slumber in the comfort of her own warm bed, nestled beneath a down counterpane until the coming of dawn.

In her mind's eye, she pictured the magic crystal dangling from a fine strand of gold still hanging about her neck. She could almost feel the bead's cold, smooth surface against her skin. Drawing in a deep breath, she closed her eyes. As she slowly exhaled, she pretended she was making a wish on the dreamstone.

She pictured herself back in the safety of Pepperton Palace, lounging in the comfort of her soft bed. Every fibre of her weary body began to relax, feeling as though it was swathed in the warmth of her luxurious, billowy goose down quilt. As she imagined wishing for a fitful night of sleep, the ambient sounds of the surrounding forest became nothing more than a distant drone as her mind floated off in a deep fog. As she exhaled another slow, deep breath, the worries of the day melted away. Her concerns about the Pooka and whether this being had been able to manipulate the powers of the dreamstone no longer entered her mind.

Rose did not even stir when Tag, in a cold sweat, bolted upright from a nightmare.

4

Broody 'ell

Tag's bleary eyes slowly opened to stare up at the bland, dawn sky. He yawned, wishing the sun was slow to appear on this morning. Between staying up late listening to Rose's incessant chatter and the strange nightmares he was unable to recall, he was feeling far from rested, and yet, he knew the desire to sleep longer was not a possibility.

He glanced over to where Rose slept; a small smile on her serene face as she continued to dream. Near her, by the now cold campfire, Cankles, his mouth slightly agape, snorted only to wake himself as he gagged on saliva. His eyes fluttered open as he coughed, sputtered, and then yawned.

"You're not lookin' so well, my friend," noted Cankles, propping himself up on his elbows to spy upon Tag. Usually, his comrade was the first to rise. He never wasted time lollygagging in his warm bedroll, preferring to prepare the horses for another day of travel. Instead, Tag lay there, staring with weary eyes, wishing he could fall back to sleep.

"How do you fare?"

"Tired… so very tired," admitted Tag, through another great yawn.

"What's up with that?" questioned Cankles, rolling up onto his feet as he stretched. "Didn't get much sleep last night?"

"I slept, but not well, my friend."

"Oh dear! Was my snorin' keepin' you awake?" asked Cankles, plundering one of the packs to prepare a morning meal.

"No more so than usual. I just kept having nightmares."

"Nightmares?" repeated Cankles.

"Yes, and I don't know if it was the same one that woke me several times or if they were completely different each time. Whatever it was, it kept me tossing and turning for most of the night."

"Bad enough havin' one in the night, but to have a spate of 'em in one sleep? That's got to mean something," decided Cankles.

"Maybe, but it can also mean nothing at all," responded Tag, refusing to believe it could possibly be an omen of sorts.

"I'm hopin' so. Probably just ate a bad piece of smoked venison, that's all."

"Perhaps you're right. Still, it's the strangest thing that I'd not recall a single memory of at least one of the nightmares," noted Tag. Throwing the cover from his body, he slowly sat up. "I kept waking up, and each time, I couldn't remember a thing."

"Well, I believe that if you were meant to remember, then you would. But in my way of thinkin', it was nothing more than my snorin' that kept you up last night. I know there were times when I'd wake myself up doin' just that; and that alone can be quite the nightmare."

"No… It was something more than your snoring," insisted Tag. "I just don't recall."

"Well mate, if you don't remember, it probably wasn't worth rememberin' in the first place," decided Cankles, tossing a water flask to his comrade.

Tag took a quick swig, swishing the cool water in his mouth before spitting it out.

The splattering of water hitting the ground near to Rose caused her to stir. Her eyes opened, only to snap shut as the cold sprinkling of back splash, a blend of saliva and tepid water flecked her face.

"What is the matter with you?" grumbled Rose, using her forearm to blot away the tiny droplets from her cheek.

"Sorry 'bout that," apologized Tag, wiping the dribble of water from his chin. "But it was about time you got up anyway."

"Fine, but there was no need for this!" snapped the Princess, tossing the bedroll off as she stretched.

"Oh good! You're awake," greeted Cankles. "I'll fetch you some brekkie once I take care of some business. I'll be back in two shakes."

She watched as Cankles darted off, finding some privacy behind a large tree to relieve himself.

"Yes, and a good morning to you, too," shouted Rose, as Cankles disappeared from sight.

"Sleep well?" asked Tag, tying his bedroll into a tight bundle.

"Slept like a baby, considering these primitive conditions," answered Rose.

"Better than me, then," said Tag.

Rather than asking him why the restless night, Rose plopped down next to the cold fire pit, waiting for Cankles to prepare the morning meal.

Rubbing the sleep from her eyes, she glanced up to see Cankles return. He hastily wiped his hands on his trousers before rummaging through the pack to serve up some bread and cheese to his comrades.

Staring at Cankles through narrowed eyes, she questioned him, "Your hands are clean, right?"

"You saw me just wipe 'em on my trousers," answered Cankles, tearing off a chunk of bread to toss to her.

"Good enough, then," said Rose, nodding in approval as Cankles used his hunting knife to shave off some hard cheese to serve with the bread.

"So, young master," said Cankles, handing over a serving of food to Tag as he addressed him, "what's the plan for this morning?"

Tag drew a deep breath, gazing up to the sun peering over the horizon. "Our only option is to hold the course; follow in the direction that damned Pooka was last seen flying off to with those crows."

"I do not know about you, but my eyes can only see so far," said Rose, washing down the bite of bread and cheese with some water. "I lost sight of them as they approached this forest. So where do we go from here?"

"Obviously, I have sharper eyes than you do," stated Tag. "Those birds landed on the tallest fir tree with its very top demolished by a lightning strike."

"So we go there?" asked Rose.

"Yes. I recommend that we travel as far as we last spied that tricky little Pooka; see if he left some clues as to where his ultimate destination is to be," responded Tag.

"I believe it is safe to assume that little miscreant plans to deliver the *you-know-what* to Dragonite," decided Rose.

"In all probability, yes, but we do not know for sure," stated Tag, stuffing a chunk of bread and cheese into his mouth. Chewing and then chasing it down with a gulp of water, he added, "There is a chance the Pooka has his own designs on the crystal."

"He is a tricky one, alright," agreed Cankles. "Methinks that little Sprite can't be trusted, even by the one who had entrusted him with the task of claiming the *you-know-what* in the first place.*"

"The most logical thing to do at this point is to go to where he had been seen last," suggested Tag. "From there, we shall see where fate guides us."

"Fate conspires against me yet again," groaned Loken. He rubbed his eyes as they squinted under the dazzling glare of the morning sun. Shining through the branches, the fractured sunlight piercing the shadows of the forest served to wake him, burning through his eyelids as he slept. "Didn't mean to sleep for this long."

By the position of the sun overhead, it had to be late in the morning by now, if not already the noon hour. The mishap that saw him take a horrific tumble from the treetop, followed by his confrontation with a cantankerous badger, and then reclaiming the magic crystal only to discover it was damaged had taken its toll on his body and mind. But more than he was physically battered, he was emotionally drained, exhausted by the abrupt elation that was immediately followed by crushing disappointment.

The long hours that followed to plot out and mentally rehearse his scheme to trick the Sorcerer passed rapidly, and when he finally drifted off to sleep, dawn was already creeping in, leaching the darkness from the sky.

The small knothole in the tree trunk he had found refuge in was perfect. He curled up for the remainder of the night, safe from harm, but it was also deep enough that the sun's light failed to enter to wake him until now. In hindsight, he wished he had slept out in the open where the sun would have shone down on him sooner.

Loken tossed off the soft hazelnut leaf he had used as a blanket, stuffing it out of the little hole so he could exit. Though now wilted, it still served its purpose, shielding him from the late night chills.

Yawning, he stretched his stiff shoulders as his new, crisp wings rattled before lifting him off the bough.

Loken smiled.

At least the dreamstone granted him one wish before losing all its magic. With ease and grace, the Sprite flew, maneuvering between the branches.

"Time to eat," muttered Loken, his eyes searched the bark for the pitch that oozed from wounds inflicted on the tree. The sap that seeped through to harden was the tree's natural defense, preventing disease and bacteria from entering the inner bark and heartwood to kill it.

"Perfect!" exclaimed Loken. He discovered a hardening glob of sap with a dead gnat preserved and suspended within. "Bonus! Extra protein."

It was the right consistency, not so hard that it'd pull out his teeth and not so soft that it was a runny mess. Still, it would be sticky, especially on his fingers so the Sprite leaned forward, using his teeth to gnaw off a small mouthful.

Like a delectable candy, Loken allowed it to melt than to get it stuck all over his teeth. This tacky substance gave him instant energy, his wings rattling with vitality. It was so delicious, his hunger overtook common sense. His teeth clamped down around a sizeable globule of pitch, filling his mouth with this syrupy sweetness.

"Broody 'ell!" groaned Loken, using his tongue to pry off the pitch gumming his teeth together. Sucking to melt it down, he then chewed at a slow, steady pace. It felt like eating hard, sticky taffy and his jaw was beginning to ache.

Using the tip of his index finger, he worked loose the melting clump of pitch adhering to a back molar. With his hunger temporarily sated, Loken glanced skyward. The sun had not slowed its journey across the sky and the hours of daylight would only dwindle if he chose to linger here.

Hopping off the branch the Sprite launched into the air. Maneuvering between the boughs swaying in the restless breeze, Loken alighted next to a bristling clump of fir needles. Kneeling down, he brushed away the debris to reveal the dreamstone. Hidden away from the eyes of curious crows and hoarding squirrels, the magic crystal rested on the fork of a twig, its gold chain wrapped around to keep it from falling.

"There you are, my broken beauty," said Loken, carefully unravelling the delicate, golden links. "It is time to take you home to the Sorcerer."

Using his hands to hoist up the sphere, he realized it would be too hefty for him to fly with in his present form. Even with the new set of wings it would still be difficult to fly with any speed or cover any distance. This would also make him an easy target for kestrels and other small birds of prey seeking an easy meal.

Just as Loken transformed into a flying squirrel, the sounds of hoof beats resonating through the air caught his attention.

"Curses, it's them!" Loken muttered beneath his breath as he peered down to the forest floor. To his frustration and dismay, there were the three human beings he least wanted to see. "How did they get here so quickly?"

Taking up the crystal by its bead cap, in the frenetic stop-and-go movements of a nervous squirrel, he ventured closer to see if he could learn anything of the trio's presence. He watched as Tag dismounted and his comrades followed him, hopping off their horses.

"This must be it," said Tag, crouching down to better inspect the forest floor.

"*It? What is it?*" questioned Rose, her perfect brows furrowing in curiosity.

"Look! Feathers… black feathers," replied Tag, pointing to the scattering of evidence amongst the leaf litter.

"They look to be from a crow," decided Cankles, picking up a glossy, ebony flight feather.

"That is exactly what it is," stated Tag, taking it from Cankles to better exam. "And look, this is blood."

"I'd say this is definitely from a crow," determined Cankles, as he picked up a stiff, black foot that was detached from a missing carcass.

"I'd say that is disgusting!" groaned Rose, recoiling in revulsion as she stared at the clawed foot curled as though locked in a permanent perching position. "And so what if it is from a crow and that feather has blood on it?"

"Since it is not obvious to you, Princess, remember the Pooka escaped in the guise of a crow?"

"So what?' responded Rose.

"The crows he made off with were last seen roughly in this area." Tag pointed to the top of the fir tree that had been damaged by a lightning strike.

"And the blood? And this nasty bird's foot?" questioned Rose. "Care to explain the relevance of these items?"

"Oh, I know! Perhaps the animals we heard havin' a spat last night were fighting over a dead crow?" suggested Cankles. "Wild animals do have to eat after all, and many resort to scavengin' to survive."

"Maybe if we are lucky, the crow those animals were fighting over was actually the evil Sprite," offered Rose. "Perhaps that little trouble-maker finally received his comeuppance last night."

"Why, yes!" agreed Cankles. "Maybe our troubles are finally over."

"Yes, and I'm a knight and she is a pauper," grunted Tag, shaking his head in ridicule.

"Is that your way of saying you disagree with us?" questioned Rose.

"As much as I wish it were so, I hardly think we'd be so lucky. I'm just hoping that the Pooka and the crows in his company came to roost here before venturing on."

"Well, obviously aside from the one that died somehow, the flock has moved on, but to where?" asked the Princess.

"I can make an educated guess or we can see if we can find a solid clue," suggested Tag. "Let's just take a good look around before we move on."

"Other than this scatterin' of feathers and this crow's foot we've found amidst these dried fir needles, I don't see anything else," noted Cankles, his eyes scanning the forest floor for some kind of evidence of the Pooka's passing.

Tag nodded in agreement, and then his eyes settled on a wilted, green leaf resting upon some brown, dried needles.

"What do we have here?" said Tag, his brows furrowing in curiosity as he knelt down.

"It is called a *leaf*," responded Rose. "A shrivelled, old leaf. What of it?"

Tag picked up the limp foliage, flattening it out in the palm of his hand to better exam. The velvety soft leaf was that of hazelnut. He glanced about, searching for a nearby shrub from where this leaf originated.

"So?" probed Rose.

"I see not one hazelnut bush in close proximity to this tree," answered Tag.

"Maybe the wind brought it to this place," offered Cankles.

"Or something else did," said Tag, staring up to the overhead branches.

Loken froze, hoping to go undetected. The inconspicuous pelt allowed this new animal form to blend in against the tree. His dark, liquid eyes did not even blink as he waited for these mortals to move on.

Tag stared, searching the shadows and studying the sun's light dancing through the tree canopy.

"What are you looking for?" questioned Rose, staring up into the tree, too.

"Don't know," said Tag, scrutinizing the trunk and the many branches. "I don't think it's by accident this leaf came to be here."

"But maybe he is correct," responded Rose, glancing over her shoulder at Cankles. "Suppose it was nothing more than the wind that blew this leaf here?"

"Possibly, but I doubt it," replied Tag, his eyes still searching about. "I just don't want to chance missing something in case that Pooka did leave a clue."

"What kind of clue? What should we be looking for?" asked Rose.

"Something... *anything* that speaks of that shape-shifting creature," responded Tag.

"Like that squirrel?" asked Cankles, pointing to the animal clinging to the side of the tree as it peered down at them.

Tag's eyes opened wide in surprise as he stared at the flying squirrel.

Upon being spotted by the trio, the animal suddenly skittered along a high branch.

"Bloody hell!" Tag gasped under his breath. "It's the dreamstone."

"What are you talking about?" asked Rose, her eyes squinting as she tried to spot the animal Cankles pointed out. "I thought you said it was a squirrel."

Tag's finger pressed against his lips as he cautioned her, "Hush! Keep your voice down."

His eyes followed the squirrel as he motioned for Rose to arm her sling.

"Are you mad?" gasped Rose. "If you think I am going to kill a cute little animal, you have another thing coming."

"It's the Pooka," insisted Tag, his eyes still trained on the squirrel darting along the branches. "And he's got the dreamstone."

"It can also be an ordinary squirrel that just happened to have found the dreamstone," argued Rose, as she reluctantly positioned a steel ball in the leather cradle of the sling.

"And remember what happened the last time you fell for a 'cute, little animal'?" asked Tag, reminding Rose of the infamous incident concerning the harmless, little bunny that attacked with murderous intent, savaging Cankles' finger in the process.

"Gotta admit, Princess, Tag could be right," whispered Cankles, catching the glint of sunlight reflecting off the crystal. "Can't be by chance that squirrel's got the dreamstone danglin' from its mouth."

"I will be so angry at you both if you're wrong," cautioned Rose, her eyes focusing on the squirrel as she took aim.

"Trust me," urged Tag. "It's the Pooka! Take him down now, before he gets away!"

The sling whirred as it spun by her ear; each revolution getting faster as Rose took aim. Just as she released the steel ball, the squirrel jumped. It sailed through the air, the membrane of skin between its wrists and ankles filling like the sails of a tiny ship as it landed on a neighbouring tree.

Loken squeaked in fright as the steel ball whizzed through the air, grazing by his broad, flat tail he used to steer his flight.

"Again!" hollered Tag, pointing at the furry thief making its escape. "Before it disappears."

Rose fumbled with the steel ball, scrambling to rest it in the sling's cradle before the squirrel made off for good with her magic crystal.

"Quickly! This way!" hollered Cankles, as he gave chase.

He watched as the squirrel made another daring leaping, landing on the neighbouring tree. It raced along the branch, the crystal clenched between its teeth before scurrying to the opposite side of the tree's trunk to avoid Rose's aim.

"See! I told you it was the Pooka," declared Tag.

"How do you know for sure?" questioned Rose, lowering her sling now that the many branches served to screen and protect the squirrel from her aim. "It could have been a regular squirrel that happened upon the dreamstone."

"There was nothing regular about the creature! That was a flying squirrel," reminded Tag, huffing in frustration.

"So?"

"Flying squirrels are nocturnal, they're not out and about during the light of day," explained Tag.

"How do you know?"

"When have you ever seen a flying squirrel active during broad daylight?" responded Tag.

"Never," said Rose. "But so what? Maybe they are just hard to see to begin with, day or night."

"Why do you think they have such big eyes? It's so they can see and move about under the cover of darkness."

"Oh…" muttered Rose.

"The little bugger's gone," announced Cankles. He held his aching side as he gasped for his breath. "Chased him as far as I could, but he made good his escape."

"Did he morph again?" asked Tag.

"Not that I saw, but he was headin' north, leapin' from tree to tree," said Cankles, blotting the beads of sweat from his forehead. "Still had the crystal danglin' from its mouth, too."

"Damn!" cursed Tag, shaking his head is disappointment. "This is not good."

"Well… at least the wicked little Sprite has not gotten as far away from us as we first thought," said Rose, tucking away the unused steel ball. "But why would it head north when the Sorcerer awaits him to the east, in the Bad Lands?"

"Who can say?" responded Tag, as he gathered their mounts. "Whether it was the quickest route, easiest route to facilitate his escape or he has designs on the dreamstone himself, it's best not to speculate. Instead, let's see if we can hunt him down."

"Good idea," agreed Cankles, giving Rose a leg up onto her mare. "Let's make haste, my friends!"

"Damn those meddling mortals!" Loken snorted in disgust. In a flash of light, the Pooka assumed his usual form as he rested on a high tree branch. "That was too close!"

He plopped down next to the crystal, his heart thundering in his chest as he fought to catch his breath.

In the distance, Loken heard the dull clatter of hooves galloping through the forest. Instead of fading away, they were becoming louder.

"Damn it all!"

The Sprite stuffed the magic crystal, as well as the chain, into a small knothole in the tree trunk. In another flash of light, Loken transformed into a hairy, brown spider. Anchoring the web to a limb, Loken lowered himself down in hopes that he'd be privy to secrets shared between the trio in pursuit.

Instead, the three on horseback charged through the forest, riding right past the tree Loken, as a spider, was suspended from. He managed to elude their eyes, but now, he was no closer to learning what their intentions were, aside from reclaiming the dreamstone.

As the horses and their riders disappeared from sight, Loken morphed, assuming his typical form. His wings fluttered, pushing him up through the branches.

He alighted upon the bough nearest to the opening he had tucked the crystal into. Reaching inside, Loken pulled hand-over-fist on the gold chain until the crystal emerged from the deep shadow.

"Idiots!" grumbled Loken, snickering as his foes continued northward. "If they only knew the dreamstone was broken. They'd end their search here and now. Mind you, better to allow them to engage on a fool's errand and suffer the hardships of another quest than to end their misery in haste."

Just as Loken was preparing to transform into a creature better designed to move undetected, unmolested and with relative ease through the tree canopy, an idea flashed in his mind. He was already in the Dimbolt Forest. The Fairy's Vale was a slight detour off his northerly destination. It had been years since he last ventured into the Fairies' realm. Perhaps it was time to pay them a visit again, or more accurately, to see Pancecelia Feldspar, the Queen of the Tooth Fairies.

'I'm already so close,' thought Loken, his fingers rubbing his chin in pensive thought. *'I believe a little side trip is in order.'*

5
Are We Lost Yet?

"We keep heading north until we have no reason to do so," decided Tag, as he spurred his mount on.

"But suppose there is no reason to journey that way," questioned Rose. "Suppose that *thing* has headed east to meet up with Dragonite there, in the Bad Lands?"

"Easy to assume," said Tag. "But what's to say the Sorcerer lingers in his former stronghold? After he turned tail, fleeing than to face defeat, I hardly believe he'd stick around, especially with Lord Silverthorn and the Dream Merchant in pursuit."

"Methinks the young master is right, m'lady," said Cankles. "I am far from brilliant, but even a simple man like me would not stick around after such a disastrous confrontation. In my humble opinion, it'd be downright foolish."

"I suppose," conceded Rose, "but if that is the case, then where would the Sorcerer flee to?"

"Dragonite is vermin, like a rat. Even rats will have more than one opening to their nest, should a snake or weasel come a-hunting," stated Tag.

"So you are saying that Dragonite has escaped, taking refuge in another lair far from his former domain?" asked Rose.

"It makes sense to me," responded Tag.

"To you, yes, but it could be completely wrong."

Tag reined in his mount, wheeling the stallion about to face the Princess. "It is bad enough having been made to embark on this quest with you when I should be training in the knighthood as we speak, but if you question and second-guess all my decisions, then why am I even here?"

Rose's mare snorted, coming to an abrupt halt as she confronted him. "It is not that I am questioning you, I am just having doubts as to where that nefarious little Sprite is heading, and if he even means to deliver the dreamstone to the Sorcerer."

"Look here! We must take decisive action right now. We cannot waste precious time speculating on the why and the where of Dragonite. Logic dictates that we head north; follow in the wake of the Pooka," countered Tag.

"Logic may not be so logical this time," argued Rose.

"Then what do you suggest we do?"

For a lingering moment, Rose mulled over this question in silence.

"Well?" prompted Tag.

"At this time, a suggestion eludes me."

"Therefore, rather than be stymied by indecision, we shall continue northward until we have evidence to steer us otherwise," stated Tag.

"Fine," said Rose, unleashing a dreary sigh. "Then north, it is."

"As I said, as soon as we have reason to move on elsewhere, then we will do so," promised Tag, his heels tapping the stallion's flanks to urge it on.

"Just how big is Dimbolt Forest anyway?" asked Rose, ducking to avoid a low-hanging bough as she coaxed her mare on to follow Tag's mount.

"Big enough," grunted Tag. "In fact, it is the largest forest in Fleetwood, even bigger than the Elves' Woodland Glade."

"If you're askin' about its actual size, I don't rightly know for sure. Never been this far north, but this is the reason the Fairies live here," explained Cankles. "It's so big; it makes it hard for people to find their Vale."

"And why would those puny beings not want to be found?" questioned Rose.

"Need you ask?" snorted Tag, shaking his head in dismay. "You were hardly gracious and rather demanding when you showed up. Not to mention how you practically trampled their circle of toadstools!"

Rose thought on the less than hospitable greeting she received after quite literally stumbling upon a Fairy's Ring, and then intruding on the Tooth Fairy's dentine palace.

"Yes, yes, but for how much farther do we travel?" asked Rose, wishing for nothing more than to change the subject. "And what is beyond this forest?"

"If we keep travelling far enough, this forest will eventually give way to the highlands," responded Tag.

"As in the Fire Rim Mountains?" questioned Rose.

"A miracle! You've actually been paying attention to the scholars tutoring you on geography," teased Tag.

"But is that not the place where dragons and all manner of dangerous beasts dwell?" gasped Rose, her breath catching in the back of her throat.

"Apparently so," confirmed Tag.

This time, it was Rose *and* Cankles bringing their steeds to an abrupt halt.

"Hold on here! So you are telling me that we will be heading directly into danger? Into dragon country?" asked Rose, as she glared at her comrade.

"If need be," answered Tag, his words, matter-of-fact.

"Dra- dragons eat – eat people," stammered Cankles, his eyes growing wide in fear.

"Then we shall take extra care to avoid hungry dragons," said Tag, speaking with confidence. "And if we do encounter one of those beasts, I shall kill it. If I successfully undertake this task *and* reclaim the dreamstone, I shall be granted the status of knight for sheer bravery alone."

"If you survive," reminded Cankles, gulping to swallow the lump catching in the back of his throat.

"This is madness!" groaned Rose, shaking her head in dismay. "What makes you think the Sorcerer is hiding out in those mountains? And do not tell me it is logic."

"This time, it's a combination of logic *and* intuition," informed Tag, dismounting to allow his horse to drink from a creek.

"*Intuition!*" groaned Rose, as she hopped down from her mare. "Now this is truly madness! Your brain has been addled by forces unknown and unseen."

"Why would you say such a thing? You always say you trust in your intuition," argued Tag, his brows furrowing in curiosity.

"That is correct, but I was speaking of *my* intuition, not yours. A man's intuition is nothing more than an educated guess at best, and never a very good one at that! A woman's intuition, for your infor- mation, is so much more than mere guesswork!"

"And my intuition tells me to stay out of this argument," sighed Cankles, his eyes rolling in frustration as he attempted to duck the verbal sniping.

"Hear me out," ordered Tag. "I think it's safe to assume Dragonite has fled his territory in the east for the time being."

"So?" grunted Rose.

"Think on it!" urged Tag. "It is not as though he would flee to the Woodland Glade where Lord Silverthorn and his people dwell. The Elves would have no qualms about capturing him. Nor would the Sorcerer take refuge in Dwarf or Troll country, for he has no allies amongst these beings. His past treatment of them left much to be desired. I believe they quite literally have an axe to grind against that deviant soul."

"Fine, but why would he take sanctuary in the Fire Rim Mountains when that region to the north is crawling with dangerous dragons?" questioned Rose.

"He would do so for that very reason," explained Tag. "He believes none would be foolish enough to venture far to the north to hunt him down."

"And for good reason," griped Rose. "The Sorcerer is insane to do so and you just pointed out that none but the foolish would follow him there!"

"So I did," admitted Tag.

"I will have you know, I am far from being the foolish type!" declared Rose.

"I meant to say; none but the brave dare venture that far north," corrected Tag.

"Foolish! Brave!" snorted Rose. "It matters not! I refuse to wander that dragon infested country searching for the demented Sorcerer."

"I agree Dragonite is crazy, however, he is far from stupid. As deranged as he is, you cannot argue that he is cunning," reasoned Tag.

"I'm guessin' it's his cunnin' mind that keeps him from being caught in the first place," agreed Cankles.

"Just think on it, Princess," urged Tag. "The desolate lands to the north would be the perfect place to hide; biding his time until it is safe for Dragonite to show his ugly face again."

"Even if this is so, do you fully comprehend how far to the north you are speaking of?" questioned Rose. "Even I know the Fire Rim Mountain Range is a vast expanse of land, and far more dangerous than any we have yet to travel! And the farther we head north, the colder it will become."

"True," admitted Tag.

"Have you forgotten I am partial to the warm, sunny climes far to the south?"

"Then it's a bloody good thing we're heading into the warm days of summer as we venture in the opposite direction, Princess," responded Tag.

"But we're only headin' that way if there's good reason, right, young master?' asked Cankles, his eyes nervously glancing northward to the distant mountains, their peaks piercing through the thick layer of low-hanging clouds.

"Of course," replied Tag.

"I knew we should have travelled with a battalion of knights," groaned Rose, shaking her head in dismay.

"And draw attention to our presence? I think not," dismissed Tag. "We must be discreet. To move with a battalion of knights is to offer up those dragons more to eat. We are better to move in secret and not allow our numbers to betray our presence."

"Now there's a lovely thought," grumbled Rose, her eyes rolling skyward, "the three of us becoming dragon fodder. I shall be the tasty morsel of an appetizer; you will be the main course; while our gangly friend becomes the toothpick the giant reptile will use to clean its teeth!"

"That won't happen if we are careful, but for now, there is no point in fretting about it," stated Tag. "There is a chance we will catch up to the Pooka before he journeys that far."

"Oh, my! You are an optimistic one!" exclaimed Rose.

"Better to be optimistic than to fold to despair," grumbled Tag, as he tried to ignore the sarcasm tainting her words.

"The young master's quite right," conceded Cankles. "If he has no intention or hope of succeedin', we may as well go home now. And if we do, we'll probably have no home to go home to anyway."

"Fine, but what if we encounter one of those fearsome dragons?" asked Rose.

"Then my father's sword will come in handy," answered Tag, his hand patting the hilt of his weapon.

"Somehow, your words do not exude confidence," sighed Rose, pulling herself back into the saddle.

"Worry not," urged Tag. "Let's move on."

"So… are we lost yet?" grumbled Rose. These words oozed with cynicism as the Princess glanced about at her all-too-familiar surroundings. The stand of trees towering over them was beginning to look identical to those in the forest where they had first entered to commence this quest.

"Of course not," said Tag, shrugging off her concern.

"Then why does it feel like we have been wandering in circles?" asked Rose, shifting restlessly in her saddle.

"What are you talking about? The sun is still to our backs, the wind to our faces."

"Gotta admit, young master, this place is lookin' mighty familiar to me," noted Cankles.

"Not true," insisted Tag, pointing to a knoll just up ahead. "Look! A rise. We haven't been this way yet. Let's see what is beyond."

"You better pray there is a village or a settlement of sorts where I can freshen up after this long, dreary ride," said Rose, glaring through narrowed eyes at Tag.

He chose to ignore her look of condemnation as he urged his mount on. Their horses plodded up the hill at an unhurried pace. Reaching the top, the trio came to a stop. Scanning the landscape before them, the trees gave way to a large clearing. A scattering of small cottages dotted this area situated by a wide, rushing creek.

"There you go! Civilization," announced Tag.

"*Primitive* civilization," clarified Rose. Her critical eyes scrutinized the simple homes with a vegetable patch growing before each humble abode.

The quaint cottages were constructed of mud and straw, plastered onto a simple post and beam frame. The mixture, air dried and then baked by the midday sun, was as hard as kiln-dried clay.

Crude in design and basic in structure, these homes bore not a single feature reminiscent of the palatial comforts found in Pepperton Palace, but still, Rose continued to hope the inside was much more pleasing than the exterior walls. She studied the thick layer of straw thatching the roof of each home and the roughly hewn wood that made up the crude window shutters.

"At least they have food," noted Cankles, spying a community smokehouse in the center of this small cluster of cottages.

From the faint scent of maple and alder smoke that continued to linger in the evening air, he detected the aroma of smoked venison and spicy sausages. It was a scent that permeated the air, seeping deep into the walls, thatched roof and clothing of every person dwelling in this village when the smokehouse was in full use during the late summer and into the months of autumn.

Near to the smokehouse, slabs of brook trout fished from the nearby creek were filleted and cured with salt. Laid out on wooden racks to dry in the heat of the sun, the fish would last well into the winter when hunting for game became more difficult with the heavy snowfall that blew in from the north during the first month of the new year.

"Since when does stinky fish left to rot in the wind and the sun classify as food?" complained Rose.

"It's not rotten," assured Cankles. "It's being cured in the sun, probably before it's strung up in the smokehouse."

"It still does not sound appetizing to me," responded Rose. "Such fare will only assault my discerning palate."

"It will be appetizing when you're good and hungry," countered Tag.

"Being a princess, I have discriminating taste. Perhaps if I was starving and my tongue had lost its ability to sense flavour, or the lack thereof, I can be convinced to eat it."

"Where we are heading, you may not have a lot in the way of choices. I'm sure these people can be persuaded to do business with us," said Tag, prodding his horse on to follow the trail leading down to this settlement.

"Perhaps we should move on," suggested Rose, turning her nose up at the modest village devoid of any signs of luxury, "travel to the next one."

"It's not fancy by any means, but I'm sure these folks are the hospitable type," said Cankles, sounding ever the optimist.

"If anything, someone here might have seen something unusual," added Tag.

"Unusual in what way?" questioned Rose.

"In the way of a wicked Sprite or a flying squirrel adorning a piece of jewelry," responded Tag.

"Oh," said Rose, as she nodded in understanding.

"Well, if anything, they've got food," added Cankles. "We might be able to replenish our supplies if we're thinkin' of continuin' northward."

"Better yet, maybe these people can give us directions so we can make sure we are not travelling in circles," suggested Rose. "The last thing we need is to get lost in unfamiliar lands."

"Har, har!" grunted Tag, in mock laughter.

"I am serious," insisted Rose. "I am in no mood to spend half the quest lost in the middle of nowhere."

"I did not say that we're lost."

"Then where are we? What is this place?" questioned Rose, her mare following close behind Tag's stallion as Cankles' mount took up the rear.

As the horses plodded by an old man tending to his crop of potatoes near the trail they travelled, he glanced up as Rose continued her interrogation of the young man in her company.

"Well, go on! What is this placed called?"

As Tag glanced about, searching for a signpost of sorts, the old man chirped up: "This is Home."

"No offense, good sir," said Rose, "I know this is *your* home, but what is this place called."

"Home." He responded again, leaning against the handle of his garden hoe.

"Are you daft? Or did you not hear me?" asked Rose, her brows crinkling in a frown.

"Heard ya jus' fine, miss," answered the man. "As I said, this little village is called *Home*."

Rose scratched her head in bewilderment as she stared at this stranger.

"Originally, this wee settlement wasn't big enough ta bother naming," explained the stranger, the blade of the hoe biting into the freshly churned soil. "But whenever we ventured inta the forest ta go huntin' or up the creek ta go fishin', we always returned home, hence the name *Home*. Might as well keep it simple, if ya get my drift?"

"Makes perfect sense to me," responded Cankles.

"Of course it would," sniffed Rose, staring with raised eyebrows at her comrade.

Ignoring the Princess, Tag spoke up, "Good day, sir. We are travellers in need of accommodations for the night and a mercantile where we can purchase some supplies."

"If you're speakin' of an inn an' a place ta buy food stuffs, you're in luck, young man."

"Excellent! Can you point the way?" asked Tag.

"There's room over there." Using the handle of his hoe, the man pointed at a simple barn.

Rose stared over at the structure designed to house several horses or cows. "Our steeds can be left out on a pleasant day like this. We were referring to accomodations for us to stay the night."

"As I was," said the man. "The horses are out with their masters on a hunt for a day or two an' that's fresh straw in them stalls. It'll be fit fer sleepin' in, an' the best part of all? It's free!"

"Free is good," said Cankles.

"If you are livestock," muttered Rose. "I was speaking of a proper inn, with or without a public drinking house attached to it where we can purchase a decent meal."

The man rubbed his balding head as he sputtered in laughter, "You're speakin' in jest, young miss! Does this place look big 'nough fer an inn, let alone a pub?"

"No need for concern, good sir," assured Tag. "The stable will be fine, thank you. As for a shop to buy provisions?"

"Ain't got no shop that you're probably used ta. We usually jus' barter amongst ourselves," admitted the old man, rubbing his stubbly chin in pensive thought. "But the fella jus' down the way, that cottage to the right at the end of this trail, can probably help ya with what you'll be needin'. He's the purveyor of all things edible an' otherwise. If you're travellin' somewhere, he'll have what you'll be needin' ta get ya there."

"The cottage at the end of this trail? To the right?" repeated Tag, glancing down the way.

"Ya heard me correctly, young sir. He's out huntin' right now, but my friend is expected back late tonight or early in the mornin'. He'll have everything ya'll need, an' then some."

"A nice, hot meal would be lovely about now," sighed Rose, her stomach rumbling in protest to be fed.

"If you ain't too fussy, my wife's got a great big pot of venison stew simmerin' an' some fresh baked bread coolin' if you'd like ta join us fer supper."

"Are you sure?" asked Tag, pleased and surprised by this unexpected invitation.

"Wouldn't offer if I wasn't, young fella. Besides, ain't often we get visitors ta these parts. My wife wouldn't mind seein' a new face or two at the dinner table than jus' my ol' ugly mug everyday."

"That would be lovely," responded Cankles, bowing in appreciation. "Venison stew sounds delightful."

"Yes, but do you have pheasant, sir?" questioned Rose, turning her nose up at this simple fare she regarded as food for the common man.

"Pheasant?" chuckled the old man. "Only in my dreams! This is grouse country, but ain't no grouse on the menu today, missy! I prefer ta hunt fer grouse in the autumn when the chicks are old 'nough ta fend fer themselves an' them birds are plumped up for the winter."

"How disappointing," sighed Rose.

"If you be wantin' fresh meat, I caught some muskrats this mornin' at the local frog pond," offered the old man. "Can roast 'em up with some fresh herbs from this garden fer ya, if that's what ya prefer."

Rose's eyes widened with horror. She recalled her first introduction to this fare when Cankles shared a meal with them when this whole misadventure began.

"I hardly think you can consider those water rats as being real meat," groaned Rose, grimacing in disgust.

"But roasted jus' so, them muskrats taste jus' like chicken," stated the old man.

"Never mind her, good sir! It was merely her attempt at being funny," explained Tag. "Your wife's venison stew sounds absolutely wonderful."

"We'd be mighty honoured to share a meal with you," added Cankles, his mouth watering involuntary at the mere thought of indulging in a bowl of fresh, piping hot stew.

Scratching his head in thought, the old man responded with a shrug of his bony shoulders, "Don't rightly know what's so funny 'bout the young lady's comment, but never mind! Supper should be ready right about now. I'll jus' have my missus set extra plates at the table."

"This is very kind and generous of you," commended Tag, nodding in gratitude.

"Our little haven ain't a fancy, bustlin' village like some of 'em places to the south in Fleetwood, but one thing we take pride in is the hospitality of our people," said the old man, using his hoe as a walking stick as he led the way to his cottage. "Jus' follow me, my young friends. Dinner's on."

Tethering their horses to the hitching post just outside the stable, the trio followed their host to his cottage. Giving the door a hard nudge with his shoulder to push it open, the smell of stew and freshly baked bread billowed forth, almost bowling Rose and her comrades over with its savoury aroma. It was a warm, inviting scent made all the more apparent as a woman used a ladle to fish out the twine that held an aromatic bundle of wild herbs together.

"Molly, we've got company," announced the old man, as he escorted his guests inside.

"Good gracious, Rupert! Why didn't ya warn me we'd be havin' company," scolded the short, round, matronly woman. She dropped the ladle, as well as the herb bundle back into the stew as she tried to make herself look more presentable, hastily removing her strained apron and primping her frizzy, grey head of hair.

"Now how am I supposed ta do that, woman?" grunted the old man, as he hung his well-worn jacket on a wooden peg protruding from the door. "Only jus' met these folks."

"I'm sorry," apologized Tag. "We didn't mean to impose on you."

"Oh no! No imposition at all, young man," responded Molly. "Jus' don't get people, especially new folks, comin' round for a meal very often. It jus' would've been nice ta have had a chance to get gussied up for company. That's all."

"You look absolutely fine," said Cankles, nodding his head in approval and greeting.

"Oh, you're jus' sayin' that," giggled the woman, as she elbowed her husband to make sure he heard this compliment.

"He probably is, but don't you go puttin' him on the spot," said Rupert, pulling out a chair for Rose to sit on as he motioned for her comrades to join them at the table.

Molly shot a baleful glance at her husband, and then smiled once more as she delivered a willow basket filled with slices of bread. "So, who are these young folks, Rupert?"

"Hell if I know," grunted the old man, as he placed a crock of butter on the table. "I told ya before, they jus' showed up here at Home so I brought 'em home."

"Home as in this village, or home as in this house?" questioned Cankles.

"Both," answered the old man. "We ain't had time for formal introductions yet."

"Rupert! You rude, rude man!" scolded his wife, her plump finger wagging in disapproval at him. "So much fer your world famous hospitality!"

"Oh, hush, Molly!" snorted her husband.

"No need for concern, Missus...?" Cankles waited for her surname.

"Cottle, Mrs. Cottle," answered Molly.

"As in *mollycoddle?*" asked Cankles, frowning in both surprise and confusion.

"Kinda, but not quite. Jus' call me Molly an' this old coot is my husband, Rupert."

"We're pleased to meet your acquaintance," greeted Tag, accepting a bowl of steaming hot stew from her serving tray to pass on to his comrades first. "This is Rose and our friend, Cankles. My name is Tagius."

"Welcome to our humble abode, now go ahead!" urged Molly, handing out wooden spoons to her guests. "It's best eaten hot, so tuck in."

"Thank you," said Tag and Cankles, their spoons eagerly diving into their serving of stew. The meaty, lean chunks of venison, now tenderized from the slow cooking process and the uniform cubes of tender potatoes, carrots, and whole pearl onions simmering in a thick, brown gravy had their mouths watering even before taking that first bite.

As her comrades devoured their food, Rose used her spoon to poke and prod at the items bathed in this dark gravy. It did smell temptingly delicious, but it was not exactly the succulent, herb crusted roast of pheasant or venison that she was used to eating at the palace.

"Is there something wrong, dear? Aren't ya hungry?" asked Molly, watching her guest as she pushed the pieces of meat and vegetables around her bowl like a picky toddler playing with her food.

"She is hungry and there is something wrong with her," answered Tag, pointing his spoon accusingly at Rose. "It's called being fussy."

"Ain't you ever had stew before, child?" asked Molly.

"I've seen the domestic staff eating it before," said Rose. "But you must admit, and take no offense, it kind of looks like the leftover scraps they throw together for the pigs' slop."

Tag and Cankles froze. Their spoons full of stew were suspended before their gaping mouths as Rose's words assaulted them and insulted their hosts.

"Your domestic staff?" repeated Molly, staring quizzically at Rose.

"Knock to the head," explained Tag. He then mouthed the words; *not right up here*. Using his knuckles to rap against his head, he then spun an index finger by his ear to indicate that Rose's mind had been addled in a mishap.

"Well then, if I were a pig, I'd have died and gone to the big pig sty in the sky," assured Cankles, happily devouring his serving. "This is the most delicious stew I've ever had the joy of eating."

"I'll second that," agreed Tag, using a piece of bread to sop up the delectable gravy.

"Oh, you boys are too kind!" exclaimed Molly, blushing with modesty. "It's jus' old-fashioned stew. Nothing fancy here!"

"I'll say," muttered Rose, glanced up from her bowl to see her comrades chowing down like it was the best thing ever. They were either extremely ravenous and wouldn't have cared if these chopped vegetables and chunks of meat were simmering in warm, seasoned mud or this bland looking concoction was indeed as flavourful as it smelled.

"In fact, if you're too fussy to eat it, I'll finish it for you," offered Tag, licking the gravy from his lips as he finished his bowl of stew.

"It is that good?" asked Rose, her mouth watering involuntarily as the fragrance of thyme and rosemary wafted up from her bowl.

"Better than good," assured Cankles, licking his spoon clean as Molly ladled more stew into his bowl. "You don't know what you're missin'."

Just as Tag reached across the table to help himself to Rose's neglected serving, armed with a wooden spoon, Rose stuck out. She smacked his knuckles as she scolded him, "Do you mind? I did not say you could have it."

Tag's smarting hand recoiled, shaking off this sting as Rose rammed her spoon into the center of the bowl to stake her claim.

There was nothing runny about the gravy the chunks of meat and vegetables were simmered in. The wooden spoon stood up unassisted when Rose let go of it to pull the bowl closer.

"See! It's so thick, it'll stick to your ribs and keep you feelin' satisfied 'til morning," stated Cankles, shoving another spoonful of stew into his mouth.

Rose tentatively scooped up a small sampling of the stew, minus the meat and vegetable, blowing on the gravy before tasting it. Once it was sufficiently cooled, she held her nose and plunged the spoon into her mouth like it was some foul-tasting medicinal tincture she was being made to swallow.

Tag merely rolled his eyes in dismay at her dramatic performance while Cankles encouraged her to eat more.

As she swallowed, her stomach rumbled, demanding to be fed this stew *now!* Rose's delicate brows arched up in pleasant surprise as her taste buds seem to come alive, dancing a jig of gratitude if they could, to thank her for not fouling them with something her comrades only pretended to pass off as delectable cuisine.

"I do say! This *is* delicious!" declared Rose, licking the gravy from her lips. Overcome by hunger, she dove in. In the most un-ladylike manner, she shovelled a heaping spoonful into her mouth, barely chewing her food before swallowing.

"You keep eatin', dear," urged Molly, pleased that her guest was finally enjoying the meal. "There's plenty more ta go around when you're ready."

"So, what brings you young folks ta our neck of the woods?" questioned Rupert.

Before Cankles or Rose could offer a revealing answer, Tag spoke up. "We're searching for a friend. Last we heard he was seen heading north."

"North to where?" questioned the old man.

"We heard he could be heading as far north as the Fire Rim Mountains," answered Tag.

Rupert dropped his spoon into the bowl as he glanced up at Tag. "Are ya sure 'bout that, young man?"

"Not really, for we have nothing but rumours to base our search on at this time," confided Tag.

"We've only had a handful of strangers travellin' through these parts in the past month," said Rupert.

"Perhaps he came and went, unnoticed," suggested Tag.

"I hardly think so. I make it my business ta know all those comin' an' goin' through these parts. Bein' that my garden is the first any traveller would come across upon enterin' Home, I'd know of any stranger passin' through as I'm always putterin' 'round in my garden. I'd be the first ta know."

"Oh, come now, Rupert! It's not like you're the eyes an' ears of the entire village," scolded his wife. "You're half deaf an' near blind ta begin with!"

"Am not!"

"Then why did you shout a *good-mornin'* to that old mare trottin' up the road, only ta get your codpiece all in a bunch when ya thought old lady Phillippa Winehouse was ignorin' ya?" scoffed Molly, slapping her generous thigh as she laughed at him.

"Say again?" asked Rupert, squinting in the candlelight as he cupped a hand to his ear to better hear Molly raising her voice in annoyance at him.

"Never mind," said Molly, heaving a weary sigh as she waved him off.

"So, have you seen any strangers or anything unusual of late?" questioned Tag.

"Anything unusual?" repeated Rupert. "Like what?"

"Like a flyin' squirrel out in the middle of the day, in particular, one wearin' a fine gold necklace with a crystal bead," responded Cankles.

The old man chuckled in response, "An' was that wee critter wearin' a frock an' knickers, too?"

"Oh, shush!" scolded Molly, giving her husband a poke with her elbow. "You were speakin' of strangers passin' through?"

"That would be a single stranger," corrected Tag, thinking on how he would even begin to try to describe the shape-shifting Sprite. "He was on his own, the last we saw."

Rupert's fingers rubbed his stubbly chin in pensive thought. "Can't rightly say I have... There was a man with his wife and child early yesterday morn, jus' passin' through ta visit family in the neighbourin' village, but that's all I can remember right now. My old noggin' ain't what it used ta be, ya know what I mean?"

"Oh, I do know," responded Cankles, nodding in empathy.

"But even if I had, why would your friend be headin' ta dragon country? Ain't nothing there but... dragons."

"An' folks who end up dead when they encounter 'em beasts," added Molly, her jowls wobbling as she shook her head is woe.

"That's why we are trying to find him, to keep him from heading directly into danger," lied Tag.

"Well, hate ta say this, young fella, but I'm thinkin' your friend's a bit daft if he's really headin' there," decided Rupert. "It'll be the death of him, if he does."

"He's more than just a bit daft," agreed Tag. "But we mean to keep him from going there."

"Well, good luck ta the three of yous," offered Rupert, giving his head a dismal shake. "Them dragons are real active right now, not like they're jus' wakin' up from their winter slumber, ya know?"

"Yes, we know," said Tag, heaving a sigh.

"Well, the three of yous are brave, young souls ta be takin' on this quest ta save your friend," praised Molly, using the end of her spoon to push the stray, wiry grey wisps of hair from her eyes. "It's an adventure most would never consider undertakin'."

"Misadventure is more like it," assured Rupert.

"We don't have much choice in this matter, but I'm sure we'll be fine," said Cankles, as he pointed to Tag and the sword hanging from his baldric. "The young master will keep us safe."

"If he does not get us hopelessly lost along the way," said Rose, heaving another disgruntled sigh.

"If we get lost, it will not be on purpose," grunted Tag, glaring through narrowed eyes at Rose.

"If you're so concerned 'bout not gettin' yourselves lost, you should talk ta my friend, the fella I mentioned before about buyin' provisions from," recommended Rupert. "I heard he had some newfangled thing that's supposed ta help ta keep you from gettin' lost on your travels."

"What is this *thing* you speak of?" asked Rose.

"Don't rightly know. Jus' heard the neighbours sayin' my friend has a way ta keep travellers from gettin' lost. Could be a special kind of map, I'm thinkin'."

"I will make sure I speak to your friend about this," responded Tag.

"You do that, young man." Rupert nodded in approval. "Worst place ta get lost in is up north in dragon country."

"Jus' make sure ya move 'bout the Fire Rim Mountains durin' the cool of the night or the chill of early mornin'," suggested Molly, her eyes wide in fear. "I've heard 'em dragons don't move as quickly as when they've been baskin' in the heat of the noonday sun."

"I suppose that makes sense," said Tag, recalling how the common snakes found in the gardens and meadows of Cadboll in the County of Wren were lethargic when they were not sufficiently warmed.

"Of course it does," assured Molly. "Don't want ta be hearin' that the three of yous met an early demise, so ya best heed this warnin' an' do what ya must ta stay safe."

"Don't often agree with this woman, but she's right," said Rupert. "An' speakin' of warnings ta heed, if you be seekin' this kind of advice, they say there's a woman with the *gift*. They say she can foretell the future, if ya believe in that sort of thing."

"If it keeps us one step ahead of danger, I am open to this kind of advice," chirped Rose. "Where can I find this woman?"

"Somewhere between here an' Far," answered Rupert.

"I heard she lives in Too Far," said Molly.

"How far?" asked Rose, frowning in bewilderment.

"I'm speakin' of a wee village, not that much bigger than ours, it's called Far, as in, it's far from Home. If ya head ta Too Far, then you've gone too far," corrected the old man.

"Huh?" grunted Cankles, scratching his head in confusion.

"Heard this teller of the future lives in, or near, ta this place," explained the old man.

"And she is good at predicting the future?" queried Rose.

"So I've heard," said Rupert.

"Couldn't hurt to be one step ahead of danger," decided Cankles. "I'm all for seekin' this woman out, if it helps us."

"Where exactly does she live?" asked Tag.

"Never been there before, but I imagine you'll have ta head somewhere up north. Shouldn't be too much trouble ta find her though, as she's the only one in the Dimbolt Forest with this gift an' since you're all headin' up toward the Fire Rim Mountain Range anyway, I'm sure you'll cross paths with the woman along the way," said Rupert.

"Maybe she'll be waitin' for us on the side of a road somewhere, if she's as good as you claim she is," offered Cankles.

"You could be right, my friend, but I suggest havin' an early night, if you're thinkin' of movin' on tomorrow toward that god forsaken dragon country," recommended Molly.

"That's the plan," responded Tag. "I'll be paying your friend a visit first thing in the morning to stock up on some supplies and I'll see if he has a map that will help us on the way."

"Good idea," praised Rose. "Getting lost is the last thing we need."

6
It's a What?

Rose's eyes slowly opened, coming awake to the sound of fresh straw rustling beneath her as she stirred from her sleep.

"Good morning!" greeted Cankles. He tightened the cinch of her mare's saddle as he readied the horses for another day of travel.

"Why are you so dreadfully cheerful?" groaned Rose, yawning as she stretched. "It's too early for that."

"Oh, I don't think so, m'lady," said Cankles. Giving the horse a poke with his elbow so the mare would exhale, he was able to adjust the cinch accordingly so the Princess wouldn't end up on the underside of her mount due to a loose fitting saddle. "The morning sun is just peekin' over them mountains and soon, it shall bathe the lands in its glorious light. In fact, it looks to be the start of a beautiful day."

"As long as it's not raining, that is all I really care about," grumbled Rose, throwing off her bedroll. "There is nothing more miserable than riding in the rain, especially if the ride is not within a well-appointed, covered carriage."

"Don't anticipate rain 'til much later today, if it comes at all," noted Cankles. He peered through the trees, gazing to the eastern horizon. There, the impending sun set the gossamer wisps of cloud snagged on the distant mountains in the Land of Big aglow in crimson.

"My, you are so very optimistic this morning," grunted Rose, stretching as she sat up.

"Thank you," said Cankles, nodding in acknowledgement.

"It is bloody annoying!"

"Oh… well, I shall try to keep my optimism contained," promised Cankles.

"You do that," urged Rose, rising up to meet the new day with her usual demeanor when she'd rather sleep in. "Besides, what do you have to be so happy or optimistic about? The day has only begun, after all."

"There are plenty of reasons to be happy, even grateful for, at this early hour," said Cankles, his words cheerful as he continued his work. Sliding the saddle blanket from high on his horse's withers, down onto its swayed back so the horse's coat would lie flat and smooth, he tossed the saddle over top.

"I hardly think so," responded Rose, her tone dismissive as she rummaged through one of the packs containing food. "Name one thing."

"You complain about waking up at such an early hour," explained Cankles. "You should be grateful that you are awake."

"As opposed to…?"

"Let me just say that dead folks don't have the privilege of wakin' up…ever!"

"I suppose I cannot argue against that statement," conceded Rose.

"Wakin' up means you're alive and kickin', hence, all the more reason to not waste all your time sleepin' away. As for being optimistic, I'd like to believe it's contagious, like yawnin', but better!"

"Yawning is not contagious," countered Rose.

"Sure it is, Princess. I'm bettin' that even reading about someone yawnin' is enough to make the reader do it, too."

Just the mention of this word was enough of a catalyst to suddenly trigger a subconscious need to yawn. The sensation overwhelmed her, causing Rose to surrender to this urge.

Cankles followed suit, his mouth gaping wide open as he inhaled, and then loudly exhaled. This in turn caused Rose to yawn involuntarily once more.

As her hand covered her mouth to stifle this yawn, Cankles gave her a knowing smile as he said, "See, as contagious as the pox, but nowhere near as deadly… another thing to be thankful for!"

It became apparent to the Princess this simple man's sense of optimism was the very thing that allowed him to wake up each morning and to greet the day with unabashed enthusiasm. Being a commoner with nothing to show in the way of wealth or power, Rose came to the conclusion that with nothing else of any real value, it gave this peasant of a man reason to live a life of purpose, no matter how simple.

"Well, I guess it is better to wake with a positive attitude than to wallow in misery," said Rose.

"Absolutely!" agreed Cankles. "I believe it can set the tone for the entire day. Misery only begets misery, and if I were able to remember my earlier life, I'd probably be drownin' in it, if I didn't choose to look on the positive side of life! Nope, it's much better to be grateful for what you have and be optimistic that the day will hold some promise."

Rose thought on the multitude of nasty scars that haphazardly marred his back, as well as those on Cankles' head, now hidden by his mop of hair. Though he swore he had no recollection how he received these permanent reminders of a traumatic beating, she was confident this was the misery he spoke of.

"Well said," praised Rose.

"Hey, as far as I'm concerned, as we venture into the unknown, I am grateful to be in the company of my two best friends," responded Cankles, offering her a congenial smile of gratitude. "I've got every reason to be happy *and* optimistic."

Rose could sense the sincerity in his voice. Knowing that aside from his mongrel of a pet dog and the mangy cat that made it a habit of coughing up hairballs, she and Tag were probably his only human friends.

"Speaking of friends, where is Tag?" asked Rose, searching about to see if he was off replenishing their water flasks.

"He woke up long before the sun even thought of showin' its face. He shouldn't be long now," assured Cankles, as he tightened the cinch on his horse's saddle. "Said he just wanted to pick up one or two things for the journey to the north."

"Oh, yes…" remembered Rose. "Did he say what items he planned to purchase?"

"I imagine some food to last us the trek there and back again. I do recall the young master sayin' something about gettin' maps or directions for our travels."

"Well, whatever Tag buys, it better be useful to us."

"It is," promised Tag. His steps were silent as he approached from behind her, lowering the pack from his shoulder.

Rose jumped with a start, and then she jumped again as the pack suddenly rustled about at her feet.

"What the heck is that?" gasped Rose, snatching up the pitchfork used to clean the stable. "It is alive!"

Before Rose could strike or poke the object inside, Tag yanked the intended weapon from her hands. "Do you mind? Of course, it's alive!"

"What can it be?" asked Cankles, kneeling down before the pack for a closer look.

"It's the latest in travel technology," explained Tag, smiling proudly over his latest acquisition. "Rupert Cottle's friend had just what we'll need to keep from getting lost."

"A compass?" offered Rose, frowning with curiosity. "For if it is, there is nothing new about a compass, you know?"

"Of course I know, and you can still get lost with one if you don't know where you are going or how to get there," said Tag. "This is better than any old compass!"

"Go on! What is it?" asked Cankles, eager to see this new technology.

"It's called a G.P.S.," replied Tag, undoing the pack's buckle.

"It's a *what?*" Rose and Cankles responded simultaneously.

"A G.P.S.," repeated Tag. "It's short for Gnome Positioning Service. It's the latest rage in these parts."

"*Eek!*" shrieked Rose, leaping behind Tag as a rumpled-looking Gnome tumbled forth from the pack he had turned upside down. "What is this ankle-biter?"

"It – or should I say, *he* is a Gnome, specially trained in memorizing the lay of the land. The service he provides is to tell us where to go and how best to get there," explained Tag.

"*I* should be the one telling *you* where to go, right about now," snapped Rose, scowling in frustration. "A Gnome Positioning Service? What were you thinking, Tag?"

"I was thinking of *you.*"

"How can this- this Gnome make you think of me?" sputtered Rose, pointing an accusing finger at the strange, little being standing before her, his pointy hat in hand.

"Yesterday, you were complaining about getting lost," responded Tag. "This G.P.S. will show us the way, as well as how far we must travel to reach our destination."

"I'm thinkin' you mean to say N.P.S." corrected Cankles, staring at the little Gnome standing shorter than his knees.

"The '*g*' in Gnome is silent," explained Tag.

"Well that's silly… You'd think the fellow who was clever enough to invent the alphabet would be smart enough to know how to spell," commented Cankles. "What a waste of a letter!"

"Never mind that," ordered Rose. "What are we supposed to do with this *thing?*"

"We take him with us," answered Tag.

"Say again?" gasped the Princess.

"I do love ta travel," said the Gnome. His voice was low and gravelly, almost grumbling even though he appeared to be quite happy as he crawled back into the pack, ready for the journey to begin.

"A Gnome that loves to travel?" asked Rose, staring quizzically at this diminutive being as he adjusted his pointy red hat, squashing the tip down so Tag could see over it. "Now, I've heard it all!"

"How'd you think I came ta know these lands as well as I do?"

grunted the Gnome. "I know where every river, hill an' significant landmark in these parts, an' beyond, are ta be found."

"Do you now?" sniffed Rose, ever doubtful as she scrutinized the scruffy little being dressed in a coarse wool outfit. His grizzled beard and wiry gray brows added to his unkempt appearance.

"You betcha!" announced the Gnome, as he settled into the pack, sitting on his stumpy, folded legs to position himself as low as possible. "Tell me where you'd like ta go, an' I'll tell ya the fastest way ta get there. Of course, if ya decide you'd rather take a more scenic route an' time is of no concern, I can show that way, too."

"See," grunted Tag, giving the Princess his best *I-told-you-so* stare. "Now there's no way we can get lost."

"So you say," responded Rose. Her tone was as skeptical as ever.

"I do!"

"And just how do we pay him for his services?" quizzed Rose. "For, until we reclaim the *you-know-what,* our funds are limited for the time being."

"We pay him with this," replied Tag, passing a small burlap bag to Cankles.

"I am afraid to ask," sighed Rose, giving her head a dismal shake.

Cankles peered into the bag. "Carrots, turnips, rutabagas and beets? It's a bag full of veggies!"

"Just like the Dwarves, they love root vegetables," confirmed Tag. "Most Gnomes have a green thumb and take to gardening with ease. Apparently, this one loves vegetables; he just can't grow them very well."

"I do love 'em veggies, but my green thumb's tainted, I tell ya," admitted the Gnome, as he flexed his small, grubby digit for all to see. "Haven't had much luck growin' my own garden, so I've gotta earn an honest livin' by other means."

"That makes perfect sense to me," decided Cankles. "A Gnome's gotta eat, after all."

"Especially 'em tasty beets! Delectable!" declared the diminutive being, as he wiped the drool trickling from his mouth down the length of his beard.

"Well, this should be interesting," muttered Rose, raising herself into the saddle.

"Interesting indeed!" agreed Cankles. "So, how does this G.P.S. work, young master?"

"It's easy," said Tag. He lifted the pack up, but instead of wearing it on his back, Tag wore it on his front with the Gnome facing forward. "Just watch and learn, my friend."

"You do know the pack is on backwards?" asked Rose.

"Of course! How else will he be able to see where we're going if he's facing the wrong way?" responded Tag, adjusting the pack before taking his place on his mount.

"Now what?" asked Rose.

"Then you give the G.P.S. the information he needs to get us to where we want to go," responded Tag.

"What is your destination?" asked the Gnome, his gravelly voice now all business.

"We want to head north, to the very fringes of Dimbolt Forest bordering the Fire Rim Mountain Range," stated Tag.

"The scenic route; the route less travelled; or the fastest possible way to get there?"

"The fastest route possible," answered Tag.

"Very good," said the Gnome.

"If we are made to travel this distance, how long will it take?" questioned Rose.

"Depends," responded the Gnome.

"On what?" asked the Princess.

"Whether ya choose ta walk or ride your horses, an' if ya ride, if the horses are made ta walk, canter or gallop most of the way."

"Ride, of course!" responded Rose.

"At a steady trot," added Tag, wanting to take into account that they'd be searching for signs of the Pooka's presence along the way.

"Three and one-half days by horse taking the scenic route; two days if you travel the fastest route. Mind you, it'd be little over one day an' one-half if ya got good, sturdy horses; not miserable old nags that'd rather stop an' eat all the way there."

"Our horses are in prime condition and when I say 'go', they do exactly that, with utmost speed," assured Rose.

"Then one an' one-half day, it is," confirmed the Gnome.

"Hey, did you not say you wanted to see that woman with the power of foresight?" asked Cankles.

"Oh, yes!" said Rose, with a nod. "Do you know the way to get to a village called Far?"

"Sure do," replied the Gnome. "In fact, if it's Lady Aglynessa ya wish ta see, her home is on the road to Far."

"You mean it's too far to get to?" questioned Cankles.

"No, I mean ta say, the lady's home is along the way to the village of Far, just on the outskirts," explained the new guidance system. "Now if ya miss it, then you'll end up in the village of Too Far."

"The point being, you know how to find this seer of the future?"

inquired Rose.

"I know exactly how to get there," confirmed the Gnome.

"How handy is that?" exclaimed Cankles, nodding in approval.

"They don't call me the best G.P.S in these parts," assured the Gnome, eager to demonstrate his navigational skills to his new customers.

"Hey... I was told you're the *only* Gnome providing this service in this forest," said Tag.

"So I am! Therefore, it makes me the best at what I do."

"Somehow, I am not brimming over with confidence," said Rose, heaving a dreary sigh. "I am not sure I want to be told where to go by a puny being that should really be tending to a garden."

"You don't like being told where to go by *anyone*, big or small," reminded Tag.

"True, but I am not keen on any kind of modern day technology that has not been rigorously tested," admitted Rose, frowning at the grumpy looking Gnome peering out from Tag's backpack. "He does not even come with a compass."

"Sure I do," responded the Gnome, his stubby fingers searching through his pockets. He pulled out a round ceramic container, opening the lid to reveal what was inside.

Peering in, Rose frowned as she remarked, "This, little sir, is *not* a compass. It is nothing more that a sewing needle pushed through a tiny piece of wood!"

"So it is," grumbled the Gnome, "but if ya fill this with water, the needle floats to the top. If ya give it time, it'll point the way ta the north."

"Brilliant!" exclaimed Cankles, his hands clapping together in delight as Rose looked on with doubt clearly etched on her lovely face.

"See! You worry all for naught, Princess," assured Tag. "Now, let's be on our way."

"Keep going straight for twenty-eight horse-lengths 'til ya reach a tree that looks like my mother growin' from a fork in the road. From there, turn northeast 'til I tell ya otherwise," directed the Gnome, his finger pointing the way.

"Wait a minute! How would we know what your mother looks like?" questioned Rose, as she stared suspiciously at the navigator. "We did not even know you until Tag brought you along, so it is not like you had introduced us to her in the first place."

"Well, don't feel bad. I can barely remember what she looks like as the only thing I recall now is that she had rather bland, forgettable features, but methinks I need something to keep the old noggin runnin', if you gets my meanin'?" The Gnome smacked his lips, rubbing his hands together.

"If it'll help us get to our destination, sure," Tag said, handing the Gnome a carrot.

"This is what ya give me? A simple carrot? To keep this wise noggin of mine functionin' at its best, I need something that is like brain food to us Gnomes!"

"Like what?" asked Tag.

"A large, sweet beet would do nicely," bribed the Gnome.

"Fine! If you say so," sighed Tag, rummaging through the burlap bag tied to his saddle. Handing over the deep purple vegetable, it was snatched from his hand.

The Gnome set his teeth into the beet, biting off a chunk like it was a hard, crisp apple. Talking with his mouth full, bits of masticated vegetable flew from between his now purple teeth. "Well, the best I can describe my ol' mummsy is that she was the gnarliest thing you can ever imagine."

The Gnome contorted his whiskered face and twisted his back like he was a gnarled old, willow tree; bent, weathered and at the mercy of the elements.

"The old biddy was a tad shorter than me, but she would've been taller if she wasn't so stooped. She was like a stubborn old tree that was knocked down flat in a windstorm an' still tried growin' up to the sun. An' her skin? It was dry like a chewed up ol' piece of boot leather an' as rough as the bark on a pine tree."

"Lovely! Now there is a wonderful image," grunted Rose, shaking her head in disgust. "So she looks just like you?"

"Aside from these whiskers, I'm supposin' you can say we don't have much in the way of looks in common. Mind you, my beard is more lush than hers was."

"She was a bearded woman?" gasped Rose.

"She was one of a kind," said the Gnome, taking another chomp from the beet. "I can tell you more."

"That is quite all right," insisted Tag. "I believe we know more about your mother than we care to."

"I'd like to hear more," chirped Cankles, intrigued by this description.

"On your own time, my friend," urged Tag, staring up ahead to where the Gnome pointed. "Allow me to concentrate on finding this old, gnarled tree our G.P.S. so eloquently described."

"Venturing on is fine, but I suggest we stop for a moment," urged Rose. "My royal bottom has endured quite enough in this saddle."

"Again?" groaned Tag.

"What can I say? I am a princess, therefore, I am more delicate than most."

"Then that is a sad thing," commented Tag, as he urged his steed on. "We still have far to go, so the constitution of a commoner like me or Cankles would serve you better for the duration."

"Oooh! That is something you can wish for, if you get the chance, Princess," suggested Cankles.

"I think not!" gasped Rose. "Come to think of it, I am getting used to the long hours in this saddle."

"You are?" questioned Tag.

"Are you doubting me?"

"I'm not, Princess, but I wouldn't mind if we stopped and took some time to eat," said Cankles. "I'm feelin' a wee bit peckish again."

"That is a good idea, Cankles!" Tag exclaimed. "We shall eat *and* give the Princess a momentary reprieve from her saddle."

"Brilliant," said Rose. "I have no problem with that."

"You are going off course," grumbled the Gnome, his stubby index finger pointing one way while Tag steered his mount off the road.

"Hush! Your service is not needed at this moment," responded Tag. "Take the time to enjoy the rest of your food."

The beet juice tinted finger stopped pointing as the Gnome used both hands to cram the remaining root vegetable into his purple-stained mouth, hoping for another to devour as the trio stopped to share in a meal.

Hopping off his mount, Tag removed his backpack to lower the Gnome to the ground. The little being scrambled out of his carrier; burping as he thumped his chest with a balled fist.

"Some dried fruit and smoked venison will have to do for now," said Tag. "Let's not waste time building a fire and cooking up a meal right now. We can do that tonight."

"We'll make time for a decent meal later," agreed Cankles, digging through his pack to share the food while Tag passed a carrot to the Gnome tugging at his trousers to let him know he was still hungry.

As much as Rose disliked the stringy, thinly sliced smoked venison Tag had bought from the mercantile that sold him the Gnome Positioning Service, she decided to take advantage of this opportunity to be free of the saddle. She paced to and fro, stretching her legs as she slowly chewed on the leathery shreds of meat, making it last to prolong this reprieve.

"Your pacing is making me nervous," stated Tag, licking the salty, greasy residue left on his fingers by the smoked venison. "Are you eager to be on our way, Princess?"

"Oh, no! Though I *am* eager to pay a visit to that woman who can foresee the future, I am certainly *not* eager to get back on my horse at this very moment. Right now, I want nothing more than to walk off these stiff muscles before they grow numb beyond repair sitting in that hard saddle."

"Then you best keep walking, for we'll be back on those horses sooner than you know it," said Tag, stuffing a piece of dried apple into his mouth.

Rose unleashed a weary sigh as she resumed her pacing.

"Hey, you're the one who is so keen on seeing that woman. If you want to do that, then we must cut this break short to make time for this detour and delay," explained Tag.

"But it could well be worth it," reasoned the Princess. "There is a chance she can provide us with information, the kind that can be crucial to our quest and ultimately, our success."

"Maybe... but I just can't help feeling skeptical about the whole thing," cautioned Tag.

"Why would you feel skeptical?" questioned Rose, sensing he wanted nothing more than to continue this mission without further delays or distractions.

"Truth be told, every person I ever heard of claiming to be able to see into the future was a phony; nothing more than a trickster praying on the gullible and those eager to part with their money, especially if they thought such information was a surefire way to make more money," responded Tag.

"I will have you know, Tagius Yairet, I am far from gullible; nor am I looking for some inside information as to where best to invest my money for a hefty return," informed Rose. "If anything, I am doing this to help *us*. If what this woman has to say about our future makes it easier to find that demented little Sprite and the *you-know-what,* then a visit could well be worth it."

"Perhaps the Princess is right, young master. Don't mean to sound like I'm takin' anyone's side on this matter, but havin' this kind of knowledge would certainly be helpful, considerin' how vast and sprawlin' these lands are," said Cankles.

"Yes, but keep in mind it will only be helpful if her predictions are accurate," reminded Tag.

"That's very true," agreed Cankles.

"Being that I have never before used the services of a fortune-teller, when we do find this seer of the future, how will we know she is truly gifted with the power of foresight?" questioned Rose.

"How would I know? I guess you'll just have to take your chances. In my way of thinking, if she really can predict the future, she'll know of our coming," decided Tag. "She'd probably have signs galore showing the way to make sure we don't miss her."

"You think?" asked Rose.

"Of course she would! That absolutely makes perfect sense to me," said Cankles. He nodded in agreement with Tag as he tied the pack of food back onto his horse's saddle.

"I suppose if she is as good as she is reputed to be, then she would know," decided Rose.

"Then let's not keep the lady waiting, Princess," suggested Cankles. "We should make haste and seek her out while the light of day still holds."

7

The Agly Truth

"It feels like we have been riding forever," whined Rose. She rolled her shoulders, twisting about to loosen her stiff back muscles that painfully reverberated with every jarring beat of her mare's hooves as it trotted along the dirt road. "How do you know we have not ridden right by the village?"

"I'm the best G.P.S. provider in these parts! You must learn ta trust in me, m'lady," urged the Gnome, his beet-stained index finger pointing the way to Tag, even though it was obvious the trail ahead was straight.

"Yes, yes! So you say, but need I remind you that you are the *only* Gnome we have seen in these parts? Hence, making you, by default, the only G.P.S. for leagues and leagues," grunted Rose. "But truly, suppose we missed the village?"

"Was I not right about that gnarled old willow tree that looked like my ol' mummsy?"

"Yes," admitted Rose, recalling the misshapened tree at the fork of the road they turned onto.

"Then trust me. If we passed by Far, then we'd have gone too far an' we'd be in Too Far, but we're not, an' I'd know it."

"How? Does this sorry excuse for a road pass right through the centre of this village, so it is impossible to miss?"

"No, Far is jus' off ta the east of this roadway," replied the Gnome, his words smug.

"So there is a possibility we did go too far," determined the Princess.

"If we had, we'd have ridden right past a huge cedar stump with a large hemlock tree growin' from it. Then for sure, we'd have gone right by it, but we haven't!" explained the pint-sized navigator, his finger weaving like a snake in a 'S' shape to indicate curves in the road ahead.

"That's fine then, after all, isn't that where we're going? To Too Far?" queried Cankles, trying to keep up with this exchange between the Princess and the Gnome.

"No, you'd be wantin' ta go ta Far, not ta Too Far. Too Far is too far away from where the seer of the future dwells," reminded the Gnome.

"Say again," responded Cankles.

"Never mind," sighed Rose, urging her mare on to keep up with Tag's mount. "All that matters is that we have not missed the opportunity to pay a visit to the lady with the gift."

"This lady awaits us with a *gift?*" questioned Cankles. "Oh! I do love presents! Can't wait to see what it is!"

"That is not what the Princess means to say. She was referring to this lady's gift of *foresight*," reminded Tag.

"Oh yes! The *lady* with *that* gift," said Cankles, with a nod of understanding.

"If it helps us to capture the evil Sprite or avoid the demented Sorcerer, it will be time and money well spent," justified Rose.

"Yes, but only if her predictions are accurate," countered Tag, as skeptical as ever.

"We shall find out soon enough," responded Rose.

"Perhaps we should make an appointment?" suggested Cankles. "Just in case she is very busy."

"I think not," said Tag, with a shake of his head. "If she's as good as Princess Rose hopes she is, then she'll already know we're on our way to see her."

"Oh! Quite right, young master, she would know!" exclaimed Cankles.

"Jus' five horse-lengths ahead, you'll be takin' the trail on the right," instructed the Gnome, pointing the way. "Lady Aglynessa's cottage is down this way."

"So this Lady Aglynessa has built a reputation on her gift of foresight?" queried Rose.

"Never been ta see her myself, but she must be good if people in the northern reaches of Dimbolt Forest all know of her," answered the Gnome. "You don't build a reputation if you're bad at what ya do."

"I suppose you are right," said Rose.

"There is such thing as a *bad reputation*," remarked Tag. "Ever think that maybe she's just been very lucky with her guesses."

"They are *predictions*, not guesses. And it sounds like you do not want to see this woman," noted Rose.

"I know you do, and you are in the habit of getting what you want, so I am not about to waste precious time arguing about it. But just don't get your hopes up too high," warned Tag. "You could be setting yourself up for a heaping big serving of disappointment."

Clucking his tongue on the roof of his mouth, Tag urged the stallion on along the well-worn dirt road as Cankles and Rose's mounts trotted on, following close behind. They squinted as the sun's dazzling light danced through the vibrant, green leaves. The tall trees leaning over the road formed a natural archway like the towering ceilings of a great cathedral. Enraptured by a sense of awe, it was as though they were in for an otherworldly experience into the unknown as they ventured forth.

This majestic setting was suddenly marred by large, unsightly signs posted along the roadside. The first sign nailed to a tree beckoned them forth. The white, watered-down paint spelled out the message: *Want to know what lies ahead? Lady Aglynessa can end your dread!*

Trotting by, their eyes were accosted by another sign. This one read: *Today only! All readings half price!* Right behind this, a third made a bold claim: *I know you're coming, I see you... so you might as well get your future told.*

After reading five more signs, all in a row, each designed to entice travellers to pay a visit to this woman for a personal reading, they found a quaint, little cottage in a sunny clearing in the midst of this forest. As they neared, they reined in their steeds as the horses panicked, nervously skittering about as a large, brindle hound suddenly bounded out from behind a shed. Barking and snarling, its mouth frothed as it snapped at Tag's steed, lunging at its rump.

The only thing that prevented the vicious hound from sinking its teeth into the horse was the rope tethering it to a stake pounded into the ground.

"Nice doggie!" gulped Cankles, dismounting on the other side to keep his horse between him and the dog. "Sit! Sit I say!"

Instead of obeying this command, the mongrel howled, prancing about on its hind legs as it strained against the rope that prevented it from mauling these trespassers.

"Careful, my friend!" cautioned Tag. Giving it a wide berth, he led his horse away from the deranged animal. "I don't believe that dog is trained, except to attack."

"Its bite is as nasty as its bark, I'm sure!" Cankles shouted to be heard above the ruckus. "It looks like it's gonna strangle itself just to get at us."

As Cankles and Tag chose to avoid the raging beast, Rose abandoned her mare. With deliberate strides, she marched straight over to the dog.

Its front legs flailed about in the air as the mutt stood on its hind legs, straining against the coarse rope that was pulled so tight, small clouds of dust puffed into the air each time the tether was yanked taut. With threads of saliva flying from its snapping jaws, its yellowed teeth clattered together as it lunged at the Princess.

Rose glared as she snapped back, "I am a princess! How dare you behave like a wild beast before me?"

"Get away from that mutt!" hollered Tag, alarmed as Rose brazenly stared down the crazed animal.

Ignoring his warning, using rolled sheets of parchment she smacked the dog across its snout as she shouted, "Shut it, you mangy cur!"

To Tag and Cankles' surprise, the dog whimpered, leaping back with its tail tucked between its legs. As suddenly as the animal lunged to attack, it retreated; ducking behind the shed it first came from.

"What did you do?" questioned Tag, bewildered by the dog's abrupt change from hellhound to frightened puppy.

"I taught that beast to act with a little respect before royalty," said Rose, stuffing the parchment back into her saddlebag. "It just called for a commanding voice and a firm hand."

"That's it?" asked Tag.

"Any creature, even an unruly man, can be tamed in such a way," insisted Rose, her words were matter-of-fact.

"Oooh! Pity the man to become her husband!" noted Cankles, surprised by her forcefulness as he gave Tag a knowing wink.

"I sense the dog was just so used to people running in fear from him that he was taken by surprise when the puny Princess turned on him," determined Tag.

"Believe what you want," sniffed Rose. "I know that beast recognized royalty when it set its crazy eyes on me!"

"If you say so," Tag sighed.

Tying the horses to a hitching post, Tag lowered the miniscule navigator to the ground.

"While we're busy inside, munch on this," offered Tag, giving the Gnome a big carrot to eat as they moved forward to meet with Lady Aglynessa, and quite possibly, their future.

The Gnome grunted in appreciation, his stout, but dulled teeth snapping off the tip of the vegetable as he settled down for a meal.

Stepping onto the stoop of the cottage, the three comrades prepared to face their destiny. Just as Rose was about to knock, the trio jumped with a start as the door flew wide open.

"Welcome! I've been expecting you!"

Tag and Cankles' mouths dropped open, but for a reason quite different from Rose's.

Instead of an old, haggard woman with years of experience a beautiful young lady, probably no older than Rose, greeted them at the doorway.

"So you were expecting us?" asked Rose, surprised by this greeting.

"Well, maybe not exactly *you*, but I knew someone was coming to my door."

"Oh, my! I'm duly impressed!" praised Cankles. "Already your predictions are provin' accurate."

"Actually, my dog's barking tipped me off. He always makes a huge ruckus when anyone sets foot on my land."

"Smart dog, then," praised Cankles.

"Are you Lady Aglynessa?" questioned Rose, staring suspiciously at the raven-haired beauty.

"Enter! Welcome to my humble abode." She beckoned them through the threshold. "And you can just call me Agly."

"Ugly?" asked Cankles, his brows arching up in surprise as he admired her fine features. "You, young lady, are far from ugly!"

"What is wrong with you? Do you have cloth ears?" admonished Rose. "*Ag*, as in agate, with a *lee*. *Agly*, short for Aglynessa, I'm sure."

"Oh…" was all the red-faced Cankles could manage to say in embarrassed response.

"No harm done! I get this all the time. I'm quite used to it by now," she giggled, motioning her new customers to follow her inside.

"Others tease you about your name?" asked Cankles, appalled by the very notion.

"When I was born, I was named in honour of my three aunts. Originally, I was named after my Aunt Agnes, but my mother couldn't handle all the squabbling when Aunt Marilyn and Aunt Vanessa felt snubbed by the name selection. Hence, my mother was compelled to combine elements from all three names into Aglynessa, just to appease them."

"I bet that shut them up pretty quickly," said Cankles. He nodded in understanding.

"It did and Agly is so much easier to say, but growing up wasn't so easy when the other kids would tease me, calling me Ugly."

"Well, the joke was on them, then," decided Tag, giving her a nod of approval and a congenial smile.

"Well, thank you, kind sir!"

"It is a pleasure to meet your acquaintance, Lady Agly," said Tag. He smiled at this beauty whose ebony tresses cascaded down past her shoulder, framing the delicate features of her face to make her alabaster skin seem luminescent in the sun's light.

"Believe me, the pleasure is all mine," responded Agly, giving Tag a coy smile and a knowing wink as she invited them to sit down at her table. "You're here for a reading, yes?"

"Why else would we be here?" asked Rose, unnerved by this stranger openly flirting with Tag.

"Well, some do come here to buy my honey," explained Agly, pointing to a shelf stocked with ceramic jars sealed with beeswax. "I've got some hives out back and my bees make the sweetest honey in these parts."

"We are not here for honey, *honey*," grunted Rose, her tone, snide. "We heard you possess the power to foretell the future."

"I sure can! Make yourselves at home. I will be right back."

"She's not at all what I expected," whispered Tag, waving and smiling at their hostess as she disappeared into a back room. "I was expecting an old hag with a dowager's hump on her back, warts on her face and crazy, wild hair."

"Like a *witch*," assumed Rose, thoroughly annoyed by the smile on Tag's face and the sparkle in his eyes.

"I suppose," admitted Tag.

"Oh, that girl is much too beautiful to be a witch, that's for sure," said Cankles.

"Maybe she *is* a witch," offered Rose. "And maybe she has you both bewitched to see what is not."

"Beguiled by her loveliness, is more like it," stated Cankles, teasing Tag with a jab of his elbow.

"You're just saying that because you're jealous," decided Tag, as he frowned in disapproval.

"What have I got to be jealous of? I am a princess, the fairest in all of Fleetwood at that!" refuted Rose.

"Yes, but aren't you also the *only* princess in all of Fleetwood," responded Cankles, as Tag chortled at his candid remark.

"Never you mind! And how do you know for certain that she is not some witch and at this very moment, you are both under a strange enchantment; one that causes you to see a beautiful, young woman rather than an ugly, old witch?"

"Why?" asked Tag. "Do you see an ugly hag?"

"I see a *female* of rather bland features. I suppose a man who'd settle for mediocrity would find her somewhat attractive."

"*Jealous!*" taunted Tag, shaking his head in dismay. "That's what you are!"

"No, really!" insisted Rose. "Whether she is gifted with foresight or not, do you truly believe that if she were an eye-sore of a witch she would have anyone wishing to use her services? I think not! It must be a spell we are all under."

"I'm thinkin' that if she was truly as unbecomin' as you believe, Princess, she'd still have regular patrons if she is good at what she does," offered Cankles.

"I was not speaking to you," snipped Rose, using her fingers to clamp her lips together as a sign for Cankles to cease his nonsensical jabbering.

"I'm thinking that I like what I see, and you're just jealous! Plain and simple," grunted Tag, as he listened to Agly rustling about in the other room.

"That girl is plain *and* simple; therefore, I have no reason to be jealous. I am just genuinely concerned that your small, easily-influenced brain has been addled when you stepped upon her threshold," responded Rose, with words meant to condemn. "Perhaps that is how she became endowed with this power. It was acquired through the forbidden arts."

"As in dark magic?" gulped Cankles, his eyes widening in surprise and fear as he nervously glanced about, searching for telltale signs of witchcraft.

"It's a bit late to be thinking about that," scolded Tag, dismissing Rose's words of caution. "And if it were true, it's not as if you can just ask her if she's a witch."

"Why not? All indications point to this fact."

"What indications?" questioned Tag, frowning in confusion. "A bubbling cauldron of magic potion? For if so, I see none!"

"Listen up, you gullible boy! Allow me to draw up a list: A beautiful young woman, here... living alone on the outskirts of town; gifted with an ability normal people like me are lacking in," answered the Princess. "Need I say more?"

"Please don't! You are lacking in many things and just how *normal* you are is up for debate," teased Tag, dismissing Rose's misgivings of this lovely stranger.

Her finger jabbed Tag's chest to make sure she had his undivided attention as she continued to state her case. "You say that now, but give that addled noggin of yours a hard shake! I find it mighty odd that she lives here alone with nothing more than her hives of bees and that vicious mutt of a dog."

"I find you to be '*mighty odd*', but I continue to associate with you, Princess! So there!" stated Tag. "And who said Lady Agly lives alone?"

"I do! And look!" Rose pointed to a cat peacefully napping on the windowsill in the warmth of the afternoon sun, "A *black* cat."

"Aaah!" sighed Cankles. His hands clasped together in delight as he gazed with adoring eyes at the sleeping feline. "It's so cute! I do like cats."

"You fool!" scolded Rose, wagging a condescending finger at her comrade. "Witches have cats – *black* cats to be exact."

Cankles frowned with concern as he noted, "That cat is not completely black. It has white mittens and socks, white whiskers, too. And in the sunlight, that black fur looks more like dark brown, in my opinion."

"I was not asking for your opinion. Just trust me, my friends. I do believe this wench is actually a witch in disguise," assured Rose, offering a judicious nod to her comrades.

"Bloody hell… And here, you were the one who was so insistent that go out of our way to come here in the first place!" Tag grumbled in frustration.

"That was *before* I became aware of the obvious," Rose argued in her defense.

"You are obviously nuttier than a fruitcake," teased Tag, rolling his eyes to the heavens.

"I like fruitcake," announced Cankles, as he smacked his lips.

"Hush!" snapped Rose. "This is no time to be thinking of food. We can be in mortal danger."

"I won't be long!" Agly shouted from the other room as she sorted through the tools of her trade. "Just getting together what I need to do a proper reading."

"Take all the time you need," offered Rose. "We are in no hurry."

Seizing Tag by the lapels of his vest, she whispered, "Hurry up! Think of something."

"You're the one who suddenly decided she's a witch," retorted Tag, prying Rose's fingers off his crumpled vest. "You figure it out."

"Oh, lovely! Rose to the rescue, yet again," muttered the Princess. "Fine! I will get to the bottom of this. I will prove to you that she is not all that she appears to be."

"This will be interesting," snorted Tag, shaking his head in dismay. "Just remember, you don't want to offend her if you're wrong, nor do you want to raise her ire if you're right."

"Oooh! The young master is quite correct, m'lady! You don't need to be settin' another curse upon yourself," cautioned Cankles, sitting on the edge of his seat like he was ready to bolt from this cottage at the most opportune moment. "One curse is more than enough for the average man... or woman, in your case."

"Worry not, I will be wise in my choice of words," decided Rose, gathering her composure by smoothing out the wrinkles of her dress. "Being that I am a princess, tact and diplomacy are my middle names."

"I thought *rude* and *inept* were," teased Tag, biting his lower lip to stifle his cry of pain as Rose kicked his ankle.

All three jumped with a start as a crystal landed with a heavy *'thud'* in the middle of the table; its rough, jagged bottom biting into the wooden surface to add more permanent indentations.

"Here we go!" said Agly. She placed a shell and its single content on the table as she occupied the chair between Cankles and Tag. "I had to find my new rune stone. This one is much easier to read than any of my old ones."

"This is one, huge rune stone!" exclaimed Cankles. He stared at the pillar of crystal, the many smooth, flat facets refracting light in all the colours of the rainbow to shine against the walls and ceiling. The clear top facets ascended to form a sharp point while the bottom of this formation rested on a jagged, cloudy nest of opaque quartz from which this large shard grew from the earth.

"Oh, no! That's not my rune stone. This old thing is my reading crystal," explained Agly.

"Kinda like a crystal ball?" asked Cankles.

"Exactly! Except mine is not all round, smooth and polished," responded Agly, gazing proudly at the crystal handed down through the generations.

"I was not expecting this *thing*. What happened to using a conventional crystal *ball?*" asked Rose, as she stared with skepticism at the largest chunk of crystal she had ever seen. "Does round and polished not make for a more precise reading?"

"Contrary to what most believe; a crystal in its purest form, ripped from the bowels of the earth and free of the manipulations of human hands to shape it, makes for the best, most accurate predictions," answered Agly, her words convincing.

"Makes sense to me," said Tag, his shoulders shrugging with indifference. "Let's do this."

"Hold on," ordered Rose, raising a dainty hand for Agly to desist. "Before we proceed, I have a few questions to ask you."

"I know... that is why you are here," responded Agly, giving her new patron a knowing smile.

"Oooh! You *are* good!" praised Cankles, nodding in approval to their hostess.

"The questions I wish to ask have nothing to do with *me*, and everything to do with *you*," stated Rose, her eyes narrowing in suspicion as she scrutinized the girl.

"Go on then. Ask away," urged Agly.

"Very well! So, just what are your credentials?" probed Rose, intent on discrediting this girl Tag seemed so taken with.

"My credentials?" repeated Agly, her delicate brows furrowing in confusion. "What do you mean?"

"What is your background? Your level of expertise?" interrogated Rose. "Exactly how did you acquire your '*gift*'?"

Agly frowned in bewilderment as she answered, "It was passed down from my momma, that's how."

"What about dabbling in certain plants for, let's say... their medicinal properties?" Rose continued her inquisition. "Perhaps you have mixed these said plants with an eye of newt or wart of toad from time to time?"

"What are you talking about?" queried Agly. "Are you asking if I run an apothecary?"

"I am not speaking of a *traditional* apothecary, if that is what you prefer to call it," sniffed Rose. "Perhaps you will better understand this question: Have you, perchance, cursed a person or two in the past?"

"I've done my fair share of cursing at customers who left without paying, but I've never hexed them, if that's what you mean."

"I mean to ask, have you ever invoked the powers of the forbidden arts to place an enchantment or curse on another soul?"

"Exactly what are you asking me?" Agly stared intently into Rose's violet eyes that glittered like perfect stones of amethyst.

"My *friend* is asking you if you are a witch," responded Tag, giving Rose a smug smile as the Princess squirmed uncomfortably.

Agly tossed her luxuriant tresses over her shoulders as she giggled, "You mean like a *witch* witch?"

"I'm afraid so," apologized Tag, as he and Cankles both joined her, laughing as Rose's cheeks burned with embarrassment, turning a deeper hue of red.

"Well, of course I am!" confided Agly. "Fourth generation witch to be sure!"

"*Ah-ha!* I am on to you, missy!" declared Rose, pointing an accusing finger at their hostess as her comrades' laughter came to an abrupt halt upon this admission.

"I prefer to call myself an enchantress though. I don't much care for the word '*witch*' and all that it implies. Has rather negative connotations, if you get my meaning?"

"Enchantress, indeed!" said Tag, giving Agly a broad smile and a nod of approval.

"And even if you wanted to call me a witch, I'm not a witch in the traditional sense. Didn't much care for learning about potions and spells. Nor did I like testing them; that was the worst part of that whole witchcraft business."

"So… it is not as though you delve into the forbidden arts?" ascertained Rose. "You do not deal in dark magic?"

"Oh, no! The only thing I delve into is sharing secrets about what the future holds in store."

"So, my comrades are not under some kind of bewitching spell at this moment?" questioned Rose, staring suspiciously at Cankles and Tag, for it was obvious to her they saw a girl of far greater beauty than she could see.

"Why would I place them under an enchantment?"

"It would explain why their jaws dropped upon seeing you," answered Rose, grimacing in pain as Tag's boot pressed down firmly on her toes to make her stop insulting their hostess.

Agly blushed upon hearing her comment.

"Look here," explained Rose, as she pointed at Tag, "*he*, of all people, needs no distractions; especially coming from a flirtatious tart of a fortune-teller!"

"Good gracious! I'd never make advances at another girl's man," promised Agly, giving Tag an innocent smile.

"Oh, believe me, this rogue of a scallywag is *not* my man!"

"He isn't?" asked Agly, as she glanced over at Tag with a renewed look of hope gleaming in her eyes.

"Not my type in more ways than one, if you get my meaning?" stated the Princess; her words were matter-of-fact.

"Why not? He is very handsome, after all," said Agly, smiling shyly at Rose's comrade.

"I am?" Tag looked momentarily stunned, but flattered as he sat up tall in his chair.

"He is?" added Rose, frowning in disgust.

"Of course!" responded Agly. Beneath the table, her bare foot lightly caressed Tag's leg, causing him to jump with a start at this unexpected advance.

"Never mind him," urged Rose. "We are here to conduct important business with you."

"Oh yes, of course!" acknowledged Agly, smiling at the flustered young man struggling to regain his composure. "Let us begin with introductions. You know who I am, so what are your names?"

"Guess!" invited Cankles, offering her a congenial smile. "I'm bettin' you already know who we are, m'lady."

"For pity's sake! We have no time for silly games," admonished Rose, pointing to her comrades as she made the introductions. "This buffoon is Cankles Moron. That ruffian with that stupid grin on his face seated to your right is my servant, Tag and my name is Rose-alyn."

"Mayron," corrected Cankles.

"And my name is Tagius, *plus*, I am *not* your servant. I am a knight-in-training."

"It is a pleasure to meet you, one and all! Let us commence," said Agly.

Greeting her guests with a friendly smile, Agly's warm demeanor served to melt Tag's heart, while glazing over Rose's, made all the colder by her frosty disposition as she bore witness to this friendly exchange between the fortune-teller and her servant.

Agly placed a large abalone shell before the trio. Inside this bowl, a single, polished rectangular pebble stood out against the iridescent mother-of-pearl. One side of this pebble was black; the other was milky white in colour.

"How does it work?" asked Cankles, staring at this small rune stone that was marked by a strange, white etching on the dark side and a black one on the white surface.

"As there are three of you, we must first determine who is the most receptive to a reading. Each of you will take a turn tossing this stone into the air, and then catching it in this bowl."

"And then what?" asked Tag, discreetly angling his legs away from this girl's amorous reach.

"It's difficult to give an accurate reading if my energies are spread thin between the three of you. This is so we can decide who gets the reading, so I can better focus on the task at hand. If your stone lands white side up, you get a reading. If black, you'll have to come back again when the divine spirits are more willing to accommodate you."

"So there is a chance you will not be doing a reading for me?" queried Rose.

"A fifty percent chance to be exact," responded Agly, nodding in confirmation.

"Spot on with her prediction again," praised Cankles, amazed by this young woman's abilities.

"That was not a prediction," countered Rose. "It was nothing more than pure logic. It will either be *yes* or *no*."

"Who should go first?" asked Tag.

"Age before beauty," said Rose, sliding the abalone shell bowl before Cankles.

"Don't mind if I do!" Cankles cupped the shell in his hands as he looked to Agly. "Should I be thinkin' of anything in particular as I do this?"

"No, just relax and empty your mind."

"That won't be difficult for him to do," grumbled Rose, eager to see the outcome.

"Release all negative thoughts," continued Agly, "and open your mind to the possibilities."

Cankles closed his eyes, clearing all stray thoughts as he tossed the pebble into the air. With a dull clatter, he caught it in the bowl. It bounced from side to side, switching from black to white only to come to rest with the black side up again.

"Nope, won't be me on this day," concluded Cankles, passing the stone and the bowl on to Tag.

Without any care or thought, Tag tossed the monochromatic pebble, not caring either way about which side it would land on. This time, there was no bouncing to and fro; it was plainly black.

"Too bad, just not my lucky day I suppose," said Tag, with a feigned sigh of disappointment.

"Hoorah! Then I am the fortunate one," announced Rose.

"To the contrary," said Agly. "It is up to the divine spirits to determine if you are worthy of a reading on this day."

"But I *am* worthy," insisted the Princess, "being royalty, and all."

"Sorry, but this is how it works," responded Agly, sliding the abalone shell and its rune stone before her. "If you refuse to abide by the rules as set forth by the divine spirits, then they will refuse to cooperate. And if they do, then what's shown could very well be questionable in terms of accuracy."

"Fine, then!" Rose snatched the shell into her hands.

Closing her eyes, and clearing her mind, she slowly exhaled. Focusing on the task at hand, she prayed for the stone to land in her favour. Tossing the pebble, in a blur of black and white, it tumbled through the air. The rune stone clattered loudly as it landed against the mother-of-pearl. Bouncing once, the natural, inward curving lip of the shell prevented the pebble from straying outside this bowl.

"Yes!" Rose exclaimed in triumph, her fist pumping the air. "I win the right for a reading."

"Very good," said Agly, nodding in approval. "So here's the Agly Truth."

"You mean to say the ugly truth," corrected Tag.

"When it comes to my predictions, believe me, it is the *Agly Truth*.

It can be ugly at times, but usually not."

"Explain," ordered Rose. "What is the meaning of this 'Agly Truth' business?"

"It is best to say that when I foresee the future, I can only interpret what I see."

"So?" responded Rose.

"So... ever since I dropped this silly thing, the crystal only reveals images to me. There are no sounds to reveal the exact context of conversations between those appearing in the course of a reading."

"Meaning, you are making an educated guess as to what these images mean," determined Tag.

"Pretty much," admitted Agly. "The images you'll see are one hundred percent accurate, but my interpretation of what it means may be slightly off."

"Slightly?" questioned Rose, her eyes narrowing in suspicion as she glared at the girl.

"Well, you're welcome to interpret what you see for yourself, but usually, I'm quite good at it."

"This is your crystal and your area of expertise, Lady Agly," said Tag. "I think we would be wise to leave the business of divination up to you."

"Oh, just call me Agly. And I take no offense if any one of you questions my abilities to foretell the future. You'd not be the first, and I can tell you right now, you will not be the last."

"I'd say my abilities would be far more questionable than yours, m'lady," said Cankles. "Please, proceed."

"I agree, so let us get this underway," ordered Rose.

"Are you sure you want a glimpse into your future?" questioned Agly, peering into Rose's eyes as though searching her soul. "For there are some who believe it does not bode well to do so."

"I am not one of these people," assured the Princess. "Besides, as far as I am concerned, things can get no worse for me than they already are."

"Alrighty, then," said Agly, using the sleeve of her frock to rub away the most obvious smudges of fingerprints from the surface of the large crystal. "Let's get this done."

"How do we start?" asked Tag.

"First, we join hands," instructed the young lady, extending hers to Tag and Cankles. "Go on now."

She encouraged Rose to do the same as the Princess merely stared at Cankles and Tag's grubby paws they presented before her.

"Must I?" asked Rose, grimacing in repulsion as Agly eagerly clasped Tag's hand into hers.

"Yes," insisted Agly. "We must, as one, invite the divine powers to do a proper reading."

"Very well, then," conceded Rose, touching, but just barely, her comrades' grimy mitts.

"Now, close your eyes, clear your mind and focus on the beating of your heart," instructed Agly. "When our hearts all beat as one, we will be ready to proceed."

All in the room did as she ordered, but as soon as Rose closed her eyes; Agly opened hers. While her new customers tried to concentrate, she began to fondle Tag's hand, her warm fingertips teasingly caressing his palm as the young man began to squirm in discomfort, not expecting these amorous advances.

One of Tag's eyes popped open, and then the other as he stared at the beautiful, flirtatious Agly. As far as he could determine, she was concentrating on things other than conjuring up divine powers.

"And we're ready to proceed!" announced Tag, yanking his hand free of this girl's adoring grasp.

"We are?" asked Rose, opening her eyes to see an innocently smiling girl sitting next to a clearly flustered Tag.

"I'm ready," said Cankles. "At least, I think I am."

"Good! Time is wasting away," said Tag, averting his eyes from Rose's unyielding stare and Agly's admiring glance. "I'd like for this reading to be underway."

"Just be patient, Sir Tagius," ordered Agly. "I must be in the right state of mind for this crystal to work properly, or at least as properly as it can for a crystal that's a bit faulty."

"Faulty in that it provides no sound, correct?" asked Rose. "Other than that, the images we will be privy to are accurate."

"Correct," stated Agly, her hands waving over the crystal as it began to glow; a warm, golden light swelling from its depth. "It's all in the interpretation."

"And what do you see?" asked Tag.

"Hush! Let the girl concentrate," scolded Rose, motioning for him to shut his mouth.

"How very intriguing!" noted Agly. Staring intently into the crystal, she then glanced up at Rose.

"What is it?" queried the Princess.

"Though you were the one to win the right for a reading, it would appear your life is so intrinsically bound to your friends' lives, the revelations to be shared concern all three of you."

"Already your reading proves inaccurate," grunted Rose.

"How so?" asked Agly.

"For one, my affiliation with these two can only be loosely defined as *friendship*, for it was nothing more than a cruel twist of fate that brought us together on this quest to begin with. Secondly, my life is very much my own and of far greater value, that I loath to have it bound to theirs, not that their lives are worthless or anything like that," explained Rose, speaking with all certainty.

"Oh my! You have a grand sense of humour!" praised Agly, seeing how Tag rolled his eyes in frustration, while Cankles scratched his head in thought, trying to comprehend the exact meaning of Rose's words.

"Yes, it's the kind of humour one would like nothing more than to take a big mace to. Club it in into shape, if you get my meaning?" grumbled Tag, as he scowled in disapproval at Rose.

"Hush! Your incessant chatter is cutting into my valuable reading time," scolded Rose, motioning Tag to be quiet.

As the mist swirling in the centre of the crystal began to dissipate, Agly said to her, "You have lost something... It was something of great value to you."

"Her mind, but it wasn't *that* valuable," teased Tag, laughing at his own joke.

He was greeted by a look of consternation as the others attempted to focus on the message the crystal was trying to put forth.

"Go on," urged Rose. Staring into the crystal, her back straightened as she listened intently.

"You have lost a... friend."

"*A friend?*" repeated Rose, as she frowned in confusion.

"It looks to be a Fairy!" explained Agly.

"You are doubly wrong," stated Rose, shaking her head in disappointment. "He is a wicked little Sprite, and he is definitely *not* a friend."

"But we *are* looking for him," said Tag.

"Like I said, there is no sound, so I must interpret what I see as best I can," explained Agly.

"Can you tell us where he is at this very moment?" asked Cankles, his eyes straining to see what this girl spied within the crystal as a fractured image played out on the various facets.

"I can foretell the future, not give details of the here and now, or I'd be rather useless as a fortune-teller, don't you think?" responded Agly.

"That makes sense," admitted Cankles.

"Fine, then," grunted Rose. "Can you tell us where that little miscreant is planning to go or where we can eventually find that marauding, little thief in the not-too-distant future?"

Agly stared deep into the crystal, scrutinizing the fleeting images that played out before her.

"Now, I see a man... He is a stranger to you."

"What about him?" asked Rose.

"You must go see this man..."

"What does he look like?" questioned Rose, her eyes straining to see what Agly saw through the veil of mist. "Does he have a name?"

"The crystal is not providing me with a name... At least, not right now."

"Then how are we to find him?" asked Rose.

"Just look for the man with a hairy mole," advised Agly, as the image faded. "He can tell you where this Sprite can be found."

"A man with a *hairy mole* can tell us where to find the Sprite?" repeated Tag, making sure he heard her correctly.

"As best as I can tell, yes."

"Can you tell us where we can find this man?" questioned Rose. "Is he near to us?"

"He has a home just outside of Far... no wait! He is in Too Far. Head north to the outskirts of this village and you will find him there."

"What else can you tell us about this man?" asked Tag.

"That was all to be revealed to me," answered Agly. "But what is this?"

Her eyes pierced through the swirling fingers of mist to see an image of Cankles. He was on his back and looking on in utter horror as a great, scaly foot was about to come crashing down on him.

"What is it, m'lady?" asked Cankles, noting the look of concern in her eyes.

Agly glanced over at him as she answered, "I see you."

"I see you, too, m'lady."

"No, I mean to say, I see you in there – in the future," responded Agly, turning her gaze into the magical crystal.

"And what do you see?" questioned Cankles, squinting as he stared through the mist swirling inside.

"I'd refrain from having any entanglements with dragons," warned the girl.

"No need for concern," said Cankles. "I have no intention of going anywhere near to those ghastly beasts."

"Well, just in case, a confrontation is not recommended," warned Agly. "It is sure to end badly."

"That is just common sense," grunted Rose. "What person, in

their right mind, would even think of confronting a dragon in the first place?"

"Apparently, *you* will," answered Agly, checking the fleeting image once more to catch a glimpse of Rose armed with Cankles' dagger as she rushed in to stab the beast.

"Me? I am not that demented!" gasped Rose. "It must be a mistake!"

Another fleeting image materialized before Agly. This time, Rose was frozen with fear as she faced a dragon that had dropped from the sky to appear before her. She watched as the creature's black, forked tongue flickered as it approached her, hissing and snarling as Tag slowly unsheathed his sword to fend off the beast.

"It is wrong to take what is not yours," warned Agly.

"She already knows that, but it doesn't usually stop her," snorted Tag, as he rolled his eyes in frustration.

"Because of your actions, your friends will endanger themselves in saving you, if you do not heed this warning."

"Warning heeded!" gulped Cankles, leaning in closer to the crystal to fully appreciate this prediction.

"Tell us more," urged Tag. "What else can you see in there?"

Agly gazed into the crystal, preparing to make her next prediction as Cankles leaned forward, eager to catch a glimpse of what the future held in store for them. He hovered over this glowing crystal, his nose almost pressing against the polished surface as his eyes squinted, peering into one of the facets.

"I don't see a thing… Methinks the future is lookin' cloudy," stated Cankles.

"It is you! You are fogging it up with your breath," grunted Rose, pulling on Cankles' vest to make him sit down.

"Oh my! Sorry 'bout that," apologized Cankles, reclining back in his chair to allow the condensation to evaporate.

"I see something now…"

"What is it?" asked Tag.

"Oh, my goodness! Now who is this man with the ill-favoured look about him?" asked Agly, as she glanced up at her patrons. "He looks none too pleased."

Tag, Rose and Cankles leaned over the table to peer at this image that Agly found so troubling. Inside the crystal a hazy scene unfolded before their eyes. Recognition was immediate! It was Parru St. Mime Dragonite. He was in a fit of rage, venting his wrath on a bat as it frantically fluttered about the cave.

"I wonder what he's saying," pondered Tag, watching the Sorcerer swallow a beverage from a pewter vessel, only to spew a fine mist at the bat hovering before him.

In a voice sounding eerily like that of the Sorcerer's, Cankles provided his version of the dialogue taking place: "Cream! I told you I wanted cream for my tea!"

His voice then became high pitched and squeaky as he pretended to mouth the words spoken by the bat, "but master, we have no cream – never did!"

They watched Dragonite hurl the cup and its contents in the bat's direction. As the vessel of wine bounced off against the cave wall, rather than repeat the words of profanity uttered by the Sorcerer, Cankles offered his version of this confrontation, "Then turn into a cow! I demand cream for my tea!"

The bat darted behind a stalactite, squeaking in protest of this treatment as a bolt of energy flew from Dragonite's staff to annihilate the rocky formation. Cankles offered his interpretation in a high pitched voice, "But master, no can moo - I mean do! I can't turn into a cow. I can only turn into a bull."

"Hush! Enough with this silliness," scolded Rose, staring intently as a grey veil of mist shrouded this image to obstruct her view.

"It appears that the Sprite continues to conspire with the Sorcerer after all," determined Tag.

"It doesn't look like it's goin' well for the little fellow," decided Cankles.

"You know this man?" asked Agly, gazing at Tag with genuine concern.

"Unfortunately, yes, but not on a social level," admitted Tag.

"I have a very bad feeling about him," said Agly, searching her crystal to see if it would reveal more.

"We all do," grunted Rose. "What more can you tell us?"

"Let me see…" said Agly, scrutinizing another image for more clues. Just as Cankles, Tag and Rose leaned forward for a better look, they jumped with a start.

The Sorcerer raged and this time, it was clear to see his mouth formed the words: *Kill them all!*

The light shining from within the crystal swelled, filling the room with a menacing red glow as a gargantuan dragon bellowed, preparing to unleash a torrent of deadly flames. A dense fog filled the crystal, refusing to reveal anymore.

"I wasn't expectin' that!" gasped Cankles, scrambling back into the chair he fell from.

Agly frowned in confusion as the image changed once more.

This time, she said, "When water turns to fire and you pass through unscathed, you shall seek what you desire, if you follow the way."

"What the heck does that mean?" asked Cankles. "Since when does fire leave *anything* unscathed?"

"I tell it as I see it," answered Agly, her slight shoulders rolling in a shrug as a fleeting image of a towering waterfall faded from sight and then there was nothing.

"I must see more! Tell us more," demanded Rose. Panic filled her heart as her knuckles rapped on one of the smooth, flat facets of the crystal to prompt it to work.

"There's nothing more to tell you," said Agly, pushing Rose's hands away from her tool of divination. "The spirits have decreed that this is all they can, or will, reveal to you at this time."

"Well, you can tell your divine spirits that they are cheating us of a proper reading," snapped Rose, heaving a disgruntled sigh. "There's nothing more you can tell us?"

"I can strongly recommend that you stay away from that deranged soul, the one that wants to kill the three of you, and to avoid any kind of confrontation with all manner of dragons. Yes, stay as far away as you possibly can from these dangers," offered Agly, tossing a black velvet cloth over the crystal before Rose could accost it again.

"And that is it?" grunted Rose, heaving a disgruntled sigh. "We are to avoid danger?"

"Unless you want me to make things up, then yes, that's all there is for now."

"I have been cheated of a decent reading," insisted Rose. "I demand to know more."

"You can demand all you want. Like I said, there is nothing more I can tell you. The divine spirits are temperamental at the best of times. They will only reveal what they wish to show you," explained Agly.

"If this is the only kind of stuff the divine spirits are willin' to share, I really don't want to know anymore," decided Cankles, pushing his chair away from the table.

"Tag, make this girl reveal more of the future to us," demanded Rose, hoping that Agly would be swayed by her companion's words of persuasion.

"I think you should just pay Lady Agly and we'll be on our way," responded Tag.

"But I'd like to know who the Sorcerer was ordering that dragon to kill," said Rose. "I just want to be sure."

"Trust me, you really don't," replied Tag, standing up to take his leave. "It's time for us to go."

"And rush off to certain doom?" gasped Rose, shaking her head in dismay. "I think not!"

"The future is not engraved in stone. And it is not as though you know what the final outcome will be, anyway," disputed Tag.

"Well, I refuse to venture forth if this is what is in store for me," argued the Princess. "Doom or despair, the future does not bode well for any of us by the look of things to come."

"Methinks it's lookin' like an equal measure of doom *and* despair," sighed Cankles, giving his head a dismal shake.

"And what do you think will happen if we don't continue on?" asked Tag. "There will be no future for us, or anyone else, for that matter."

"So, you are saying I have no choice," grumbled Rose.

"You always have a choice. It's only a matter of whether you can make the right one."

"You are trying to make me feel guilty."

"Yes, I am," admitted Tag, "if it's the only way to make you do the right thing, then absolutely."

Rose scowled, her lower lip protruding in a stubborn pout as she glared at Tag.

"There is nothing more for us; no point in lingering here any longer than need be," stated Tag, waving Cankles on to follow him to the door. "Pay Lady Agly and we shall take our leave."

"Fine! If I pay you the full amount instead of your discounted rate, will you at least tell me when these events will happen?" questioned Rose, digging out a silver coin from a velveteen pouch to tempt the fortune-teller.

"Sure, I can do that," replied Agly, accepting the coin from her customer.

"Well?" coaxed Rose. "When exactly will these predictions take place?"

"They will happen sometime in the future, and they shall unfold exactly when the divine spirits decides that will be so," answered the girl, as she pocketed the silver.

"What?" gasped Rose, her brows arching up in dismay. "Is that all you can tell me?"

"Yes, and it was the absolute truth," responded the girl.

Rose unleashed another disgruntled sigh.

"There you go! You asked; she answered honestly," said Tag, in Agly's defense.

"But I was expecting a concise answer; a chronological unfolding of events, not this vague response," argued Rose.

"Well, you know these spirits... they are as fickle as you are," teased Tag. "Come, we leave now."

Just as they were about to exit through the door, Agly dashed across the room, snatching up a small ceramic jar from one of the shelves.

"Take this," offered Agly, passing the jar to Tag. "You might be in need of this."

"What is it?" asked Tag, sniffing the hardened beeswax sealing the opening of the jar.

"Honey, it will come in handy."

"Yes, *dear*, but what is it?" snipped Rose, glaring at the girl bearing this gift.

"It's honey," explained Tag. "This jar is full of honey."

"Wonderful! I do love honey," exclaimed Cankles, smacking his lips as he eyed the delectable treat.

"You tend to love anything that is edible, especially if it is sweet," grumbled Rose, snatching the jar from Tag's hand.

"Thank you, Lady Agly," said Cankles, bowing his head in appreciation and respect. "Thank you for your time and for makin' me privy to information, that in hindsight, I'd rather not know about."

"You are most welcome, Master Mayron." She curtsied politely before Cankles. "Just remember, such information can be used to your advantage."

"Yes, I suppose a thank you is in order," decided Rose, nodding in acknowledgement to the girl.

"You have already thanked me with coin, but the thanks shall be hollow if you do not heed my warning," cautioned Agly, as she politely curtsied to Rose.

"We will certainly consider your words," promised Tag.

Before he could bow in parting salutation, rather than curtsy as she did to the others, Agly threw her arms around the young man, planting a kiss upon his mouth.

Though surprised by her actions, Tag's bid to resist was futile as these soft, warm lips pressed against his. As though he was under a strange enchantment, everything and everyone around him seemed to magically vanish. His will simply melted in her embrace as he answered this kiss.

"They do make for a lovely couple," commented Cankles, nodding in approval.

Rose's mouth dropped open in awe and disgust, and then slammed shut as she growled through clenched teeth, "Enough of these shenanigans! We must be off!"

"We're in no hurry," sighed Tag, staring dreamily into Agly's emerald green eyes.

"Oh, yes we are! We leave *now!*" demanded Rose, prying the girl off of Tag. "Get your mouth and hands off of him!"

"But he will never come by this way again," lamented Agly, as she stared lovingly at Tag. "I just wanted to wish him well."

"A handshake would have sufficed," grunted Rose, giving Tag a shove as she physically barred Agly from making another advance at him. "We must be off now!"

"No need to leave at this very moment," sighed Tag, staring mesmerized into the eyes of his beautiful, new admirer.

"Why not stay?" invited Agly. "Darkness falls quickly on this forest. You can spend the night here."

Before Tag could accept this invitation on their behalf, Rose grabbed his arm, steering him out through the door before Agly could further entice him.

"Oh, I'm on to you, you brazen, little hussy! We leave now!" insisted Rose, pushing her comrade toward his waiting horse.

8
A Momentary Distraction

"Desperate, little trollop!" Rose cursed beneath her breath. Her eyes, aglow like pinpoints of fire, burned with resentment as she glared at her comrade.

This stare was so intense, Tag could swear they'd burn a hole clear through his cloak and vest to permanently brand the skin on his back.

"I heard that," muttered Tag, shrugging off this uneasy feeling pressing down on him like an ominous shadow of doom.

"Good! And I will have you know that what I said was true; every word of it."

"So… you're saying that a beautiful, young lady like Aglynessa would have to be *desperate* to fall in love with someone like me?"

"Believe me, she was no lady! And, as you are a typical male and you are too dense to know it; it was *lust*, not *love*, shining in her beady, little eyes!"

"Really?" snapped Tag.

A baleful glance over his shoulder did nothing to deter Rose, as she continued to verbally run roughshod over the fortune-teller.

"A respectable lady does not throw herself at a man like that. And take no offence, Tag, but yes! That girl was clearly desperate. Living way out here – alone, she probably hadn't seen a living, breathing male of the human species in ages."

"Offence taken," grumbled Tag, ignoring the Gnome as the little navigator frantically pointed to the main road while horse and rider veered off onto the little trail to the left. "I believe she, unlike you, has excellent taste. That young lady knows a man of good quality and sound character when she meets one!"

"Surely you jest! She could not even differentiate between a *boy* and a *man*," snorted Rose, turning her nose up at Tag.

"Turn back at your first opportunity," instructed the Gnome, madly pointing back at the road leading to Too Far. "You've strayed off course."

"Bloody hell!" snapped Tag. Scowling at the Princess, he reined in his mount, wheeling his steed about. "Look what you've done. We could have gotten lost."

"Oh, whoop-dee-do! I hardly think so. Is that not what your little friend is for? To keep us from losing our way?" snorted Rose, her voice tightening with sarcasm as she pointed at the Gnome. "So we must turn back? Big deal!"

"It *is* a big deal!" snapped Tag. "Had we gotten lost, I'd never hear the end of it from you."

"And rightly so!" rebuked Rose, urging her mare to follow Tag's horse, as Cankles took up the rear on his mount.

"Oh, my! Someone's in a foul mood," noted Cankles, grimacing under Rose's scathing tone. He was just grateful he was not caught in the middle of this debate and now, he could only hope he would not to be drawn into this altercation or downed by the stray, hostile words deflected in this verbal volley.

"Speaking forcefully, and with conviction, does not mean I am in a foul mood," argued Rose, her heels vigorously tapping the mare's flanks to urge it on.

"Well, you can sure fool me," snorted Tag, guiding his horse back onto the road as the Gnome continued to point the way.

"So I was wrong, m'lady," conceded Cankles, nodding in acknowledgement to the Princess. "Being mad is not quite the same as being jealous, that's for sure."

"*Jealous?* Are you insane? Who said that I am jealous?" snapped Rose, scowling in resentment.

"Oh, no need to say it, m'lady," explained Cankles. "It's in your actions and I can see that glint in your eyes. They said it all, especially when you pried Lady Agly away from the young master's arms."

Tag said nothing, merely giving the Princess his best self-satisfied, *I-told-you-so* grin.

"Just because we were in a hurry to leave, it does not mean I was jealous," insisted Rose.

"She likes me. You're jealous. She likes me. You're jealous," chanted Tag, his voice annoyingly chirpy as he tormented her.

"*Owww!*" Tag yelped in pain as one of Rose's small, steel balls bounced off the back of his head.

"You are being infantile! I have nothing to be jealous of where you and that little trollop are concerned, you incorrigible ruffian!" Her hand reached into the pouch containing the never-ending supply of ammunition for her sling, threatening to assault Tag again if he failed to refrain from antagonizing her.

"Was that really necessary?" grumbled Tag. He rubbed the back of his smarting head that would now, undoubtedly swell with a small goose egg to mark the point of impact.

"Yes, it was!" snapped Rose, pleased that her aim was still accurate in the dimming light. "And if anything, you were probably nothing more than a momentary distraction for that girl! She was undoubtedly bored out of her puny mind, living way out in the middle of nowhere all on her own."

"Call it what you will, but if that is how she wants to treat *'this distraction'* as you so eloquently put it," snapped Tag, his thumb jabbing his chest in defiance, "then I liked it! So there!"

Hoping to put an end to this verbal sniping, Cankles spoke up. "Perhaps we should rest for the night, my friends. Darkness will be upon us before we know it."

"Good idea," decided Tag, steering his stallion off the road into a small clearing, even as the Gnome continued pointing north to Too Far. "This is as good a place as any. We'll rest for the night; journey on at first light."

As dusk surrendered to the coming of the night, a pair of amber eyes glowed, intensifying as the shadows of the great oak tree deepened with the setting of the sun.

Disguised as a great horned owl, with eyes now perfectly suited to see in the growing darkness, Loken scrutinized his surroundings. It had been years since he was last in the Fairy's Vale, but even with the passing of time, little had changed in his absence.

The Fairy's Ring, a circle of white toadstools with the distinct, red caps flecked by white spots continued to thrive in the forest clearing. By the path worn by many tiny feet, it was obvious the Fairies still congregated at this very spot, dancing under the silvery light of the full moon, weather permitting.

The tufts of feathers protruding from his head and the flat, disk-shaped face all assisted in gathering and transferring the faintest of sounds to his sensitive ears. In fact, his sense of hearing was now much keener than his eyesight.

As dusk melted into the impending darkness, the only thing Loken could detect was the steadily growing chorus of tree frogs drowning out the symphony of crickets. Their croaking seemed to grow more urgent as the sky deepened to a cobalt blue and tiny stars twinkled on high like sparkling diamonds.

Loken's eyes, his pupils now completely dilated to take in the celestial lights, glanced about. Set in this owl's head that was designed to swivel right around; allowing him to see directly behind, the Sprite searched about for the telltale orbs of golden light that betrayed the presence of the local Fairies inhabiting this region of the Dimbolt Forest.

In the distant trees, lights began to flicker on, but the size and intensity of these golden spheres was indication to Loken that these were nothing more than the male fireflies taking to the air to make their presence known to the females in search of a mate.

Peering down through the branches of this grand old oak tree, Loken spied on the mouth of the tree hollow. It began to glow, becoming brighter as darkness enveloped the lands.

Fireflies positioned along the entrance of the tree hollow emitted a golden light, reflecting off the pearly white, dentine edifice that formed the palace inhabited by the leader of the Tooth Fairies.

It would only be a matter of time before she would gather her underlings, inspecting her workers and giving final instructions prior to sending them off into the night on their nocturnal foray to gather discarded teeth.

Loken watched with eager anticipation, hoping to catch a glimpse of the Queen as she departed on her quest for the perfect incisor. The light within the hollow grew brighter as Fairies, fifty strong, marched out in single file from the palace to assemble in the courtyard. Their combined aura as they prepared for this night's trek continued to swell, becoming brighter as Pancecelia Feldspar, the Queen of the Tooth Fairies appeared, ready to preside over the inspection before sending them on their way.

The Fairies stood shoulder-to-shoulder, standing at attention as Pance's aide, Sparks Firestar checked off the preparation list, making notes as per the Queen's instructions.

Each row was ten Fairies wide and five deep. The uniform space in between the rows provided sufficient room for Pance and Sparks to maneuver as they began this nightly review.

Pance's wings hummed as they carried her; floating gracefully between the rows as she made sure each of the Fairies had their little bag supplied with coins. These magical coins would transform into the local currency when exchanged for teeth. She also checked to make sure each Fairy had their wand at the ready, secured in their belt holster at their left hip. The wand was a necessary tool to transform the tiny coins to human size proportions, as well as shrink down the teeth to a manageable size so they could be collected and carried in the bag that hung from the left shoulder to rest on their right hip.

Approaching the last Fairy in the back row, Pance could not help but notice how this one, instead of standing at attention; staring straight ahead, back erect, and chest puffed out, slouched like he had no spine. His bleary, blood-shot eyes wandered nervously, trying to avoid direct contact with hers.

"What say you, Jinx?" questioned Pance. "You do not appear fit to fly on this night."

Jinx's eyes rolled forward, struggling to stay fixed on the back of the head of the Fairy standing in the row directly in front of him as Pance neared to better inspect him.

"Meanin' no – *hiccup* – no disrespect, Your Majesty," responded Jinx, "but I'm rarin' ta go ta work."

"I hardly think so," countered Sparks. He frowned in disgust as this worker's speech and demeanor clearly indicated he was inebriated.

"What do we have here?" asked Pance, noticing the sticky, telltale stains of fermented honeydew on this Fairy's tunic. "Have you been imbibing, Jinx?"

"Nope… no imbibin' here. Did have one dr- drink," slurred the intoxicated Fairy, as he inadvertently raised four fingers to indicate just how much he had actually consumed.

Sparks leaned forward, sniffing the Fairy's breath as Jinx exhaled heavily into his face.

"For pity's sake!" exclaimed Sparks. His face grimaced in revulsion as he recoiled from Jinx's sour breath that was tainted by the sweet liqueur. "You are as drunk as a skunk!"

"Skunks get drunk?" gasped Jinx, a crooked smile adorning his face as he imagined a wild drinking party in the company of these monochromatic cousins to the weasel and mink. "They'd be like little stinky minkies having little drinkies."

Stifled giggles rippled through the assembly, coming to an abrupt halt as Pance cleared her throat to regain their attention.

"You are being pulled from duty, sir," ordered Sparks, motioning for Jinx to remove himself from the row of Fairies that were fit to fly.

"I am?" mumbled Jinx. "Why?"

"You have been drinking to excess. Judging by your condition, it has been within the last two hours prior to roll call," explained Sparks, staring at his crumpled raiment and badly creased wings.

"Might've been drinkin' a wee bit, but come on, it's not like I'm – *hiccup* – *drunk* drunk. It was jus' a shot or two of liquid courage ta get me primed for the night, in case I have the misfortune of encounterin' another beastly child lyin' in wait ta cap – *hiccup* –capture me."

"I understand you are still traumatized by the events of last night," said Pance, "and I can empathize completely, having had the misfortune of enduring such a fate, but drinking yourself to oblivion is not the remedy to overcome your fear."

"But really, I'm not that bad off," insisted Jinx, as he made a valiant attempt not to slur his words and stand upright without wavering.

"You are so impaired you have no idea how truly intoxicated you are," countered Pance, her head shaking in disapproval.

"Maybe a little tipsy, my Queen," corrected the wavering Fairy; "but not so much that I can't fly straight."

"You cannot even stand up straight before us," countered Sparks, scowling in disgust.

"Can so," insisted Jinx. "I *am* standin' straight, but it's my back that's kinda crooked."

"Say no more! And if you believe your own words, your judgment is so impaired you have no business venturing from this place, if you wish to remain safe and survive the night," warned Sparks.

"N- not so," protested the intoxicated Fairy. "I can – I can still do my job."

"You know we do not allow Fairies to fly under the influence, especially when on official duty," reminded Pance.

"Not only are you a disgrace to our profession, but to undertake this task with your senses dulled and your mind addled by alcohol will prove hazardous to you, if you are caught in the act," rebuked Sparks. "And it can certainly prove to be deadly to us if you should be captured and made to reveal the location of the Fairy's Vale."

"But – "

"You know the rules, Jinx," said Pancecelia.

"Fall out of line. Retire for this night," demanded Sparks, jotting down this latest violation on Jinx's already-blemished record. "One more infraction and you will be cut from service until you pull up your bootstraps and prove you can fly straight."

"You're makin' notes of this one, little incident?" gasped the Fairy, swaying to and fro as he struggled to keep the row in an orderly line. "It'll mar my exemplary record."

"What exemplary record?" scoffed Sparks. "You never had such a thing from day one of service."

"I protest!"

"Protest and I will have you removed from service permanently, if the Queen so desires," warned Sparks, his writing quill poised in his hand to record this new infraction. "I recommend you retire for the night, sir."

"Bloody hell! Now I *really* need a drink," groaned Jinx.

"I recommend no more drinking and far more sleeping," ordered Pance, watching as Jinx reluctantly complied, staggering across the courtyard to find solace in sleep, or perhaps another helping of honeydew liqueur.

"Please accept my apologies. I will make it a point to have all Fairies review their flight orders and service guidelines to ensure none imbibe prior to calling for duty," promised Sparks, bowing in respect to Pance.

"Yes, see to it. We do not need another incident like this in the future," said Pance, heaving a weary sigh.

"Now, where were we?" said Sparks. Glancing down at his notes, he then pointed his writing quill at the young Fairy maiden standing at attention as her wings trembled with nervous excitement. "Oh, yes! A new recruit; our newest member to the teeth harvesting brigade."

"Welcome, Lily," greeted Pance.

"Thank you, Your Majesty!" The Fairy maiden curtsied in respect. "I am truly honoured to be counted as a member of this league of legend! I promise I will do my utmost to perform my duties to the best of my abilities."

"I am confident you will, my dear. Since this is your first time, Lily, as tradition dictates, you will accompany me on this night," invited Pance. "I will oversee your maiden flight; ensure you learn some of the methods we use to go undetected and to provide instructions on what to do if your *'customer'* should wake in the midst of your duties, and so on."

"Oh yes, Your Majesty," said the youngest of the Fairies, as she curtsied in respect once more to Pance. "I am eager to learn from the best!"

"Very good then," praised Pance.

She offered up one final reminder to her staff, "Remember, do not award the mortal offering a decayed tooth that is only fit to line the palace dungeon with any more than a ha'penny."

"Yes, Your Majesty!" The Fairies answered as one, their crisp wings crackled, snapping to attention as they made final preparations before taking flight.

"And one more thing," added the Queen.

"Yes, Your Majesty?"

"Do not get caught!"

"Of course, Your Majesty!" The Fairies answered in unison once more.

"Then, let us be off," urged Pance, pointing with her wand into the world beyond this protected tree hollow. "Though the night is young, there are many teeth to be gathered. Dawn will arrive sooner than you think."

With these final words of caution, the Fairies streamed out of the courtyard. Their golden aura glowed brightly against the night sky as the tiny beings headed off in different directions.

"Are you ready, Lily?" asked Pance, extending her arm for the anxious, young Fairy to grasp.

Lily offered a nervous smile, nodding in response as her hand wrapped around Pance's wrist.

With a flick of the Queen's wand, in a brilliant flash of golden light they vanished, leaving Sparks standing alone in the courtyard.

By the intensity of the light that swelled from the tree hollow, Loken knew immediately the Queen of the Tooth Fairies had departed, too. His chance to sneak a glimpse of her now disappeared, fading with her dazzling aura. He ruffled his breast feathers as he heaved a dreary sigh. Spreading his wings, Loken pushed off into the air. With short, downy feathers covering his talons, they worked in tandem with the soft, ragged edges of his flight feathers to allow the Sprite to fly silently, gliding down to a lower branch.

Loken peered inside the abandoned hollow housing the royal domicile, hoping against hope he had not missed his chance to see her.

It was at this very instant, Sparks froze. An uneasy chill seized his heart. It was an unnerving sensation, as though an evil soul with deadly intent was staring at him, scrutinizing his every move.

Sparks suddenly spun about. He spied upon large, amber eyes glaring at him from the mouth of the tree hollow.

Whipping out his weapon, a bolt of energy flew from the tip of his wand as he shouted, "Be gone! There is no room to roost in here! This hollow is occupied."

With a disgruntled 'hoot', Loken's feathery head ducked, missing the charge meant to drive him away. Launching off the low-hanging branch, the Pooka, still in the guise of a great horned owl took to the air. Circling the oak tree, Loken settled on a high branch, out of sight and safe from the powers of the Fairy's wand.

Sparks darted over to the entrance of the hollow, searching about for signs of the large bird of prey as he muttered beneath his breath, "Methinks the Queen better acquire more teeth to expand on this palace, and do so quickly; make it so squirrels and owls will think twice before attempting to make their home in here."

Surveying the dark forest, Sparks saw nothing of concern. In the branches of the neighbouring trees, he spied upon the warm globes of golden light as other Fairies inhabiting the Vale were coming awake to venture forth from their homes, glowing brighter than fireflies as they took to the air.

Confident the owl would not be returning; Sparks tucked the wand back into the holster of his belt. Spinning on his heels, he marched across the courtyard to retire into the palace, but not without first posting two guards at the mouth of the hollow to take defensive action should the owl return. Glancing back at the Fairies assigned to sentry duty, Sparks entered the palace, retreating into the main library to bide his time until Pancecelia's return.

"Damn that little bugger!" Loken cursed as he ruffled his feathers in agitation. "How dare he attempt to accost me? And how dare he even think he can replace me in my absence?"

With a disgruntled snort and an abrupt show of light, Loken morphed into his usual form. His new, crisp set of wings rattled with indignation as he peered down from his hiding place to stare at the hollow.

"In due time, I shall return for you, Sparks Firestar. In the end, you will be ousted from your position of privilege. Better yet, when I get my way, not only will you be ousted, you will be as good as dead! But how to gain access to the palace right now?"

The Pooka paced the tree branch, pondering this dilemma now that the way was guarded.

"I've got it!"

With a snap of his fingers, under a swell of light, the shape-shifting Sprite transformed. His hands smoothed out the lapels of his vest, adjusting the belt and wand holster as he flicked the stray strands of flaxen hair over his shoulder.

"This will do nicely," said Loken, with a nod of approval as he inspected the reflection of his new form shining off the smooth surface of the dreamstone.

Pushing against the branch, the Pooka took to the air once more, spiralling down to the tree hollow. As he appeared before the two sentries, the Fairies lowered their pikes, crossing the tips to block entry to this intruder.

"Halt! Who goes there?" asked one Fairy, staring at the golden orb of light hovering closer.

"Make yourself known!" demanded the other.

"You are both dolts!" snapped Loken, grunting in disgust. "It is I, Sparks Firestar."

The Fairies exchanged confused glances, as one spoke out: "Master Firestar? What are you doing here?"

"I thought you retired for the night," said the second guard.

"Obviously, you two are negligent in your duties! Either you had abandoned your post or were slacking off, totally oblivious to your surroundings," rebuked Loken, staring with disdain at the two Fairies standing guard at this threshold. "If you had been paying attention, you would have seen me flying overhead, out of this hollow to make sure the owl was well away from here."

"Really?" responded one Fairy.

"Are you doubting me; calling me a liar?"

"Oh, no! That was not what I meant, sir!" explained the Fairy, his words apologetic. "I suppose we were momentarily distracted when you exited from here."

"You're bloody right, you were distracted!" snorted Loken, pushing by the sentries as he stormed off toward the palace. "Make sure you do your job and do it well, or your Queen will hear about this."

"Yes, sir!" responded the Fairies, their bodies stiffening as they stood at attention.

"Good! Just keep an eye out for anything suspicious," ordered Loken, as he marched up the stairs into the keep. "You never know what unscrupulous character may be lurking about."

Stepping through the magnificent, pearly-white archway designed to inspire awe, the Pooka glanced about as he slipped inside. "Some things never change… and then again, maybe not."

The grand entranceway into the main hall leading to the two libraries and the spiral staircase to the bedchambers looked identical to when he was last inside the palace. The only difference was that all evidence that he had been part of the daily life in this royal residence were now gone. All paintings of him in his former glory were stripped from the walls. It was as though he had never existed.

As the telltale aura of a Fairy maiden illuminated one hallway as she approached to deliver a lilac floret-drinking vessel to the real Sparks Firestar; Loken silently ducked into another. He took refuge in the shadows of an alcove, careful not to bump the life-size statue housed here as he hid from view.

He peeked around the corner only when he was certain she had passed by and he could hear the maiden conversing with Sparks in the privacy of the royal library.

"Will there be anything else, Master Firestar?"

"Not on this eve, but once I am done with the Queen, everything will change, Iris," answered Sparks, offering the Fairy maiden a disarming smile as he embraced her in his arms. "And enough with the formalities, my dear, we are much too *familiar* for that."

"Hush, my love," whispered Iris. She pressed an index finger to his lips as her delicate wings fluttered in anticipation. "The palace has eyes and ears. You can never tell who might be listening in to our every word."

"Anyone of importance is out for the night, engaged in business outside of this palace," assured Sparks. "But most importantly, Pance is well out of earshot."

"What is this?" gasped Loken, his eyes widening with dismay. He couldn't believe what he was hearing. Taking measured, cautious steps, he crept closer to the library door to listen, taking in the discreet words shared between these lovers.

"Better to side with caution, my love," urged Iris, as she kissed Sparks' throat.

"Let them hear," defied Sparks, his attitude cavalier as he motioned her to stop this demonstration of affection so he could have a sip of the honeydew liqueur she had delivered to him.

"To be bold is one thing; to be foolish is a whole other matter. All your work and planning will be for naught if the Queen catches wind of our plot."

"Perhaps you are right, my dearest," admitted Sparks, nodding in agreement. "It is better to act with discretion; to be careful if we are to see my scheme come to fruition."

Loken inched closer to the double doors that were left ajar when Iris floated into the library with refreshments. Pressing an ear to detect these hushed words, the Sprite listened intently.

"This is no scheme," whispered Iris, drawing Sparks closer to kiss his lips. "This is a grand plan, one that shall ensure the Queen is ousted from her high position and a new order set into place."

"And that day will come soon, my love," promised Sparks, giving her a knowing smile.

"When?"

"On the eve of the summer solstice," revealed Sparks, taking another sip of the sweet beverage.

"The longest day of the year?"

"Yes, it will be most fitting! It is during the night when her powers are at its full strength. When it is the shortest night of the year, she will be at her most vulnerable."

"See! That is not a scheme. It is a cunning plan concocted by a clever man!" praised Iris, her delicate hand stroking his cheek.

"Clever enough to not rouse suspicion in the Queen's eyes in all these years as my loyalty and devoted service continues to lull her into this false sense of security," assured Sparks, giving Iris a knowing smile.

These words, the revelation of a plot to overthrow Pancecelia Feldspar, caused Loken's blood to boil, and with this, his aura glowed more intensely. It was enough to shine through the crack between the doors.

Sparks' eyes narrowed in suspicion. He pressed a finger to his lips for Iris to be silent. Creeping closer to the entrance of the library, one hand rested on the hilt of his wand. Yanking the door open, he gasped in surprise, stumbling back.

A flea sprang onto his chest before hopping out an open window to disappear from sight.

"Bloody hell!" gasped Sparks, gaining his composure as Iris rushed to his side.

"What was it? Did you see someone?" asked the Fairy maiden. Her worried eyes strained to see what he saw, but there was nothing, only the cold light of the moon streaming through the window.

"It was a damned flea, no doubt from the dormice living in the nest above this hollow."

"Thank goodness that was all it was and not some spy lurking about," sighed Iris, her skin crawling at the thought of a parasite as large as a flea was so close to her.

"Yes," agreed Sparks. He stared at the window, waiting to see if the pest was about to return. "It is all the more reason to be discreet in our words and actions, my dear."

'*I have returned none too soon,*' thought Loken. The articulated joints of his powerful hind legs pushed off against the dentine walls of the palace to land him on the parapet of the balcony leading to the royal bedchamber. '*I knew the little bugger was up to no good from the very start! But now it begs the question, how does that scoundrel intend to hatch his plan?*'

Confident that Sparks suspected nothing and had retreated into the main library, Loken hopped down from this low wall onto the balcony. Scrambling on all six feet, he easily fit through the gap between the balcony door and the floor to enter the room. Once inside, safely hidden away from the eyes of those guarding the palace courtyard, Loken morphed, assuming his usual form.

His wings rattled, trembling with malice at he pondered his rival's devious plan. He always believed Sparks despised him. Being a Sprite rather than a Fairy, Loken always thought this intense dislike was forged by racism, to drive a wedge between him and Pance because he disapproved of their relationship. He now understood why the Fairy had planned his banishment to begin with, for he was the one thing that stood in the way, preventing Sparks from initiating his dubious plot to usurp the Queen, casting her from a position of power to assume it for himself.

"Curse that wretched soul," swore Loken, his words tainted with spite. "Firestar will get his comeuppance! It shall only be a matter of time, and I will be the one to make it so. I will do everything in my powers to keep Celia safe from harm."

As his eyes adjusted to the gloom, he glanced about this grand bedchamber. Loken heaved a weary sigh as he felt the splinter in his heart pierce a little deeper. It had been long since he last roamed the corridors of this palace and even longer still, since he was last in the Queen's royal bedchamber.

Just as in the main hall, all evidence of Loken's existence that was once prevalent in this room was also gone; banished as he had been. All that lingered now were the ghosts of memories long past.

Loken's eyes adjusted to the pale light of the moon seeping into the room through the cracks of the door and through the windows adorned by the lacy, sheer curtains made of silk spun by spiders. Soon, it was enough light for the canopy bed against the far wall to come into focus.

Creeping to the edge of the bed, Loken stopped. His fingertips fondly caressed the counterpane draped neatly over the thistledown stuffed mattress. Inspecting the floor around the bed, it was obvious the domestic staff had already swept away all traces of Fairy dust; the fine, iridescent scales that were shed from Pancecelia's wings. Hoping against hope, Loken peeled back the down counterpane. Sure enough, the celestial light shining through caused the trace of Fairy dust to glow, sparkling like diamonds.

"Brilliant!" exclaimed Loken, his hand brushing the dust together in a tiny pile before sweeping them into the remnants of a tattered rag of a kerchief. "This will do nicely!"

Folding in the corners of this cloth, he concealed the glittering dust inside for safekeeping. Tucking it into his belt, Loken headed across the room; back to the balcony doors to escape the same way he had arrived. He suddenly froze in his tracks.

Spying his reflection in the looking glass over the dressing table, Loken scrutinized his haggard face. Leaning in toward the mirror, he remembered the bygone days before he was cursed. It was difficult enough for a Sprite to be accepted into the Fairies' realm, especially one with the ability to change his form at will, but now, in this cursed state, it was no wonder his former love no longer recognized him.

"Celia…" whispered Loken, staring at the small, framed portrait of the Queen resting on the dressing table. He was the only one who ever addressed her by this name and since his exile; none were permitted to utter it. He stared with sad, recessed eyes, studying his gaunt features that made him appear well beyond his true years. He was now a mere husk of his former self. Not even his mother or siblings, had they lived, would recognize him in this condition.

Loken released a disheartened sigh as he turned away from his reflection. Glancing down, he noticed the brush Pancecelia would use to tame her beautiful tresses. He picked it up, inhaling deeply to revel in the faint perfume distilled from the attar of wild roses. It was a fragrance he had long regarded as being synonymous with his Celia; fresh, sweet but not overpowering.

Strands of silken hair caught on the bristles glistened in the moonlight. Using his fingertips, Loken carefully removed three strands, winding them together before tucking the hairs into his belt.

"Ah-ha! I should have known!" Sparks shouted as he burst into the bedchamber.

Just as the tip of his wand glowed to unleash a blast of energy to incapacitate the Pooka, Loken morphed. The power shooting from the Fairy's wand exploded in a shower of white sparks as it deflected off Loken's protective armour of thick, overlapping scales.

Rearing up, the top of his scaly head scraped against the ceiling. Loken's forked tongue flickered. He hissed as he struck out, attacking the Fairy.

Sparks cried out in fear. Dropping his wand, he fell back against the two guards accompanying him. Instead of raising their pikes to make their stand against this serpent, they dropped their weapons. Screaming in fright, they retreated into the hall. Slamming the door behind them, they left Sparks trapped in the room with his nemesis.

"I should just kill you now!" hissed Loken. The black, slit-like pupils floating on these amber orbs stared in utter disdain at the Fairy cowering before him. "Be done with you, once and for all!"

"If you dare, the truth will die with me!" snapped Sparks, scrambling on his hands and knees to reclaim the wand as his eyes remained fixed on the snake towering before him.

"Make no mistake, you will die, but not before the truth is known to Celia!" declared Loken. Lashing out with the tip of his tail, he knocked the wand away from Sparks' reach.

With his back pressed against the door, the Fairy trembled in utter terror. He flinched, eyes closed, face turning away as the tip of the shape-shifter's tongue flickered before him.

"I can taste your fear," hissed Loken. Staring at Sparks through glassy, unblinking eyes, he then added with a smirk, "And it tastes like... chicken."

"What?" gasped Sparks, forcing an eye open only to be greeted by that snaky tongue gathering scent particles from the air.

"You heard me! You are a mindless, cowardly winged creature no better than a chicken. I'd crush your measly body; swallow you whole this very minute if it did not serve me better to keep you alive for now!"

Sparks yelped surprise as the door he was pressed up against suddenly flew open as the guards returned with reinforcements. Kicking this barrier in, the blow sent the Fairy tumbling head-over-heels to land right before Loken's coiled body.

Leaping into action, the small army charged toward the Sprite's serpentine form; the tips of the pikes held high to keep him at bay as Sparks scrambled to safety. Though Loken could have easily attacked and killed the Fairies coming to Sparks' rescue, he chose to retreat. His long, scaly body undulated in snake-like fashion as he escaped through the balcony door and over the parapet. His tail whipped about to bowl several of the guards over to prevent them from following. Moving at an unnerving speed, the Sprite slithered across the courtyard and through the entrance of the tree hollow.

Loken disappeared from sight as the Fairies watched from the balcony, cheering their success at driving off this dangerous serpent.

"Thank goodness, you are safe," gasped the guard who had inadvertently locked Sparks in the bedchamber with the snake.

"No thanks to you!" grunted Sparks, thoroughly incensed. He brushed the dust and humiliation from his raiment as he struggled to compose himself.

"Who were you speaking to?" asked the other guard, glancing about the now empty room.

"What are you talking about?" questioned Sparks, smoothing out the creases of his vest.

"We thought we heard another voice in here with you."

"Are you mad?" snapped Sparks. "Since when do snakes take to speaking? If you heard anything, it was merely my own voice threatening that cursed beast, ordering it to leave or I'd be forced to kill it."

"Mighty brave of you to face that creature on your own," praised another Fairy. "It could have been the death of you."

"I hardly think so!" snapped Sparks, reclaiming his wand from the floor. "I had the situation well in hand in spite of you two, clumsy oafs!"

"I suppose we should warn the Queen of this intrusion," decided the Fairy leading the rescue charge.

"You will keep your mouth shut, all of you!" demanded Sparks. "There is no need to alarm her when the danger has already passed."

"But suppose the snake returns?" asked the Fairy.

"Fear not, that foul creature has no reason to come back here," answered Sparks, motioning the others to leave the room immediately, should Pance return unexpectedly. "In the meantime, assign more guards to sentry duty just in case that serpent does make another attempt to invade this hollow."

"But you just said – " the guard's sentence was cut short as Sparks' hand lashed out, slapping his startled face.

"Do not question my orders!" snarled Sparks, shaking the pain from his smarting hand. "Do as I command."

Slithering along on his belly, the large ventral scales delivered the Sprite higher. Loken crawled into the lofty branches of the old oak tree, becoming one with the long, twisting boughs. Coiling about the dreamstone he hid on a forked branch, the Pooka contemplated his next move. He had hoped to remain until dawn, hiding and waiting in secret for the return of Pancecelia Feldspar, just to catch a glimpse of her again, but knowing what he knew now, Sparks Firestar had forced his hand once more.

Loken knew he had no choice but to return to Parru St. Mime Dragonite and somehow exchange this damaged crystal for the potion the Sorcerer had long promised to him.

"Then go, I must," Loken whispered. "But first, I must see a man about a mole."

9
The Man with the Hairy Mole

"For such a small being, he sure snores like a full-sized human," complained the Princess. She watched the backpack the Gnome was transported in. Now doubling as a bedroll, it slowly rose, and then fell, as their navigator exhaled loudly as he slept.

"Yes… He's almost as loud as you are," teased Tag, glancing up from the campfire as the Gnome snorted, gagging on his saliva.

"I *do not* snore!" protested Rose. Her delicate brows furrowed in resentment as she pointed to Cankles as he slept peacefully, totally unaware of the mosquito that had landed on his hand to feed. "He does. You most certainly do, but I am a princess. Princesses are not that vulgar."

"How would you know what you're doing when you're fast asleep? You're oblivious to everything and everyone around you."

"I know what I know and only commoners sleep with their eyes half open and their mouths agape as they drool in their slumber."

"Ha! You're not as oblivious as I first thought, and more common than you'd like to believe!" heckled Tag.

"What is that supposed to mean?"

"You just described yourself when you're fast asleep!" In feigned slumber, Tag's head flopped over onto one shoulder. The whites of his eyes showed through the half-closed lids as his tongue lolled, dangling from the corner of his mouth.

Rose's eyes opened wide in dismay as she gasped in denial, "I do not sleep with my eyes open, nor do I drool!"

"Want to bet, Princess? I'm surprised you haven't drowned in your own pool of drool as you snooze."

She was momentarily mortified. The very thought of anyone, even Tag, seeing her in this less-than-dignified state of unconsciousness; eyes staring vacantly as her tongue dangled from the corner of her mouth to leave a trail of saliva was not the becoming image she wanted to leave in any person's mind, especially his.

"So you say!" Rose attempted to brush away his words with a flat out denial.

"I do!"

"If it were so, it would be more like little kitten snores without the drooling!"

"Kittens do not snore," insisted Tag. "They purr, but in all my life I've yet to hear a single cat snore."

"Never you mind! You should be more concerned by today's predictions, but instead, you seem unworried by what that fortune-teller revealed to us," scolded Rose, attempting to change the subject.

"What are you talking about?"

"Good gracious! Were you too busy gawking at her to listen to her words of warning? That girl made some dire predictions as to our future and this quest."

"I am not about to be held prisoner by a few fleeting, though dire, images swirling about in a faulty crystal," explained Tag.

"That is rather foolish of you."

"Think what you will. I shall take heed of these warnings with a grain of salt, for I prefer to be the master of my destiny."

"You are the master of nothing, not even your sword," scoffed Rose, giggling at his response.

"Had I been allowed to train as I should have, I'd be a master of this weapon, as well as the longbow, pike, mace *and* spear."

Knowing Tag was only going to remind her how it was her fault he was prevented from entering the knighthood as a youngster, Rose worked quickly to pacify him.

"I tell you what, if and when I reclaim the dreamstone, I shall wish for you to be bestowed with all the knowledge and skills that will allow you to use these weapons like a fully trained knight."

"You should not make promises you have no intention of keeping, Princess," grunted Tag, shaking his head in disapproval.

"I speak the truth! It is only fair, after all."

Though Tag knew this offer was motivated more by guilt than genuine concern or a need to make amends, he was not about to turn down this offer.

"Fair, indeed!" agreed Tag, as he unsheathed his sword from its scabbard to hone the blade.

"But surely you will regard that trollop's warning of things to come?"

"What trollop?"

"You know? That fortune-teller you are so smitten with," grunted Rose, still annoyed she was made to bear witness to Tag's first real kiss.

"She was no trollop. And why should I hang on her every word just because she made these predictions?"

"Because if you do not, it is madness and you will be deemed as being mad for deliberately ignoring your destiny! You will be playing directly into the hands of fate," warned Rose.

"And you are so willing to believe in the words of this so-called *trollop*. So, who is truly the mad one, you or me?"

"So that girl was indiscriminate in her choice of men," sniffed the Princess, her shoulders shrugging with indifference. "I will not begrudge her for her stupidy or poor taste."

"What?" gasped Tag, frowning in resentment.

"Hush, I am still talking! I just know what I saw in her crystal. With or without her interpretation of events, it does not bode well for us."

"Those images were hazy at best! But if it makes you feel better, I will bear in mind her predictions. I will use this knowledge to my advantage, than to be dogged and hampered by what we know."

"Hmph," grunted Rose. "I suppose that would be the prudent thing to do than to let this knowledge paralyze you with fear."

"My thoughts, exactly!"

"But are you not alarmed by her last prediction?" questioned Rose, staring with certain dread into Tag's seemingly unconcerned eyes.

"The one about the Sorcerer ordering a dragon to kill?"

"Well, yes… but I was thinking more of her last words to *you* as we parted company."

"Remind me," prompted Tag, he stopped sharpening the blade to listen.

"When she kissed you, she said it was because you'd never be coming back this way."

Tag grew silent as he mulled over these words.

"What say you, Tag?" asked Rose, studying his face as he tried to recall Agly's exact words. "Are you not concerned for your life?"

A knowing smile crept across his face as he answered, "She could have meant nothing more than we'd be going home via a different route, not backtracking on our own steps."

"You think so?"

"That is what I choose to believe."

"But suppose she meant…" Rose's words faltered as she slowly drew an index finger across her throat. "You know?"

"If I entertained this notion, do you not think this quest would end prematurely? There would be no point in going on if I thought I'd be killed rounding every corner along the way."

"I am not sure if your mindset makes you brave or foolhardy," noted Rose. Her brows furrowed in confusion as she glanced over at her comrade as he calmly resumed honing the blade of his sword on a fine-grained whetstone.

"Well, you have a tendency to believe whatever you want, even if it was not the whole truth. I prefer to live my life unfettered by half-truths and premonitions of doom that can potentially be altered if I simply take control of the situation."

"Brave words spoken by a foolhardy fool," decided the Princess, giving her head a dismal shake.

"Why are you still here, if you think so little of me?"

"Who said I think little of you? If you were not brave enough to undertake this quest to begin with, we would not have come as far as we already have."

Tag frowned, stunned by these unexpected words of praise. Staring through the flames of the campfire to gaze at Rose, he asked, "Was that a compliment?"

His smile caused the Princess' face to flush with embarrassment, but her saving grace was the glow of the fire. Its amber flames served to diminish the rosy hue of her cheeks.

"Let me say that I am just grateful you chose to undertake this mission with greater zeal than I could ever muster. If anything, I am thankful for that."

Knowing that it probably took more nerve for Rose to divulge this tidbit of information and words of praise than it took to convince her to accompany him on this quest, Tag decided to still his tongue and curb his desire to tease her.

"To become a true knight requires more than just a steady hand to wield a sword. It also demands the man to have steady nerves, enough to face any and all challenges with unwavering conviction."

"I suppose…"

"Have you ever known a decent knight to run in fear than to face a challenge, no matter how daunting?" questioned Tag. "My father was certainly one to live up to his title and I have no intention of ruining his good name and reputation by falling short of his expectations."

"But what about your expectations?"

"I am my father's son. I plan to meet, hopefully exceed, his expectations had he lived."

"But I am speaking about what *you* truly want in life," stated Rose.

"See this sword?" asked Tag, holding forth the weapon so the reflection of the dancing flames shone brightly against the polished blade as though the sword was forged of silver.

"What of it?"

"You see nothing more than a weapon – a sharp, pointy blade used to cut down the enemy," explained Tag.

"And it is."

"But to me, it is so much more. Other than my memories, this is all I have left that was once my father's. It symbolizes all that I respect of him as a man and a father, as well as the order of knights he held in such high and noble regard."

"*That* silver sword?" asked Rose. She stared at the blade that looked like so many others she had seen in the hands of the knights in her father's service. She understood its sentimental value to Tag, but how this simple weapon of war could come to represent so much more was beyond her.

"Yes, this sword symbolizes integrity and honesty; selfless service and the courage to stand up and do what's right, even if it means to stand alone. It represents the best of the knighthood and all that my father once exemplified."

"I suppose I understand," responded Rose.

"What I truly want is to be a knight, like my father. To me, there is no greater calling."

"So, it is not just to please him, had he lived?"

"To become a knight will be to honour his memory, but if my heart were not set on this, I hardly think I'd have what it takes to rise to the occasion, especially knowing what we know now from the fortune-teller. Besides, I don't believe doing things in half-measures. I have every intention of becoming a full-fledged knight and living by the code of chivalry all in this brotherhood live and die by."

"Live by, I can accept, but to *die*?" responded Rose, shuddering at the thought. "I am not so keen on that."

"But to put duty before all else, even in the face of death, this is what allows the knight to stand out from the common man."

"Yes, but the common man tends to live longer than the average knight," reminded Rose.

"In my mind, it is better to die an average knight than to live a common man," stated Tag, speaking with all certainty.

"You do know that living by this code will also mean pledging an oath of fealty to the monarch?" reminded Rose.

"Of course I will do so to your father. It will be my duty and my honour to serve the King."

Rose began to giggle in response.

"What now?"

"It also means doing so to me, if and when I should ascend to the throne," answered the Princess.

Tag grew silent, contemplating the whole notion of being at her beck and call, answering to her every command.

"Well?" probed Rose. "What say you now, *Sir* Tagius Yairet?"

"When that time comes, I will do what any respectable knight with an ounce of sense in him would do… Run for the hills and never look back!" Tag laughed out loud.

"Very funny!" grunted Rose.

"Like my father, I will do what is expected of me."

"You better! Or you will have to answer to me," cautioned Rose, wagging a condescending finger at him.

"Look here, I've suffered in your company for this long," teased Tag, unleashing a feigned sigh of defeat. "I am sure, some way, some how, I will endure."

"You make it sound like it will become a miserable term of servitude when that time comes," noted Rose.

"That shall all depend on how you will manage when entrusted with the power that comes with the crown and throne."

"So you are concerned this *power* will go to my head?"

"All I will say is that you will not be the first, nor will you be the last, to abuse this kind of power," explained Tag. "I just pray your father remains in good health for a long time to come… at least long enough to allow you to have a better grasp of how to run the kingdom without running rough-shod over your subjects."

"And you think I'd do this? Mistreat my underlings?" gasped Rose, appalled by his suggestion.

"We are not your *underlings* and I suspect you would have been more tempted to do so before."

"Before what?"

"Before your forced interaction with us *commoners* during our last misadventure made you more empathetic to our plight and our daily struggles," answered Tag.

"Yes… I certainly appreciate my life of privilege even more so now, while dreading the possibility of living in the shoes of a peasant," revealed Rose, shuddering at the hardships she was made to endure when she was banished from the palace.

Tag stared with raised eyebrows at the Princess.

"I mean to say, I better appreciate what my life of privilege can do for those less fortunate."

"Ah… so there is still hope for you yet, Princess," said Tag, nodding in approval.

"Are you mocking me?" Rose's eyes narrowed in suspicion as she glared at Tag.

"I am attempting to keep you in line, on the straight and narrow, so you will have the chance to evolve into the type of monarch your parents, and the entire nation of Fleetwood, can be proud of when that time comes."

There was a tinge of sincerity in Tag's voice, enough to prevent Rose from questioning his words.

"Well, I suppose we both have more to learn to better ourselves in many respects," decided Rose. "But in the meantime, I need your word that you will take heed of Agly's warnings, that you will not throw caution to the wind and ignore her predictions."

"Will you go to sleep if I make this promise?" asked Tag, wiping away the filings from the sword's blade with an oiled cloth before sheathing the weapon.

"Yes, but only if you vow to seriously consider her warnings."

"I will heed her words, if only to use her predictions to alter the outcome of the future to my liking," swore Tag, hand over heart in solemn promise. "Will that do?"

"Yes."

"Good! Now go to sleep," ordered Tag, tossing the bedroll to the Princess. "We have a busy day ahead of us in the morning."

"Remember, keep your eyes out for that man, the one with the hairy mole," reminded Tag, steering his horse in the direction of the Gnome's pointing finger.

"I wish Agly had given us a better description of this man than just that one, disturbing feature," grumbled Rose.

"I'd say a *hairy mole* is descriptive enough," said Tag. "It must have been prominent, enough for the lady to make mention of it."

"But suppose we are heading to a village inhabited by *moley* people? It would serve us better if we knew if this fellow we seek is tall or short, young or old," reasoned the Princess. "Suppose we pass right by him because the mole in question is on his back, hidden under his shirt so none can see it?"

"Or maybe it's on his hand!" offered Cankles. "If he were one of those slave-drivin' types, I'm bettin' he'd order people around, whippin' them with the long hairs protruding from the mole on his hand!"

"What?" gasped Tag and Rose, staring with disbelief at Cankles as he flicked his wrist as though he was cracking a great whip.

"Yes, as if *that's* going to happen," Rose sighed.

"Or perhaps it's on his bottom," said Cankles, a hand smacking his rump to home in on this possibility. "And he has this special patch on his trousers so those bristly hairs can grow right through, that way he won't be uncomfortable when he's sittin' down!"

"That is too bizarre!" rebuked Rose, shuddering in disgust as she tried to push this image from her mind.

"But it could also be on his forehead, growin' from between his eyes, and lookin' like a hairy third eye," continued Cankles, as his imagination ran rampant. "And he might have to tie the hairs growin' from the mole back along with the hairs on his head because it'd get in the way of his sight."

Rose and Tag both grimaced at the thought as Cankles' vivid description took form in their mind's eye.

"*Or*, and I'm just thinking something *CrAzY*, it could be small, with only a few short bristles growing from his chin," suggested Rose, as she rubbed her temples in frustration.

"True, but then he might have this odd habit of twirlin' it between his fingers," said Cankles, pretending to twist invisible whiskers growing from his chin like he had a luxurious beard.

"I believe your imagination is getting the better of you, my friend," decided Tag.

"You think so?" asked Cankles, reining in his wild imagination.

"All we need to keep in mind is that however big, or small, that mole is, and wherever it is on his person, it must be obvious enough for Agly to take notice of it," reminded Tag.

"I suppose," agreed Rose, her heels gently tapping against her mare's flanks to coax it on. "However, I hardly think it will be as large and obtrusive as Cankles believes it to be."

"Just be watchful," urged Tag. "This fellow could be out and about. There's even a chance we'll meet him somewhere along the way."

As the trio rounded the bend of the roadway, their horses cantered right past an elderly man. Glancing back as the old man waved in greeting at them, Cankles' eyes opened wide in surprise.

A large, dark mole with white hairs sprouting forth, long enough to braid, protruded from the man's left cheek. This protuberance was strangely eye-catching; the hairs hanging like a little pony-tail from his otherwise clean-shaven face.

"It's him! The man with the hairy mole," exclaimed Cankles, his thumb jabbing over his shoulder for the others to look behind them.

As the three wheeled their horses about under the Gnome's ardent protest that they were going the wrong way, the man panicked. He jumped off the road, dashing into the safety of the forest to avoid these strangers in pursuit.

"Come back!" hollered Tag, his heels sinking into his stallion's flanks to set his steed on a hard gallop.

"Turn back! Head north!" ordered the Gnome, as he frantically pointed in the right direction.

"Shut it!" snapped Tag, ducking beneath low-hanging branches as he gave chase.

"My goodness! For an old man, he's very spry," noted Cankles, taking off to follow Tag and his mount.

"Hey, you! Wait!" shouted Tag, steering his horse between the trees to cut off the moley man's path.

With two riders coming up from behind and the young man charging up ahead to intercept him, the old man dropped to his knees. He cowered in fear as he declared, "I didn't do it! I didn't steal 'em chickens!"

"*Chickens?* What chickens?" asked Tag, hopping off his steed as the Gnome grunted in annoyance, his finger still defiantly pointing to the north.

"I didn't steal 'em! I swear," declared the old man. With fingers entwined and hands clasped to the back of his head like an escaped prisoner admitting defeat and eager to surrender, he trembled in fear before Tag.

"We're not accusin' you of stealin' anything," explained Cankles, raising his hand in a gesture for calm. "Isn't that so, m'lady?"

Instead of answering him, Rose stood utterly dumbfounded before the man. With mouth agape, her eyes stared with an equal measure of awe and disgust, at the mole and the snowy-white hairs cascading from this growth. The only thing that would have been more disconcerting was if this mole had been a second head growing from this man's face, and it was speaking back at her. Such a phenomenon would have solicited even more gawking from the Princess.

"Then what do ya want from me?" sputtered the man, scrambling to stand on his quaking legs.

"We mean you no harm," promised Tag, raising his hands to show they were empty and his sword was still sheathed in its scabbard. "We only want to speak to you."

"About what? If it's about those missin' hens, I already told ya; I don't know a thing about 'em."

"This has nothing to do with chickens, good sir," assured Cankles, his hand passing before Rose's face to break her trance as she continued to stare, unblinking, at the hairy mole on the man's face.

"Then what are ya wantin' from me?"

"Answers," responded Tag. "We are merely seeking some answers."

"I told ya before, don't ask me no questions about chickens. I know something 'bout those missin' eggs, as they went first, then came the chickens."

"The chickens came before the eggs?" asked Cankles, frowning in bewilderment.

"Better ta say the eggs disappeared before those damned chickens did," grumbled the old man, the whiskers of his mole flapping about in the breeze as he spoke. "But never mind that, I thought this had nothing to do with 'em birds."

"That is correct, sir. We understand you know the whereabouts of someone we have been searching for," explained Tag.

"An' who might that be? 'Cause I know pretty much everyone in these parts, even beyond Too Far."

"We are looking for a Sprite," revealed Tag.

"A *Sprite*?"

"Not just any Sprite. This one can change," added Cankles.

"Change what, his clothes? What's so special 'bout that? Even I've been known ta change my undergarment once in a blue moon."

"No, my friend means to say this Sprite is a Pooka; one of those shape-shifting Sprites that can change its form to any other living creature," explained Tag, ignoring Rose as she stared, mesmerized by the hairy mole.

For a long moment, the old gaffer pondered this question, his fingers twirling the hairs dangling from this mole as though he was fidgeting with long strands of a beard or moustache.

"Ya do know the Dimbolt Forest is home more to the Fairies than the Sprites these days?" questioned the man. "Sprites are few an' far between in these parts this day an' age, most – at least those still left in this realm prefer the Land o' Lakes north of the Bad Lands."

"We are aware of that," answered Tag.

"I wasn't," admitted Cankles, as Rose continued to stare.

"One of 'em shape-shiftin' Pookas, eh?" The old man tugged on the whiskers as he deliberated on the young man's question.

"Well?" probed Tag. "Do you know of this Sprite? He goes by the name of Loken, if that helps."

"Nope, that don't help at all an' I can't say that I know of this rascal," declared the old man.

"What?" gasped Cankles. "But you're the one! You're supposed to know."

"Says who?"

"Lady Aglynessa, the seer of the future," answered Cankles.

"Oh, *that* seer! She's a sweet girl an' all, but she's as cracked as that crystal she reads from," chuckled the man, slapping his thigh as he laughed.

"Are you saying she lied to us?" questioned Tag, stunned by this revelation.

"Naw, but they don't call her predictions the Agly Truth fer nothing, my friend!" snorted the old man.

"She did say something about this *'Agly Truth'* business," recalled Rose, finally snapping out of her self-induced trance as the stranger chortled loudly.

"She speaks the truth, but only as she sees it, which ain't necessarily a hundred percent accurate all the time, dependin' on her interpretation," explained the old man.

"But she told us a man with a hairy mole will know of the Sprite we seek," informed Cankles.

"Hairy mole..." muttered Rose. She stared once more, her eyes drawn, as though hypnotized, by this hirsute facial protuberance.

The old man started to chuckle as he answered, "Methinks that girl meant ol' Scizzyfig, the man who *owns* the hairy mole."

"I'd say you're the owner of a pretty hairy mole, if I do say so myself," commented Cankles, staring at the long whiskers floating like a mini banner caught in the wind as the man talked.

"Look here, did the lady make it clear that it was one of these," asked the old man, tugging on the hairs growing from his large facial mole, "or did she tell ya it was a man with a hairy mole *critter?*"

"Like one of those animals?" asked Cankles, using his hands like a mole digging through the earth.

"All Lady Aglynessa said was that we were to seek out a man with a hairy mole," answered Tag.

"So ya didn't bother ta look inta the crystal ta make sure, did ya?"

"We just assumed," said Cankles.

"Well, you know what they say 'bout folks who assume?" responded the old man, shaking his head in regret.

"You make an *ass* out of *you* and *me?*" offered Tag.

"I was gonna say, it makes ya one stupid dolt of a fool, but I like what you said better, so let's use that."

"So you're not the man we're looking for," decided Tag.

"No, I believe you're lookin' fer ol' Scizzyfig. He happens to own the hairiest mole in these here parts."

"Impossible!" gasped Rose, her trance broken this time by talk of a hairier mole than the one she was already faced with.

"I'm speakin' of a real mole; one of them little critters that live in the earth, diggin' around for worms an' such," explained the man. "Ol' Scizzyfig keeps one fer a pet!"

"Why would anyone in his right mind want to keep a mole for a pet?" asked Rose.

"Scizzyfig is a professional mole hunter. He catches an' kills 'em critters, but he won't kill an' skin this little bugger 'cause it's the damned hairiest little mole he ever dug up. Personally, I think it's kinda ugly, especially those little tentacle-like feelers stickin' out from its nose. It's jus' the way they keep wigglin' about."

The old man used the fingers of his grubby hand, waving them around like the snout of a star-nosed mole, blindly groping about for an earthworm to eat.

"Oh… so she meant *that* kind of hairy mole," said Rose, only now making a concerted effort not to stare at the man's unique facial feature.

"Why would anyone hunt for moles?" questioned Cankles. "It's not like they'd make for a very big meal and they probably taste real… earthy."

"They are hunted for the moleskins," answered Tag. "That silky soft fur makes for an excellent lining in gloves, shoes and boots."

"It does?" questioned Cankles.

"Yes, but you would not know," said Rose. "After all, it is only used in the best quality gloves and footwear."

"There you go then," responded Cankles, nodding in acknowledgment. "That explains why I didn't know."

"Do you know where this particular mole hunter lives?" questioned Tag.

"Of course! Jus' head north, ta the outskirts of Too Far," instructed the old man, pointing in the same direction the Gnome continued to point at.

"Say! That is exactly what Lady Agly told us," declared Cankles, nodding in approval.

"All the more reason to heed her words of warning," decided Rose, giving Tag one of her mincing, *I-told-you-so* stares.

"Where exactly on the outskirts of the village?" questioned Tag, as he turned his back to the Princess to ignore her.

"Oh, ya won't be missin' ol' Scizzyfig's hut," assured the old man. "It's on a stretch of land that's been all turned up from his diggin' for moles. An' if that ain't enough, there'll be lines of 'em little moleskin pelts, all tanned an' hangin' up outside his hut fer curin'."

"Do you think that is possible?" questioned Rose, turning to Tag. "Could Agly have made a mistake?"

"Maybe she was correct with what she saw, but we were the ones who were mistaken in our interpretation," offered Tag. "After all, none of us did bother to look into the crystal to make sure.

"Well, easy enough to do," decided Cankles. "Who would have thunk it possible: a man with a hairy mole as opposed to a man with a mole that's hairy?"

"Well, if anyone's seen this Sprite you're seekin', it'll be my ol' friend Scizzyfig."

"What makes you say this?" questioned Tag.

"Cause he's the only person in these parts with the patience ta sew moleskin cloaks and coats fer 'em wee folks wantin' something extra warm ta wear when the weather starts ta take a turn for the worse."

"That makes sense!" decided Tag.

"So we ride on? Search out this Scizzyfig fellow?" asked Cankles, watching as the old man scurried off.

"Yes, we head north," answered Tag.

"Finally!" grunted the Gnome, his finger still pointing the way.

"That was very rude," commented Tag, scowling at the Princess as he glanced over his shoulder at her.

"What are you speaking of now?" Rose urged her horse to stay close behind Tag's mount so she could better hear him.

"You were staring at that man's face, or more precisely, that mole on his face. You were gawking at it like it was the most god-awful thing you had ever seen."

"Yes, it was the most god-awful, unsightly thing I had ever been witness to," admitted Rose, "but I was *not* staring."

"Well, you certainly were not glancing in admiration."

Rose shuddered involuntarily as she thought back on the fountain of white hairs cascading from the large, dark mole.

"Fine! So I stared. It was hard not to. If it were able to speak, that thing would have been begging to be stared at."

"I must admit, it was hard not to want to just look at that thing on his face. It was akin to ridin' past a horse and carriage accident along a roadway and tryin' not to stare," said Cankles, nodding in agreement with Rose. "Never seen anything quite like that before."

"Still," said Tag, shaking his head in disapproval.

"Look here! The man did not care in the least," insisted Rose. "He seemed quite proud of it; flaunting that *thing* before us, as he did."

"I hardly think he was flaunting anything," defied Tag.

"Then what was the meaning of that?" countered Rose, scowling at her comrade.

"Of what?"

"If he did not mean to flaunt that hairy little beast on his cheek, then why does he bother to so meticulously shave his face of whiskers so there is no beard or moustache, and yet somehow, his razor miraculously misses removing that luxuriant growth cascading from that mole? I swear! There was enough hair it could be mistaken for a pony's tail growing out of his face!"

For a moment, Tag mulled over Rose's words, thinking back on how the man, in pensive thought, would twirl the strands like he was fondling the end of a long moustache. Perhaps she was right. After all, if the man was embarrassed by this growth, he would have gone out of his way to pluck, trim, shave or do all three to remove the strands sprouting from the mole so it'd be less obvious.

"Even though you are right, it was still rude to stare like that," reiterated Tag. "I could have sworn it looked as though your eyes were going to pop right out of your head."

"So you say! Perhaps you are just so used to being surrounded by oddities on a regular basis, it did not seem so strange to you," justified Rose.

"I suppose I have gotten quite used to being around you, but still, I've learned not to stare," teased Tag.

"Are you saying I am odd?" sputtered Rose, as she glared at her comrade.

"Methinks he means *odd*, as in *rare*, like a beautiful flower amongst a tangle of brambles," interjected Cankles, sensing this argument was about to reach new heights.

"I truly *am* a rare beauty," agreed the Princess, as she gave Cankles a coy smile.

Upon hearing these words, Tag spurred his horse on, to gallop away from her.

"Hey! Where are you going?" shouted Rose.

"I mean to put some distance between us! I fear my eyes will burn as you bask in the glow of self-adoration," hollered Tag.

"Ha! You are not funny at all!" scolded Rose, only to glare at Cankles as he sputtered in laughter at Tag's comment.

"Actually, I thought it was quite funny," commented Cankles. "Tag's eyes burnin' from the glow of your…"

"Hush, my foolish friend," ordered Rose. "It is obvious to me that you have much to learn about being a court jester and what is truly funny! Like that!"

Rose giggled aloud, pointing at Tag as he turned about in his saddle, only to get smacked in the face by a tree branch as his stallion listened to the Gnome's instruction to keep moving straight ahead.

"That was not funny!" grunted Tag, rubbing his accosted face. "I could have lost an eye."

"If you had, at least it wouldn't be from basking in my glow!" scoffed Rose.

"Ooh! That was funny, too, m'lady!" declared Cankles. "You are quite the witty one."

"When the occasion calls for wit, I have been known to deliver," said Rose.

"You are now enterin' the village of Too Far…" announced the navigating Gnome, sitting low in the backpack as Tag's horse sped along at a gallop. "And now, you are about to leave it."

Tag reined in his stallion, slowing it to an easy canter as Rose and Cankles' horses caught up.

"Blink and you'd miss it," noted Cankles, glancing about at the small cluster of mud and straw homes topped with thatched roofs that lined either side of the road.

"This is what I'd call a one-horse town," decided Tag, gazing over at the solitary mare drinking from a trough outside one of the humble cottages.

"There is not much here," noted Rose, glad she dwelled in an opulent palace that was a bustling metropolis compared to this place.

"Why did ya think they called this place Too Far?" grunted the Gnome. "It's too far north for most people ta want ta live here."

"And how far away does the mole hunting man live from here?" queried Rose, as her mare trotted past the last home to her left.

"The old gaffer did tell us that this Scizzyfig fellow lives on the outskirts of Too Far," reminded Tag.

"But how far on the outskirts?" questioned Cankles.

"Let's ask that man," suggested Rose, pointing back to the center of the tiny settlement where a fellow was lugging a bucket of water from the community well to his home.

"Are you sure that's a man?" whispered Tag, staring at the non-descript, bland features and the body hidden by loose fitting apparel.

Rose's eyes narrowed as she studied this person, thinking if the facial features and clothes would not reveal gender, then surely the feminine sway of the hips would determine if this indeed was an ugly specimen of a female or a rather unattractive male. With the weight of a full bucket causing this person to walk tilted over to one side, it did nothing to reveal a masculine or feminine gait.

"Well? Male or female?" whispered Tag.

As this person tottered ever closer with the heavy load, Rose determined it had to be a gangly stick of a girl with exceptionally plain features heading their way.

"Hey you! Young lady!" called Rose.

Instead of responding to the Princess, the person set the bucket down, glancing about to see who this stranger was addressing.

"You! Yes, you!" called out Rose, pointing at the person in question. "The one with the water bucket."

"Are ya blind or something?" snapped the skinny man clad in baggy, threadbare clothing.

Realizing her mistake, Rose responded, "Terribly sorry, Sir! My vision is not what it used to be."

"Aren't ya a bit young ta be usin' that excuse," said the villager.

"The company I am forced to keep is aging me prematurely, even as we speak," said Rose, in her defense.

"So, what can I be doin' fer ya?" asked the man.

"We are looking for a fellow who goes by the name Scizzyfig," said Rose. "Do you know of him?"

"You must be speakin' of Hairy Moe," decided the man.

"Oh no, we already made the mistake of accostin' a man with a hairy mole and we don't mean to do so again," said Cankles.

"I'm speakin' of Moe Scizzyfig, or Hairy Moe as the locals call him."

"I'm afraid to ask," sighed Tag.

"Oh, ain't nothing ta be afraid of where that old gaffer's concerned! We jus' call him Hairy Moe 'cause when he takes off his shirt, it looks like he's wearing a big ol' sweater, when really, it's all that hair growin' from his back an' chest."

"We really did not need to know that," said Tag, "but since you know of this man, do you know where he lives?"

"You're on the right trail. Jus' keep headin' north, less than half a league or so from here. You'll know his place when ya see it. An' if ya don't, then you're blinder than 'em moles he catches."

"Thank you," said Tag, nodding in appreciation.

With his tongue clucking against the roof of his mouth, Tag urged his horse on. The Gnome diligently pointed the way as Cankles and Rose followed behind.

"You are now on the outskirts of Too Far," announced the Gnome, just as their horses trotted by the last shack of a house to the right of the roadway.

"That is pretty apparent," said Rose.

"Keep your eyes on the look-out for the mole hunter's plot of land," ordered Tag, his eyes glancing at the treed expanse lining the roadway.

As they ventured farther from Too Far, Rose was beginning to think they had been misinformed.

"Look up yonder! Could that be the land of the mole hunter?" asked Cankles, pointing ahead to a large clearing.

Tag brought his steed to an abrupt halt as his eyes surveyed the patch of forest denuded of trees. This plot of land, much like a farmer's field, was cleared of stumps and large rocks. Instead of long, straight rows of tilled and furrowed earth churned up by the blade of a plow, mounds of dark, rich soil pocked the earth, here and there. These mounds dwarfed the smaller mole hills where the small creatures would excavate their tunnels, pushing the unwanted dirt up to the surface and out of the way.

"If this isn't the doin' of that mole hunter, then it's a farmer gone mad," decided Cankles, inspecting the chaotic landscape.

"I have a feeling we are at the right place," determined Tag.

"I think you are right, but I do not see anyone," said Rose, her eyes searching about for a hairy man tearing up the earth in search of moles.

"Maybe he's inside," said Tag, hopping off his steed.

"No harm in checkin' to see," responded Cankles, helping Rose down from her mare.

Tag lifted the Gnome from the pack, giving him instructions. "Stay here. Mind the horses."

"I'm your navigator, not your stable boy," grunted the Gnome.

"Here," said Tag, passing him a big carrot. "Consider this payment to watch our horses. Eat this and don't go helping yourself to more. That bag of vegetables must last the trip."

Just as the trio approached the door to the ramshackled cottage, a large man appeared, rounding the corner of this home.

"Thought I heard horses comin' this way," said the stranger.

Rose scrutinized the man. The sleeves of his dirty shirt were pushed up to his elbows to expose a furry abundance of hair that thinned marginally along the back of his hands to the first set of knuckles. In one hand, he held a small spade; in the other, he held a cracked, wooden bowl filled with moist earth and writhing with plump earthworms.

"Good day, sir," greeted Cankles, pointing to the container of bait.

"I see you're plannin' on goin' fishin'."

"Nope! Gonna feed my pet," he responded, raising the bowl of worms in casual greeting.

"Please tell me your pet is a hairy mole," pleaded Rose.

Yellowed teeth appeared through the tangle of beard as the man smiled, "Indeed it is! Not that I'm boastin', but it's the hairiest little mole in the whole world, if I do say so myself!"

"Are you Master Scizzyfig?" questioned Tag.

"Yep, an' jus' who might you be?"

"This is Cankles. Her name is Rose and I am Tagius. We were told you might have some information that we're seeking."

"Most people come ta me fer moleskin, not information." He invited the trio to follow him onto the rickety porch. Here, on a small, wobbly table leaning against the wall of the cottage, he pulled the dark cloth covering a small, wooden cage.

"This is Harry, Harry Mole," introduced the hunter. He plucked the dark grey creature from the loose dirt, holding it by the scruff of its neck. Instead of short, soft fur, this animal's coat was as dense, but the hairs were at least five times the length, making for a rather shaggy looking mole.

"Oh, my!" gasped Rose, her eyes opening wide in fascination. "That is one hairy mole indeed! Certainly, the hairiest I have ever seen."

"Harry is his name," explained Hairy Moe. "I figured if I named him Hairy like my nickname, it'd jus' get folks confused."

"Too late," sighed Cankles, scratching his head in thought as he stared at the little insectivore.

The star-nosed mole struggled, its spade-shaped paws armed with sturdy claws flailing in the air as though it was digging through invisible soil. Tiny, beady eyes squinted under the harsh light of day. It made the mole even more frantic to retreat into the dark earth lining the bottom of the cage.

Plopping the animal on the pile of dirt, Moe emptied the wooden bowl of earthworms, soil and all, on top of the creature.

As soon as a writhing worm brushed by one of the little feelers protruding from the mole's sensitive snout, the voracious animal began to feed. Sharp, little teeth made short work of the earthworm. The mole devoured the thrashing invertebrate.

"That was disgustingly fascinating," commented Rose, grimacing as she watched the mole's tactile sensors feel about for another worm to feast on.

"So… jus' what kind of information were you folks seekin' from me?" asked Moe, as he used a bit of twine to secure the door to the cage. "Cause if you're here wantin' ta know 'bout some stolen eggs, I know nothing 'bout that. Might know something 'bout some missin' hens, but that's about it."

"Methinks Hairy Moe and the man with the *hairy mole* are in cahoots somehow," decided Cankles, his eyes staring in suspicion as he scrutinized this hirsute specimen of a man.

"If you're speakin' of wily Simon, that ol' codger has been known ta steal a hen or two from time ta time."

"We are not here about chickens or eggs," explained Tag.

"Fine, but first, who are you folks - *really?* Do ya represent the law?"

"No, sir," responded Tag.

"Did the Mayor of Too Far send ya ta collect taxes from me? Cause if that's so, as far as I'm concerned, I'm beyond village limits, hence, beyond his jurisdiction for any kind of taxes to fill his coffers."

"As I said before, this is my friend, Cankles. I am Tagius, servant to King William of Fleetwood and this is his daughter, Princess Rose-alyn."

"Royalty! Why didn't ya jus' say so?" The man's eyes widened in surprise as he bowed in respect. Spitting into the palm of his hands, he used the saliva to slick back the long, dark, oil clotted strands he side-combed over his balding head.

"So, Princess Rose-Alyn, how may I be of service to ya?" asked Scizzyfig. "If you're here lookin' ta purchase the finest quality ridin' gloves lined with the best moleskin fur, I still have a few pairs left I'm sellin' fer cheap now that the winter's over."

"We are not here to buy, we are here seeking information," explained Tag. "For reasons unbeknownst to us, a lady with the gift of foresight told us that you have the answer we seek."

"If it's an answer to a mathematical question, I stink at 'rithemetic," confessed Moe. "Can't help ya with that."

"Look here, sir, we are seeking a specific person and it is our understanding you had dealings with the one we are searching for," explained Rose.

"So you're not wantin' ta buy any of my moleskin products?" asked Moe, the disappointment in his voice was obvious.

"Not at this moment," answered Tag.

"Hey, a man has got ta make a livin'; if ya won't be wantin' ta buy my merchandise, then ya best take your leave an' let me get back ta the business of mole huntin'. Time is money, ya know? An' I ain't gonna make any money standin' around yakking ta you folks."

"I understand your time is valuable to you, Master Scizzyfig, but if you have information that is important to us, won't you *please* help us?" asked Rose, hoping the addition of 'please' would work to sway him.

"Let me ask you this, m'lady," responded Moe.

"Go on," invited Rose.

"Jus' how valuable is this information that you be seekin'?"

"It can prove to be invaluable to us," admitted the Princess.

"Ya don't say…" responded Moe, stroking his beard in pensive thought.

"Oh, we do!" exclaimed Cankles.

"Well then, since you understand how valuable my time is ta me an' ya seem insistent that my answers could be of great value to ya, it seems only right that if you be wantin' to engage me with a bunch of questions, I should be duly compensated."

"You ask for payment in exchange for words?" asked Tag.

"Not jus' any words. These are words that ya claim ta have great value ta the three of yous."

"A *bribe* to have you answer our questions?" asked Rose.

"That word makes it sound so underhanded," dismissed Moe. "I'm jus' askin' ta be compensated fer my time. Not even askin' fer that much."

"How much qualifies as not much?" questioned Rose, unwilling to loosen the purse strings until a fee was established.

"Well, it's been a while since I've had the means ta buy some ale ta lubricate my throat so I can speak properly. Even now, I can feel my parched throat closin' up. It'll jus' be a matter of time before I won't be able ta speak at all ta help ya."

"Suppose I give you a piece of copper for each answer you provide?" negotiated Rose, palming the burgundy pouch in her hand so the man could hear the jingling of coins to tempt him.

"Sounds fair ta me. Ask away, m'lady!"

"First of all, is it true you have dealings with Fairies and Sprites?" asked Rose.

"Depends on how ya mean. If you're askin' if I've squashed any of them wee folks of late, then the answer's no, not even accidentally."

"She means, is it true you sew apparel for them?" said Tag.

"Oh, I used ta, but that was when my sight was better. Now I sell 'em tiny folks the mole pelts an' they do their own sewin'. The only thing these damn eyes will let me sew fer them are the simple capes or cloaks; none of those tiny, fancy coats." Moe extended his hand, waiting for Rose to pay before he proceeded with the next question.

"So, have you seen a male Sprite, one standin' about a tad taller than my thumb?" asked Cankles, as he wagged this digit before the man's face so he'd have a comparison.

"I'd say they're all 'bout that size, but yeah, I had a Sprite here early this mornin'." Again, Moe extended his hand, smiling as the coin Rose dropped into his awaiting palm clinked against the first one he received.

"Was his name Loken?" asked Tag.

"How the hell would I know?" grumbled Moe.

"I thought you said you do business with these wee people?" asked Tag.

"I do, but that little vermin wasn't about doing legitimate business. I caught him in the midst of tryin' ta steal away with one of my moleskin pelts I had hangin' up ta cure," replied Moe, as he waited for payment. "That'll be two coins now, before I'll be answerin' anymore of yer questions."

"Look here, why do I not just give you this one gold coin if you answer all of the questions we ask, than to have me dole out copper for each 'yea' or 'nay' you give?" offered Rose, holding up the shiny piece of gold to tempt him.

"Sounds reasonable ta me," said Moe, nodding in agreement, as he pocketed the coins he already earned so she couldn't take them back.

"So you didn't get the name of this Sprite?" ascertained Tag.

"On this occasion, there was no time fer proper 'howdy-dos'. I was too busy swattin' at that damned pest. I was tryin' ta make him drop the moleskin."

"Did he say why he was stealing or where he was going?" inquired Tag.

"Nope, didn't give the little bugger a chance."

"Well, this was an utter waste of time," grumbled Rose. "We do not even know if this is the right Sprite."

"Well, I wish I could tell ya more, m'lady," said Moe. "But I wasn't 'bout ta stand around an' challenge that Sprite, especially when it gone an' morphed inta a huge brown bear!"

"It changed?" gasped Cankles.

"As soon as it did that, I bolted. Grabbed my pet mole an' locked ourselves into my home."

"Ah-ha! That Sprite was here!" exclaimed Rose.

"I suppose you don't know where he was heading?" questioned Tag.

"After I tried smackin' that little pest, I'd be bloody stupid ta try askin' it any questions once it became that bear. By God, it sure surprised the hell outta me! It was my first encounter with a Pooka."

"At least Agly was right about this," said Tag.

"True, but we are no closer to finding out where that Sprite took off to," decided Rose, heaving a weary sigh.

"Well, by my estimation, I'd say it's safe ta say that little bugger plans ta head far ta the north, probably up ta the Fire Rim Mountains," offered Moe.

"What makes you say that?" questioned Tag.

"When the Fairies an' the odd Sprite comes ta me for my moleskin pelts, it's ta make warm clothin' in preparation for the comin' of winter. We're jus' heading inta the warm months of summer an' if that little thief was wantin' that pelt ta wear, it'd only be 'cuz he's headin' ta the north where there's still snow on 'em distant mountains."

"That must be it!" decided Tag. "Loken is heading north and he plans to meet up with the Sorcerer there."

"Well, if you folks are plannin' on headin' that way, all I can say is good-luck ta ya."

"Thank you," said Cankles.

"You'll need all ya can get, considerin' you'll be headin' straight inta dragon country."

"No need to remind us," said Rose.

"We'll be fine," assured Tag, his hand patting the hilt of his weapon. "I've got my sword by my side."

"Oh, goody!" exclaimed Moe, his voice oozing with sarcasm. "The dragon can use it ta pick his teeth after he's done eatin' ya fer lunch."

"If we move with stealth and do nothing to draw the attention of those beasts to begin with, we'll be fine," responded Tag, speaking with confidence.

"Yeah, that's what all 'em other folks said before they got eaten by a dragon," grunted Moe.

"Are you tryin' to scare us? For if that's your intention, it's workin'," said Cankles.

"Jus' speakin' the truth, my good man," responded Moe.

"It is not as though we're blindly stumbling into the unknown," said Tag. "We know we are heading to dragon country, so we shall proceed with caution. We'll just keep our wits about us as we venture forth."

"Somehow, you're words offer little in the way of confidence," sighed Rose.

"Well, at least we now know Lady Agly was right in her prediction," said Cankles, smiling in approval. "Mind you, that part about the man with the hairy mole as opposed to the owner of Harry, the hairy mole still leaves me scratchin' my head."

"Yes, and now we can look forward to the Sorcerer ordering a dragon to kill us," grunted Rose, giving her head a dismal shake as she recalled one of the fortune-teller's predictions.

The smile on Cankles' face abruptly vanished as the image from Agly's crystal flashed in his mind.

"Look here, it's more important than ever we stop the Sprite," reminded Tag. "If anything, at least we can focus our efforts to the north than to ride about willy-nilly."

"You make it sound as though we should rush headlong into danger; meet our destiny as Agly predicted," responded Rose.

"We avoid danger wherever and whenever we can, but we have a chance to change this destiny she predicted," stated Tag.

"You sound so sure," said Rose, staring through suspicious eyes at her comrade.

"I am. Now, pay the man and let's move on," ordered Tag.

"You're more than welcome ta ask me more questions," invited Scizzyfig, hoping to profit some more from this exchange.

"I think you've provided us with all the answers we need," said Rose, as she handed him the single gold coin.

10

Dream On!

"Into the pack," ordered Tag, motioning the Gnome to step inside.

"We're movin' on?" asked the little navigator. Grinning in excitement, his worn teeth were framed by equally stained lips. Both were now a deep shade of magenta.

"Hey… didn't I give you a carrot to eat?" questioned Tag, staring suspiciously at the Gnome.

"Why'd you ask?" He replied with a question as his wiry brows crinkled into a frown of confusion.

"Your teeth! They look awful!" remarked Rose, grimacing in revulsion.

Realizing the deep reddish-purple vegetable must have coloured his entire mouth, the Gnome drew his lips over his teeth to conceal the evidence as he gummed the words, "Don't know what you folks are speakin' of!"

"You helped yourself to a beet, didn't you?" interrogated Tag, peering into the burlap bag to see how much was left. "I told you only *one* piece of vegetable."

"But I did eat jus' one!"

"I *know* without doubt, I gave you a single carrot," argued Tag.

"So you did, but I switched it for one of 'em sweet, tasty beets. So, when it comes right down to it, I still only ate jus' one piece of veggie," confessed the Gnome.

"The little fellow really didn't do anything wrong," reasoned Cankles. "There's still the same number of veggies in that bag as when you left it with him."

"What is the big deal, anyway?" gasped Rose, rolling her eyes in frustration. "We have more important things to worry about than how many vegetables your G.P.S. ate."

"You're right," conceded Tag, raising himself, along with the navigator, back into the saddle.

"Of course I am," said Rose, getting a leg up onto her mare from Cankles. "Let us move on. Perhaps we will be able to catch up with that dreadful little Sprite before he meets with the Sorcerer."

"Are you ready?" asked Tag, pressing down on the top of the Gnome's hat so his view was not obscured.

"Always," answered the Gnome, eager to be on the way. "Where to now?"

"We need to head north, to the Fire Rim Mountains."

"Are ya sure 'bout that?" questioned the Gnome, his brows furrowing with concern. "There are dragons up there; big, hungry, nasty dragons, ya know?"

"Yes, no need to remind us of that," responded Rose, rolling her eyes in frustration.

"Well then... what about all 'em volcanoes? They don't call 'em the Fire Rim Mountains fer no reason, ya know?" added the Gnome.

"*Volcanoes?*" gulped Rose, her eyes were like daggers as she stared at Tag.

"*Active* volcanoes to be sure," confided the Gnome. "There's some real hot spots where the lava flows freely; a regular river of molten hell."

"You never said anything about active volcanoes!" gasped Rose, smacking Tag on his arm.

"*Owww!* Do you mind?" snapped Tag, rubbing the point of impact where her hand accosted him.

"Not really, considering you deliberately withheld this crucial bit of information from me."

"I thought the name said it all, not to mention your studies," explained Tag. "Or were you not paying attention to the scholars appointed to teach you about the world outside your palace?"

"I knew there were volcanoes, but I did not know they were still spewing lava," confided Rose. "How dare you not tell me?"

"Consider it an oversight, but if anything, what good would it had served you? You're already upset knowing that there is a chance we will encounter a dragon or two," reasoned Tag, rolling his shoulders in a shrug.

"I'm thinkin' that we can outrun flowin' lava, but not a dragon," decided Cankles. "Dragons are probably much faster than that."

"Like the Princess needed to hear that," grumbled Tag, rolling his eyes in dismay.

"Probably not, but at least she can be less worried about a volcano, should it erupt," said Cankles.

"I do not like the prospect of either meeting a dragon *or* encountering an erupting volcano," grunted Rose. "Both offer a promise of a fiery death."

"Not if we're careful," said Tag.

"*Careful?* Is that the best you can offer?" whined Rose.

"Well, if you choose to be reckless rather than careful, you will pretty much guarantee yourself an early demise," argued Tag.

"Careful is an *excellent* idea," stated Cankles, nodding in agreement with his young comrade.

"A better idea is to avoid dragons and volcanoes altogether," said Rose, speaking with utmost certainty. "Head somewhere other than north."

Tag glanced over at the Princess, staring with raised eyebrows at her.

"It was just a suggestion." She unleashed a dreary sigh. "I have every intention of reclaiming the *you-know-what,* even if it takes us to that god-forsaken land of fire and *death*; deadly beasts and *death*; the dreaded Sorcerer, and did I forget to mention: the very real possibility of *death*?"

"Now that's what I wanted to hear from you," praised Tag, offering her a smile. "But I'll ignore the death part. Instead, we shall venture forth fearlessly."

"I believe you'll do so with less fear than me, my young friend," decided Cankles.

"My confidence is buoyed by the fact the Princess is still prepared to proceed with the quest, albeit with a degree of trepidation."

"Woo-hoo…" grumbled Rose, sarcasm tainting these words. "Let us journey to the north to meet our fate, and why do we not smack destiny in its face while we are at it?"

"Remember, we do not have to fall victim to it," stated Tag. "We can alter the course of our destiny."

"So you say," sighed Rose.

"I do. We head north," said Tag, speaking with conviction.

"Very well then," said the navigator. "So, the scenic route or the fastest, most direct one?"

"Time is of the essence. The fastest way to get us there, please," answered Tag.

The Gnome's stubby, nail chewed-to-the-quick index finger automatically pointed ahead. "When you're back on that main road, turn right."

Following the portable navigator's instructions, their horses galloped northward. As their mounts tired, they slowed down to an easy canter to give the horses a reprieve from this gruelling pace.

"What's wrong with you?" asked Tag, watching as Rose shuddered.

"Did you not see?"

"See what?" responded Tag, frowning in curiosity. "I have no idea what you're talking about."

"That mole hunter lived up to his nickname, Hairy Moe! You could see the hairs on his back bristling through his shirt." She shuddered again.

"Ooh, yes! And his mole, Harry was as hairy as his friend Simon claimed the creature to be," added Cankles, coaxing his mount on to keep up with the others. "I was most impressed, in a bizarre sort of way."

"*Ewww!* That man and his hairy little friend were both rather detestable, but more so the hirsute man," groaned Rose.

"If it bothers you so much, try not to think about him," urged Tag.

"Easy for you to say," grunted Rose. "I was the one who ended up touching his grubby, furry hand when he accepted the coins. And to make matters worse, he broke with protocol. He had the gall to touch royalty when he grabbed my hand to shake it! *Yuck!*"

Tag began to laugh aloud in response.

"What is so funny?" asked Rose.

"I just find it amusing that you are so put-off by touching his 'furry hand' when I thought you'd be more disturbed about touching Moe's *dirty hand*... the one he used to dig up those earthworms with."

"*Argggh!* He *did* touch those disgusting things!" bellowed Rose, dropping her reins to wipe her hands on her frock. "I've been contaminated!"

Cankles and Tag both began to laugh as she frantically brushed her hands off.

"Whatever you think is there, I'm sure it'll disappear in its own, good time," said Tag. "For now, we have a Pooka to catch."

"Why does this always happen to me?" grumbled Loken. He blotted the drying blood from a wound high on his back between the shoulder blades.

Aside from being of greater stature than the average Fairy and possessing the rare trait amongst Sprites, this ability to shape-shift, Loken was beginning to have serious doubts as to its worth. To change at will was a gift intended to keep the Pooka safe. With this ability to assume the form of all manner of creatures, great and small, Loken had the unfortunate luck of morphing into animals that, more often than not, ended up threatening his life. Whether he adopted the form of a benign moth or a great dragon, unexpected danger always seemed to be lurking just around the corner to ambush him.

This time was no different and Loken was beginning to wonder if part of the curse inflicting him was also a regular dose of bad luck. He wadded up another handful of dried moss, pressing it against the cut made by the edge of the steel bodkin tipping the hunter's arrow. The projectile had grazed him on his shoulder as he raced northward in the form of a buck.

The last thing he expected was to encounter hunters looking for some fresh venison so deep in the Dimbolt Forest.

With great, bounding strides that delivered him with ease through the large stands of trees; it was probably the only thing that spared him from being downed by the deadly arrow. One of the hunters had trained his sights on him as Loken, in the form of a deer, raced along a trail commonly used by the local wildlife. The man released the arrow, intent on killing the large buck. Instead, the projectile glanced against a wind-blown branch. The arrow ricocheted off the bough, skimming high against Loken's shoulder. Ignoring this stinging pain as the bodkin sliced his skin and lanced through flesh, the Sprite dashed away at top speed, disappearing into a dense thicket.

Once he had safely distanced himself from the hunting party, Loken morphed, assuming his usual form. Removing the necklace from about his neck, he used the chain to hoist the dreamstone into a tree. Once he was hidden away from the hunters, he was able to tend to this superficial wound.

"Knowing my luck, had I turned myself into a predator like a wolf, those bloody hunters probably would have tried killing me for going after their herds of deer," muttered Loken, as he pressed the absorbent clump of moss against the arrow's bite. "So much for a hasty retreat to the north. Dragonite will have to wait a little longer."

The bleeding had all but stopped; still, there was a risk of infection setting in.

"I need some honey to dress this wound. I wonder if there's a beehive around here?" Loken muttered to himself as he glanced about, searching for the telltale signs of an active colony. Seeing nothing, the Pooka had an idea. In a flash of light, he transformed into a black bear. Now, with the heightened sense of hearing and smell gifted to these creatures, Loken's sharp claws allowed him to cling to the tree trunk as he assessed his surroundings. His furry, rounded ears twitched as they listened for the droning hum of bees while his sensitive snout sniffed the air, smelling about for the sweet scent of honey.

"Aha! Now there's a hive that's just crying to be raided!" announced Loken, his beady little bear eyes following a couple of bees flying toward the waxy home filled with honey, tucked away in a tree hollow not far from the one he was in now.

Loken's bear form shimmied down the tree trunk to the forest floor below. Rising up on his rear legs, his ears rotated about as his snout pointed skyward, sniffing for the exact direction that would lead to this hive.

'There it is!' thought Loken, his keen senses homing in on the apiary. With shuffling steps, his bear form lumbered over to the tree in question. The mouth of the tree hollow was alive with frenetic activity as honeybees buzzed in and out in a steady procession.

Sitting on his big, hairy rump, Loken gazed up to the hollow, staring wistfully as the nectar-laden insects returning home with their liquid gold performed a wiggling dance to direct the other hive-mates to a bumper crop of blossoms burgeoning with sweetness.

"All I need is a little dab," said Loken, as he pondered how he was to get the honey. Already being a black bear, this thick, shaggy coat would shield him from the stings of angry bees. It would be easy enough to use his powerful claws to tear open the hollow and steal away with some of that golden liquid. Of course, his bare nose and his vulnerable eyes would be made to bear the brunt of the assault if he took offensive action, destroying the hive to get what little he needed.

Staring at the busy little insects arriving at the mouth of the hollow, he watched as the bees greeted each other. They used their antennae for a tactile introduction before granting entry to the returning bees.

"That's it!" declared Loken.

In a flash of light, Loken transformed once more. As a bee he'd greatly reduce the risk of being harmed by blending into the hive's general population.

Taking to the air, his wings hummed, making that distinct buzzing sound that has become synonymous with these hardworking insects.

"I should grab some pollen or a bit of nectar, that way, I won't rouse suspicion should I arrive empty-handed," surmised Loken.

He hovered in the air to scan the open, sunny patches of the forest floor for clumps of wild flowers. It then dawned on the Sprite that he was a drone, a male member of the colony. To arrive at the hive with a floral bounty would certainly rouse suspicion, considering it was only the female bees that were relegated to the task of harvesting nectar and gathering pollen to feed the queen and her colony, including the gadabout, non-industrious drones.

Loken alighted upon the ground at the base of the hive tree. Here, worker bees had unceremoniously dumped dead and dying bees that had worked to exhaustion. The Sprite, in this insect form, proceeded to rub up against these carcasses. In doing so, not only did specks of pollen migrate onto his bee body, but the invisible chemical signature that distinguished these bees from all the other colonies, granting them safe access to the hive when they were active workers, was now transferred on to him.

A row of bees blocking the entrance used their wings to fan the air. This helped to maintain an optimal temperature within the hive to prevent the wax combs from melting on hot, summer days. This circulating air also helped to reduce the moisture content of the regurgitated nectar stored in the yet-to-be-sealed wax cells, turning this liquid into the thick, concentrated sweetness of honey. These bees stopped their work upon Loken's arrival. They resumed fanning as several of the bees greeted this mysterious drone. Through their compound eyes, they recognized him as being a male bee, but by using their antennae in tactile greeting, they were able to determine if this drone actually belonged to their colony. Recognizing the pheromones dispersed by the queen bee, that specific scent that identified Loken as one of their own, the worker bees returned to fanning the air through the hive. Loken's larger drone form pushed through the row to enter the protected colony, unmolested by the others.

He crept inside, crawling around the bees performing their whirly-gig dances to show the others the direction and distance to be flown in relation to the sun to find a bounty of nectar-rich flowers.

Inside this hive, Loken marvelled at the workings of this miniature city. Combs filled with honey and sealed for winter consumption gave way to the nursery where female workers fed the grub-like larvae, each housed in an individual waxed cell until they matured to join the work force.

Glancing about with his insect eyes that allowed Loken to take in far more of his surroundings, Loken searched for the chambers consisting of wax combs ready to be sealed. These would contain the true honey; the thick, concentrated amber liquid, not the watery nectar that had been freshly harvested.

While taking in the sights of this bee colony, Loken spotted the object of his desire, begging to be stolen. Syrupy thick honey dripped down from a section of comb that had been shattered by a marauding mouse that had attempted to steal away with some of this liquid food.

By the swarm of activity, the Sprite could see it had not ended well for the mouse. Stung to death, worker bees joined in a group effort to remove the dead mouse before its body rotted to contaminate their harvest. Other bees were relegated to the morbid task of removing the bodies of the bees that sacrificed their stingers, and their lives, to protect the hive from the thieving mouse.

Loken, as casually as a bee could, flew to the honey. The other bees were too busy to take notice of him, absorbed in their work to see anything beyond the dead carcass they were attempting to discard.

He carefully sipped on the honey, stealing enough to cover his wound and a little more to sate his hunger.

Loken flew out of the hive, escaping attention by departing from the hive with a group of bees on their way to harvest more nectar. He winged away, flying off to where he was left the dreamstone.

Alighting upon the branch, Loken regurgitated the honey, the sticky droplet adhering to the bark. With a flash of light, Loken assumed his usual form.

"Better… much better," murmured Loken, dabbing the sticky honey directly onto the laceration. "This should stave off infection."

Holding up the dreamstone, he scrutinized the crystal. Examining the reflection of his wings, he had to make sure the arrow had not somehow ravaged them.

"Thank goodness," sighed the Sprite, relieved his new set of wings remained intact. They were still in pristine condition in spite of his latest ordeal. "Now, to make up for lost time."

'To change into a fleet-footed deer again will likely mean becoming those hunters' supper,' thought Loken. *'To become a horse should prevent me from being eaten, but in all likelihood, some fool will probably try to capture me to be his beast of burden. So… what will it be this time?'*

Loken sat on the magic crystal, contemplating this conundrum. If the Princess and her cohorts in pursuit were nearby, the last thing he needed was to be spotted by them. He had to take the shape of a creature large enough to transport the dreamstone, but small enough to go unnoticed. It had to be an animal that would be ignored by predators, especially the human kind, but a creature that can move with speed.

"I know!" exclaimed Loken. He draped the gold chain over his neck as he prepared to morph.

With a snap of his fingers, in a flash of white light the Pooka transformed into a falcon. Now, he would be able to fly high out of the reach of any hunter and he'd be fast enough to out-fly and out-maneuver the marauding crows and even large birds of prey like an eagle.

With the magic crystal safely around his neck, Loken pushed off the tree branch. Taking to the air, the Sprite's sickle-shaped wings carried him high on a rising bank of warm air. Gliding effortlessly, he circled several times on this thermal. When he was nothing more than a dark speck against the pale blue sky, Loken winged his way northward.

"I wish we could just magically transform into a bird like that falcon," said the Princess, staring wistfully to the cloudless sky as a little raptor glided overhead. "It would be so much faster and far less uncomfortable than enduring hour after endless hour in these hard saddles."

"Wouldn't that be grand? To fly as free as a bird," marvelled Cankles, squinting to see the falcon as it headed north toward the Fire Rim Mountains.

"No point in wishing for the impossible," reminded Tag. He focused on the road ahead, ignoring the bird of prey flying off in the distance.

"I was just making conversation," responded Rose, shifting restlessly on her mare.

"I believe you were hinting that you're getting tired of riding," said Tag, reining his stallion in.

"A break would be lovely," admitted Rose.

"We shall ride on a little farther, and then we'll stop for the night," offered Tag.

"And some supper?" asked Cankles.

"That, too," replied Tag, nodding in agreement.

"If that is the case, then I can endure for a little longer," decided Rose, tempted by the promise of rest and a meal.

As the skies dimmed and a velvety dusk smothered the lands, Loken folded his wings, gliding back to earth. Diving down at a frightening speed, the Sprite's falcon form headed straight toward a tree that remained erect even after a lightning strike. Just as he neared the dead, bare branch, he fully extended his wings, fanning out his tail feathers. Instantly slowing down on approach, he landed safely on this perch.

In a flash of light, the Sprite assumed his usual form. He held tight to the dreamstone to keep it from falling to the forest floor below. His amber eyes squinted as he gazed to the west, watching as the sun stole away with the last of its light. Although his eyesight was as exceptional as a falcon, with the impending darkness his vision was about to become compromised. To transform into an owl would solve this problem, but the mournful calls of a neighbouring owl establishing its territory to other rival males nullified this plan.

The last thing Loken needed was to be attacked by an owl after his harrowing encounter with a hunter's arrow. To enter dragon country smelling of fresh blood was a sure way to solicit unwanted attention from those overgrown, flying reptiles in search of a small, easy snack.

With the golden necklace firmly in his hands, the Sprite huddled against the tree trunk as he contemplated his next move. One thing was for certain, to spend the night on this dead tree that stood out from all the others in this patch of forest was out of the question. Loken had to make his move, and do so quickly.

Draping the strand of gold around his neck, in a flash of light Loken morphed once more. Clasping the branch with his clawed feet as well as the thumbs protruding from the apex of his wings, the Sprite scrambled on all fours to the end of the branch than to dangle upside-down as bats typically do.

Now, as this creature of the night, Loken no longer needed to rely on his vision to see in the growing darkness. Plus, the configuration of skin shaped like a tiny horseshoe around his nostrils would serve to amplify the ultrasonic sounds he can now emit to navigate effectively, even through the darkest of nights. As a greater horseshoe bat, Loken would be free to fly on to his destination unmolested, even by the owls that would not think twice of catching the smaller species of bats that inhabit the northern reaches of the Dimbolt Forest.

Launching off the branch, Loken extended his leathery wings. The night wind filled the thin membranes, drawing them taut between the finger joints as he flew northward to meet his partner and nemesis.

"In spite of these primitive conditions, we dined well on this eve," praised Rose. "The roasted grouse were absolutely delectable!"

"Thank you," responded Cankles. He was pleased his efforts to create a hot meal were well received, rather than to serve up more of the thin, leathery sheets of smoked venison and stale bread. "Mind you, if it hadn't been for your deadly aim with that sling of yours, I doubt we'd have feasted as well as we had."

"Well, though I was the one to strike those silly old birds from their lofty perch, you were the one to dress and roast them to perfection."

"Aah, but if your keen eyes did not spot those grouse huddled up in that tree in the first place, I'd have had nothing to roast to begin with," stated Cankles.

"True, but if you had not knocked them from that bough they had landed on after I downed them, we would have had nothing to dine on," reminded the Princess.

"Yes, but if – " Cankles' sentence was cut short as Tag interrupted this praise session.

"If I had not made the fire, those grouse that *she killed* and *you had dressed* would not have been roasted, hence, we would have been eating smoked venison instead," reminded Tag.

"Very true," agreed Cankles.

"Yes, but I hardly believe that qualifies as a true contribution to the effort," remarked Rose. "We were going to build a fire anyway."

"It does so," retorted Tag. "I hardly think you'd eat raw game bird, so a fire was necessary to cook the grouse. And who took the time to build this roaring campfire? I did!"

"Well then, perhaps I should have let you go hunting while I stayed behind to build the fire, instead," countered Rose. "After all, I do know how to do that, too, now."

Cankles knew this was a deliberate jab at Tag and his last ill-fated attempt at grouse hunting, when he and his young comrade failed miserably at dislodging, with a barrage of stones, a couple of birds from a high tree branch. He also knew this matter could potentially explode into a full-blown argument.

"Just because you are gifted with this unnaturally precise aim that allows you to kill innocent, little birds – " snapped Tag, as Rose cut him off.

"Innocent, little birds *you* so eagerly devoured after I killed them!"

"That I roasted over the fire *Tag* made," reminded Cankles, hoping to pacify his comrades. "And that brings us to this one conclusion; we worked together as a team to share in this lovely meal."

"And what a great team we are," grumbled Rose, her voice dripping with sarcasm.

"But we are," insisted Cankles.

"We cannot even get it all together," sighed Tag.

"Aah, but together I do believe we have it all, at least, all that we need to engage in a successful quest," surmised Cankles, speaking with conviction. "We are a team."

Seeing that spark of hope ignite in Cankles' eyes, Tag was not about to be the one to extinguish it. "You are right, my friend. Together, we are much stronger than individuals standing alone."

Rose glanced over at Cankles, the man whom so happily saw the elevation of his status from lowly village idiot to royal court jester as monumental. She then gazed over to Tag as he stoked the flames of the campfire. She had known this young man since they were small children. He had always been headstrong with a deep sense of justice; a quality he had undoubtedly inherited from his father.

"I suppose there are worse people to be standing next to," decided Rose.

"Like whom?" questioned Tag.

"Like the man with the hairy mole and the hairy mole man," answered Rose, as she burst in to a fit of giggles.

Tag merely rolled his eyes as Cankles joined her, laughing at her comment.

"Do you understand that she actually made a slight at us?" questioned Tag.

"No harm done. If it makes her laugh, I'm good with it," responded Cankles. He was just relieved this moment of levity was enough to diffuse a potential argument.

As the night wore on, the trio found a warm spot by the campfire to spread out their bedrolls under the starry sky as the Gnome curled up in his pack, the sack of root vegetables lovingly embraced in his arms, like a lumpy, hard rag doll.

Made weary by the long day on horseback, Rose was the first to drift off, ignoring her usual urge to talk late into the night.

Tag eventually nodded off, lulled to sleep by the drone of Cankles' snoring and the chorus of tree frogs peeping in the surrounding forest. As his mind meandered, wandering in his nocturnal subconscious, Tag was off on another one of his rousing adventures where he was the ultimate hero and feats of derring-do were mandatory before waking with the coming of the sun.

It was quite common for Tag to dream of single-handedly capturing murderous villains, battling vicious dragons and rescuing beautiful damsels in all manners of distress.

Of course, all this was accomplished with uncommon valour, amazing flair and unparalleled success!

This latest dream was no different from the others, but this time, the deadly confrontation unfolded on one of the highest peaks of the Fire Rim Mountain Range. On this towering plateau, against a crimson dawn, Tag, dressed in a full stand of armour and wielding nothing more than a shield and his father's sword, squared off against a gargantuan, fire-breathing dragon.

Man and beast prepared to wage war surrounded by sheer cliff walls.

It was a majestic backdrop, perfect for battles of legend. The sweeping vista far below appeared, only to vanish again as swirling banks of misty clouds hugging the shoulders of this great pinnacle added to the drama by lending emphasis to just how high they truly were.

Chained to a massive stone pillar, Evelyn, Rose's beautiful handmaiden paled in fear, trembling as she waited for Tag to save her, but between her and her rescuer was a winged leviathan of nightmarish proportions.

With a slow, lumbering gait, the dragon advanced. Its heavy footfalls boomed, sending tremors through the earth to reverberate through their bodies.

Standing steady, Tag braced for the assault. With no long-range weapon like a bow or spear to deploy, he was not within striking distance to engage the beast, but the dragon was certainly within range to mount its own attack.

Crouching low to the ground, Tag raised his shield, using it as a protective barrier.

What had started as a guttural rumble from deep within the dragon's throat became a thunderous roar. It sounded like the giant bellows of a blacksmith's furnace; raking at his nerves and rattling him to his very core. The noise was so deafening, it drowned out Evelyn's horrified screams as swirling tongues of orange flames and searing heat gushed around him as the beast exhaled.

Tag could feel the rising temperature of the intense fire through the steel boss of his shield where the handle and the leather strap that secured it to his forearm grew uncomfortably hot. As soon as the flames changed to a pale shade of yellow, Tag knew the beast was about to lose its fiery breath.

As the creature's massive head recoiled, inhaling fresh air to unleash another volatile blast, Tag waited. He waited for the precise moment when the large, overlapping plate-like ventral scales stretched apart, revealing the vulnerable underside protected by this armour when the lungs were not fully expanded.

Just as these scales separated to expose these narrow gaps, Tag dropped his shield. Dashing toward the beast before it could unleash another fiery breath, he raised his sword.

Tag lunged.

The tip of the blade pierced through the vulnerable skin exposed between the ventral plates on its chest. Instead of driving the weapon deep into the dragon's heart, the creature suddenly reared up, the blade coming short of striking its mark.

Tag gasped in surprise as the monster's foot came crashing down.

The earth shook with the percussion of the blow, sending him tumbling to the ground. Bellowing in rage, the dragon's foot smashed down again to crush the knight.

Rolling away, Tag avoided the impact, but donning full battle regalia, he was unable to stand up quickly. Just as he struggled to sit upright, the dragon slammed its foot down once more.

Unable to move away in time, Tag watched in horror as the dark, leathery sole of the dragon's foot rushed toward him to smear his body into the ground.

The beast suddenly bellowed in agony.

Retracting its foot, the dragon recoiled in pain as the tip of Tag's sword sank in.

With the blade still lodged in the sole of its foot, the dragon struggled like a dog trying to remove a painful thorn piercing its tender paw.

Unable to maintain his grip on the sword's hilt, Tag surrendered his weapon. Scrambling, he rolled from side to side to keep from being trampled by the beast's erratic movements. Driven by sheer adrenaline, he leapt onto his feet. Instead of racing off in fear, Tag knew the closer he remained to the dragon, the safer he'd be.

This close, the beast was less likely to discharge its incinerating breath, and if his luck held, positioned just so, he'd avoid detection by staying within the creature's blind spot.

This one bit of knowledge Tag's father had shared with him when he was a young lad was about to be put to the test. He had learned that dragons have terrible visual acuity, relying more on sudden movement to detect prey. And just like a horse, this creature's eyes were positioned on the sides of its head to create a blind spot in its field of vision.

Any man who was brave enough to stand this close to a dragon would land in this zone of invisibility, at least in theory.

An angry growl rumbled from the dragon's throat as its teeth snagged onto the sword, yanking it from its foot. With a flick of its head, the weapon was tossed aside.

Tag held his breath, watching in wide-eyed horror as his father's sword came to a skidding stop at the very edge of the cliff. The blade hovered over oblivion as the hilt of the perfectly balanced weapon kept it from tipping down the mountainside. The brilliant light of the morning sun danced across the silver blade as the sword perched precariously, waiting for a sudden breeze or the tremor of the dragon's footfalls to send it toppling over to disappear forever.

He sighed in relief to see his precious sword did not take a tumble, but any thoughts of retrieving it were dashed as the dragon's head whipped about to face him.

Tag froze. Holding his breath, he came nose to snout with the giant reptile.

He stood stock-still, not even blinking as the dragon gazed straight ahead, as though staring right through him. Not even Evelyn moved, her breath catching in the back of her throat as she watched in stunned amazement and fear as this brave knight boldly confronted the monster.

As the dragon swivelled its head about to search for its prey, Tag moved accordingly, quickly sidestepping to remain at the very tip of the reptile's snout. He was so close he could reach out and touch it. When the reptile tilted and turned its head to stare ahead with its other eye, once again, Tag scrambled, trying frantically to remain out of its field of vision.

Just as the dragon's head settled back to point straight ahead, still unable to see its intended prey, the beast suddenly snorted. Its spent breath gushed right into Tag's startled face.

Though equipped with eyes of questionable ability, there was no doubt the dragon's sense of hearing was far better than it's sight. As Tag gagged on the foul stench of its breath, the dragon acted instinctively. With jaws agape, it lunged forward to seize its prey, only to have Tag launch himself bodily onto the dragon's snout.

Accustomed to its food fleeing in terror, the reptile was startled by this unexpected move. Snapping its head back, it flung Tag skyward. Twisting through the air, he landed on the dragon's scaly head.

Though unable to see its prey, through the tough scales the dragon could still feel Tag's suit of armour banging about as he struggled. His hands grabbed a hold of the ragged edge of its right ear to keep from falling to the ground below.

Issuing another angry bellow, the coat of scales rattled like loose armour as the behemoth shook its body to be rid of this pest.

Instead, Tag landed at the base of its ear. Holding on for dear life with one hand, he used his other to seize the dagger from its holster. Before the dragon could use one of its clawed feet to dislodge him, Tag plunged his blade into the thin temporal bone at the base of its ear that was not protected by thick scales. Once, twice and then thrice, he drove the dagger in to its hilt, stabbing into the dragon's disproportionately small brain.

Just as Tag was about the ram the bloodied blade into the creature's head once more, it abruptly stopped its attempt to dislodge him. It was as though the dragon forgot it was being attacked. The amber orbs of its eyes seemed to glaze over as it glanced toward the desperate female chained to the pillar.

Evelyn began to panic, screaming in terror as the dragon set its sight on her.

Drawn to her frantic movements as she struggled against her bonds, the dragon charged. With the creature's ungainly steps, Tag lost his grip on the dragon's ear. Bouncing off its head, he slid down. The tip of his dagger sent sparks flying as Tag used it against the scales to slow his descent. Sliding down between the creature's eyes, his ride came to an abrupt stop on a spur protruding from the dragon's snout.

As it neared its shackled prey, Evelyn screamed as she watched the beast rear up. Towering over her, its head recoiled as it filled its lungs to capacity to unleash a fiery blast of heat and flames.

"No!" hollered Tag. The tip of his dagger deflected off the scales as he slipped on the rivulets of blood streaming from the wounds at the base of its ear.

Just as the dragon's massive head shot forward, its great maw opened wide to exhale this fire, its legs suddenly buckled beneath it. The behemoth came crashing down, flinging Tag from its snout.

He hit the ground, the visor of his helmet slamming down as he came to a skidding stop before Evelyn.

Before she could say her first 'my hero', Tag sprang to his feet with the kind of agility only possible in one's dreams. He dove for his sword as the percussion of the dragon's dead weight slamming into the earth caused his sword to tip over the edge. Lunging forward, he moved to seize the weapon by its hilt just as it went over, but he missed. As the leather wrapped handle slipped from his fingertips, he snagged it by the brass pommel, catching it between his thumb and index finger.

Sighing in relief, Tag snatched up the sword. Leaping onto his feet, he brandished the weapon once more. Hoisting it aloft, Tag charged toward the dragon before it could come to its senses.

The silvery blade slammed down, striking the beast on its snout. Raising the sword once more, it became clear to Tag the dragon had finally succumbed to the wounds he inflicted on its head. Perhaps the small brain was slow to register the true level of trauma it received from the dagger's assault.

Reluctantly lowering his weapon, Tag scrutinized the dragon sprawled out before him. It was still, silent, and staring with glazed, vacant eyes fixed on the infinite horizon.

"Good as dead!" declared Tag, nodding with approval at his handiwork.

Strutting over to Evelyn, he was greeted with tears of joy and relief.

"Look away," ordered Tag, as he wielded the sword in his hands.

White sparks flew in the air as the blade hacked through the iron chains that shackled her wrists to the granite pillar.

"My hero!" exclaimed a grateful Evelyn. She threw her arms around Tag's neck as she embraced him in an adoring hug. "I knew you'd come to my rescue!"

"Of course! It's what I do," stated Tag. In a grand flourish, he tossed aside his helmet to receive his well-earned reward.

Taking her up in his arms, he dipped her, leaning forward to kiss Evelyn's dewy, soft lips.

Just as he was about to receive this token gesture of gratitude, the dragon stirred, slowly lifting its dazed head.

Before Evelyn could scream, without even glancing behind him, Tag nonchalantly reached behind, thumping the dragon on its snout with the pommel of his sword. This seemingly harmless assault caused the beast to drop dead.

"This is like a dream come true," sighed Tag, as he turned his attention back to Evelyn for that much anticipated kiss.

"Of course it's a dream, you dolt!"

This strangely familiar, know-it-all voice raked at Tag's nerves. He cringed as it was followed by, "And why in heaven's name are you wasting your time saving *her* when you are supposed to be protecting *me?*"

"Go away!" grunted Tag, annoyed that Evelyn felt compelled to follow protocol.

She immediately released her embrace to politely curtsy and then bow in servitude before Princess Rose.

"Excuse me, but I am not here by choice. This is your silly dream and you obviously wanted me to be here," snapped Rose, rolling her eyes in frustration.

"Well, you just changed this grand dream into a bloody nightmare," growled Tag. "Now leave!"

"Look here, I know you are big on all this chivalry stuff and performing foolish acts of bravery, but save it for me. Do not waste it on this commoner."

"But these acts of chivalry and bravery will certainly be wasted on you, Princess, for these are qualities that are quite foreign to you," reminded Tag, as Evelyn abruptly disappeared in a puff of smoke, much to his chagrin.

"Well, here is the deal served up with a big, healthy dose of reality, Tagius Oliver Yairet: I am a princess. You are a knight. It is your duty to do as *I* command. And I command that you reserve your knightly acts of chivalry for me, not waste it on that common commoner peasant girl, Gwendolyn."

"*Evelyn,*" corrected Tag.

"As long as she knows her name, who really cares?" snipped Rose, her shoulders rolling in a shrug of indifference.

"I care! And she is your subject," corrected Tag. "You should be more respectful."

"Dream on! I am the one to be respected."

"By virtue of your title, yes. But if you want it to truly mean something, you must earn respect; not expect it to be handed over on a silver platter."

"*Earn?* That sounds like work..."

"The best way to earn respect is by simply being respectful to others," reminded Tag.

"Oooh... It *is* work," decided Rose.

"Never mind that, what are you doing in my mind?" questioned Tag. Snatching up his helmet from the ground, he crammed it back on his head. Raising the visor, he watched as the great dragon morphed into Loken. The shape-shifting Sprite simply vanished, vaporizing like mist in the morning sun.

"Obviously, you were thinking about me."

"I was thinking about Evelyn. We were about to kiss before you so rudely interrupted."

"Well then, you can just thank me now."

"For what?"

"I spared you the distasteful task of receiving this token gesture of gratitude from that peasant girl," teased Rose, pretending to pucker up for a kiss as she sauntered over to the edge of the cliff where Tag almost lost his father's sword.

"Not that it is any of your business, but suppose I wanted to kiss her?"

"Then I say you must set your standards higher," snipped Rose, peering over the ledge.

"If I did not know better, I'd say you are jealous," decided Tag, flicking the dragon's blood off the sword's blade before sheathing it. "And if you're smart, you'd step away from there."

"I *am* smart and you only wished I was jealous," sniffed the Princess, the toe of her shoe shoving a pebble over the cliff to watch it disappear in the swirling clouds below.

Before Tag could warn her again, Rose screamed. She dropped straight down, the earth beneath her feet crumbling away. Her fingers latched onto the ledge and just as it dissolved under her grip, Tag lunged forward, seizing her by the wrist with one hand as the other continued to hold his sword.

"Good God! You're heavy!" gasped Tag, as he lurched dangerously over the cliff as her weight and gravity worked against him.

"I am not!" snapped Rose. Her breath snagging in the back of her throat as the edge of the cliff continued to crumble under Tag as she dangled in his grip.

As Tag slid further, lowering the Princess ever closer to the bank of clouds below, the panic escalated to an all-new level.

"Don't drop me!" screamed Rose. "Don't let go!"

"Stop struggling!" hollered Tag. Fighting to keep his grip on her, he rammed the pommel of his sword into the earth in an attempt to end this downward slide.

Rose screamed once more as Tag's helmet fell from his head, almost striking her on the shoulder as she fought to hold on.

"Grab my wrist with your other hand!" ordered Tag. The sweat beaded on his forehead as he struggled to hold onto both Rose and his weapon.

"Let go of the sword!" shouted Rose, the tears streaming down her face as fear and panic continued to grow.

"I can't!"

"You *won't!*" argued Rose, the toes of her shoes scrambling to find a foothold on the sheer cliff.

"I can't lose this sword!"

"We'll both die if you don't!"

"Shut it!" growled Tag. He fought to hold on as Rose's hand grew slick with sweat. He knew she didn't have the strength to pull herself up, nor was he properly anchored to prevent them both from slipping over this cliff to their death.

Pushing against the pommel, Tag attempted to set the sword into the earth while at the same time, giving himself the leverage to pull Rose to safety.

On his belly, Tag inched his way back onto firmer ground. Just as he released the hilt of the sword to pull Rose up, Parru St. Mime Dragonite appeared.

A sinister smile curled the Sorcerer's lips as his gnarled finger pushed against the broad edge of the blade as he said, *"Oopsy!"*

"NO!" screamed Tag. Lunging for the sword as it toppled over the cliff, he lost his grip on Rose.

The look of terror in her eyes as she slipped into the clouds below burned into his memory. Her scream, echoing all around him, rang in his ears.

Tag's heart was pounding, rising in his throat and thundering in his ears as Dragonite whispered, "No need to make a choice now."

"Rose!" shouted Tag, watching as the Princess disappeared through the clouds. At mid-scream, he bolted upright, trembling as he glanced about in utter confusion.

"Hush! I am trying to sleep," mumbled Rose, not even opening her eyes as she rolled over to resume her slumber.

11

A Deal is a Deal

For once in Loken's difficult life, his travel, at least this leg of the journey, was unhampered by a catastrophe or the near misses he was usually plagued by.

Winging his way through the labyrinth of subterranean tunnels, his leathery wings whisked him through the gloomy maze. The rows of burning torches, the amber flames dancing and twisting in the wake of his flight, cast a great, distorted shadow as he neared the mouth of the Sorcerer's secret lair. Coming to rest on the archway leading to this large chamber, Loken slipped off the chain of the necklace from about his neck. Leaving the magic crystal on the stony ledge for safekeeping, he proceeded with caution.

"Phew! I made it unscathed," whispered the Sprite.

Just as he fluttered into the chamber, he was greeted by words of rage bellowing from the Sorcerer.

"*You!* How dare you show your face to me!" shrieked Dragonite, the wine he sipped spewing from his mouth. This carmine liquid splashed over the rim of the pewter vessel that trembled in his angry grip.

"You fool!" squeaked the Pooka, his wings flapping madly as he ducked away from the vessel hurled at him. With a loud clatter, the cup bounced off the wall, the wine splashing in all directions. "It's me, Loken!"

"I know!" snarled the Sorcerer, levelling his staff at the Sprite's bat form.

A blue bolt of energy flew toward Loken just as he darted behind a large stalactite hanging from the cave ceiling. It narrowly missed his wing to send a shower of sparks cascading from the cave wall where it deflected off the stalactite. The calcareous formation shattered as it fell to the ground.

Loken retreated. His bat wings frantically pushed him through the air to make his escape. Taking refuge behind the archway making up the mouth of the chamber, the Sprite morphed back into his usual form. Clambering down, he lowered the dreamstone to the cave floor. Tossing the new moleskin cloak he stole from the hairy human, Loken concealed his new set of wings that were now folded neatly against his back before approaching his nemesis.

"Are you out of your mind?" hollered the tiny being, peering into the chamber. "Is this how you greet an old friend?"

"I have no friends, old or otherwise," snapped the Sorcerer.

"Yes, I wonder why?" sighed the Sprite. "You are as rash as ever!"

"I have good reason to kill you, you audacious little miscreant! How dare you show your face after failing me?"

"Who said I failed?" grunted Loken.

"Say again!" ordered Dragonite, momentarily stunned by these words. "What news have you?"

"At this rate, you will never know."

"Look here, you were the last person I thought I would see alive again. You took me by surprise, and if anything, I thought you were here to taunt me," lied the Sorcerer, raising his hand in a gesture of calm. "Do you have news of the dreamstone?"

"None of your questions will be answered if you assault me again," responded Loken. "If you do, I will take my leave, *immediately!*"

"How you leave shall depend on the manner of your return," growled Dragonite.

Abandoning the magic crystal, the Pooka pushed the dreamstone into the shadows first, before presenting himself to his master. With cautious, measured steps he advanced.

"So, by some strange miracle you survived your encounter with the Princess," noted Dragonite. His final memory of the Pooka was seeing a bloated Loken sailing over the trees after being drop-kicked by Cankles. "When I last saw you, you were twice the size and in a hurry to abandon me and my mimely minions to face the Dream Merchant and his allies on our own."

"I did not abandon you, and if you remember correctly, nor was I in any condition to assist you, if I could."

"Excuses, excuses!" muttered the Sorcerer, staring suspiciously at the Sprite as Loken neared his throne. In all the years he had been acquainted with him, this tiny being *never* walked when in his usual form, always taking to the air with his tatty old wings than to risk being treaded upon. "So what brings you here?"

"Our deal."

"What of it? No dreamstone. No potion," grunted Dragonite,

dismissing the Sprite with a wave of his hand. "It is as simple as that!"

"What makes you say I did not return with the magic crystal?" questioned Loken, his arms crossing his chest in defiance.

"I do not see it... And do not tell me you have it hidden beneath that moleskin cloak, for if you did, you'd have a great malformation between your shoulders as big as dowager's hump on an old witch's back!"

"I'm no fool! Do you truly think I would simply hand it over without first making sure that potion is ready to be exchanged, as you had promised?"

"I am insulted by your insinuation!" snapped Dragonite, his fist slamming down on the armrest of the throne. "The promise is as good as the man making it."

"Yes, that is why I need to make sure. Show me the potion and I will show you the dreamstone."

"Very well," conceded the Sorcerer, nodding in agreement. His hand fished about, searching through the great folds of his flowing robe. Holding forth a small vial for Loken to see, he announced, "Here we go! The potion you desire."

Just as the Pooka rushed toward the throne to claim his reward, Dragonite's foot came up, the sole of his worn, ragged boot ready to stomp down on him.

"Not so fast! Where is the dreamstone?"

"Will you hold true to your promise?" asked Loken, as he peered out from the shadow of the Sorcerer's foot.

"A deal is a deal," responded Dragonite. "Now, show me the dreamstone!"

"I will retrieve it."

"Make haste, or I shall renege on my offer," grunted Dragonite, waving the Sprite off.

Instead of flying away to retrieve the dreamstone, Loken scurried off on foot, like a cockroach fleeing the light of day. Rounding the corner of the chamber's entrance, he seized the crystal by the bead cap. Dragging the gold chain behind him, he trudged along as though he was shackled by a great ball and chain.

The two mimes standing guard on either side of Dragonite's throne put on a grand display, their gestures and exaggerated facial expressions of surprise and excitement becoming more exuberant as the light of the overhead torches reflected off the dreamstone.

With a snap of Dragonite's fingers and a point to the floor before the throne, the mime on his left dropped on all fours. He pretended to be a footstool as the Sorcerer propped his scrawny legs up on his swayed back.

"I am more than just a little surprised to see you had not returned empty-handed, after all," praised Dragonite, nodding in approval. "And I am even more surprised that you had chosen to return with the dreamstone. A wise, or foolish, decision based on one's point of view."

"I know you enough that had I returned without the dreamstone, I would be denied that potion and you would have killed me. And had I opted to flee with the dreamstone to use for my own devices, then I'd spend my remaining days fighting to stay alive. Either way, you would see me put to death," reasoned Loken, his words convincing.

"True, very true," admitted Dragonite, peering over tented fingers to study the crystal in Loken's possession. "So, give it to me!"

"Give me the vial first."

"No! You give me that dreamstone first," snorted the Sorcerer, his hands balling into angry fists.

"Are you mad?"

"I will be, if you do not hand it over!" Dragonite snatched up his staff, lowering the black obsidian crystal mounted atop his staff as the man-made footstool issued a silent scream, scrambling to be out of the line of fire as the second mime ducked behind the throne.

"You try; I die," warned Loken, rattling the gold chain at the Sorcerer, "and this crystal will be destroyed along with me."

Dragonite grunted in disdain as he slumped back in his throne, contemplating this stalemate.

"What if we make the exchange at the same time?" suggested Loken.

"That is fair," decided the Sorcerer.

"First," said the Sprite, transforming in a glow of light, "this will make it real fair if we are equal in all ways!"

In excitement, Dragonite's bony hand slapped his gaunt thigh. He admired Loken's adopted form while the two mimes stared in wide-eyed fascination at the Sorcerer's doppelganger.

"Ooh! I do like what I see!" crooned Dragonite, nodding in approval.

"Of course you would! I look just like you, and deliberately so!" Loken adjusted the tattered sleeves of this well-worn, black robe, preparing to grab the vial of potion at the first opportunity.

The Sorcerer forced his back erect. The bones of his normally stooped spine popped audibly, one after the other, as he stood upright, circling around Loken, now of whom was his spitting image.

The Sprite watched through narrowed eyes, staring suspiciously as Dragonite inspected his likeness, slowly limping around to admire this facsimile of his greatness.

With the dreamstone in his hand, Loken made his demand, "This crystal, for that vial of potion, like you had promised."

"Yes, yes!" Dragonite's clenched fist opened up to reveal the tiny vial, the liquid inside glowing with magic.

"On the count of three, we make the trade," instructed Loken.

"Fair enough," agreed the Sorcerer.

"One…" counted Loken.

"Two…" said Dragonite.

Before they both shouted 'three', each lunged for their prize while simultaneously withdrawing their hands.

Denied of their respective reward, Loken and Dragonite bellowed in rage, attacking each other. Tumbling to the cave floor, they rolled about, kicking and punching as they grappled for control.

"Hit him!" Dragonite shouted at the mimes as he struggled beneath Loken. "Use my staff! Hit him!"

Just as the Sprite thought he had the Sorcerer pinned, Dragonite shifted his weight, raising his bony, right hip to throw Loken off balance. Rolling over top of him, this time the Sorcerer had the Sprite against the floor.

"I said, hit him!" commanded Loken, ordering the mimes to strike the Sorcerer with his own staff.

"No, I said to hit him!" reiterated Dragonite, struggling to keep the Pooka pinned beneath him.

"No, I did!" shouted Loken.

The one mime wielding the staff looked to the other holding a club, his shoulders rolling in a shrug of confusion.

The club wielder scratched his head in bewilderment. Shrugging his shoulders, he was just as confused.

The other mime, nervously gripping the Sorcerer's staff, pointed at Dragonite, and then at the Sorcerer's double.

The club wielding mime studied both versions of the Sorcerer, but was still baffled.

"Bloody hell, hit the damned Sprite!" ordered Loken, struggling to push Dragonite off.

"Don't listen to him!" snarled Dragonite. "Listen to me, I'm the real Sorcerer!"

"No! I am!" snapped Loken.

Just as Loken shoved the Sorcerer off, both assailants fell on their side, still refusing to let go of each other.

The mimes shrugged their shoulders, and, with weapons in hand began clubbing both versions of Dragonite.

Loken snarled, and in a fit of rage and a brilliant show of light, he transmogrified into a massive brown bear. Rearing up on his hind legs, he bellowed, roaring in the faces of the startled mimes as his huge paws armed with knife-like claws slashed at the air.

The mimes unleashed a silent scream, dropping the offending weapons. In a blind panic, they slammed into each other before running into the cave wall. Knocking their heads against solid stone, they fell unconscious.

Loken towered above Dragonite, his lips curling in a ferocious snarl as the Sorcerer attempted to reclaim the staff. A paw slammed down, his entire weight driving the weapon into the cave floor to prevent his nemesis from picking it up to use against him.

Dragonite stood up, slowly backing away as his hands came up in surrender. "So much for a fair trade…"

"I knew I had no reason to trust you," growled Loken, rearing up once more in a threatening posture.

"Nor do I trust you!"

"So now what?" asked Loken. "We both have something the other desires, but neither is willing to part with it."

"There is no reason for such animosity," decided Dragonite.

"Of course there is! If I was stupid enough to trust you from the start, I'd be long dead."

"Not so! I would be inclined to torture you for a good measure of time before killing you, if I had my way."

"There's a lovely thought," grunted the Sprite; "all the more reason to withhold my trust."

"So, we are at a stalemate, yet again." Dragonite held the tiny vial between his finger and thumb. Loken gasped in surprised as the Sorcerer let it drop, only to catch it in his other hand.

"Careful!" cautioned the Sprite. "Don't break it."

"Aaah, I see you still want this potion."

"Yes! As much as you want *this*," stated Loken, the crystal suspended from the gold chain dangled from one of his claws.

"Let us be civilized about this," urged Dragonite, palming the vial in his hand. "It is difficult enough dealing with a shape-shifting Sprite, even harder when you take the form of such a formidable creature. Return to your usual form, and perhaps, I will attempt another trade with you."

"No tricks?"

"If there are no tricks on your part, absolutely!" agreed Dragonite.

"I am willing to cooperate."

In a flash of light, Loken assumed his regular form. He quickly adjusted the stolen moleskin cloak over his slight shoulders to conceal his wings.

"Much better!" praised Dragonite, settling on his stony throne, staff of power back in his hand. "But we agreed: no tricks."

"Yes, I have nothing to hide," said Loken, lugging the crystal in his arms as he neared the Sorcerer.

"I beg to differ," grunted Dragonite, staring suspiciously at the Pooka.

"What do you speak of?"

"What are you hiding from me?"

The Sprite lowered the crystal to the cave floor as he opened up his hands to show he was unarmed. "See… nothing!"

"I mean to ask about what you hide beneath that new cloak," questioned the Sorcerer.

"This old thing? I picked up for the journey north. You know how cold some of these chambers and tunnels can be, even in the warmer days of summer."

"Do you really expect me to believe that?" snorted Dragonite, shaking his head in disgust.

"Why not? I speak the truth."

"You are a liar! It is like a bad, unbreakable habit for you."

"*Me?* What are you speaking of?" Loken nervously clasped the edge of the moleskin cloak, pulling it tighter over his shoulders. "You know these caves can be downright freezing until you venture into the bowels of the earth."

"I find that mighty odd, considering you have ventured to the north without need of such protection in the past."

"I am getting older. I feel the cold more so these days. But before you cause my blood to boil with all these asinine questions, let us do an exchange and I shall be on my way."

"Hmph!" grunted Dragonite, his beady eyes scrutinizing the Pooka standing before him. "Why are you in such a rush? We can do a swap, and then celebrate our individual victory with a shared drink."

"Sounds lovely, but I need that potion for good reason. The sooner I get it, the sooner I can right a wrong," reasoned Loken. "Hence, my need for a hasty departure."

"You sound most convincing, but not convincing enough. Now, speak the truth!" demanded Dragonite, his fist slamming down on the throne's armrest caused Loken to jump.

"But – but…" stuttered the Sprite.

"Shall I dispose of this vial now?" Dragonite held it to his mouth, threatening to swallow it.

"No! Wait!"

"Then speak the truth! What are you hiding? Remove that cloak now!"

Loken released a dreary sigh. "As you wish."

The moleskin cloak slipped from the Sprite's slight shoulders.

"See! I have nothing to hide," declared Loken.

His folded wings suddenly popped open, extending above his shoulders for Dragonite to see. A pristine set of translucent wings as crisp as those found on the backs of newly hatched dragonflies rattled with anxiety.

"Well, well, well! What do we have here?" grunted Dragonite, leaning forward to better examine these new appendages protruding from the Pooka's back.

"It is not what you think!"

"At this moment, you have no idea what I am thinking!" snapped the Sorcerer.

"Let me explain!" pleaded Loken, clutching the dreamstone to his chest as though it would somehow spare him Dragonite's wrath.

"Why? Because you think it will save your life?"

"Yes, but more importantly, I *need* that potion more than you need this crystal."

"I will be the judge of that." Dragonite's fingers drummed impatiently on the armrest. "So, explain yourself. Just how did you acquire this fine set of wings? And do not feed me some cock-and-bull story that you had partially morphed into a dragonfly, just enough to give you these appendages! I know you must do a complete transformation, or not at all."

"True, but these wings came to me quite by accident," responded Loken.

"Accident? Bah! Speak the truth. You used the dreamstone, did you not?" interrogated Dragonite.

Loken's eyes nervously glanced about, as though searching for the correct answer to get him out of this fix.

"Well?"

"I am no dolt! Of course I tested out the dreamstone," snapped Loken. "There was no point in making this long journey to deliver a faulty crystal. It would only raise your ire and get me killed in the process."

"And yet, here you are!" grunted Dragonite, pointing the black, menacing chunk of obsidian crowning his staff toward the Pooka.

"Should I kill you now?"

"Whoa!" shouted the Sprite, raising his hands in a gesture of calm as he took to the air. "Let's not be hasty!"

"Why not? You did break the dreamstone, after all."

"It was not my fault, it happened in a struggle to wrestle this crystal from those rotten mortals."

"And what makes you so sure it is faulty?" queried Dragonite.

"If it was still working, do you truly believe I would have settled for nothing more than a new set of wings? Believe me, when I decided to test it out to make sure it was still fully functioning, I would have wished for a major transformation, to appear as I once did."

"Knowing you, even with the threat of death hanging over your head, you would have stolen away with this crystal if it was indeed working," decided Dragonite.

"Well, you will never know for sure now, but no matter," dismissed Loken. "The point is; you can have the dreamstone now."

Dragonite lowered the crystal atop his staff at the Sprite. "And what the bloody hell am I to do with it?"

"You said yourself: a deal is a deal!" argued Loken. "I retrieved the dreamstone for you."

"Well then, why do I not just render the magic in the potion impotent, and then do a trade. That will make it fair."

"Wait! You can still use the dreamstone! Perhaps, not how you originally intended, but it still has its uses," insisted Loken.

"Are you positive it no longer works?"

"It fell from a great height. When I was finally able to retrieve it, I took it upon myself to test it; to see if it still worked. It dispensed one, and only one, wish before it ceased to glow or work again."

"Hence, the new set of wings?" determined Dragonite.

"No matter how hard I tried, this bloody thing refused to grant anymore wishes. I tried repeatedly to wish myself here to present you with the dreamstone, but all attempts failed," explained Loken, holding up the crystal for the Sorcerer to see.

"You are not lying…"

"I swear on my life, I speak the truth!"

"I would be more inclined to believe you if you chose to swear on something of real value."

"Say what you will, but I tried in vain to make it work. If you do not believe me, you are welcome to try it yourself," offered Loken.

Before the Sprite could hold it up for Dragonite to take, the Sorcerer snatched it away. He knocked the Sprite over, yanking on the gold chain that was trapped under his foot.

Loken pushed off the ground, his wings lifting him onto the throne's armrest. He watched as the Sorcerer set to work.

Dragonite used the ragged sleeve of his robe to clean away the smudges and dirt, polishing the crystal to a shine. Holding the dreamstone by its bead cap, the Sorcerer examined it for any obvious imperfections. True to Loken's word, the tiny sphere merely reflected the torchlight. If anything, it looked like a rather ordinary bead of crystal.

"How did you make it work before?" questioned Dragonite.

"I simply commanded it to give me a new set of wings."

"Sounds easy enough... I wish for a big chest made of solid gold that is brimming with gold coins!"

There was no brilliant flash of light to herald the arrival of this bounty of gold; not even a single coin manifested.

"Let it be..." Nothing happened.

"Make it so!" Still, nothing happened.

"I want it, now!" demanded Dragonite, shaking the dreamstone in frustration. "Damned crystal! It *is* broken."

"I told you so," grunted Loken, watching this pathetic display of avarice.

"You failed me! Now you die!" snapped the Wizard.

"Do not be rash," urged Loken.

"I am not being rash. This is what we had agreed to! You failed, and yet, you have the unmitigated gall to return with a crystal that is no good to me. You probably broke it out of spite!"

"Why the bloody hell would I do that when my life is at stake as well as any hope of claiming that potion you promised to me?"

"Crazy people do crazy things! You are no exception."

"Enough with the insults! If you are as wise as you claim to be, you would still find use for this crystal."

"What good is a damaged dreamstone to me?" snapped Dragonite, slumping down on his stony throne.

"They do not know it is damaged," informed Loken.

"*They?*" repeated Dragonite, his wiry brows knitting into a frown of confusion.

"Yes, the Princess and those two buffoons that helped to annihilate your army of mimes," reminded Loken. "At this very moment, they journey northward in hopes of reclaiming the magic crystal."

"So... they still believe it works," said Dragonite. His bony fingers stroked his tangled beard as he contemplated this bit of information.

"They must... why else would they continue this quest?"

"So what?"

"Revenge! You can still get revenge," reminded Loken. "You always said the next best thing to riches was revenge."

Dragonite mulled over these words. Sitting upright on his throne, his dark, recessed eyes gleamed with malice as he cackled, "Yes... and vengeance will be mine!"

12

Dropping the 'If' Bomb

"You had another restless night," noted Cankles, as he secured his bedroll to the saddle.

"Yes, Tag woke me in the dead of night, disrupting my beauty sleep," grumbled Rose, answering through a great yawn.

"I was speaking to the young master," responded Cankles, glancing over at Tag. "He was tossin' and turnin' most of the night."

"Oh, it was nothing," dismissed Rose. "He was probably just having a wonderful dream about me."

"It was a nightmare, and if I recall correctly, you were in it," said Tag, rubbing the sleep from his tired eyes as he readied for the next leg of their journey.

"It was a nightmare because I was in it? Or I was in it, and then it became a nightmare for other reasons?" queried Rose, staring suspiciously at Tag. "There is a difference you know?"

"Yes, I do know," he grunted, rolling his eyes in annoyance.

"So what caused this dream to become a nightmare?" questioned Rose.

"I was battling a huge dragon. It was all going very well and then…" Tag's voice trailed off as a fleeting glimpse of his nightmare flashed through his mind's eye.

"And then what?" probed Rose.

"I lost my father's sword," answered Tag.

"Is that it?" gasped the Princess, groaning in disbelief. "You dreamed you had lost your sword?"

"Yes," lied Tag.

"Good gracious! That hardly qualifies as a nightmare. I thought you were going to say that someone important, like me, had died in your sleep," muttered Rose.

"No need for concern! It was only a dream after all," reminded

Cankles. "You were probably just worried about losin' that sword somehow after waitin' all these years to get it back again."

"Yes, you're probably right," decided Tag. "And I worry needlessly. There is no way I'd ever lose my father's sword – not now."

"There you go then," said Cankles. "Now, we really should make haste while the day is young."

"Yes, we head due north," responded Tag, holding the backpack open for the navigational Gnome to climb back into.

"So what happens when we get to the edge of Dimbolt Forest and stare across the vast expanse of the Fire Rim Mountains?" asked Rose.

"We shall face the unknown together," answered Tag.

"Somehow, I find no comfort in your words," sighed the Princess. "It does not speak of a clever plan."

"I must rebuild my army of mimes," decided Dragonite, as he contemplated his best strategy.

"What is it with you and those mimes?" grumbled Loken, heaving a disgruntled sigh. "You know they are utterly useless when it comes to matters of warfare. Bloody hell! They couldn't even pretend to *act* like soldiers the last time they were called to war."

"You know my reasons. And unlike you, they do not talk back! So add that to my list."

"Well, if you choose to surround yourself with mindless minions unable to think for themselves to save their own lives, you may as well say farewell to me. I am not foolish enough to become embroiled in your ill-planned follies that are doomed to fail from the get-go."

"Where is your faith in me?" growled the Sorcerer, a feigned look of disappointment shadowed his scowling face.

"My faith skipped out of here, hand-in-hand with trust, when you and your army of mimes were soundly trounced by those aligning themselves with Princess Rose and her cohorts," answered Loken. "And come to think of it, you never even bothered to seek me out after that despicable girl used the dreamstone to turn into a wasp, paralyzing me with her venom in the process."

"And when did you think I'd have the time to search for you? Silas Agincor and those damned Elves lead by Rainus Silverthorn were hot on my heels!"

"And deservedly so!" retorted Loken, his wings rattling with indignation. "You were a fool not to anticipate their coming."

"I knew they would come. I just never thought they would show as soon as they did, in the numbers that they had. And had they not interfered, the dreamstone would have been mine! Mine, I tell you! I would have had them grovelling on their knees, begging for death than to suffer my rage."

"Well, you have the dreamstone now, so it is only fair that you hand over that vial of potion," reminded Loken, extending an expectant hand to the Sorcerer.

"Think again, Pooka!" The glow of the vial disappeared in Dragonite's hand as it balled into a quivering fist.

"This is not fair!" snapped Loken. "You have the dreamstone. I have nothing!"

"*Boo-hoo!* Pity for you, but it is the way of the world."

"You promised me. I did as you asked!"

"That deal was applicable only if the dreamstone was returned in working order," snorted Dragonite, tucking the tiny vial of magic potion into one of the many deep folds of his robe. "We both know this crystal is as defective as you are!"

"Then when will I get the potion?" asked Loken, his hand slowly withdrawing in disappointment.

"When, and only when, I get my revenge. Once you help me lure those mortals to my lair, and more specifically, Princess Rose into my trap, then you will be rewarded accordingly."

"I suppose that is fair."

"Of course it is! However, if you choose to forego the potion and assist me in this plot out of the goodness in your heart and as a sign of goodwill, I will not refuse it," said Dragonite.

"Have you taken leave of your senses more so than usual?" snapped Loken, his tone incredulous. "I will not be deprived of that potion. If it means to aid you in your scheme; then so be it, as long as I get what I'm deserving of."

"Oh, you shall most definitely get what you deserve, and then some," promised Dragonite, the corners of his thin lips that drooped in a constant scowl curled ever so slightly into a forced smile. "So you will do it?"

"As if I have a choice!" grumbled the Pooka. "Mind you, I have suffered in your company for this long, I am confident I can endure a little longer."

"Endure you will! If all goes as planned, you shall be rewarded with the potion you so desire, as well as my esteemed gratitude."

"I can do with the potion. I am indifferent to your gratitude."

"Suppose I reward you with the potion and refrain from killing you out of spite?" offered the Sorcerer, eyeing the Pooka with obvious contempt.

"That will do," answered Loken.

"Brilliant! We have a deal!" Dragonite's bony hands slapped together in delight.

"So, what form will this revenge take?" asked Loken. "I assume you intend to kill those fools?"

"That is no bloody good!" grunted the Sorcerer, dismissing his accomplice off with a wave of his hand.

"You do not plan to kill them?"

"I have a reputation to uphold! Of course I do, but it must be carried out in such a way it shall be etched permanently into the annals of history and into the minds of all," grumbled Dragonite, his gnarled index finger tapping his chin in pensive thought. "What to do? Or should I say: how to do the deed?"

"Why waste your time? Just kill them," suggested the Sprite, his words blunt as he drew an index finger across his throat. "Dispatch them! Quick and easy."

"Love to, but methinks the dreamstone is not so much broken as it is conditioned to work only for Princess Rose… a precaution, so to speak, put in place by Agincor to prevent the likes of me from tapping into its powers."

"You could be correct. The Dream Merchant is a crafty one, but I doubt it. It did grant me one wish before ceasing to work again," reminded Loken. "And that being said: Kill them for all the grief they've caused me!"

"No… I need to know for sure. If this dreamstone will only work for the Princess, I shall force her to grant the powers of this crystal to me."

"And then what?"

"And then I will kill her and her cohorts, but only after I cause them emotional and physical trauma of immeasurable magnitude. So much so, it will be their undoing. And the best part? They will not even know I am the cause of it until it is too late!"

"Are you mental? It sounds nefarious enough, but how do you plan to pull this off?"

"*Doubt!*"

"*Loo-py!*" grunted Loken. This word was tainted with sarcasm as the Sprite's index finger spun by the side of his head. "You *are* mental."

"I am speaking of *self-doubt*. It can undermine the stoutest of hearts and the soundest of minds," stated Dragonite, a sinister grin curling his lips once again.

"Now, I'm intrigued," admitted Loken.

"I can do it in such a way they will suspect nothing. They will second-guess their own actions and decisions. They shall question every move they make. Eventually, they will turn on each other."

"Sounds devious, but killing them will be less time consuming, the results: immediate."

"True, but I need the girl alive for the time being, her two cohorts are dispensable though. But until I kill them, the enjoyment will be in watching them suffer in each other's company," explained the Sorcerer. "If luck and fate conspires in my favour, those two fools travelling with the Princess will abandon the quest, leaving her alone and vulnerable!"

"It's rather bizarre and twisted, but appropriate, in a sick sort of way," determined Loken.

"I know... it is perfect!"

"Fine! But how do you plan to accomplish this?" asked the Sprite.

"There is a way, but it will require much thought and planning on my part to incite the level of self-doubt and resulting chaos I intend to dispense."

"It would be so much easier to simply annihilate them! Bombard them with oil-filled canisters set ablaze," insisted Loken. "Pain, suffering and eventually death, if your goal is to make them suffer!"

"Sounds delightful, but my form of torture can only be appreciated by other intellectual villains and criminal masterminds like me. Instant gratification will not do! I must savour their misery!"

"So no lobbing of flaming oil canisters at her or her comrades?" asked Loken.

"I shall bomb them, all right! I shall hit them with a spell that will raise such doubt, such trepidation; they will question their every step, decision, even their motives."

"And that's it?" asked Loken, scratching his head in bewilderment. "An enchantment?"

"Picture it now," said Dragonite, staring dreamily into the dark shadows of his lair. "*If* we did this instead of that, *if* he had listened to him instead of her, *if* we had turned back than gone ahead! They will question each other to the point that chaos shall reign supreme! Doubt will shake the very foundations of their quest. It will put into question their loyalty, devotion and the integrity of their friendship. As surely as flaming canisters had bombarded them, this insidious spell will destroy them on so many levels. It will be a much crueller fate!"

"And what will you call this '*bomb*' of a spell?" snorted Loken, disappointed a truly devastating weapon of war was not going to be deployed.

"Those three will be asking *'what if'* so much I shall call it the devious enchantment of deceit, deception and doubt!"

"That's a bit wordy. Why do you not just call it the *if-bomb?* At least it's easier to say and sounds much more dangerous!"

"Perhaps you are right for once, my demented little friend," agreed Dragonite, nodding in approval. "The *'if'* implies the nature of the spell, the *'bomb'* represents its destructive force. Yes... I like that! The *if-bomb...*"

"And will you be dropping this *if-bomb* on the Princess and her cohorts any time soon?" questioned Loken.

"As soon as you can lure them to my lair," responded the Sorcerer.

"Why do you not attack while they are in the Dimbolt Forest? Catch them unawares?"

"Love to, but there is a fly in the ointment!"

"A *what?*"

"It comes in the form of a pesky Elf lord," revealed Dragonite, lowering his obsidian crystal to reveal an image to Loken. In the menacing glow of this black, volcanic glass the Sprite spied upon Lord Rainus Silverthorn. The Elf was working with Silas Agincor to retrieve the dreamstone, if Princess Rose failed to do so. "As we speak, Silverthorn conspires with the Dream Merchant to reclaim the magic crystal. At this very moment, they journey through the Dimbolt Forest."

"What else had been revealed to you?" asked Loken. He forced down the rising tide of panic. The possibility that the Sorcerer spied on him when he dropped the crystal during his mishap with the marauding crows or during his attempts to make the dreamstone work filled him with dread.

"Are you mocking me?" grunted the Sorcerer. "You know since the run-in with my brother Wizards my powers are no longer at full strength. That is why I need the dreamstone to work."

"Brother Wizards?" scoffed Loken, chortling under his breath. "You deal in the forbidden arts, hence the reason you are brother no more to the clan. Nor does your choice of company reflect well on you."

"Cruel fate had brought us together," grunted Dragonite. "It is not by choice that you are here with me!"

"I was speaking of those idiotic mimes!" snapped Loken.

"You speak ill of my minions, and yet, they are loyal to me! They never question my leadership."

"Of course not! And it's only because those dim-wits refuse to speak, all in the name of this so-called *art* you think so highly of!" snorted Loken, shaking his head in disgust.

Dragonite's eyes narrowed in resentment as the obsidian crystal swelled with menacing light. "What say you now?"

"I say the art of mime is growing on me," gulped Loken, watching as the light within the black crystal faded accordingly with the Sorcerer's diminishing anger. "So we focus on the Princess, ignore the Elf and the Dream Merchant for the time being."

"Those two are minor details to contend with in the big scheme of things! The point being, this obsidian crystal will only reveal what it wants to, leaving me in the dark about most matters beyond my lair. And you have noticed how it is taking longer than it should to power up before I can discharge its magic."

"Aaah! So *that* is the reason why you are resorting to spells and potions; ergo the if-bomb," surmised the Sprite.

"I will neither confirm, nor deny it. Just know that I want to see my enemies suffer before they meet their demise."

"So Silverthorn and Agincor believe you have the magic crystal," determined Loken.

"It is apparent they believe you managed to escape Pepperton Palace with the dreamstone and had delivered it to me. I sense that the outcome of Princess Rose's last quest forced them to question her abilities, as well as those in her company, to reclaim it," stated Dragonite, as he fondled the crystal bead dangling from its gold chain. "And now that I have it, they will do whatever they can to steal it away from me."

"If you are so paranoid that they are set on killing you to get it back, perhaps you should just return the dreamstone to Agincor?"

"If I do, I shall make it a point of killing you first for annoying me to no end! I need to know from the Princess if this dreamstone still works, and if so, I shall use it to turn on my enemies, you included if you do not mind your words!"

"No need to get testy!" urged Loken, taking to the air with his new wings. "Remember, you need my help to get the Princess here."

"Yes, and just how long you live will be in direct relation to how well you serve your purpose," reminded Dragonite.

"I recommend taking action before the Elf and the Wizard catch up to the Princess. It will be easier to pick them off one at a time than to contend with them simultaneously."

"Yes, we do not need them combining their efforts to steal away with this dreamstone. Therefore, I shall deploy the if-bomb tonight."

"Tonight?"

"On this very eve," confirmed Dragonite, his eyes gleaming with malice. "Once this magic is unleashed on them, they will be at their most vulnerable. You shall use the opportunity to learn if there is a secret to using this crystal or if the Princess is indeed the key to manipulating its powers."

"Behold! As per your request, the vast wastelands of the Fire Rim Mountain Range," announced the Gnome. In a grand flourish, he presented the dismal landscape to the courageous trio, as Tag steered his mount to the very edge of Dimbolt Forest.

"It looks mighty forebodin', if I do say so myself," noted Cankles, as he surveyed the broad expanse before him.

The dark storm clouds gathering on the distant horizon threatened to steal away with daylight before the sun even disappeared with the coming of night. The jagged mountaintops, like great fangs, pierced the sky, snagging billowy clouds drifting by while heat and the malodorous reek of sulphur hissed as it escaped from deep cracks in the earth.

"The lands look inhospitable and desolate," stated Rose. "You would think dragons would seek out a better habitat."

"Consider yourself lucky they don't and haven't taken to making the pastures and farmlands of Fleetwood their home," grunted Tag. "Aside from the threat they face against knights willing to protect crown land and property, the only thing that keeps them here are these volcanoes. They like to hibernate in the warm, subterranean caves during the long winter months and they still find refuge within when the summer nights become unseasonably cold."

"For some reason, your words made sense to me," decided Rose, nodding in agreement. "But where to from here?"

Tag stared across the tortured landscape.

Islands of trees and shrubs dotted the rugged terrain scarred by lava flows now hardened over time. These clumps of vegetation that managed, by sheer luck, to escape the path of molten lava or the fiery breath of the resident dragons battling for male supremacy were the only patches of green against an otherwise barren, but treacherous landscape.

"You got us this far; do you know your way beyond this forest?" Tag asked the Gnome.

"Are you mad? My people are considered a delicacy to 'em dragons. I have no intention of becomin' a snack. An' besides, venturin' beyond this point requires danger pay, of which ya don't have," grunted the little navigator, raising the near-empty burlap bag.

"But I will promise to double your pay; offer you all the beets you could ever want," bribed Rose.

"Sorry, missy! There ain't enough beets in this world to make me journey beyond this point. From here on in, you folks are on your own," stated the Gnome, as he emptied the final parsnip and the last three remaining rutabagas from the bag into his pockets for his long trek home.

"So, you'll go no further?" queried Tag.

"Not on your life, or mine, so ya may as well let me down. If ya feel a need to meet your appointment with death, then by all means, you're free ta venture on if ya like, but this is where my service ends. I mean ta live a good, long time. This is where we'll be partin' company. I'll jus' hoof it on home from here."

"Surely you would be safer travelling with us, than to journey home alone," said Rose.

"Safety in numbers, I always say," added Cankles.

"Have ya folks taken leave of yer senses?" asked the Gnome, stretching his stubby legs after the long ride in the backpack. "Don't know what would ever compel ya ta travel beyond this point, but that's yer business. My job was ta get ya here fer as long as the root veggies lasted. I lived up ta my end of the bargain an' I ain't about ta waste my life on a fool's errand, leadin' ya through lands crawlin' with 'em ferocious, scaly beasts."

"I can understand your apprehension," said Tag, watching as the Gnome turned away, "but will you reconsider?"

"Nope! Trust me; I know what I speak of. I'll be much safer partin' company with you three fools than ta set a single foot on that land," stated the Gnome, not even glancing back as he waved farewell.

Cankles gasped and Rose squealed in surprise as a golden eagle swooped down. With curved talons, it plucked the Gnome up by his thick wool coat.

Before Tag could unsheathe his sword or Rose could arm her sling, the bird of prey soared skyward.

Spewing profanity in the language of his people, the little Gnome struggled to keep his red hat from flying off his head as the raptor flew ever higher into the sky.

"Oh, my goodness! That eagle is going to make a meal of him!" gasped Rose, staring in wide-eyed disbelief as the bird and Gnome shrank against the azure sky.

"No... Methinks that bird is just takin' our little friend to her nest ta play with her eaglets," decided Cankles, refusing to assume the worst.

"I don't think so," said Tag, pushing his sword back into its scabbard.

"You don't?" asked Cankles. He gulped down the lump catching in the back of his throat as his eyes filled with horror, thinking on the fate of this small being.

"It was part of the deal," lied Tag, watching as the great eagle winged southward, struggling to keep its grip on the squirming burden. "When we were done with the G. P. S., an eagle was appointed to return him home."

"Oh… I suppose that makes sense. They were heading in the right, general direction, after all," decided Cankles. He was quite prepared to accept this explanation than to believe the Gnome was about to become an easy meal for a family of eagles.

"Whatever the case, we will never catch up to that bird now," stated Rose, tucking away her sling.

"True," agreed Tag. "And it won't matter, not to the Gnome or any other living being including us, if we don't retrieve that dreamstone from Dragonite before he does something crazy with it."

"Whatever the case, I'll pray that little fellow does not meet an untimely demise," said Cankles.

"If you're concerned the eagle is going to eat the Gnome, I don't think that will happen," determined Tag, attempting to ease his friend's concern.

"What makes you say that?" asked Cankles.

"During the last leg of this trek the Gnome had eaten up all the beets and carrots first, saving his least favourite vegetables for last."

"So?" responded Rose.

"What I am trying to tell Cankles is that I believe, unless the eagle has developed a taste for parsnips and rutabagas, that's exactly what that bird will be getting if it sinks its beak into the Gnome," reasoned Tag.

"Well, I, for one, believe in the old adage; you are what you eat," said Cankles, speaking with conviction. "Never been keen on rutabagas myself and I can't say I've ever know an eagle to like them either."

"So, we are not going to attempt rescuing the Gnome?" asked Rose, seeking Tag's confirmation.

"We can't, even if we wanted to. And we may not need to in the end," reminded Tag.

"Oh yes… reclaiming the dreamstone from the Sorcerer," said Cankles. "I suppose it won't matter to anyone, including the Gnome, if Dragonite unleashes his evil unto the world."

"So what do we do now?" asked Rose, her eyes staring off to the distant north where a column of black smoke swirled skyward. Any hope that it was nothing more than a mountain belching to relieve some internal pressure was soundly squelched as the thunderous roar of two dragons engaged in battle shattered the still air.

"We wait," decided Tag, dismounting from his stallion to lead it into a protected clearing. "Once darkness settles on the land and night steals away with the last of the warmth from the air, we will advance. If we are lucky, the moon and stars will provide enough light to guide us on our way."

"I have an idea," said Cankles.

"Go on, what is it?" asked Tag.

"Less than half a league from here we passed by a solitary, little lake. By all the activity on the surface, I'd say it's teeming with trout."

"You want to go *fishing?*" groaned Rose, her nose wrinkling in disgust.

"It'd be wonderful to have a nice hot meal of fresh-caught fish for a change," responded Cankles. "And if we turn back now, we'll arrive at the lake well before sunset, the perfect time for fishin'."

"Brilliant!" praised Tag. "It will help to pass the time."

"*Ugh!* Fishing is for commoners," muttered Rose, "an activity reserved for those starving and desperate for something to eat."

"Have you ever fished before?" queried Tag, as he turned his steed about.

"Of course not!"

"Then you obviously have no idea how relaxing it can be," stated Tag.

"Oh, *please!*" The Princess rolled her eyes for the umpteenth time.

"The young master is quite right, m'lady," insisted Cankles. "They say an hour spent fishin' can add a year to your life."

"Really? And who are *they?*" questioned Rose.

"Old folks who do a lot of fishin' I suppose."

"I think our friend has a brilliant idea," said Tag. "It'll give me a chance to rest and freshen up."

"Good idea," teased Rose, as she fanned the air with her hand. "You smell like a sweaty horse. Your gamey aroma will only attract every dragon in the area once we venture northward."

"*Ugh!*" groaned Rose.

She grimaced in disgust as she watched Cankles carefully impale a big, fat earthworm onto a barbed hook, forcing its body around the curved piece of metal. She shuddered as she imagined the poor creature unleashing a scream of pain so high-pitched only dogs and other worms could hear it.

"Can you not just tie that *thing* on?"

"Sorry, but it's the only way to keep the worm from fallin' off the hook once you begin castin'," explained Cankles, his words apologetic as he spied the Princess wincing in sympathy as the worm writhed, its posterior thrashing about wildly. This undulating body wrapped itself around the pointed piece of metal to effectively disguise the hook from the eyes of the most discerning trout.

"I do not know what is worse: to be impaled, drowned or swallowed whole by a fish," said Rose, as she contemplated the earthworm's fate.

"Just be glad you're not a worm."

"Of course I am glad for that," responded the Princess. "What a terrible existence it would be."

"In my way of thinkin', God would never have created worms, nor would he make them so tasty to fish if they were made for no other purpose than this," explained Cankles, wiping his hands clean on his trousers before casting the baited line.

"Whatever eases your conscience, I suppose," said Rose, her shoulders rolling in a shrug.

"It's the way of nature, m'lady. I'm sure this very ground you kneel on would be squirming beneath you with an overabundance of worms and other such grubs, if fish and birds did not feast on them."

"*Yuck!*" yelped Rose, leaping onto her feet. The very thought made her skin crawl. "Then it is a very good thing! Feed them to the fishes, I say!"

"If we are lucky, the trout will be hungry, snapping up the worm, hook and all."

Cankles tossed the line out, the baited hook hitting the water with a small splash that sent quivering rings rippling outward to diminish before reaching the shore. The doomed worm sank until the cork float bobbing on the surface prevented it from disappearing on the silty, weed clogged bottom.

"Now what?" asked Rose.

"Now, we wait."

"That is it? We *wait?*" groaned Rose, plopping down on the ground next to Cankles.

"Like the young master said, '*Patience is a virtue*' and this is the relaxin' part of fishin'," reminded Cankles, crouching low to the ground. In this position, his compact size and movements were kept to a minimum so any trout swimming near to shore would not be frightened away to deeper waters by his presence.

"Waiting is not relaxing, it is *boring*," insisted Rose, heaving a dreary sigh.

"Believe me, after a long day of choppin' firewood, ploughin' fields or cleanin' a stable; this *is* relaxin'," insisted Cankles, thinking on the odd jobs he'd take on to eke out an existence. His eyes trained on the piece of cork floating on the placid water, waiting for subtle, telltale movements to indicate a fish was nibbling on the morsel of worm.

"When you put it like that, I suppose it can be considered relaxing, as boring as all this inactivity is."

"The reward is when the fish takes the hook," assured Cankles, staring hopefully as a large trout jumped, leaping into the air to snap at a dragonfly hovering over the surface of the water near to the cork float. "It becomes a test of skills to land the trout, once that hook is set."

"If you say so," responded Rose, still in need of convincing.

"Oh, I do! You just wait and see, m'lady. Trust me when I say it is no easy feat to bring in a nice size trout. This is the true test of one's fishin' skills."

"I am in no need of such skills, but I am willing to watch you."

"Everyone should know how to fish," insisted Cankles, working in the slack line, hand-over-fist, so it would be easier to set the hook once a fish snapped up the worm.

"Why, when I can have someone else do it for me?"

"Because you will be forever reliant on another to keep you fed, however, if I can teach you to fish, you can eat whenever it pleases you."

Rose thought seriously on Cankles' words. "I suppose that is very true. Profound words of wisdom from my newly appointed court jester. I am impressed and surprised at the same time."

"Thank you, m'lady," said Cankles, as he blushed with modesty. "Who would've thunk it comin' from one reputed to be the Village Idiot of Cadboll? And here, I thought I was just statin' the obvious."

"Well, it was not obvious to me until you spoke those words. Therefore, being that I am so much smarter, it just stresses the fact that they truly were words of wisdom."

"When you put it that way, then I suppose it was downright brilliant of me to say!" decided Cankles, nodding in approval.

"I wouldn't go as far as that, but it did indeed make sense."

"Oooh, quite right, m'lady! Only a dolt of a fool would boast of his brilliance. A smart man would remain humble, stayin' his tongue, allowin' others to speak of his wisdom."

"I am not sure of what you just said, but if you mean it is better not to be a braggart, that is probably true."

"I'm sure the young master would agree, being so full of knightly wisdom and all," whispered Cankles.

"Speaking of Tag, where did he go?"

"I think he took your insult to heart and decided to do something about it."

"Which insult? There has been so many. And just because I candidly speak the truth, it does not mean I am being insulting. All it means is that I am honest enough to say what is on my mind. So, which one were you referring to?"

"You know the one," said Cankles, his hands tightening their grip on the fishing line.

"The one about Tag still being a silly, little boy? Or the one about him being in love with that *precious* sword he is always fawning over?"

"I was speakin' of when you told the young master he reeked and his *'gamey aroma'* would attract all manner of dragons as we venture to the north," reminded Cankles.

"Oh… that one."

Before Rose could defend her words, Cankles leapt onto his feet. He whooped with glee, yanking on the line to set the hook as a large, speckled trout exploded to the surface of the lake in a flash of silver and iridescent flecks of black and magenta. It thrashed wildly to be free.

"I've got us some dinner! We'll be feasting like royalty tonight!" exclaimed Cankles, working with haste to retrieve his catch.

"Hoorah!" cheered Rose, clapping her hands in delight. "I will fetch Tag. We shall make a roaring campfire to cook that fish by."

"You do that!" Cankles struggled; pulling on the slick, wet line as the trout swam to and fro, fighting for its freedom.

Rose dashed off, running to the clearing by the edge of the lake where she left Tag to set up a temporary camp while she and Cankles went off to catch some fish.

Just as she rounded the grove of willow saplings growing along the reedy shore, Rose came to a skidding stop. She gasped in surprise, her mouth dropping open.

Tag shrieked, startled by her abrupt appearance. His hands instinctively dropped to his nether regions as he fell to his knees, crouching down so he was waist deep in water.

"What are you doing?" asked Rose, staring in wide-eyed amazement.

"I was bathing! What do you think I was doing?"

The water dripping from his hair ran down, beading on his shoulders before gathering to dribble along the grooves of the muscles defining his chest and abdomen. Feeling the intense burn of her eyes as she blatantly stared at him, Tag's feet nervously shuffled about, stirring up the silt so the cloudy water concealed him from the waist down.

"I did not think you would heed my advice to get cleaned up. How was I to know you were bathing?"

"Well, I was! So what are you doing here?" snapped Tag, using one hand to pull a large lily pad closer in case she decided to join him in the lake. "Were you spying on me?"

"Spying on you? Why would I..." Her voice trailed off as she came to the sudden realization that Tag had evolved.

He was no longer the little boy she grew up with. Instead, his naked body, at least what was exposed above the water line, had transformed. He was not bulging with over developed, vein-popping, grotesque muscles like the strongmen that would appear when the travelling carnival rolled into the neighbouring villages.

Instead, Tag's once rake-thin, skeletal boyish form had gone through a metamorphosis. He had muscles that were now shaped by the hardships of life and these quests; sculpted by the many hours he spent training to wield his sword with a degree of proficiency.

"Stop staring at me!" ordered Tag. The only part of his body burning with heat was his face as it flushed with embarrassment.

"What happened to you?" questioned Rose, creeping closer to the water's edge for a better look.

"It's bloody cold in here, that's what!" responded Tag, in a disgruntled huff as his hands, in modesty, continued to cup his groin.

Ignoring his words, Rose's delicate brows arched up in surprise as her finger pointed to the pectoral muscles on his chest and the toned abdominal muscles that glistened in the light of the late afternoon sun.

"When did you get those?" asked the Princess, staring with wide-eyed fascination at the muscles that had been hidden away from her beneath layers of clothing.

"Get what?" grunted Tag, glancing down in case she was pointing at leeches that had decided to prey on his blood while he washed up.

"Those things that look like muscles. When did you get them?"

"When I last went to the market, what do you think?" snorted Tag, rolling his eyes in dismay.

"Are you being sarcastic?"

"Of course I am!" Tag sank into the water until it was up to his neck to hide from her scrutinizing eyes. "And yes, they *are* muscles!"

"But when did you get them?"

"You do not just *get* muscles and it's not as though they just happened. I guess they began to develop about the time when those *happened* on you," muttered Tag, freeing one hand to point at the mounds of Rose's breasts that were accentuated by the cinched waist of her frock.

Rose blushed, pulling the edges of the cloak around her. "I never thought you noticed…"

"Well, they are kind of there!" stated a flustered Tag.

"They are? Have you been staring at them?"

"Of course not! It's not as if they're really obvious," grunted Tag, pretending that he only noticed because she brought it up for discussion.

"They aren't?" gasped Rose. Suddenly insulted by his words, she threw back her cloak and thrust her chest out in defiance, proud of her womanly charms.

"Never mind that! What are you doing here? Did you want something from me?" asked Tag, quick to change the subject before Rose could interrogate or incriminate him.

"Yes… Ah… Oh yes!" stammered Rose. "Fire! We need to build a fire. I caught a big fish."

"*You* caught a trout?" Tag's words were tinged with doubt.

"Well, I was more or less learning how to fish and supervising the task, so our friend was the one to actually land the beastly thing," admitted Rose. "So, unless you want to eat it raw, a fire is in order."

"Fine, but look away," urged Tag. "Better yet, just go away."

"Why?"

"Are you daft? I'm not coming out of here with you standing there, gawking at me," Tag used one hand to wave her off while the other continued to hide his masculine bits and pieces.

"I promise I will not laugh," giggled Rose.

"I'm not worried that you'll laugh, I am concerned it'll be more than your eyes can handle!" scoffed Tag, bracing himself for a round of ridicule and mock laughter.

"Oh, dream on!"

"If you insist on staying and you refuse to look away or go away, then make yourself useful," ordered Tag, standing up so he stood waist deep in the water.

"What are you doing?" gasped Rose, watching as the sun's fading light glistened off his wet body.

"I am not about stay in this water another minute longer," decided Tag, his teeth beginning to chatter with the cold. "Either look away, go away or make yourself useful by tossing my raiment to me."

Rose's inquisitive eyes were oddly drawn to Tag's developing form. It was mesmerizing to behold, and yet, being that it was Tag, it was somewhat disturbing. Even as she tried to avert her eyes, her peripheral vision still caught a glimpse as he proceeded to wade to shore after issuing his warning.

"Where is your sense of modesty?" asked Rose.

"*Modesty?* You are the one who can't stop staring! Besides, I can't stay in this water forever, and I did warn you I'm coming out."

Rose resisted the urge to peek. Squeezing her eyes shut, she hurled his trousers in the general direction of his splashing before dashing off to their camp.

"I'm so glad we had fresh fish for a change. It will provide us with the energy we'll need for the journey. A job well done, Cankles, my friend!" praised Tag, as he discarded the spiny bones into the fire.

"Thank you, but there was nothing to it, really," Cankles responded modestly, a blush on his cheeks for a simple task he enjoyed doing. "What I'm grateful for is gettin' this fire goin' and keepin' the smoke to a minimum, bein' that we're so close to the Sorcerer's domain."

"I quite agree. The last thing we need is to bring attention to ourselves," said Rose, nibbling on her portion of trout served up on a leaf to keep her hands clean.

"Have some tea as well, Princess. It's brewed with chamomile so it'll help you to have a restful night of sleep before we have to move on," offered Cankles, passing her a tin cup of this steaming beverage.

"Thank you, the nights here to the north are colder, so this should help to drive off the chill, if nothing else," said Rose, grateful for the cup of hot tea to warm her hands on.

"Just don't forget to drink it so you're not up all night," reminded Tag, unsheathing his sword to sharpen the blade. "Try to steal away with a few hours of sleep before we venture on."

"I wonder what dangers await us once we leave the cover of this forest to venture on into the Fire Rim Mountains?"

"Well, we all know it is dragon country. We also know there are lots of volcanoes, both dormant and active," said Tag.

"As long as we know what we are heading into, I would like to believe we will be fine," decided Rose.

"I'm sure we can also expect a confrontation with the mimes, those who continue to serve Dragonite. I'm confident many followed him northward, and that is only the dangers we do know about," informed Tag, not noticing the colour draining from his comrades' faces with each word he spoke.

"Wha- what if we do encounter a dra- dragon?" stammered Cankles, his mind swirling with worried thoughts. "How do we fend it off, let alone survive? They've got to be huge! And how does one even escape their fiery breath?"

"Or even worse, what happens if one of those volcanoes were to erupt while we are standing in its shadow? How do we save ourselves from incineration? And what if burning ashes were to rain down on us? I can't allow my hair to burn again!" exclaimed Rose; shuddering as she recalled the first time she created fire. As successful as she was, the Princess accidentally sacrificed some of her hair in the process.

"Or the worst thing possible, the mimes find us and make us watch one of their shows before feeding us to a dragon or dropping us into one of those volcanoes!" Cankles cried out, as all three shuddered at the mere thought of sitting through a performance.

"No! I believe the worst thing possible would be being captured by the mimes, and then made to perform along with them," gasped Rose.

"And near the end of the performance, a giant dragon swoops down to attack us just as a volcano erupts, making the ash fall from the sky to burn your royal head of hair!" added Cankles, trembling at the mere thought of these potential dangers.

"I recommend you both rein in your imaginations," suggested Tag, sliding the whetstone against the blade in long, even strokes. "It is better to hope for the best, but prepare for the worst. Allowing your imaginations to run amok will do you no good. It will only serve to feed your fears."

"My fear is pretty hungry," admitted Cankles. "Maybe I should stop thinkin' on this."

"Good idea," said Tag.

"And should any of Lady Agly's words come to pass, then what?" asked Rose.

"Fear not," dismissed Tag. "If anything, those were merely images of what may be, *not* what will be. If there is any truth to her predictions, I will use what I know to my advantage so we can circumvent catastrophe."

"I suppose that is one bit of good fortune on our side," decided Cankles, choosing to be hopeful. "We have insight that the Sorcerer is not privy to."

"It will give us a distinct advantage, I'm sure," said Tag, using the pad of his thumb to test the blade's sharpness.

"You sound mighty confident," noted Rose.

"So? There's nothing wrong with being confident," stated Tag. "Or would you rather have an indecisive coward, one who is too afraid of the possible outcome, leading the quest? In my opinion, I'd side with the person proceeding with confidence, than to follow someone who will second-guess his every move or doubt his every decision."

"But confidence to the point of arrogance?" questioned the Princess, staring with raised eyebrows at the knight-in-training.

"Just because I speak the truth with conviction, it does not mean I am arrogant," corrected Tag.

"Now you are sounding smug *and* arrogant," responded Rose.

"Think what you will, but I know what I speak of, and if I can use this knowledge, the predictions made by Lady Agly, to help right a wrong, then that is what I must do."

"A little humility would serve you well, for you are coming across as all I had said plus, you are also sounding rather pious and boastful in boldly declaring that you will do what is right."

"I think not, m'lady," said Cankles, speaking in Tag's defense. "In my way of thinkin' the young master is far from being boastful; his humility intact."

"What makes you say that?" questioned Rose, challenging her court jester. "I dare you to prove me wrong when I know I am right."

"In my way of thinkin', a humble person is more concerned about *doing* what is right than always *being* right."

"Now that is a profound observation, my friend!" praised Tag, smiling broadly as he nodded in approval.

"Not really, I think it's just common sense," dismissed Cankles, shrugging off this compliment.

Rose frowned in confusion as she thought on Cankles' words. "I do not believe I like your way of thinking, sir! I am not sure why just yet, so I will have to think on it."

"Why do you not sleep on it instead," suggested Tag. "Take some rest while you can, for we shall be on the move at the midnight hour."

Taking advantage of this time, Tag and Cankles soon drifted off to sleep while Rose tossed and turned. Surrendering her body and mind to the whole notion of a restful slumber, but finding none, the Princess got up. It seemed that the chamomile tea Cankles had brewed up helped both her comrades to achieve a calm, restful sleep, but all this tea did was make her want to pee.

Answering the call of nature, Rose rolled onto her feet. Plucking a handful of soft leaves from a hazelnut tree to use, she ducked behind a large pine tree for some privacy.

Before she could hike up the hem of her dress, the light of the moon shining off an object at the base of the tree caught her eyes.

"What is *this?*" gasped Rose, crouching down for a better look.

A large, emerald green egg as big as her head rested against the tree's gnarled roots protruding from the ground. This egg was trimmed with gold, adorned with a multitude of brilliant-cut gems of topaz and studded with marble-sized creamy white pearls that glimmered in the moonlight.

"I have never seen anything quite like this before. I wonder how you got here?" Rose whispered beneath her breath as she admired this treasure. "Did someone lose you?"

The Princess stood up, staring into the shadows of the forest for signs of a traveller searching for this beautiful ornament he had lost. The only movement her eyes could detect came from the boughs and branches swaying restlessly in the evening breeze. The only sounds Rose could hear came from the chorus of crickets as they resumed their symphony. The world was at peace.

"I believe the old saying, '*I find, I keep; you lose, you weep*' applies in this case," decided Rose.

Tossing aside her handful of leaves, the call of nature was suddenly forgotten, overwhelmed by the harping of avarice sounding like an alarm in her brain. Staking her claim; her hands greedily wrapped around the bottom of this ornate egg.

"Mind you, if I should encounter a stranger claiming to have lost such a thing of extraordinary beauty, they are welcome to reclaim it, if they can prove it is theirs."

Rose was surprised to find this egg was light, like it was completely hollow. The real weight came from the gold trim, the gems and pearls decorating it. She skipped back to camp with her treasure. Placing it on her bedroll near the dying embers of the campfire, Rose tossed some more wood onto the smoldering remnants, breathing life into the red-hot chunks of charcoal. As flickering flames grew into great tongues of fire consuming the fresh supply of wood, Rose marvelled at the magnificence of her find.

The lustrous sheen of the luminescent pearls glowed in the firelight as the many facets of each topaz sparkled, as brilliant as the highest quality diamond.

As Rose silently *ooohed* and *aaahed*, cooing over her newfound treasure, she turned it around, examining it for any special markings that would betray its ownership.

To her surprise, on one side of this large, adorned egg was a hinge. On the opposite side was a latch and it became immediately obvious to Rose this ornament was fashioned in such a way it could be opened.

"I wonder what is inside?" whispered Rose, her finger working the latch free.

"DON'T!"

Rose gasped in surprise as Tag snatched the egg away from her, shouting: "Don't do it!"

"Do what?" snapped Rose. Her heart thundered with fright, startled by her companion.

"You were going to open this, weren't you?" asked Tag, holding the egg an arm's-length from her grasp.

"And so what if I was? It is mine, after all."

"This is *not* yours," argued Tag. "At least, I don't recall you taking such a thing from the palace, if it was even there to begin with."

"I found it, so by all rights, it now belongs to me," justified the Princess.

"What's goin' on?" asked Cankles, rubbing the sleep from his eyes as he sat up.

"Tag is trying to claim what is rightfully mine," complained Rose.

"Not so! Is your name etched somewhere on it?" questioned Tag, daring her to prove ownership.

"No, but neither is anyone else's name. But I tell you what, if we should run into a stranger claiming they lost this beauty and can prove it is rightfully theirs, I am more than willing to return it," reasoned Rose. "Until such time, it belongs to me!"

"What is it?" asked Cankles, crouching next to Tag for a better look.

"It is a rare egg laid by a rarer still monster-sized chicken," determined Rose.

"There are *monster chickens* in this forest?" gasped Cankles, his eyes darting about nervously.

"That was the Princess' *monster-sized imagination* at work," snorted Tag, giving her an incredulous stare.

"Fine then! What do you think could have made such a humongous egg, Mister *I'm-too-humble-to-admit-I'm-always-right-even-though-I am-even-when-I'm-not?*" questioned Rose. Her tone was as intimidating as his condemning stare.

"What?" asked Tag, bewildered by her words.

"You heard me! I was speaking of you!" With an accusing finger, Rose jabbed Tag in his chest.

"Well, I knew you couldn't have been talkin' about me, cause I'm rarely ever right about anything," admitted Cankles. "So, what's this thing you're lookin' at?"

"Judging by the size, the emerald green colour and these striations along the surface, I believe this to be the egg of the mace-tailed dragon," responded Tag.

"Mace-tailed dragon?" repeated Cankles, as he scratched his head in thought. "Why is it called a mace-tailed dragon?"

"Because the end of its tail is studded with spikes, like a mace," explained Tag.

"Well, I'm sorry I asked," gulped Cankles, now fearing a potential encounter.

"Worry not, my friend," assured Tag, as he examined the egg. "The mace-tailed dragons are a rare breed these days. Some scholars believe them to be extinct. And of all the dragon species known to man, they were one of the smaller ones. Reputed to be the least aggressive, they prefer to shy away than to confront a human."

"That is good to know, but who would have ever thought these dragons would create such exquisite eggs, bejewelin' them in this manner," commented Cankles.

"Are you for real?" asked Rose, staring in awe, but not in a good way, at Cankles.

"As real as you are, m'lady," replied her court jester, his words matter-of-fact.

"This old dragon egg was decorated by human hands. It had to be," determined Tag, scrutinizing the workmanship.

"Well, now that you have confirmed it was once a dragon egg, let me see what is inside," insisted Rose.

"Are you mad?" gasped Tag.

"I will be, if you do not hand it over," grunted Rose, her hands extended expectantly before her to receive this treasure. "But more than mad as you imply, I will grow mad with curiosity, if I am not permitted to find out what is hidden within."

"Does common sense not warn you that this *thing* is an omen of evil?" cautioned Tag.

"Or maybe it was an *omelette of evil*," chortled Cankles, laughing at his own pun.

"Has common sense abandoned you?" questioned Rose, as she glared at Tag. "For it is evil to deprive me of what is mine."

"Where did you get that?" asked Cankles, staring at the object of her adoration.

"I found it," said Rose, her thumb jabbing over her shoulder. "Just over there, behind that tree."

"Surely you find it bizarre that a thing of such rare beauty is out here in the middle of nowhere?" reasoned Tag.

"Thank you for the compliment, but I was speaking of this egg," responded Rose.

"So was I," grumbled Tag. "But listen up! Do you not think it strange that this valuable, jewel-encrusted dragon egg would be left here in this forest where *you* would so conveniently find it?"

"I must admit, the young master is quite right, m'lady. It is an odd thing that it'd be left here; odder still that you'd be the one to find it," commented Cankles.

"Beauty is drawn to beauty, that is the reason I found it, and you did not," explained Rose.

"That may be so, but I've got a bad feelin' about this," warned Cankles.

"Oh, pooh-pooh to you!" muttered Rose, dismissing these cautionary words as she reached for the dragon egg.

"I forbid you to open it!" ordered Tag. "Don't even think about it."

"Why not?" pouted the Princess.

"Because in my heart and in my mind I sense there is something evil about it."

"How can this lovely thing be evil? It is much too beautiful to be evil *or* dangerous."

"That is the very reason why you must not open it."

"That is like saying I am evil or dangerous just because I am beautiful," countered Rose.

"There you go!" teased Tag. "Enough said."

"Oh, hush! I will just take a little peek. What harm will that do?" sniffed Rose.

"Remember the old saying, curiosity killed the cat?" asked Cankles.

"Yes, and satisfaction brought it back," said Rose, her tone dismissive as ever.

"I just find it mighty odd this valuable work of art would be sitting here in the middle of nowhere," explained Tag. "It could be a trap."

Rose rolled her eyes in frustration. "*A trap?* If it was indeed being used as bait, a very elegantly decorated bait mind you, to lure a person of refined taste like myself into a trap, then why was one not sprung on me when I picked it up the first time?"

"Did it ever occur to you that if it wasn't lost, its previous owner chose to abandon it because there is something very bad locked inside?" responded Tag.

"I doubt it, but if it was left as a trap, why did it not go off when I initially picked it up?"

"She does have a point, young master," stated Cankles.

"So you agree that I should open it up?" asked Rose.

"Oh, I didn't say that," corrected Cankles, as he shook his head. "I just agreed that if it was some kind of trap, then it probably would've been set off when you removed it."

"Suppose the trap is on the *inside*?" cautioned Tag, still highly suspicious of this ornate egg.

"Then I would say that you are as cracked as this egg will be if I am made to fight you for it," snipped Rose, daring Tag to deprive her of this precious find.

"I command you! Do not open this egg!" ordered Tag.

"I am the Princess of Fleetwood. If you truly are a knight in my father's service, then you will do as *I* command!"

"By the will of your father and in his good name, I am responsible for keeping you safe. If I deem that *thing* to be of potential danger, then so be it! You will do as *I* say before something bad happens!" argued Tag.

"I say that all the bickerin' between you two is bad for *me*," announced Cankles, his hands firmly clamping over his ears as Tag and Rose engaged in this verbal joust. "How about you both reach a friendly compromise of sorts?"

"Like?" asked Rose, waiting to hear his recommendation.

"How about Tag lets you have that fancy egg back, if you promise to him that you will not open it?" offered Cankles.

"I'm amenable to that," said Tag, nodding in agreement.

"I suppose that is reasonable," decided Rose. "However, I do sense there is something of extraordinary beauty or immeasurable value concealed within. Perhaps a rare, pink diamond the size of my fist!"

"Or some kind of trap," reminded Tag.

"I hardly think so," retorted the Princess.

"Whether it is a valuable gem or a deadly trap, I'd say you keep it closed until the wise scholars in your father's court have a chance to determine its origin and devise a safe way to open it, in case it is a trap of sorts," decided Tag.

"So I do not have to discard or abandon this beautiful piece of art?" asked Rose.

"It is yours, as long as you hold true to your promise that you will not open it," answered Tag. "At least, not until we know it's safe to do so."

"I am agreeable to this compromise," said Rose.

"I have your word?" questioned Tag, staring into her violet eyes for the truth.

"Absolutely!" vowed Rose, her hand over her heart in solemn promise. "I will not open this egg. At least, not until I know from one wiser than me, that it is safe to do so."

"It's a deal," declared Tag, handing the bejeweled egg back to the Princess. "Now, I suggest we try to steal away with a little more sleep before we move on. Before you know it, it'll be midnight."

"Quite right, young master," agreed Cankles, scampering off to his still warm bedroll. "I want to be keepin' my wits about me as we venture north, so sleep, it is."

Rose snuggled down, her coveted prize wrapped in her arms like she was getting cozy with one of her prized, porcelain dolls as she waited for sleep to take over her body and mind. As Cankles' long, loud snoring became nothing more than a distant drone, Rose slipped into a peaceful slumber. Instead of dreaming of home or indulging in a grand banquet consisting of only desserts, the object of tonight's controversy meandered into her mind to vex her.

In her mind's eye, Rose attempted to admire this egg for it's external beauty, trying desperately to ignore the faint tinkling inside. It sounded like shards of glass tumbling about each time she rotated this ornate container.

"Glass... or perhaps a fistful of priceless, loose diamonds," whispered Rose, her fingertip caressing the latch that locked it closed. "I do wish I could just take one quick peek inside."

The more she thought on it and the longer her finger lingered on the latch, the desire to peek inside began to fester like the urge to scratch at a terrible rash.

"But I cannot... I promised not to."

"Aah! But you want to!" A voice that was strangely familiar whispered to her.

Rose turned with a start. "*You!* What are you doing here?"

"Being the Dream Merchant, obviously, you summoned me in your dream."

"This cannot be real... I must still be asleep," decided Rose.

"Then open your eyes and tell me if I am still nothing more than a figment of your imagination."

Rose squeezed her eyes shut. Slapping her cheeks, she made sure she was wide-awake.

When Rose opened her eyes, there indeed stood Silas Agincor. She stared at the Dream Merchant. There was no mistaking that ghastly robe adorned with a plentitude of gaudy, glowing moons and stars along with that bulbous nose surrounded by a wild mane of grey hair and whiskers.

"Hey... you said that you would appear in the manner I had imagined you," said Rose, staring suspiciously at this entity.

"And so I did."

"Excuse me, but I gave you a major makeover when we first met. If ever I were to see you again, you were supposed to appear as a handsome young man of princely proportions; donning tasteful attire, not that atrocious eye-sore!" She pointed at his garishly adorned robe.

"Oh, yes! One handsome young man coming up!"

In a swell of light, he transformed, reappearing many years younger, cutting a dashing figure in stylish wool trousers, a crisp white linen tunic and a fine brocade vest.

"Oh my goodness! *Tag?*"

The same old, crotchety know-it-all voice came forth, "You silly girl! It is I, the Dream Merchant. You imagined me as a handsome, young man, so I adopted the form you most desire."

"I do not desire Tag! So he looks more... mature than he used to," argued Rose, thinking on how the sun shone down, glistening on his wet body as he bathed in the lake, "but it does not mean I desire him or even find him to be mildly handsome."

She gasped, her hands slapping over her eyes as this version of Tag suddenly appeared naked from the waist up. His tunic and vest miraculously vanished, vaporizing like mist in the heat of the morning sun.

"Oh, so this is more to your liking?" determined this version of Silas, giving her a wink. His hands rested on his hips as he proudly thrust his bare chest out for the Princess to admire.

"Put your shirt back on!" demanded Rose. One eye peered through a gap in her fingers as she stared at Tag's half-naked doppelganger.

"As you wish!" With a snap of his fingers, the Dream Merchant was donning his apparel once more. "But if you want me to appear as another '*handsome, young man*', you will have to remind me of what I was to reappear as."

"You do not remember?"

"It is not my job to remember how all of you wish-grabbing mortals choose to have me appear. It is in your mind and your imagination. Obviously, you imagined me as him just now," grunted Silas, pointing over to the sleeping Tag.

"It must be the stress of this dreaded quest," sighed Rose, clutching the ornate egg to her chest.

"That may be so, Princess, but whatever the case, I am here now. What is it you desire?"

"Just a minute, I've summoned you in the past, even quoting that atrocious rhyme you made up. You never appeared before. Why now?"

"Did you repeat the rhyme, word for word, as I had told you?"

"I think I did."

"That implies you are not sure, and as such, you probably said it wrong. But no matter! I am here now, at your service."

"You can start by changing back to your usual form. It is too unnerving speaking to you like this while the real Tag lies sleeping over there," said Rose, glancing over at her comrade as he stirred.

"Ghastly eye-sore of a robe and all?" asked the Dream Merchant. "I suppose that will have to do."

With a snap of his fingers, Silas transformed, returning to his usual appearance.

"So, where were we?" asked the Dream Merchant.

"As you are here, I wish to return the magic crystal to you," offered Rose. "The dreamstone had a way of turning things into a real nightmare."

"I take it, you have reclaimed it from the clever Pooka?"

"That foul, detestable creature is far from clever. When I last saw him, he still had it, and if I am correct, that loathsome pest has turned it over to the Sorcerer by now."

"No need for name-calling, young lady! The poor thing is nothing more than a slave to Dragonite's will, after all."

"I hardly think so," disputed Rose.

"The point being, the dreamstone was entrusted to you. Therefore, it is up to *you* to return it to *me*."

"If it were up to me, I'd wish it back, just to do so," said Rose, heaving a disheartened sigh.

"So why the long face?" questioned Silas. "You have in your grasp something of just as much importance and power as the dreamstone."

"This fancy dragon egg?"

"Oh, it is not just any fancy dragon egg. It is the bejeweled magical canister from the…" said Silas, making up an appropriate name as he hauled up his drooping trousers, "the Crack of Doom."

"So it is a magical container of sorts?"

"No, what is hidden inside it is what's magical. The dragon's egg is merely festooned in such a manner so those in the know will see it is no ordinary thing."

"Oh… I do wish I could open it, just to see what magic it contains," sighed Rose, clutching it to her chest.

"You found it, therefore, it is for you to open," encouraged the Dream Merchant.

"But I made a promise to Tag that I would not open it; not until someone wiser tells me I am permitted to do so."

"Excuse me, my dear, but I *am* the Dream Merchant; a powerful, benevolent Wizard. Does that alone not make me wiser than you *and* him, combined?"

"Hey... I suppose it does!" exclaimed Rose, nodding in agreement.

"There you go then! It is for you to open up, if that is what you wish."

"What I wish for is this quest to be over with; to be home in time for my sixteenth birthday gala."

"Well, you will never find out what magic is waiting in store for you unless you open it. And why not now?"

"Should I?" asked Rose.

"There is no time like the present! Think of it as a gift, excuse the pun," urged Silas, staring longingly at the exquisite ornament.

"You are absolutely right! Maybe what is inside can even change the outcome of this quest for us," decided Rose.

"It could very well do just that and more, but whatever you decide, I must go now!"

"You are not going to wait to see what is inside?"

"Oh, I already know, but I want you to be surprised. In the meantime, another wanting, wasteful human being wishes for me to appear before him as a firefly."

"A what?"

"You heard me! He claims to find me much less intimidating as a wee, glowing insect than in my usual form," explained Silas.

"It could be that robe he finds so disturbing," responded Rose, pointing at the glowing moon and stars embroidered on his robe.

"No matter, it is his dream after all. If this fellow wishes for me to appear before him in a fancy gown with a low-cut, lacy bodice or as a firefly, then so be it."

In a glow of light that quickly diminished, he shrank in size, a golden orb of light floating off into the darkness.

Rose glanced over at her comrades. Tag and Cankles were still fast asleep. By the light of the dying campfire, she studied the bejeweled egg. Giving it a gentle shake, the tinkling sound coming from inside was like a tiny voice begging to be freed from this opulent prison.

"The Dream Merchant is wiser and he did say it was fine for me to open," whispered Rose, as though convincing herself it was true.

Her thumb pried the latch free as a seam of white light seeped through the crack. Before Rose could flip back the top half of the egg, it burst open! In a great explosion of radiant energy that swelled in a flash, it washed Rose and everything and everyone around her in an eerie white light as a disembodied shriek echoed through the night.

13

A Very Bad Idea

"What did you do?" gasped Tag.

He leapt onto his feet, now wide-awake as the brilliant flash of light vanished into the darkest shadows of the forest and the eerie cry faded, echoing off the distant mountains to the north.

Rose slammed shut the dragon egg container.

"You opened it, didn't you?" growled Tag.

Before she could make up an answer, he snapped at her.

"You look as guilty as sin. You lied to me! You promised you wouldn't open it."

"What just happened?" asked Cankles, through a great yawn as he rubbed his bleary eyes. "Was that lightning, thunder or both?"

"I don't know what it was," answered Tag. "All I know is that it came from the dragon's egg she's holding."

"Say it isn't so, Princess!" cried Cankles, as he stumbled to his feet.

The sudden, brilliant glow had seared the retina of each eye, even through closed lids. It produced blobs of phantom light that floated before him, even with his eyes squeezed shut in an attempt to vanquish them.

"Tell me you did not break your promise to the young master," prayed Cankles.

"Before you both jump to the wrong conclusion, I did not break any promise," confided Rose, calmly securing the latch on the egg.

"Did you not just open that thing?" interrogated Tag, staring suspiciously at the Princess.

"Yes, but I did not break my promise. I vowed not to open it unless someone wiser said I could. And that is exactly what I did."

"Unless Cankles or I told you to do so in our sleep, it is obvious there's no one else here to give you such instructions," snapped Tag, his arms crossing his chest in defiance as he adopted his *I-told-you-so* stance.

"Hey... are you saying *he* is wiser than I am?" asked Rose, glancing over at her court jester.

"Well, he wasn't stupid enough to open that egg, was he?" grunted Tag.

"Let me explain," urged Rose. "It was the Dream Merchant. He told me it was safe to open this dragon egg. In fact, he insisted on it!"

"Silas Agincor was here?" Tag glanced about, searching for signs of the Wizard.

"He appeared before me, telling me it was quite safe and that a special magic lay hidden inside."

"Methinks you were dreamin', m'lady," said Cankles. "I don't see the Wizard about."

"He was here, I tell you! He spoke to me. The Dream Merchant told me the power inside could affect the outcome of this quest. That is the only reason I opened it."

"The only thing that would change the outcome of the quest is if we had the dreamstone in our hands, here and now," argued Tag, "instead of being made to travel about these lands looking for something that you never should have had in the first place."

"I think the young master is quite right, m'lady," said Cankles.

"How would you know, you fool? You would believe Tag is right even if he was wrong," snipped Rose.

"Watch your mouth!" growled Tag, coming to Cankles' defense.

"Is it wrong for me to speak the truth?" responded Rose.

"You wouldn't know the truth if it smacked you on the side of your head," retorted Tag. "Why the hell did I agree to your promise? If I had only listened to my conscience!"

"You did! And you only listened to your conscience because I *did* keep my promise!"

"You really want me to believe the Dream Merchant was here? That he told you to open the dragon egg?" questioned Tag.

"He *was* and he *did!* If you had only woken up a few minutes earlier, you would have seen him with your own eyes. He left here just moments ago, taking off in the form of a firefly."

"Oh, no…" groaned Tag, his hand slapping his forehead in frustration.

"What?" asked Rose.

"You were duped! That was the Pooka!" exclaimed Tag.

"I think not! I would know the Dream Merchant if I saw him! It was most definitely the Wizard, Silas Agincor."

"Are you sure, m'lady?" asked Cankles.

Rose's confident smile withered as she answered, "For some reason, I am now having my doubts. I could have sworn it was the Dream

Merchant. Maybe if I had another look..."

"Too late for that! You were tricked, Princess," groaned Tag.

"So it was the shape-shifting Sprite. He was remarkably convincing then," decided Rose. "You should have stopped me, Tag."

"How could I? I was fast asleep! And you made a promise!"

"Well, I kept my promise! Am I to blame for being so trusting of others?" questioned Rose.

"If I had only listened to my intuition," groaned Tag. "I knew this was going to happen!"

"Then it was *your* fault!" decided Rose. "If you knew, then you should have done everything in your powers to keep that cursed thing away from me."

"I didn't actually know *know*. I just had an inkling something like this would happen. If anything, you should have questioned the *Dream Merchant's* sudden appearance, after all this time.

"I did, ergo; I was convinced it was him!"

"Should've trusted that inkling of yours, young sir," stated Cankles. "If you had, this wouldn't have happened."

"Yeah, wouldn't have happened," reiterated Rose, her tone mocking.

"If you had only used a little common sense and a modicum of restraint, whatever you unleashed would still be in there!" Tag pointed accusingly at the ornate egg.

"Well, knowin' the Princess as you do, you should've known better that she's lackin' in both," reasoned Cankles.

"Did you just insult me?" gasped Rose, jabbing an index finger into his chest.

"If I did, I don't know what came over me," groaned Cankles, his hands slapping over his mouth to stay his tongue.

"He's right. I knew this could happen, and yet, like an idiot, I chose to trust in you, Princess."

"Well, you are not that much of an idiot, for I *can* be trusted. I suppose it was slightly foolish of me for being so eager to believe it was the Dream Merchant, especially now, in hindsight."

"Hindsight?" repeated Tag, his brow furrowing in confusion.

"Yes, after he rebuked me for speaking of the Sprite in such derogatory terms."

Tag's hand smacked his forehead in frustration once more. "Did that not seem odd to you? Did even a smidgeon of doubt cross that mind of yours?"

"Only after the fact, I suppose," admitted Rose, "but it is a little late for that now."

"If only we had gotten rid of that cursed thing from the beginning," lamented Cankles.

"Why didn't you say so from the start?" asked Tag, glaring at his comrade.

"Didn't think it was my place to do so," replied Cankles. "I thought *you* knew what you were doin'."

"If you had, I would have agreed with you," said Tag.

"Really?" asked Cankles.

"Yes... Probably... Maybe not," stammered Tag.

"I rest my case," sighed Cankles.

"Well, if you had voiced your concerns, I would have certainly considered them."

"If he had mentioned his concerns, you were too busy harping at me to hear the man in the first place," snorted Rose.

"I doubt it!" snapped Tag.

"Doubt, indeed! I am beginning to doubt if you have what it takes to lead this quest," grumbled Rose. "If you were so smart, I would never have been placed in such a compromising position that would tempt me to begin with."

"If I knew you'd be so gullible and easily tricked by the Pooka, then yes, I would have taken that bloody egg away from you!"

"Oh, *woe* is you!" snipped Rose, dismissing Tag's insult. "If you had tried to keep me from this object of beauty, you would have my wrath to deal with."

"It probably wouldn't have been any worse than what you've unleashed from that egg!" grunted Tag.

"I guess it was a bad idea," admitted Rose, hanging her head in shame.

"It was a *very* bad idea," declared Tag.

"Hey... what was unleashed anyway?" questioned Cankles, as he scratched his head in contemplation.

"I do not know," answered Rose. "Truth be told, I was momentarily blinded by a resplendent white light bursting from it; then deafened by a horrid shriek that followed."

"That can't be good," said Tag, giving his head a dismal shake.

"Well, it cannot be that bad either," reasoned Rose. "How harmful can a glow of light be? And that noise? Your singing is worse! I would be more concerned if it was some vile plume of black, stinky smoke bellowing forth to choke us."

"I suppose you're right," agreed Tag. "That would be more indicative of dark magic."

"I'm scared," admitted Cankles.

"Why?" asked Rose.

"Because he just agreed with you, just like that! That's givin' me cause for concern," replied Cankles, a bead of sweat breaking out on his forehead.

"What are you talking about?" asked Tag, staring in confusion at his friend.

"Has your mind gone wobbly? You never just agree with the Princess. You'd always question her reasonin' and so on. All of a sudden, you think she's right? That alone is a sign of things to come, and I'll tell you right now, it won't be good!"

"I didn't say she was right. Then again, maybe she's right this time," responded Tag.

"There is a chance that flash of white light was a good thing," said Rose.

"We can only hope," responded Tag.

"I'll hope," said Cankles, his hand popping up. "Better than thinkin' something evil was let loose."

Attempting to down play her actions, Rose said, "Look here, if I did unleash something evil from this beautiful canister, then why are we still here and in one piece? I am still intact and as lovely as ever while you two look like... like you always did."

"I'm still the same," decided Cankles, his hand patting his backside. "It's not like I suddenly grew a donkey's tail or have cloven hooves."

Tag stared at his comrades. Rose was still undeniably beautiful while Cankles looked the same, just more agitated than usual.

"Perhaps the magic that was concealed within is more insidious. Maybe it was meant to work its evil while we slept?" suggested Tag.

"Oooh! I won't be sleepin' now!" groaned Cankles.

"Now you are grasping at straws in an attempt to make me feel bad for what I did," decided Rose.

"Well, you should!" snapped Tag.

"But it would not have happened if you had confiscated this beauty from me in the first place," reminded the Princess.

"If that was indeed the Pooka, and I'm thinking it was, then obviously whatever was inside that egg was meant to destroy us or prevent us for reclaiming the dreamstone."

"But suppose you are wrong, and it was the Dream Merchant?" offered Rose, hoping to pacify Tag.

"Highly unlikely!" Tag grunted in a dismissive tone. "I don't think so."

"Then exactly what do you think?" asked Rose.

"I don't know..."

"Pardon me?" gasped the Princess, her brows arching up in dismay.

"Did I hear you correctly?"

"I said, *I don't know!*"

Dumbfounded, Cankles' mouth drooped open in slack-jawed amazement.

"There! I said it!" admitted Tag, his heart steadily sinking with the unfamiliar sensation of dread and doubt that he had never known before.

Cankles and Rose exchanged nervous glances.

"Your mind *has* gone wobbly," determined Cankles, his index finger spinning by his head, as Rose nodded in confirmation.

"Just because I don't have an answer, it doesn't mean I've lost my mind!" snapped Tag.

"Then what do we do now? How will we know if that magic is real? If it's evil or benign?" questioned Rose.

"How would I know? Do you want me to guess?" asked Tag.

"I want you to do *something*. If you must guess, then so be it!" responded Rose.

"Even if I made an educated guess, then what? What happens if I'm wrong?" asked Tag.

"Then I will blame you later," said Rose.

"That's what I'm afraid of," grunted Tag.

"I suppose you'll both think it's too optimistic of me to hope that whatever was in that dragon egg was harmless and the magic was nothing more than that great show of light and sound?" asked Cankles. "Maybe it was meant to scare us?"

"I think you're being ridiculously optimistic," sighed Rose.

"So, you do believe you unleashed something foul?" asked Tag.

"Well, I believe *something* was unleashed, but as for how foul? It could all be a matter of opinion," answered the Princess, her small shoulders shrugging with indifference to downplay how serious the situation could really be.

"Maybe we should move on," said Tag.

"*Maybe?* You give me *maybe*? What happened to a decisive: 'we move on, *now'?*" questioned Rose.

"Don't you think we should? Just in case that light was some kind of beacon for the Sorcerer to find us by?" Tag answered her question with one of his own.

"Perhaps that's all that light was," hoped Cankles.

"Then we'll be doomed!" gasped Tag.

"We will?" asked Cankles.

"If he means to prevent us from reclaiming the dreamstone, I get the sense he means to find us so he can destroy us," concluded Tag.

"As in *kill?*" gulped Cankles.

"I hardly think that demented soul means to hurt or slightly maim us," rebuked Rose. "He will do everything in his power to keep that magic crystal away from us."

"Then I agree with the young master, we should move on," decided Cankles, snatching up his bedroll and belongings.

"We should turn back," said Rose, tucking the bejeweled dragon egg into her pack for safekeeping.

"But don't you think that's exactly what the Sorcerer believes we'll do?" questioned Tag, as he hastily rolled up his bedding. "That we'd turn-tail and retreat?"

"Are you suggesting that we continue northward?" gasped Rose. "Straight into the Sorcerer's domain? That will only hasten our demise."

"How about east?" suggested Cankles. "Bet that devious soul would never guess we neither retreated nor advanced."

"That makes sense!" agreed Tag.

"Now *you* are scaring *me!*" exclaimed Rose, staring in disbelief at Tag. "Since when did our friend make sense to you? You are going to entrust my court jester with leading this quest?"

"It's better than staying here," replied Tag, lashing his belongings onto the saddle.

"Hey! I never said anything about leading us on this quest," gasped Cankles, his eyes wild with fear. "I am here to bring some levity, not offer strategy to ensure our longevity!"

"Fine! But if I were the one leading this quest, under this situation, I think heading east offers the best chance of survival," said Tag.

"You *are* the one leading this quest," reminded Rose.

"Maybe I should rescind the offer to do so."

"What?" Rose gasped in confusion.

"If things hadn't gone awry with that cursed dragon egg, the situation would have been different," reasoned Tag. "Besides, if you have such little faith in my abilities and refuse to accept accountability for what you did, why should I be the one to shoulder the brunt of the responsibility for this farce of a quest?"

"You said reclaiming the dreamstone was crucial in protecting our realm," argued Rose. "I will have you know, this is no farce."

"Well, I could be wrong," countered Tag. "Whatever the case, your misguided actions are definitely turning this into one farce of a mission!"

"Well I'm absolutely gob-smacked, my friend!" commented Cankles, shaking his head in disbelief. "You just insulted the Princess!"

"Did I? I thought I was merely doing what she does: speaking the truth," grunted Tag, tightening the saddle's cinch before mounting his stallion.

"I think Tag meant to speak of my actions, not of my good character," decided Rose, trying to salvage her pride.

"If you say so," responded Cankles, struggling to untie the knot that kept his horse tethered to a tree. "But I really think we should leave this place in case the Sorcerer is homing in on us.

"There they are!" A voice rumbled forth from the shadows of the dark forest.

"Run! Run away!" shouted Tag, spying a flameless light glowing brighter. "He comes!"

"Scatter!" hollered Cankles, pushing Rose off in the opposite direction.

With no time to untie their horses, the trio fled on foot. Before they could dash away, a flash of light and a powerful force like an invisible tidal wave of energy bowled them over. They tumbled to the ground, engulfed in an unnatural sleep as blackness instantly filled their minds.

Tag's eyes squinted, struggling to focus as darkness gave way to the wavering, unsteady flames of a torch.

"What do we do now?" gasped Rose, searching for a hiding place.

"Now you will die," hissed Dragonite, thrusting the jagged chunk of obsidian atop his staff at Tag's chest.

Tag pushed Rose behind him, shielding her from danger. With his father's sword out of reach, its silver blade, shattered; Tag reached behind his back, unsheathing a dagger from its holster.

"Do you truly believe you stand a chance against me?" grunted the Sorcerer, annoyed by the boy's audacious actions. "Now, hand the Princess over to me."

"Never! I would rather die protecting her than to surrender Princess Rose to you!"

"That can be arranged!" snapped Dragonite. An eerie blue light swelled within the heart of the black crystal as the Sorcerer summoned his powers. In a flash, a bolt of energy surged forward, erupting into fire.

Just as Rose ducked, cowering behind Tag, the flames engulfed him. The rapacious tongues of fire and heat burned hair and clothes, melting skin and flesh. The sound of roaring flames drowned out Rose's screams as she tried to dowse the fire with the meager supply of water in her drinking flask.

Tag bolted upright, gasping for his breath. The icy water, like a brisk slap of a gloved hand striking his face, startled him. He was jolted wide-awake. His heart thundered in his chest, catching in the back of his throat as his eyes tried to focus. They stared through the stream of water dribbling from his wet mop of hair and down his face as his hand instinctively reached across to draw his sword.

Before Tag could unsheathe his weapon, the touch of cold steel against his throat caused him to freeze as a warning voice muttered: "That is ill-advised, young sir."

Tag's hand retreated, using his forearm to blot the water from his face as he sputtered, "What do you want with me?"

"Nothing. It is my lord wishing to have a word with you."

Tag struggled to stand, but his knees buckled beneath his weight. He fell forward, almost planting his face in the dirt as his hands came up to break his fall.

"This one is completely lucid now, my lord, still a little shaky, but awake. Should I give the others a similar prompt to rouse them as well?"

"That is quite all right, Halen. I need to speak to this mortal more so than the others," answered Rainus Silverthorn, waving off his personal guard and the captain of his Elven army. "They will wake in their own time. Instead, gather our men so we will be ready to move at a moment's notice."

"As you wish, my lord," responded Halen Ironwood, as he stepped over the fallen mortal.

"At ease, my friend," urged Rainus. "There is no need for concern, for we mean you and your friends no harm. I just thought it prudent to wake you, for you were lost, trapped deep in a nightmare."

Tag's racing heart calmed as this voice became strangely familiar. His eyes focused on a pair of legs sheathed in greenish-gray tights. Turning his gaze upward, the ornately embroidered tunic and charcoal coloured cloak immediately told him it was an Elf. It was the unmistakable toss of his golden hair that told Tag it was none other than the Elf Lord of the Woodland Glade.

"Lord Silverthorn, what are you doing here?" gasped Tag, struggling once more to stand on his unsteady legs.

"I recommend sitting," suggested Rainus, motioning for the mortal to remain seated. "It was quite the jolt you received last night."

"The Sorcerer! Did you capture him?"

"Parru St. Mime Dragonite?" responded Rainus, his perfect brows furrowing in curiosity.

"Yes, he struck us down last night. We tried to run, but we were not quick enough."

"You are mistaken, young sir. It was not the Sorcerer who struck you down," corrected Rainus.

"It wasn't?"

"Let me just say, Silas Agincor was a wee bit zealous in preventing the three of you from bolting willy-nilly into the dark forest, all heading off in different directions, and potentially smack-dab into danger," explained the Elf.

"The Dream Merchant was the one to render us unconscious?" asked Tag, rubbing his now throbbing head.

"He meant no harm. He merely wanted to prevent you three from racing headlong into danger or becoming irretrievably lost in the forest," said Rainus. "Unfortunately, he was a little closer than he anticipated when he discharged his magic."

"I'm confused," said Tag.

"After being bowled over by Silas' magic, of course you'd be," stated the Elf.

"No, I mean, what was he, in fact, what are *you* doing here?" asked a bewildered Tag.

"We received word from Pancecelia Feldspar the Queen of the Tooth Fairies, to be exact, that the shape-shifting Sprite working under the Sorcerer's directives had indeed been successful in escaping from Pepperton Palace with the dreamstone," informed Rainus.

"That is true." Tag nodded in confirmation.

"It is for this reason we are here now. When we initially confronted Dragonite and his army of mimes when he first attempted to steal away with the magic crystal entrusted to Princess Rose, the Sorcerer made good his escape. We had been on his trail, hunting for him ever since, steadily heading northward to the Fire Rim Mountains in a bid to capture him before the Pooka hands over the dreamstone."

"So we are on a common mission," said Tag, nodding in approval.

"Yes, to thwart a common enemy. It was only because luck and fate had conspired, bringing us here to find you and your friends before you ventured any further."

"But how did you find us?" questioned Tag. "We are in the middle of nowhere, the farthest north we've ever been in the Dimbolt Forest."

"A Gnome in the clutches of a great eagle shed some light as to your whereabouts when we rescued him."

"You rescued a Gnome?"

"Yes, he was on his way home after terminating his service with a young knight-in-the-making from Fleetwood. He made mention of the maiden you travel with as well as a fool of a jester in your company, so there was no mistaking it was the three of you he spoke of."

"No… it can't be!" gasped Tag. "We were sure he had met his demise when that eagle swooped down, whisking him off before we could do anything to spare his life."

"As odd as it sounds, it is true, Master Yairet. We parted company upon the Gnome's rescue; he, heading south with a pocket full of rutabagas while we continued northward in the direction he set us on to find you."

"Still, this is a big forest. It must have been near impossible," determined Tag.

"I am an Elf, therefore, I have excellent hearing, as keen as the ears of a fox. I can often hear things before I see it coming."

"You heard our voices?"

"How can we not? You three were arguing up a storm! *'What if we did this, instead of that? If you did this, then that would not have happened!'* And so on and so forth!"

"We were that loud?"

"Look at it this way, Master Yairet, I sense that even if I were not an Elf with such keen hearing, I would have still heard you a league away. But what caught our attention and immediate concern was that bold flash of light and atrocious bellow that filled the forest."

"So you saw and heard it, too?"

"It was so bright, I think even a blind man would have seen it," responded Rainus, "and that is no exaggeration! It was like a great beacon of light in the blackest of nights, summoning us to come hither."

Tag glanced about nervously. "I think it was."

"Was what? Bright or a beacon?"

"Both! I believe it was a foul magic the Princess unleashed, one meant to help the Sorcerer pinpoint our exact location."

"It was bright enough to do just that, but according to the Dream Merchant, it was nothing more than a clever way for Dragonite to unleash one of his spells," revealed the Elf.

"Wha – what happened?" groaned Rose, her eyes fluttering open upon hearing their voices. She squeezed them shut as the brilliant light of the late morning sun stabbed at them.

"I see you are no worse for wear, Princess Rose," greeted Rainus, his head bowing in salutation.

"Lord Silverthorn…" Rose sat up, stretching her weary muscles as she used her foot to prod the still unconscious Cankles. "What brings you here?"

Cankles woke with a start. Suddenly aware of movement and strange voices wafting about. His wobbly legs crumpled beneath him as he winced in pain from the throbbing in his head.

"Steady on, my friend," said Rainus, catching Cankles by his shoulders. "First things first."

With a snap of Rainus' fingers, Halen Ironwood reappeared, an opened flask in hand that he passed on to the Princess.

"What is it?" asked Rose, reluctantly accepting the small, cobalt blue vial. "A cordial of sorts?"

"In your condition, it is better than any cordial," answered Rainus. "It is a special tincture made from the willow to ease that throbbing in your head. One small sip is all you need."

Just as Rose held it to her nose to sniff it first, the Elf scolded her, "It is meant to be consumed, not inhaled. Now quickly, before it loses its potency."

Rose pinched her nostrils and took a swig, almost gagging on the bitter liquid. She swallowed, forcing it down her throat. With a face contorted in a sour pucker, she passed the vial on to Cankles.

"To the young master, first," insisted Cankles, thinking Tag was in worse shape, dripping in sweat when in reality, it was nothing more than the water Halen had splashed on him to hasten his awakening.

Tag was in no condition or mood to argue with Cankles. He eagerly accepted the tincture. Swallowing down the vile tasting medicine, he shuddered as he passed it back to Cankles.

Knowing how bad it was going to taste, Cankles still graciously accepted the vial. He emptied what was left, deliberately pouring it down the back of his throat to minimize contact with his tongue.

"Now, just give it time to work and that pounding in your head shall subside nicely," promised Rainus, slipping the empty vial into his vest pocket for safekeeping.

"What happened? Did you save us from the Sorcerer?" asked Rose. "Did you drive him off before he could do us in?"

"I, or should I say, Silas Agincor intervened, saving you from each other," answered Rainus.

"Huh?" gasped Cankles.

"What do you mean?" questioned Rose.

"Lord Silverthorn was just about to explain what happened," said Tag. "Allow him to speak."

"Yes. Well, upon seeing that great swell of light and hearing that hideous bellow, we first thought it was Dragonite," admitted the Elf. "We were certain he was in the midst of annihilating the three of you."

"But he wasn't?" asked Tag.

"Truth be told, Dragonite was nowhere in the vicinity, but by all the squabbling going on as we neared your camp, it became apparent that the Sorcerer had woven a strange magic; one that would cause conflict and dissension amongst you and your comrades."

"How do you know?" questioned Rose. "We did not feel any different."

"That may be true, but from what we heard, it was evident Dragonite had placed a hex on you three; one that caused doubt and chaos. It seemed most prevalent on Master Yairet in particular. His confidence and ability to make concise decisions were evidently missing."

"It was?" gasped Tag, trying to recall the strange events of last night."

"The three of you were saying the *'if'* word so often, it was practically in every second sentence you spoke," confided Rainus.

"We were?" gasped Cankles. "I rarely, if ever, use the f-word. And when I did, I only said it once to tell my hound to fetch off – oops! Didn't mean to say that."

Cankles' hand slapped over his mouth as a muffled, "I'm sorry!" squeezed out between his fingers.

"No, I mean the word *if* as in *I-F*," spelled the Elf. "You were at each other's throat, literally and figuratively; second guessing your own, and each other's, actions and words. If we had not stumbled upon your camp when we did, I have no doubt it would have escalated into a physical altercation or all three of you would have chosen to abandon this quest; or worse yet, throttle each other out of contempt."

"Are you saying that brilliant flash of light I had *accidentally* unleashed from the lovely dragon egg was an enchantment?" asked Rose.

"It would appear so, Princess."

"Well, it was not a very enchanting enchantment, if I do say so myself," grumbled Cankles, shaking the cobwebs from his cloudy mind as the willow tincture worked its magic.

"As I said, it was a spell conjured up to bring discord and uncertainty, to either cause your little group to disband and go your separate ways or drive each other mad with all that bickering to the point of killing each other," explained Rainus.

"I knew there was something evil about that light," exclaimed Tag, "and I am having no doubt about it this time."

"That is because the spell had run its course," responded Rainus. "The worst of its power wore off, like sleeping off a bad hangover... not that I would know anything about that."

"I suppose it was a good thing the Dream Merchant did what he did when he did it," decided Cankles.

"If the Sorcerer wanted to be rid of us, why didn't Dragonite just come and do the deed himself, than to have the Pooka deliver that dragon egg filled with magic?" questioned Tag.

"I can only surmise that the Sorcerer was dealt a great mental or physical blow during his altercation with the Dream Merchant. He wishes to remain in hiding, seeking refuge in one of his many lairs to the north where he can lick his wounds in relative safety."

"*Ewww!*" exclaimed Cankles, as he shuddered. "It must be nasty to lick if those wounds are infected and festering with pus."

The Elf grimaced in disgust.

"Never mind him, Lord Silverthorn," urged Rose. "Where is the Dream Merchant now? I wish to return the dreamstone to him."

"You have it?" gasped Rainus, his pointed ears pricking up.

"No, but if I tell him he is welcome to have it back, he can just wish it away from the Sorcerer," said Rose.

"If it were only that easy, Princess," sighed the Elf, shaking his head in disappointment.

"It isn't?" she asked.

"If it were, do you not think the great Silas Agincor would have just wished it away from Dragonite's evil grasp from the very start?" responded Rainus.

"Well, he really should," said Rose. "It would spare me – I mean *us*, a great deal of grief if he did just that."

"I believe it has something to do with the fact that you made a binding deal with the Dream Merchant," reminded Tag. "Did he not say that when you had your fill of the dreamstone, you and only *you*, can return it to him to terminate the deal?"

"He did say something like that," admitted Rose. "But you would think he would make an exception this time. If the Dream Merchant knows that the magic crystal has fallen into the hands of Dragonite, why does he not just wish for it back, if he is so concerned the Sorcerer will unleash some kind of evil unto the world?"

"I asked that very question of him," responded Rainus.

"And his reasoning?" probed Rose.

"The agreement is such, that even if he is able to locate that necromancer, Silas will not be able to secure the dreamstone. It will still be up to you to reclaim it, and then return it to him."

"Oh my! The Dream Merchant is quite the stickler when it comes to details," decided Cankles.

"Never had he encountered a situation in which the recipient of a dreamstone had this much difficulty in returning it to him," said Rainus, staring with raised eyebrows at the Princess.

"But I did try! From the very start when things began going wrong I repeated that silly rhyme numerous times, but to no avail."

"Perhaps you quoted it wrong," suggested the Elf. "Do you remember what it was?"

"Of course I do," replied Rose. "Oh, great Wizard, the Merchant of Dreams, answer this wish to put an end to my schemes."

When the Princess opened her eyes, there before her stood Tag, Cankles and Rainus Silverthorn. "See! I told you he gave me the wrong rhyme to summon him."

"Maybe a *please* would do the trick?" offered Cankles.

"What are you speaking of?" snapped Rose, her words sharp with agitation.

"I was thinkin' if you said *please*.... Then it's askin' politely for the Dream Merchant to reappear. If anything, it's the proper thing to do, m'lady."

"I hardly think so," grunted Rose.

"Try it," ordered Tag. "After all, it's not a word you commonly use. Maybe you just forgot to say it."

"Very well," said Rose. Heaving a dreary sigh, she closed her eyes and repeated this incantation. "Oh great Wizard, the Merchant of Dreams, *please* answer this wish to put an end to my schemes."

In a flash of golden light, Silas Agincor appeared. In the eyes of all others, he was the same, old Wizard ensconced in his gaudy robe decorated with moons and stars, but before the Princess, he appeared as a shirtless, handsome young man.

"There ya go, m'lady! A simple '*please*' made all the difference in the world!" exclaimed Cankles, slapping his thigh in glee.

"What are you doing?" gasped Rose, trying desperately to avert her eyes from the Dream Merchant.

"I came as you had imagined in your mind," answered Silas, flexing his biceps as he admired his new form. He then rubbed the ridges of muscles plating his abdomen as he commented: "Say... Look! You can wash some laundry on these babies; it's like a scrub-board."

"Stop it!" ordered Rose, her hands slapping over her eyes.

"What is she talking about, Master Wizard?" questioned Tag.

"Oh, I think she is a wee bit embarrassed because you are here and when she conjured me up in her mind's eye as a handsome young man, she had pictured you - "

Rose's hand jumped from her eyes to slap over the Wizard's mouth.

"He means to say your... brother! Yes, your brother, if you had one," explained Rose.

Tag and Cankles exchanged confused glances.

"Then the young man must have a twin that is his spitting image," announced Silas, prying the Princess' hand from his mouth.

"You can go away now," demanded Rose, her face flushing with embarrassment as she continued to see what the others could not.

"Wait a minute… Did you ask the Dream Merchant to appear in my likeness?" gasped Tag.

"I asked him to appear as a handsome, young man of princely proportions, not a knight-in-training of mediocre looks!" explained Rose. "It was a random, fleeting thought, if anything!"

"Oh, my then! You must be having many random, fleeting thoughts of this young fellow," teased Silas, striking a manly pose in his much younger body for his own enjoyment as much as hers.

"Stop it! And put your clothes on!" ordered Rose.

"The Wizard is appearing as a *naked* me?" gasped Tag, his cheeks turning a rosy hue of red.

"He is wearing trousers, but where his shirt is? Who can say?" responded Rose.

"I feel violated!" snapped Tag. "Stop staring at him being me, being half naked!"

"She cannot help but stare," assured Silas, giving the young man a knowing wink. "I'm quite the work of art in her eyes; a regular vision to behold!"

"I'm starting to get real creeped out now," groaned Cankles, trying to figure out what the Princess found so attractive about the withered old man of a Wizard he was looking at.

"Forgive me if I am wrong, Master Mayron, but if I guess correctly, the Princess sees the Wizard as a naked version of the young master," explained the Elf.

"Good gracious!" gasped Cankles, tossing his cloak at the Wizard. "Hide your shame, sir!"

"Yes, hide my shame!" agreed Tag. "Not that I have anything to be ashamed of."

"Believe me, there is nothing to look at!" snapped Rose.

"What?" gasped Tag.

"Enough!" shouted Rainus, as he barked out his orders. "We have important business to conduct and are in no need of distractions. Princess, look away until your version of the Dream Merchant is fully clothed. Silas, for your part, in her mind's eye, don a shirt will you? As for you, Tagius Yairet, feel no shame, for even though your mortal form will never achieve the same level of perfection gifted to the Elfkind, take heart in knowing that at least the Princess finds you mildly attractive. And you, Cankles Mayron, fret not for the Princess is not oogling at neither a naked Wizard nor your young friend."

"Phew!" said Cankles, shaking the image of a nude Wizard from his head. "Take no offense, Master Wizard, but it was an image I could do without."

"Well, I do not know about the others, but I find it very distracting to talk to you in the form of Tag, whether you're fully clothed, or not!" grunted Rose.

"You hear that, young man? She finds you mighty distracting!" announced Silas, nodding in approval to Tag.

"She does?" gasped Tag.

"Oh, she does," confirmed the Dream Merchant.

"She, I mean, *I* do not!" protested Rose. "At least, in a good way, if that is what you mean!"

"Who truly knows, Princess? After all, I am merely here in the form you most desire," said Silas.

"She *desires* me?" asked Tag, his eyes wide in disbelief as he gazed at the Princess.

"What I *desire* is for you to just go away!" snapped a flustered Rose, dismissing the Dream Merchant with a wave of her hand as her cheeks burned red with an all new level of embarrassment.

"For pity's sake, girl! Get a hold of yourself! You were the one to summon me, and it better be for a good reason, for I was in the midst of some very important business. Now what do you want?"

Rose drew a deep breath, trying to compose herself. Gathering her thoughts, she spoke: "I wish for you to take back the dreamstone."

"Say again, young lady," responded the Dream Merchant.

"I wish I could wish for you to have the dreamstone, but since I cannot, I give you permission to wish it away from me."

"If you had the magic crystal in your possession, I would happily free you of it, but as you do not, I simply cannot wish for it to be in my hands."

"So it is true, what Lord Silverthorn said, that I must have the dreamstone in my possession in order to hand it back?" asked Rose.

"It is what we agreed to, Princess."

"Can you not make an exception?" hoped Rose.

"What would this world come to if there were none to make good their promises, especially when the times prove trying?" groaned Silas, shaking his head in disappointment. "A man's word, my word and any deal I strike up, will mean nothing if I do not adhere to my promise and abide by what we had agreed to."

"So this deal cannot be undone?" asked Rose.

"I am a powerful Wizard, my dear girl. Of course it can be undone, but at great cost and grave consequence."

"To me, is that correct?"

"That is correct, Princess. Dare you relinquish yourself of one responsibility to take on another, one that can be potentially of even greater risk?"

"Come to think of it, I believe it is better to complete one task at a time. I must first reclaim the dreamstone," decided Rose.

"I am pleased to see you have come to your senses, Princess. We have already discussed the ramifications should the magic crystal fall into the wrong hands," reminded Silas. "If it means anything to you, then you must find a way to reclaim the dreamstone from the Sorcerer, even if it means to do so at great sacrifice."

"How did I know you were going to say that?" moped Rose, her shoulders drooping in defeat.

"Fret not, Princess," said Rainus. "Anything is possible if you put your heart into it."

"Trust me, Lord Silverthorn, her heart is not set on this at all," warned Tag. "That is why Cankles and I accompany her."

"To increase her misery and prolong her suffering by two-fold because she deserves to be punished for what happened?" questioned the Elf.

"No! We mean to keep her focused on the task at hand," snapped Tag. "We are here to help her retrieve the dreamstone; her punishment will be severe enough if we fail in our quest to aid her."

"Mind you, I don't think she fancies our company all that much," commented Cankles. "I sense we're more of a burden for her to bear than anything else."

"Aah, but two friends to help bear the burden may be all the Princess needs to see this task done," offered Silas, giving Rose a knowing smile. "One should never undervalue the power of true friendship."

Rose blushed, unable to meet Tag's sparkling blue eyes and kind smile, albeit the Dream Merchant in the young man's form.

"So, my friend, any luck in ferreting out the Sorcerer from his lair?" questioned Rainus.

"I was in the process of inspecting one of Dragonite's former haunts when I was abruptly called upon."

"Sorry," gulped Rose.

"So, what did you see, Master Wizard?" questioned Rainus. "Any sign of the Sorcerer?"

"Well, I was in the process of inspecting the lair I had found, and it was evident it was once used by the Sorcerer," responded Silas.

"Where is this place?" asked Tag.

"It is a cave in a mountain far to the north, but it almost went unnoticed because there was so much foliage that grew, concealing the entrance."

"It was fortuitous you did not pass it by," said Rose.

"The only reason I noticed it was because there was a scattering of deer bones and some ash from an old firepit at the base of the shrubs flourishing at the narrow passage leading into this cave."

"And what else did you see?" asked Tag.

"Once inside, I ventured through a narrow passageway lined with old torches. They were covered with dust and cobwebs, obviously having gone unused for quite some time. Creeping further down the tunnel, it became dank and musty. I travelled deeper into the earth, until I could smell the foul reek of brimstone heavy in the air. At one point, I came upon a pile of bones, but I had no desire to touch them to figure out whether they were human or not. It was apparent no one had been there for a long while, but before I could complete my investigation, the Princess summoned me."

"Well, I did not mean to disturb you, but this is important," insisted Rose.

"No need for concern, Princess," responded Silas. "I will resume my search where I left off. If I should come across the Sorcerer, I shall return with word."

"But how will we find you, should we locate Dragonite first?" asked Tag.

"It would seem the Princess has finally remembered the so-called *silly* rhyme," noted Silas, as he nodded in approval. "If it is urgent, she can summon me, but I wish to be left to search the lands without being bothered needlessly."

"So you will find us?" asked Tag.

"If need be, yes," answered the Wizard. "In the meantime, I recommend another dose of willow tincture."

In a resplendent flash of golden light, the Dream Merchant vanished, leaving Tag, Rose and Cankles wincing in pain as the brightness caused their heads to throb once more.

With a snap of Rainus' fingers, Halen rushed up to his side, another opened flask of willow tincture at the ready.

"*Ewww!* Not again," groaned Rose.

"I think I'd rather suffer this aching head, than to suffer another taste of that wicked medicine," stated Tag.

"Too bad we have no honey to lessen its bite," whined Rose, her face screwing up in disgust just thinking about the bitter concoction on her sensitive tongue.

"But we do," stated Cankles, searching through his pack.

"We do?" said Rose.

"Here we go!" Cankles lifted out a ceramic pot sealed with a layer of melted beeswax. "It was a gift from Lady Agly."

"That would work, my friend," said Rainus, nodding in approval as he passed the vial on to the Princess first. "A sip of this tincture and a spoon of this honey to chase it down will do the trick quite nicely."

As the sweet taste of honey masked the bitterness of the medicine, the shadow of a menacing fear swelled in Rose's heart as she listened to Cankles remind Tag of how Lady Agly said they'd find need for the jar of honey.

The seer of the future was right when she offered this gift. Now, the possibility that her other predictions were going to come to fruition began to plague Rose with dread. The colour drained from her cheeks as the image of Dragonite commanding a great dragon to kill them all replayed in her worried mind.

14
Learning the Hard Way

"Get some rest while you can, my friend," urged Rainus. "There is no need to rush northward into dragon country while the light of day still holds."

"I think we rested plenty, especially after sleeping off that *jolt* dispensed by the Dream Merchant," responded Tag, as he continued to pace to and fro.

"That may be so, young sir, but even your friends know it is a waste of energy to restlessly pace about," stated the Elf, pointing to Cankles as he busied himself with picking out clots of drying mud and pebbles from the frog of each horse's hoof, and then at Rose. "Even the Princess is preoccupied with learning the skills of archery, than to expend energy walking about as you do, but going nowhere in the process."

Tag glanced over to spy on Rose as she quietly watched the Elves partake in a contest of skills. It became clear to him the Princess' eyes were not following the flight of the arrows as they pierced the trunk of a tree they were targeting.

Instead, her amethyst eyes sparkled with delight as she admired the Elf men, each with perfectly chiseled high cheekbones framed by flowing flaxen hair that Tag was sure Rose was envious of, for it rivaled hers in luster and silky texture.

Like Rainus, these Elves were statuesque not only in height, but also perfect in posture. Their lean, toned muscles flexed with every move, accentuated by the skin-hugging tights and form-fitting tunics and vests that were created with wide, quilted shoulder-pads. Their raiment, designed to lend emphasis to a manly man physique, bore exaggeratedly broad shoulders for this purpose. The vest then tapered down, narrowing at the waist to accentuate their form.

"See! Princess Rose is completely engrossed, studying their

technique," said Rainus.

"I beg to differ, Lord Silverthorn. From my observations, I'd say it is not their technique she is studying," countered Tag.

"How so?" questioned Rainus.

"Princess Rose is not learning, she is merely gawking at your men-folk; no doubt admiring what she sees."

"They are Elves. What is there not to admire?" responded Rainus, his words matter-of-fact. "But contrary to what you say, true the Princess is *'gawking'*, as you so eloquently put it, but she learns at the same time."

"You cannot learn from merely watching," contested Tag. "One must also *do*."

"Yes, but by observing others, what they do and just as importantly, what they *do not* do, is an important step in learning. My people believe the mind is a powerful tool. If one observes, and then, for lack of a better word *rehearses* the exact actions in one's mind, it will be ingrained in the muscles. When it is time to act, the body instinctively knows what it is to do."

"In theory, I suppose," said Tag.

"Perhaps to the human race, but we Elves know it to be true," corrected Rainus. "It is as important to train the mind as it is the body."

"Unfortunately for the Princess, it is only her eyes getting any exercise as they *train* on the bodies of those Elves."

"So you are jealous," determined Rainus, giving Tag a knowing smile. "You wish for her eyes to be fixed on *you*, and only you."

"I'd be inclined to poke her eyes, if she looked at me in that way."

"What way? As an object of desire?" questioned the Elf. "Is it not normal for a human male to want to be admired as man-meat by a fair maiden?"

"*Man-meat?* That sounds rather disgusting and not to mention, completely shallow!"

"Come now, what red-blooded male does not want to be admired for his manly attributes!" asked Rainus, striking a pose just so that the sun's light shone like a halo off his golden hair and backlit his form as he flexed a muscle or two.

"I'd like to be admired for more than just my physical appearance," stated Tag.

"Aah, so you are attempting to appeal to her intellectual side," decided Rainus, rubbing his perfect, dimpled chin in pensive thought.

Before Tag could say he doubted Rose had one, Rainus continued with dispensing unwanted advice.

"You are as smart as a whip, young man," praised the Elf. "If one wishes to have a lasting relationship, there must be more than just physical attraction if you wish to have something enduring with your lady love."

"Whoa! Slow down, Lord Silverthorn. *My lady love?*" chortled Tag. "You are sadly mistaken. She is more like the lady I *loathe!*"

The Elf gave Tag a knowing smile as he responded, "So you say, but I sense there is more between you two than even you care to admit! And I can tell you right now; a loving relationship is something that must be nurtured."

"I don't know what you have in mind, but where the Princess and I are concerned, I am here out of duty. There is no relationship, loving or otherwise, to speak of."

"You say that with such conviction, my young friend," said Rainus, giving Tag a wink and a knowing smile.

"What relationship there is, is nothing more than a working one to see her through this quest. And you forget; I am a knight, or at least one in training. I bear no title; therefore in her eyes, I am well below her station."

"*Title?* A title is easy enough to come by if you are in the know," dismissed Rainus. "The point is, if you wish to win the Princess over – "

"I wish to survive this quest *and* her company," interjected Tag, rolling his eyes in frustration.

"And if you do survive this quest in her company, a quest that ends happily, I can only imagine how her admiration for you will grow exponentially." Rainus gave Tag a jovial poke with his elbow as he nodded in approval.

"I do this because I have a duty to uphold. I pledged my fealty to my liege, therefore; I am obligated to assist his daughter on this mission. More than her admiration, I seek to circumvent an evil that will touch us all if Dragonite has intentions of exploiting the powers of the dreamstone."

"A grand plan, young master! The greater the exploit, the grander the reward, should things go your way," stated Rainus, winking at Tag as he nodded at the Princess.

"I don't know what is going through your mind, but mine is focused on completing this quest and doing whatever I must to make it so."

"Well, you are undoubtedly a man of action. Why do you pace when you should be training?" asked the Elf.

"*Training?*" repeated Tag.

"Did you not say you are a knight-in-training?"

"Yes, I did."

"And yet, your sword is safely tucked away in its scabbard. That is the last place it should be if you plan to venture into the Dragon Lands. When we are well into the Fire Rim Mountains, it is better to have your weapon at the ready; be equipped with the skills to use it."

"I would feel honoured if you indulged me with a little sword play, Lord Silverthorn. I understand your people are as deadly with the blade as you are unerring with your arrows."

"Forgive me if it sounds like I am boasting, but you do speak the truth, Master Yairet. However, like anything else, as perfect as the Elfkind is as a whole, there are many of us who are better at some things than others."

"You don't say!" gasped Tag, assuming the Elves all possessed equal talents that made the human race pale in comparison.

"My area of expertise is with the longbow," explained Rainus, as his weapon and a quiver of arrows suddenly appeared from somewhere within his flowing cloak. "Now, you take Halen Ironwood. He is skilled with the bow, but naturally gifted when it comes to mastering the sword."

"He is?"

"Captain Ironwood, will you grace us with your presence?" called Rainus, waving the Elf over to join them.

"What is it, Lord Silverthorn?" asked Halen, bow and quiver still in hand.

"The young master wishes to learn some of the finer points of swordsmanship, if you will?" said Rainus.

"It would be my pleasure," responded Halen, bowing politely to the young man as he set aside his long-range weaponry.

Tag reciprocated with a bow of his own, but gasped in surprise. As he uprighted himself, the cold touch of steel pressing against his throat caught him by surprise. The Elf had quickly and silently drawn his sword, pressing the broad edge of the blade to his neck.

"Rule number one: never be caught off guard," warned Halen, flashing a mischievous smile at the mortal.

"Very true," gulped Tag, as Rainus used a finger to guide the Captain's deadly blade away from the boy's throat.

"Play nicely now, Halen," urged Rainus. "Master Yairet is a knight to King William, so we must make sure he remains unhurt for the quest, and that he returns to his liege in one piece; unmarred and unscarred."

"As you wish my lord," said Halen, his eyes remaining fixed on Tag as the tip of his blade now pointed to the boy's heart.

"Very good! In the meantime, I shall see if Princess Rose has a genuine interest in the art of archery, or if her interest is merely in the archers."

"Of course, Lord Silverthorn," said Halen, respectfully bowing in acknowledgment.

"I am eager to learn from the best, Captain Ironwood," said Tag. "Teach me what you will."

"I *am* the best, but first, what do you already know?" questioned the Elf.

"In all honesty, I have fallen well behind on my training, having come into this vocation late in life. What I've learned, I have learned from my father who once captained King William's army, but that was long ago. What knowledge I possess and skills I have fostered comes from years of practice."

"So, you have practiced against other squires training for the knighthood?"

"Unfortunately, my training partners have been restricted to the scarecrows in farmers' fields," admitted Tag.

"They are hardly worthy opponents," noted Halen, his thumb pad testing the keen edge of his sword.

"It has helped in teaching me where to aim my sword."

"Yes, but I have yet to see a scarecrow fight back," said the Elf. "A sedentary opponent is no opponent at all."

"That is why I am so eager to learn from you."

"Then let us begin. As important as it is to strike your opponent with your weapon, it is just as crucial not to take a strike," explained Halen. "If your foe is stronger than you, yes, blocking his blows will keep you safe, but repelling these powerful blows will eventually wear you down."

"Then what do you suggest? Running away?"

"If it spares your life; yes. However, what I am saying is to *move*. And not just your body. You have two feet; you best learn to use them."

"I am a knight. I will not retreat."

"That is not what I am saying," responded Halen. He raised both arms as though in surrender, exposing his body. "Attack me."

"What?" The tip of Tag's sword suddenly drooped.

"You heard me. And keep your weapon at the ready. This is not the time to get sloppy. Now attack me. I do not care how, just come at me like you mean it, with every intention of cutting me down."

"But shouldn't I warn you if I intend to go for your head or your body?" questioned Tag. "Just so you'll be prepared?"

"Do you honestly think the Sorcerer will tell you what he plans to do? I think not! That madman will strike without warning. Now, I say again. Attack me!"

Tag swung the blade about, aiming to slash the Elf from his left shoulder across to his right hip.

Instead of using the tip of his sword to block and parry the blow, Halen stepped back, using his blade and the momentum of Tag's swing to send the boy spinning right around. Just as he came about to face Halen once more, the Elf had his sword at the ready, resting it gingerly against the boy's throat.

"There are times when the enemy will be larger, more powerful. It is better to use his momentum and redirect his energy than to wage war full on when it will be far more efficient to use his power against him."

"I see," gulped Tag, as Halen removed the blade from his neck.

"I do not believe you do. Now again," ordered Halen. Assuming a wide stance so he stood at Tag's height, the Elf then pointed to the top of his head. "Aim to cleave my head in two."

Immediately, Tag's eyes focused on the crown of golden hair, only to be scolded by Halen.

"Never tell the enemy where you plan to strike by staring at your intended target. Use your peripheral vision. Take in your enemy as a whole so you will know what he is doing, as well as remaining aware of your surroundings in case there are others coming to the enemy's aid."

"Right!" Tag nodded in understanding. Adopting a stance to bring the blade down on the Elf's head, his eyes stared straight ahead instead of signaling where he planned to strike.

"Now!" ordered Halen.

Just as Tag's blade swung down, Halen stepped forward. The two blades crashed together; the Elf's sword just inches before the crossguard, catching Tag's at mid-blade.

His young heart rejoiced with victory as he pressed down with all his might, blade grinding against blade as Halen seemed to buckle under the pressure.

Tag gasped in surprise, freezing as Halen used this downward pressure and his own sword as a fulcrum. Angling one foot back, the opposing energy caused the tip of the Elf's sword to swing up, poised to slice the boy's throat.

"I see! I see!" yelped Tag. He dared not move a muscle with that Elven blade pressing lightly against his flesh.

"Yes, I believe you are starting to," said Halen, nodding in approval as he removed his sword from Tag's neck.

"You're amazing!" praised Tag, impressed as much by the Elf's sense of control as his skill with the sword.

"Yes, and I understand so, too, is my swordsmanship," responded Halen, his words nonchalant.

"So it is as much about the efficiency of movement as it is about using the enemy's own energy and momentum against him."

"To put it in its simplest terms, yes."

"Well then, I shall take these lessons to heart and never be without my trusty sword," announced Tag.

"And should you lose your weapon in the heat of battle, then what?" asked Halen.

"Then I suspect my luck has run out and I am as good as dead," determined Tag.

"With that kind of attitude, yes, you will be."

"What possibility is there to win a contest of swords when one is so severely disadvantaged?" asked Tag.

"Even unarmed, it is possible to defeat an opponent who is armed to the teeth," said Halen, as he sheathed his sword in its scabbard. "Now, attack me."

"With my sword?" gasped Tag.

"Yes, before I take it and use it on you."

"But this isn't fair. I now have a distinct advantage over you," argued Tag.

"So you say."

"I do! I cannot see how it is the other way around."

"Then find out," urged Halen. His hands devoid of weapons, he held them up as though in surrender.

"And if I hurt or kill you, then what? I cannot live with the blame!" reasoned Tag.

"If I invited such an assault and get myself killed in the process, then I will have no one to blame but myself. I bloody well deserve to die, if that is the case."

"But how do you intend to keep safe when I'm the one with the weapon, and you are not?" questioned Tag. "I fail to understand this."

"It is simple. Keep your friends close, your enemies closer still," replied Halen.

"What?"

"The sharpest, most deadly part of your sword is the tip and the first hand-span length of the blade. If you cannot stay away from the sword's tip, the safest place to be is to situate yourself as close as you can to your adversary. Now, strike me down."

As Tag's blade came down to cleave the Elf's head, instead of stepping back, Halen angled his body toward Tag's right. The blade came so close it skimmed past the wooden toggles of Halen's vest.

Missing his mark, before Tag could raise his sword to take a sideways swipe at the Elf, the boy immediately realized any blow he could administer would have no power behind it, being so close to his intended target.

Tag groaned in pain as Halen's clenched fist snapped down, striking his right hand.

The sharp blow weakened Tag's grip on the sword's hilt.

In one fluid movement, Halen's right hand seized the pommel of the sword. As his left hand pushed down on the dull portion of the blade just before the cross-guard, Halen's right hand pulled up. Easily working against Tag's thumbs to break his hold on the sword, the Elf turned the weapon on the mortal. Tag leapt back as the blade suddenly popped up between his legs, threatening to castrate him.

"See what I mean about staying in close?" asked Halen, turning the sword to safely present it by the hilt to Tag.

"I do now," squeaked the young man, his hand dropping to his nether regions to make sure his manhood remained intact.

"Good! Now, I want you to lunge at me. Plunge that sword into this fine set of abdominal muscles," urged Halen, as he patted his rock hard midriff. "I know it is hard not to admire them, but remember, resist signaling with your eyes where you intend to strike."

Tag nodded in understanding as his eyes locked with Halen's, trying hard not to be unnerved by the Elf's piercing blue eyes. Focusing on the task at hand, Tag extended his arm, leaning forward in a stabbing motion as the Elf merely angled away from this feeble lunge.

"Freeze!" ordered Halen, as he examined the boy's poor posture. "Never overextend your body."

"But you said to lunge at you. That's what I'm doing, *lunging!*"

"No, you are overextending your body, therefore, losing all sense of balance."

"I am?"

"Again! Do what you just did."

Once more, Tag lunged. His feet remained planted and his arm fully extended as he stretched toward Halen. The Elf merely sidestepped to avoid the tip of the blade. Using Tag's forward momentum as he lunged, Halen lightly grasped him by the wrist, pulling forward and down in a wide, circular motion.

With no sense of balance and what he had left, stolen from him in this simple gesture, Tag somersaulted over. He landed flat on his back as the sword flew from his hand.

"See! No balance," stated Halen, staring down at the mortal. "And there was no power in that thrust either."

"But I put everything into it," insisted Tag, brushing off the dust and humiliation from his raiment as he stood up.

"No," countered the Elf. "You put your entire *arm* into it, but that is the extent of it."

"I did?"

"Do not thrust with your arm. Put your whole body behind it," ordered Halen. "What you do now will merely prick a dragon's hide just enough to annoy the beast to hell, enough to kill you. You must extend with your arm, but drive the weapon in with the weight of your body behind it, if you wish to pierce the creature's heart."

"Please show me."

"Very well. Hold this before you, just so." Halen took the pack Tag doubled as a pillow when he slept. Rolling it up for extra padding, he had the boy hold it at chest level.

"Now what?"

Halen's gloved hand rolled into a tight fist. "This is how it feels when you punch using only the power of your arm."

The Elf chambered his arm, and then punched with all his might at the padded shield that protected Tag. With his arm fully extended, the impact was enough for the young man to take a half step back.

"I felt that," acknowledged Tag.

"Now feel *this*."

Before Tag had a chance to fully brace himself for the blow, Halen's fist came up, aiming straight for the centre of this makeshift shield. The Elf's arm was not even fully extended, but stepping in with the delivery of the blow and sinking down to send the full weight of his body behind the punch, he sent Tag flying off his feet. The boy tumbled head-over-heels, coming to a skidding stop in some shrubs.

"Oh my! Your man is giving Tag quite the beating," noted Rose, wincing in sympathy as she watched Halen send her appointed protector flying with a well-placed punch.

"Fret not, Princess. Captain Ironwood is merely hastening Master Yairet's ability to learn the skills required to master the sword, for the young man has much to learn before facing the dangers that await us as we head north."

"It is a brutal way to dispense a lesson," stated Rose.

"Some are just predisposed to learning the hard way and sometimes, the hardest lessons to learn and endure are also the ones that sink in the fastest and remain with the student the longest. No need for concern, my lady. The young man is resilient for a mortal and he is keen to master his weapon."

"I suppose he'll be rather useless to me – I mean this quest, if he is unable to wield a sword as he should," decided Rose, as she watched Tag slowly sit up. He groaned in pain, rubbing his chest where the padded shield took the brunt of the impact.

"These are dangerous times and we are heading into dangerous lands, Princess," reminded Rainus. "Even a beautiful, young maiden can die upon the point of a sword if she is unable to defend herself."

"I have no intention of letting a sword get that close to me," assured Rose.

"Oh, so you fancy the long-range weapons. That is why you are watching my archers."

"Yes," lied Rose, as she admired the Elves as they took turns firing their arrows. "I have always been fascinated by archers, I mean *archery*. Alas, it is a skill I have never learned."

"It is never too late to learn, my lady," said Rainus. "If you wish to do so, the finest marksman here would be honoured to be your teacher."

"Oh, please tell me he is the one," pleaded Rose, casting her gaze to the youngest of the Elves partaking in the contest. Though the focus of her admiration was undoubtedly several hundred years older than her by the mortal's calendar, this handsome specimen of an Elf appeared to be the equivalent of a young man only two or three years senior to Tag.

"If you are to learn archery, then it will be from the best," said Rainus, as he nocked an arrow onto the sinewy string of his longbow. "That would be me."

As easy as breathing, he let the projectile fly. With a sharp *'crack'*, it split the arrow fired by the object of her adoration.

"That is a wonderful idea, but I recommend that *he* show me how to stand, hold the weapon, and so on; while you oversee the whole exercise to make sure I am doing it just so," suggested Rose, as she smiled at the handsome, young Elf standing the farthest down the line.

"If you believe it will advance your learning, then why not?" agreed Rainus, motioning the Elf over to assist them.

With light, graceful steps he joined Rainus and the Princess.

"How can I be of service, Lord Silverthorn?" asked the Elf, bowing in respectful acknowledgment.

"Princess Rose-alyn of Fleetwood, allow me to introduce you to Argon Greenleaf of Driven Hill. This young man, at least young by Elven standards, is the newest recruit to my battalion of elite archers," said Rainus.

"I am pleased to meet your acquaintance, Princess," greeted the Elf, bowing in salutation.

"Believe me, the pleasure is all mine," responded Rose, her eyes shining like dazzling gems of amethyst as she smiled coyly at Argon.

"The Princess wishes to learn the fine art of archery as mastered by the Elfkind," explained Rainus, gesturing to Argon to step closer.

"Yes, your people are renowned in this realm for your marksmanship," explained Rose. "I can only dream of being even marginally as skilled."

"A goal is simply a dream with a beginning and an end," stated Rainus, motioning Argon to hand his longbow over to the Princess. "Let us put this dream into action, so you may achieve your goal."

"I have never handled such a formidable weapon," admitted Rose, her voice meek as she batted her lashes at the junior Elf.

"Worry not, Princess, I am here to help you learn," offered Argon. His congenial smile; perfect white teeth framed by an equally perfect set of lips, melted her heart and caused her knees to wobble.

"Let us begin immediately. Starting with grip and stance," instructed Rainus.

"You want him to *grip* my *stance*?" asked Rose, her perfect brows arching up in surprise as she grinned with eager anticipation.

"Take Argon's bow. Stand as though you are preparing to launch an arrow," said Rainus.

Rose grasped the weapon, her arm straining as she hauled back on the string of sinew, using all her might. Pulling as far back as she could, the bow quivered in her trembling grip.

"Relax," ordered Rainus. "Let us try that again, but with some Elven wisdom to assist you. Argon, give her a hand."

Sidling up next to Rose, the younger Elf guided her, his hand resting lightly on hers. "There is no need to grip the bow like this, for it is not about to leap from your hands and run away. Instead, hold it just so; nice and easy."

Rose's grip instantly loosened under his light touch.

"Now, using these two fingers, inhale as you draw back until the string is just at the corner of your mouth," instructed Argon.

"Like this?" asked Rose. This time, she did not overextend the draw to the point that she was quaking as she was before.

"Yes," said Argon. "Keep your back nice and straight."

She felt the Elf's chest pressing against her back, forcing her to straighten her spine and pull her shoulders back.

"Focus. Clear your mind. Take aim, and do not forget to breathe," ordered Rainus.

Rose remained poised as the younger Elf's hands rested on her shoulders.

"As you exhale, allow the string to slip from your fingertips. Do not pluck it," instructed Rainus, as he inspected the Princess for proper form.

Rose smiled inwardly as Argon placed his broad hands on her hips to correct her stance, her back fitting nicely against his chest as he adjusted her posture.

"Now, do not be disappointed if you come nowhere near the target," cautioned Rainus. "Only those who are incredibly lucky or naturally gifted tend to hit the target spot-on with the very first try."

"I will do my utmost to get this arrow as close to that tree as possible," vowed Rose, her eyes staring at the grouping of arrows tightly clustered on the tree trunk.

"Remember to focus on your target. Allow the string to slip off the tips of your fingers," reminded Rainus.

Rose took heed of the Elf's advice. She employed the same level of concentration she used in hurling one of her shoes at her bedchamber door or when she targeted the Pooka with her sling.

Taking a deep breath, she inhaled as she drew the string back to the corner of her mouth. As it slipped from her fingertips, Rose exhaled. The twang of the string signaled that the arrow had been sent flying. It whistled through the air, heading straight for the tree. With a '*thunk*', the arrow landed dead centre, nestled within all of the other arrows the Elves had fired.

All witnessing this feat gasped in surprise. They spoke amongst themselves about the natural skill this mortal possessed or the incredible luck that aided her.

"Remarkable!" exclaimed Rainus, applauding her efforts.

"Oh, that was nothing. I do not think I was *that* good. I bet anyone would be able to hit the target with the help of an Elf, considering the innate ability that allows your people to be such excellent marksmen," said Rose. She waved off the comments, smiling modestly as if it was nothing more than a lucky shot.

"Oh my! You have a gift, my lady!" praised Rainus, still amazed by her level of accuracy.

"No, I believe it was nothing more than luck, Lord Silverthorn. I think Master Greenleaf better show me again, just to make sure I am doing this right," insisted Rose, deliberately nocking the arrow so the feathers fledging the shaft were positioned incorrectly.

Rather than rough and calloused like Tag's grubby paws, this Elf had velvety smooth hands. Argon's touch was so gentle, yet scintillating, as he helped to position the arrow properly before nocking it. The sensation sent a shiver down Rose's spine, causing her breath to catch in the back of her throat.

"Are you alright, Princess?" questioned Argon, gazing with concern into her eyes.

"I am fine now, Master Greenleaf. I was momentarily unnerved when I realized all eyes were cast in my direction," lied Rose, glancing at the other Elves waiting and watching to see if she could hit the target again.

From an early age, the Princess was used to being the centre of attention. This time, she was the one distracted. Between Argon's delicate touch, enchanting smile and those eyes that shone like perfectly cut gems of sapphire, Rose struggled to regain her focus and composure.

"Remember; grip and stance," reminded Rainus.

"Stance?" repeated Rose, as her posture suddenly drooped.

"Yes," said Argon, one hand resting on her shoulder as the other pressed firmly against the small of her back to correct her posture. "It would be a tragedy if an arrow should misfire. I do not want you shooting out one of those beautiful, amethyst eyes."

Rose smiled inwardly. Only Tag had ever referred to her eyes as the colour of this precious stone. Most would say they were violet, or purple, but coming from this Elf; amethyst had taken on a whole new meaning.

"You think my eyes are beautiful?" questioned Rose, feeling the warmth of his breath on the nape of her neck as he leaned in to check her aim. "Most think they are unusual."

"They are beautiful indeed, and if others say they are unusual, it is only because they lack the way to describe how unique they truly are," responded Argon. "I have only seen brown, blue and the rare green or hazel eyes on members of your race. I have never seen eyes of this exquisite colour, even amongst my people."

"Ahem!" coughed Rainus. "I believe the flattery can wait. We were in the midst of teaching the Princess the fine, but serious art of marksmanship with the Elven longbow."

"My apologies, Lord Silverthorn." Argon's words were contrite as he resumed with the lesson, correcting Rose's grip.

Before Rainus could remind the Princess of all the small details needed to be addressed before unleashing the arrow, Rose let the projectile fly.

A collective gasp of surprise rippled through the crowd as Rose's arrow hit its mark. With a sharp crack, the steel bodkin struck the tree trunk, sending shards and splinters of wood flying as the shafts of tightly grouped arrows exploded on contact.

"Brilliant!" declared Rainus, praising her precise aim. "Absolutely amazing!"

"There is nothing amazing about a little luck," dismissed Rose, her cheeks flushing with modesty as the Elves applauded her aim. "If anything, Master Greenleaf made it so I could *not* miss."

"I hardly think so," stated Argon, as he marvelled at her expertise. "I was barely even touching you."

"Perhaps your light touch was just enough Elven magic to prevent my arrow from straying," offered Rose, staring adoringly at Argon as he scratched his head in bewilderment. "I say we try it again, but this time, with a firmer hand, just to make sure."

"We shall try it again, but this time, Master Greenleaf shall step well away from you," instructed Rainus, motioning Argon to return to his place in the line of archers. "If you believe it to be a transference of Elven magic to accomplish the near impossible, let us put your theory to the test, Princess."

"How?" asked Rose.

"If what you say is true, then any Elf wishing to teach you should have the same affect," reasoned Rainus. "Let us test this out on another one of my men."

"Like him?" asked Rose, pointing to another fine, young specimen of Elven manliness standing next to Argon.

"No, I was speaking of my personal guard and the captain of my army, Halen Ironwood."

"The one busy brutalizing Tag with a lesson on swordsmanship?" gulped Rose, watching as Halen easily parried Tag's blows, only to rush in, bopping the boy's chin with the pommel of his sword to send a stunned Tag reeling to the ground.

"He would be perfect."

"Perhaps, but being that I am a princess, I will fare better with a lighter touch," recommended Rose, uneasy about the largest and oldest member in this company of Elves dispensing his idea of a lesson.

"Oh, come now! I am curious to see if what you said is true," responded Rainus.

Noticing that Halen seemed all too eager to share in his knowledge of warfare, Rose declined, "I sense Master Greenleaf's magic continues to linger."

Rose quickly nocked an arrow, but before Rainus could remind her of the finer points of archery, the Princess let the arrow fly.

Once more, the arrow sliced through the air, travelling on a straight path. With a sharp '*crack*', it wedged itself between the first two projectiles she had unleashed, nestled within the tight grouping.

"No once, not twice, but thrice you hit the target spot on!" gasped Rainus, marvelling at her marksmanship.

"What do you know?" exclaimed Rose. "It must be my lucky day, aided by some of Master Greenleaf's Elven magic."

"That was not luck, nor magic, Princess," assured the Elf, inspecting the placement of the arrow. "If I did not know better, I would say you have been at this for a number of years."

"Oh, no! This is the first time I have even picked up a weapon like this," stated Rose, handing the bow back to the Elf.

"It is evident to me that you are well practiced, for your aim has been unerring," surmised Rainus. "You must have expertise in a similar weapon that allows you to have such precision in your targeting. A crossbow perhaps?"

"The only thing I know how to use is this," revealed Rose, pulling out her leather sling and a single steel ball.

"Care to demonstrate?" asked Rainus, pointing to the target. "See if you can land one of those balls as near to the center of that grouping of arrows."

"I shall do my best," said Rose, setting the smooth sphere of metal into the cradle of the sling.

Using her wrist than her entire arm to set the sling in motion, with each revolution, it picked up speed, whirring as it spun in her grip.

Rose's eyes focused on the target. With a flick of her wrist, she released one end of the sling to send the steel ball flying.

It moved so quickly, none knew where it landed until the feathers fledging the arrows quaked in it wake. Rainus' keen eyes spied on the silvery ball, embedded amongst the grouping of arrows.

The Elves were astonished by her aim, knowing that such precise targeting using a sling required more skill than needed to use a longbow and arrow.

"Brilliant!" praised Rainus, nodding in approval. "You were spot-on!"

"I suppose I have had many years of practice," responded Rose.

"How do you practice?" questioned the Elf.

"Throwing things… I am good at throwing things at moving targets," admitted Rose, not prepared to reveal that the '*things*' were usually her shoes and the '*targets*' were often the domestic staff who raised her ire.

"It is evident to me that you are naturally gifted, Princess Rose," stated the Elf.

"Gifted?" repeated Rose.

"There are many who can be trained and develop a specific skill, and then there are those born with a natural gift that can be further enhanced with training," responded Rainus. "You have an incredibly accurate aim. I can only imagine what you would be able to accomplish if you received intense, formal training with the longbow."

"I must admit, the longbow is much more elegant than this old sling," said Rose, admiring Rainus' weapon.

"This longbow is befitting one of your status and one so naturally gifted, Princess Rose," stated the Elf. "If it is something you believe you can use on this quest, then by all means, please accept it as a present."

"Truly? Are you sure?"

"It is my gift to you," insisted Rainus, bowing politely as he passed her the bow and a quiver of arrows. "I pray it will always keep you safe."

"Thank you, Lord Silverthorn," said Rose, accepting this Elven longbow. "I will use your lessons to better my skills."

Rose and the Elves in her company turned with a start as Tag shouted in triumph.

"Finally!" exclaimed Tag, his blade resting lightly against Halen's throat. "I did it!"

"You most certainly did, Master Yairet," agreed Halen, nodding in approval as Tag removed the sword. "You have caught on quickly."

"Thank goodness for that! I don't believe my body could handle much more abuse."

"It is always difficult to break old habits and to adopt new ones. I sense you will make good use of your newfound knowledge," said the Elf, as he sheathed his sword.

"I am indebted to you Captain Ironwood, I will take your lessons to heart; use them to keep my friends safe."

"Your skills will help protect you, but it will take courage to use it against the enemy, especially if confronted by Dragonite," warned Halen.

"I am hoping my determination will compensate for any courage I may be lacking in," responded Tag, placing his sword into its scabbard.

"Determination and courage working in tandem will see you far in this world," stated Halen, giving the mortal a proud pat on his shoulder. "Just practice and keep in mind what you learned on this day so you can call upon it, if these two virtues should abandon you during your darkest hour."

"This sounds more like a dire warning than words of advice," determined Tag.

"It is both," responded Halen. "For with the coming of night, we will venture into the Dragon Lands to meet up with the Dream Merchant."

15
Oh... Pooh!

"It looks even more foreboding by night," stated Rose. She stared through the darkness, spying on molten lava flowing down the mountainside to glow a sinister red. It trickled slowly, like coagulating blood oozing from the wounded earth.

"It is what you do not see that you should be the most concerned about, Princess," cautioned Rainus, as he motioned for silence. "Hush! I hear something coming."

Quickly and silently Halen Ironwood unsheathed his sword, hoisting this weapon aloft. The flat edge of the blade glistened in the moonlight as a signal for his archers to arm their bows. Automatically, the front line of Elves dropped down on one knee, as the row behind remained standing. All turned their arrows, taking aim in the direction of the sounds of twigs crackling underfoot, heading toward them.

"No need for alarm." A whisper of a voice carried on the night wind wafted to Rainus' sharp ears.

"Stand down, men," ordered Rainus. "It is only Silas Agincor."

"*Only?*" repeated the Dream Merchant, feeling snubbed as he emerged from the darkness.

"*Only* in a good sense," responded the Elf. He nodded in greeting to the Wizard. "Consider yourself lucky, for a dragon or the Sorcerer would have been greeted by the tips of many unforgiving arrows."

"Point taken, no pun intended," said Silas, pushing the steel bodkin of Halen's arrow away from his chest.

"I am pleased to see you have not ended up in the belly of a dragon," said Rose.

"Not likely to happen," grunted Silas.

"Because you would be too hard to kill?" hoped the Princess.

"I'd like to think so, but more because I would cause the beast severe indigestion," chortled Silas. "An old Wizard is hardly a delectable morsel. I'd be too chewy, being so old and gristly!"

"So what did you see?" asked Tag. "Any sign of the Sorcerer?"

"Alas, Dragonite remains hidden from my eyes. By all indications, that fiend is lurking about somewhere in the Dragon Lands, that is all I know for sure," revealed Silas, glancing over his shoulder to the vast expanse to the north.

"By what indications?" asked Rose.

"I inspected some of the caves he had used in the past, but they were empty – long abandoned."

"But you said you found signs of his presence," reminded Tag.

"Yes, I came upon a great dragon dining on a mime."

"And that is it?" gasped Rose. "A mime being feasted upon by a giant lizard? How is that proof the Sorcerer is about?"

"Believe me, Princess Rose, a mime would not be this far north unless he swore his allegiance to Dragonite, and is here to do the Sorcerer's bidding."

"That is proof enough that deviant soul is in hiding somewhere out there," confirmed Rainus.

"So how do we proceed?" asked Tag.

"What is your recommendation, Halen?" asked Rainus, turning to the captain of his army.

"The land is rimmed by mountains to the east, west and north," stated Halen, pointing to the great land formations in question. "No doubt, time is of the essence. With this in mind, I recommend we split into three parties; spread out our search, for there are many caves riddling these mountains – many places for Dragonite to hide."

"I will travel with the Elves," offered Rose, hoping to find safety within this elite battalion of warriors.

"I doubt you will be able to keep up with us, Princess," responded Rainus.

"Surely my horse can keep pace, Lord Silverthorn?"

"We will be travelling on foot," explained the Elf. "Unless you plan to use your lovely mare to draw the attention of a dragon or two, perhaps offering it up as a meal while you escape, then forget it. If you come with us, it will be by foot as well. You must be able to maintain a gruelling pace to keep up with us, for we move with speed."

"Oh," said Rose, in disappointment.

"Fear not, Princess Rose, you will be in good company if you remain with your comrades. Young Master Yairet was an excellent student. He handles his sword with skill," said Halen, giving Tag a nod of approval.

"And you now have my longbow, Princess," reminded Rainus.

"With an aim like yours, *you* could well be the one keeping your friends safe from harm."

"You think?" asked Rose, gripping her weapon with newfound respect and confidence.

"I believe it will prove to be a powerful tool, more so than your sling as you venture forth," stated the Elf.

"As for me, I will travel alone," announced Silas, as he turned to the Elf Lord. "However, it would be prudent if some of your men accompanied the Princess and her friends."

"A wise idea," agreed Rainus, motioning for the archers in the front line to step forward. "You four will advance with Princess Rose and her comrades."

Rose's heart sank with disappointment. Argon Greenleaf was not included with the Elves appointed to accompany them.

"Oh, I do like the idea of your men coming with us," said Cankles, nodding in gratitude. "We'll be much safer; no offense to the Princess and the young master."

"None taken," responded Tag. "It makes perfect sense to have some of Lord Silverthorn's men with us on this trek, just as it does to divide into several parties to cover more ground."

"Do we leave now?" asked Rose.

"This is the best time to travel through the Dragon Lands," stated Rainus. "The chill of the night makes those reptiles sluggish. Many retreat deep into caverns warmed by thermal vents."

"Are we not looking into these caves for the Sorcerer?" questioned Rose, her eyes filling with dread.

"Unless he has found a way to tame the dragons, he will be as welcomed into one of their lairs as we would be," answered Silas.

"So we are to avoid the lairs already occupied by dragons," assessed Tag.

"That would be the safest thing to do," confirmed Silas.

"But how will we know if a dragon already inhabits a cave?" asked Rose.

"There will be telltale sign," replied the Dream Merchant.

"Like?" probed Cankles.

"Bones... lots and lots of bones," said Silas, giving him a nod.

"Belonging to cows? Goats, perhaps?" wondered Cankles.

"Yes, and throw in some human bones and the rare few of the Elfkind to the pile for good measure," added Rainus. "They are usually strewn about at the mouth of the cave."

"Bugger me!" gasped Cankles.

"You will be, if you stumble into one of those dragon dens," warned

Silas. "Just be aware of the signs. If you do, you should be fine."

"Bones… all kinds of bones," muttered Cankles. His eyes, now filled with certain dread, were as large as saucers as he pondered this warning.

"So which way shall we set off?" asked Tag.

"I will search the mountains to the north, as they are the farthest, but easy enough for me to access with a little bit of magic," stated Silas. "Master Yairet, you will take your party to the east."

"Why east?" questioned Rose. "Fewer dragons?"

"I do hope so, but being that you and your friends are frail mortals requiring more water than the Elves do, I am sending you to the eastern mountain range. There, the only safe source of flowing water can be found. You can replenish your water supply, for all other rivers and creeks are contaminated with sulphur and other noxious substances secreted from the earth.

"So, it is not fit for human consumption," determined Tag.

"Only the hardiest of dragons dare drink that swill," confirmed Rainus.

"East, it is!" announced Rose, nodding in agreement.

"Lord Silverthorn, you will take the rest of your men and journey to the westerly mountains," instructed Silas.

"And if we fail to locate Dragonite, then what?" asked Tag.

"Then we shall meet back here, at this very place, in two day's time," answered the Dream Merchant.

"And if we find the Sorcerer?" gulped Cankles, wringing his hands in woe. "What then?"

"If you should locate that villain, do not attempt to capture him on your own," warned Silas. "Instead, if you find his lair, send a flaming arrow into the night sky. From there, we will come to you."

"Brilliant!" praised Cankles. "I like that plan."

"Good! Then make haste," ordered Silas. "Remember, before dawn breaks, find shelter. Once the sun warms the lands, the dragons will be active again."

"We shall heed your warning, Master Wizard," said Tag, as he watched Rainus and his men slip away into the darkness.

With nothing more than the light of the moon and the stars to show the way, two Elves took up the rear. The other two leading the way moved with confidence, guiding them through the darkened landscape.

"So far, so good," whispered Cankles, taking Rose's arm to steady the Princess as she felt the uneven ground with her foot before taking another cautious step. Moving with speed, Cankles felt a degree of safety with the added company of the Elves.

Even for Rose, her new longbow made her feel safer, even if it was a false sense of security. At this point, venturing into lands seldom visited by mortal men, and for good reason, the Princess knew that even if she forgot all she had learned about handling this weapon and Tag's sword failed them, the Elves would not. Their expertise and precise aim would surely be the end of any foe, Sorcerer, mime or dragon, wishing to launch an assault.

Failing that, Rose was confident Rainus' loyal men would willingly sacrifice their lives to keep her safe. And should a dragon be their end, she was sure these creatures would rather dine on succulent, tender Elf flesh first, than to consume run-of-the-mill, tough mortal meat.

"*Oof!*" groaned Rose, landing on the ground as she tripped over an unseen rock.

"Up you go, Princess," Cankles hoisted her back onto her feet. "You must keep up with the Elves."

"Thank you," she whispered, as she trudged along, brushing off the dirt from her hands.

"Hasten your pace," urged Tag, ushering them on. They were forced to run to catch up with the Elves as they advanced at a brisk pace. Stumbling along in the dark, the trio occasionally grabbed onto each other for balance while treading on this uneven terrain.

As they journeyed on, Cankles' imagination started to run wild. "Wait... What if there are dragons that come out at night?"

"What are you talking about?" questioned Tag.

"How do we know there aren't some dragons that come out at night? You know, so there's less competition for food?"

"I hardly think so," muttered Rose. "Those creatures do not like the cold."

"But if there are, we'll be defenseless!" gasped Cankles. "Unable to see in this blackness, we'll be hunted down. Those dragons will make an easy meal of us!"

"Fret not, Master Mayron. It is a well known fact that dragons do not come out at night, for it is too cold for them to move about with any speed, especially to catch prey," informed one of the Elves.

"But how do you know for sure?" questioned Cankles. "Suppose there are species of dragons none have ever seen or heard of before? Ones that scuttle about in the black of night, not carin' how hot or cold it is?"

"I think if there were such creatures, we would know about them," answered the senior Elf leading the way.

"And how frequently have you been to these lands to know such things?" queried Cankles.

"Frequently? We try to avoid this place at all cost! However, just think of these dragons as being like overgrown garden snakes. With this in mind, how many snakes have you seen out and about after the sun has set?"

"None," answered Cankles.

"There you go then," said the Elf. "Now, come along."

"Can we rest for now?" whispered Rose, drawing in a weary breath as she motioned for Tag and the others to stop.

"Here? Not possible! We are in the open," said Tag, waving her on to follow.

"Just ahead," said the Elf leading the way, as he pointed to the dark silhouette against the night sky. "There is a small island of trees up yonder. It will provide adequate shelter if you need to rest, but you must get there first, for we cannot stay here where we are vulnerable."

Following in the Elf's light steps, Rose ventured on with her comrades, disappearing into the shadows cast by the trees.

"We shall stop for only as long as it takes for you to have a drink and a quick rest so you may catch your breath," stated Tag, passing a water flask to the Princess before taking a swallow himself.

"That is it?" groaned Rose, her hand pressing against her aching side as she inhaled deeply.

"Yes," replied Tag. "And if you can't keep up, perhaps you should do away with that bag. Carry only your bow and the quiver of arrows to lighten your load."

"Are you mad? I cannot leave this behind," insisted Rose, shouldering the bag containing her prized possession.

"Why not? What's in it?" questioned Tag.

"My bejeweled dragon egg."

"What?"

"You know the one? The emerald green beauty gilded with gold, studded with pearls and bedazzled with gems of topaz."

"You brought that thing along?" gasped Tag, rolling his eyes in frustration.

"I was not about to leave it behind. Even without all the glitter, if the mace-tailed dragon is indeed extinct, this egg is worth a fortune – it would be priceless."

"Have you lost your mind?" grumbled Tag.

"Had I left this egg behind, then it would certainly mean my brain had been addled. Besides, it does not weigh that much, being hollow and all," reasoned the Princess.

"That's fortuitous, because none of us will carry it for you," stated Tag. "You bring it; you carry it."

"I can manage, but mark my words, this special egg can prove to be invaluable, if we survive this quest."

"You keep telling yourself that," grunted Tag. "We should move on now."

"But we barely had a chance to rest," protested Rose.

"Master Yairet is quite right, Princess," said the Elf leading their party. "It is not wise to linger here any longer than necessary. We still have a distance to travel in the open expanse of this land before we reach the cover of trees prior to the sun showing its face."

"And remember, we do not want to be caught out here when the dragons wake," reminded Tag. "Once those creatures are sufficiently warmed, the first thing they will do is to go on the hunt for food."

"I have no desire to become a dragon's meal," stated Cankles, pushing the flask to Rose's lips to make her drink. "Quickly now! Rest time is over."

There was no chance for Rose to argue as the most senior of the Elves crept to the edge of the shadows. Searching for signs of potential danger, he saw none, waving the others on to follow him.

Rose forced down a quick gulp of water, passing it back to Tag. He allowed himself a sip, capping the flask before tossing its strap over his shoulder.

"Hurry!" urged Cankles, waving Rose on. "We don't want to get left behind."

The lead Elf continued on, not even glancing back to see if the mortals could keep pace with him. Instead, his sharp ears listened. Whenever he heard the Princess' steps falter and her breathing hasten, he slowed his pace, allowing her to catch up to them.

Stopping only when the sparse cover of trees allowed it, the party ventured eastward, moving steadily through the dark landscape as the celestial lights dimmed with the approach of dawn.

In the distance, as a volcano belched, releasing a trickle of lava that glowed against the darkness, several juvenile male dragons clustered together in a cave, not yet ready to venture into the cold, still morning air. They could be heard, growling and snapping at each other, as they jostled for the warmest corner of this chamber.

With jagged mountains rimming this expanse, these great land formations caused the cantankerous dragons' bellows and snarls to amplify, echoing all around them.

"Oh, no!" yelped Cankles, his eyes nervously darting about, searching for signs of danger.

"Quickly! Hide behind that hill," ordered Tag. Grabbing Rose by her hand, he pulled her along as the Elves charged ahead to take cover.

"What is that wretched stench?" gasped Rose. She drew the edge of her cloak over her mouth and nose to filter out the smell.

"Dragon," whispered the Elf, peering around this formation to make sure no creature had followed.

"Where?" gulped Rose, her breath catching in the back of her throat as panic filled her heart.

"I should say, it is a dragon you smell," he corrected himself. "Dragon *dung* to be exact."

"What? Where?" asked Rose, lifting her foot in case her shoe had treaded on some.

"You are leaning against it," informed the Elf. "That is a dragon midden."

"A *what?*" asked Rose, jumping away from the smelly heap.

"A dragon will empty its bowel in one place, allowing its dung to accumulate; piling up higher and higher," informed the Elf.

"Oh… Pooh! That is disgusting!" gasped Rose.

"True, but it is very practical. It is used to mark their territory and to allow other dragons to know how big they are."

"This is one huge pile of dung," gulped Rose, glancing up at the tower of excrement.

"Oh, holy dog's bollocks!" cursed Cankles, as cold beads of sweat formed on his forehead. "This is one, bloody big dragon to make a pile this humongous."

"Yes, but it is not such a bad thing," whispered the Elf, motioning for Cankles to calm down and lower his voice.

"It's not?" responded Cankles, frowning in bewilderment.

"In general, the bigger the midden, the bigger the dragon. That being said, the larger the dragon, the bigger its territory is reputed to be. This dung hill marks the center of the said dragon's domain."

"And we are to find comfort in knowing we are stumbling about in the dark in a territory staked out by a terrifyingly huge dragon?" asked Rose, her words, cynical.

"This dragon is bigger than big, make no mistake about that. In fact, it is probably the largest in all the lands, but that means we will only have to contend with one beast while we remain within its territory. All others of its species, even the female dragons, unless it is breeding season, will stay well away from this territory."

"I think I prefer encountering a whole bunch of smaller dragons instead," gulped Cankles.

"The smaller they are, the faster they can run and fly," warned the Elf. "Plus, the last thing you need is to be hunted down by a herd of juvenile males."

"Why?" asked Rose.

"They tend to roam in herds, hunting and living together in relative safety in case they stumble into a territory already established by a larger, dominant male. A creature of such formidable size would not think twice about taking on intruders, even cannibalizing one of its own if another dragon is foolish enough to fight than flee."

"So you're saying that our odds of surviving an encounter is better against one massive beast than several, smaller more agile ones," determined Tag.

"Yes, for even the smaller ones have the same insatiable taste for blood. Competing with larger adults forces these creatures to be hungrier... meaner; more determined to make a kill," stated the Elf.

"I think I understand what you're gettin' at," said Cankles.

"If luck is with us, there is a chance we will not even encounter the creator of this midden," said the Elf.

"I pray for luck! I pray for luck!" chanted Cankles, terrified of encountering a dragon of any size.

"We still have a distance to go," said Tag, pointing to the small forest of trees nestled at the base of a sheer cliff.

"I doubt we can make it that distance before the sun rises," said Cankles. "Even if the Princess ran all the way, I don't think we'll reach cover in time."

"What will we do?" asked Rose.

"I believe we can, but I have a suggestion, although you will not like it, Princess," warned the Elf, speaking with all certainty.

"I do not care! I will do whatever I must to avoid an encounter with one of those beasts!"

"Are you positive?"

"Of course I am."

"Then you must smear this dung on your clothing," ordered the Elf, his words matter-of-fact as he pointed to the midden.

"What?" gasped the Princess, frowning in utter disgust. "Surely you jest?"

"Dragons do not possess great eyesight, however, they have an exceptionally keen sense of smell," stated the Elf.

"I see," responded Tag, as he nodded in understanding. "We should go by unnoticed, if we smell like the resident dragon."

"You mean, if we smell of dragon *pooh!*" corrected Rose, grimacing in revulsion.

"Even better! What dragon will want to eat its own dung? None that I know of," stated Tag.

"Clever! The fresher stuff is higher on the pile," announced Cankles, scooping up a handful of excrement. "Shall I smear some on you, Princess?"

"Must you?" groaned Rose, her nose wrinkling in disgust.

"If you wish to increase your chances of survival, I would recommend it," said Tag, smudging the feces onto the shoulders of his cloak. "If you find it repulsive, I'm sure the dragons will, too. You will hardly smell appetizing. And if anything, we can shed our cloaks later when we are done."

"Very well," sighed Rose, cringing as Cankles smeared a dollop of dragon dung in a big *X* on her back. "Just do not allow it to touch my skin."

"Right-o, Princess!" responded Cankles, as he eagerly set to work. After helping Tag and Rose mask their scent, he turned to the Elves in their company.

"What about you and your men?" asked Cankles, picking up another heaping handful of reptile dung. "To spare you handlin' this mess, I'd be happy to apply some on you and your friends."

The leader raised his hand in polite refusal. "No need, my good man; for it is not necessary."

"Not necessary?" asked Cankles, frowning in confusion. "But you said to wear this stuff to disguise our scent."

"That is true, sir," responded the Elf, as he went on to explain. "We always smell of lavender essence and the attar of wild roses, whereas you mortals smell like, and take no offense, meat worthy of being fed to a dragon."

"What do you know?" exclaimed Cankles, leaning in to sniff at the Elf. "You do smell like flowery perfume. How delightful!"

"Thank you," said the Elf, tipping his head in gratitude.

"In other words, the Elves smell like lovely flowers and dragons are not vegetarians; they are meat eaters," explained Tag. "Unfortunately for us, we smell like a tantalizing meal to those creatures."

"But not anymore," assured Cankles. He nodded in understanding as he slapped another generous dollop of dung on Rose's back, for good measure.

"Will you stop that? I have had enough of this dragon pooh contaminating my apparel!" groaned the Princess.

"Better too much than not enough," said Cankles, wiping his hands on his trousers. "Even I would not want to be anywhere near you, now."

"Fine by me," grunted Rose. Doubling the fold of her cloak over her mouth and nose, she filtered out the worst of the stink from assaulting her olfactory senses.

"We move now," ordered the Elf, waving the mortals on to follow.

Rushing across the expanse of land toward the pre-dawn sky and the cover of trees, the party moved with stealth. They came to rest briefly in what Rose first thought was nothing more than broken tree trunks, perhaps struck by lightning and denuded of foliage, bark and branches. They protruded from the earth with smaller branches scattered about the ground.

"This is odd," commented Tag, staring up at the formations that loomed in a uniform row to arc over him.

"What kind of trees were these?" asked Cankles, his hand rubbing against the object. "It feels like stone, polished smooth by the winds and the rains."

"Dragon bones," answered the Elf, walking around a thighbone that was too big to step over.

"Good gracious," gasped Rose, stepping back to take in this macabre scene. "The dragon was huge!"

Cankles stepped away from the bone he had been admiring, realizing he and Tag were standing in what was left of the creature's ribcage.

"Oh my! A full-size covered carriage could easily fit in here with still room for us to move about," noted Cankles, marvelling at the size of the chest cavity.

"It must have been the largest animal to wander these lands," determined Tag, sitting on a disk of a backbone that once formed the creature's shattered spine.

"This is great news!" declared Rose.

"What do you mean?" asked Tag.

"It means that humongous dragon that created the huge dung hill is dead," decided Rose. "We have nothing to fear now."

"Sorry to disappoint you, Princess," said the Elf leading the way, "but that is not quite right."

"What do you mean? This dragon was gargantuan!"

"True, but if you examine what remains, you will see that a dragon much larger in size killed and ate this one." The Elf used the tip of his bow to point above Tag's head where half of the left ribcage was missing. Huge, serrated teeth in jagged rows had sunk in, twisting and tearing to deliver a death-delivering bite to this creature.

"Oh…" was all Rose managed to squeak out, as her mind tried to grapple with the size of this dragon's killer.

"Goodness!" gulped Cankles, stumbling over a bone fragment as he backed away. "We best be going, then. No point in lollygagging here."

"Definitely," agreed Tag, backing out of what was left of the dead dragon's chest.

"I recommend we move with speed," suggested the Elf. "Take cover immediately."

"I agree," said Rose, as she charged off. She didn't even wait for the Elf to lead the way. As though propelled by a burst of renewed energy or fuelled by absolute fear, the Princess was off, sprinting with all her might.

"Quickly, men!" ordered the Elf. "We do not want her getting too far ahead, only to get lost."

"Fret not, for this is Princess Rose you're speaking of," assured Tag, giving the Elf a knowing smile.

Before long, they caught up to Rose as her mad dash was reduced to a plodding stagger.

"Almost there," whispered Cankles, relieved the shadows of this cluster of trees would shield them from the eyes of the hungry, resident dragon.

"Thank goodness for that," groaned Rose, gasping for her breath as the promise of safety drew closer.

"Just another thirty paces or so and we'll be under cover," said Cankles, coaxing her on as her steps began to lag behind the others.

Rose and Cankles screamed in fright as the others gasped in surprise. A bloodcurdling shriek shattered the still morning air as a cloud of dust swirled around them from a powerful downdraft.

"Look out!" hollered the lead Elf. He nocked an arrow, drawing his bow.

With an earth shaking 'thud', a dragon the size of a large carriage fell from the sky.

As the dust settled, amber eyes glowed brightly, shining against an armour of iridescent green scales. An angry hiss rumbled from the creature's throat. With its black, forked tongue flickering, the dragon tasted particles in the air, transferring it to an organ situated in the roof of its mouth to analyze the chemical signatures wafting from them.

"Do not move!" whispered the Elf, his arrow poised to launch.

"I – I thought you said it'd be a huge dragon," gasped Rose, as she and the others froze where they stood.

"It's big enough!" gulped Cankles.

"It is not the one," stated the Elf.

"It's not the gargantuan creature you claimed had made the dung hill?" asked Rose, glancing to the Elf for an explanation.

"Yes, you heard me correctly."

The dragon advanced, moving much like a bat using the thumb on the apex of each wing to scramble along the ground in an awkward hopping motion.

"But I thought you said no other dragons would dare invade the territory of another?" gasped Rose, her eyes wide in fright.

"Another dragon of its *species*," clarified the Elf, drawing back on his arrow in case the creature attacked. "That is a mace-tailed dragon!"

"What? You lied to me!" gasped Rose, turning to Tag to smack him on his shoulder. "You said they were extinct!"

"I said they were rare to the point most *believe* them to be extinct," explained Tag, grabbing Rose's arm to yank her out of the way.

The ground beneath their feet shook as the creature spun about. Its club-like tail smashed down, the spikes biting into the earth.

Clumps of dirt flew in all directions as the dragon yanked its tail free, its leathery wings opening wide to make it look larger and more imposing.

It spun about again, glaring at the Elves and mortals as its tongue flickered, tasting the air once more.

"Watch out, it might breathe fire," warned Tag, slowly unsheathing his sword as Rose stood there, her bow held unarmed in her trembling hand.

"Not this one," said the Elf, still poised to shoot. "That is why it uses its tail."

Once more, the dragon spun about. The tip of its spiky tail whipped about, smashing down to narrowly miss Rose as Tag pulled her from harm's way.

With an angry hiss, the dragon turned to face the Princess, its black, snake-like pupils narrowing as it glared at the small mortal.

"Why me? Why is it after me?" gulped Rose. She was so frightened she was unable to nock an arrow to save her life.

"It prefers girls over boys?" whispered Cankles, arming himself with his hunting knife even though he knew it probably couldn't penetrate that scaly hide.

The dragon scuttled closer to her, its tail raised in threat as its tongue darted from its mouth.

"Don't panic…" whispered Tag, brandishing his sword as he inched closer to Rose's side. "I think it likes what you have."

"What? My charming personality? My good looks?" responded

Rose, fumbling about as she dropped an arrow she tried to discreetly remove from her quiver. "What do you mean?"

"The egg," answered Tag. "The egg in your pack!"

"What?" gasped Rose.

"I think the dragon can smell it," said Cankles, his knife trembling in his hands as the Elves aimed their arrows at the beast's scaly chest.

"Slowly now," warned Tag, his words a whisper. "No sudden movements."

Rose barely breathed. Her hand slipped into the pack, fishing out the bejeweled dragon egg. As she pulled it from the pack to present to the dragon, the creature's tail lowered. Its bristling scales suddenly lay flat as the dragon's attention focused on the egg.

"It must've belonged to her," whispered Cankles, watching as the dragon cautiously ambled closer; its snout lowered as its tongue darted in and out.

Just as Rose was about to return it to the beast, her nervous hands, slick with perspiration and trembling with fear, fumbled, almost dropping the egg.

The dragon bellowed in Rose's face. Her hair flew back and her eyes opened wide in fright only to squeeze shut from the reek of the creature's spent breath as every arrow turned on the beast.

"Don't hurt her!" cried Rose, showing the dragon that the object of its intense interest was still intact. "She just wants her egg."

"That is quite the egg," muttered the Elf, his aim remaining fixed on the dragon as the first light of the morning sun glistened off the pearls and gems of topaz.

The dragon's tail began to rattle with excitement. The beast crouched low to the ground, like a great cat waiting to pounce on a mouse. Rose slowly lowered the ornate egg, placing it gently onto the ground before the creature.

"But it's empty," whispered Cankles, taking another step back.

"That dragon either doesn't know or doesn't care," said Tag, pulling Rose behind him.

"I believe the beast can still smell the scent of that egg; probably recognizes it as hers," whispered the Elf. With a subtle nod of his head, he gestured his men to slowly back away.

To Rose's surprise, the dragon was extremely gentle, carefully nuzzling the egg with her snout as the tips of the forked tongue flickered. Though decorated with gold and studded with jewels, it still detected the lingering scent signature as its own.

Before they could retreat into the shadows of the forest, the dragon roared with delight. Snatching up the egg in her jaws, the reptile pushed off the ground, launching herself skyward with her prized possession.

"Thank goodness!" gasped Cankles, following the Elves into the shadows of the trees hugging the base of the cliff. "That encounter could have ended badly for us."

"Indeed," said Tag, nodding in agreement as he sheathed his sword.

"It was a lucky thing the Princess had that egg with her, after all," stated Cankles.

"Yes... it was most fortuitous indeed! Did I not tell you that egg would prove invaluable?" reminded Rose, glancing over at Tag as she thought back on Agly's prediction about confronting a dragon. No doubt, that was what the fortune-teller meant by her warning about *'taking something that was not her own'*.

"Yes, but it was not invaluable for the reason you first thought," sniffed Tag, shaking his head in dismay.

"Well, I do not know about you, but I consider my life to be absolutely priceless," grunted Rose. "And just think! My quick thinking and brave actions saved our lives."

"I'm the one who told you to give the egg back to the dragon, but I will give you that. You did the right thing without hesitation," said Tag, with a polite nod of acknowledgement. "Just don't let it go to your head."

"So what now?" asked Cankles, wishing for nothing more than to change the subject to prevent his friends from bickering again.

"We shall take cover over here," replied the Elf, waving the party on to follow him to the center of this stand of trees where the shadows were the deepest. "Take some rest now. We shall wait for darkness to fall before we move on."

"Sounds like an excellent plan to me," said Cankles, heaving a weary sigh as he tossed his pack to the ground. Exhausted, he slumped down against a tree.

"For once, I agree with you," said Rose, plopping down by his side as she motioned for Tag to pass her the water flask.

Tag shook it first, its contents sloshing about loudly. "It's almost empty."

"That's not good," responded Cankles, peering into the opening of his flask. "I'm running low, too."

"Fear not, my friends," said the Elf. "There is water near to us. I can hear it."

"There is? I don't hear anything," commented Tag, listening for the sounds the Elf detected.

"Listen... It is a waterfall," said the Elf, glancing through the trees toward the cliff wall.

"That must be the fresh supply of water the Dream Merchant was speaking of," determined Rose.

"If it's flowing and coming from on high, it must be. At least it's better than water that's been sitting stagnant down here in one of those sulphur tainted ponds," responded Tag, only now hearing the distant sound of water thundering over a cliff to fill a deep pool.

"Drink sparingly for now," advised the Elf. "Make it last, for we cannot attempt to collect water until the sun retires. In the meantime, remain here. I will take my men; have a look around. I want to make sure we will be safe for the time being."

"Good idea," agreed Tag, watching as the Elves slipped into the shadows of the forest. He then passed the container on to Rose. "Take a sip or two, Princess. Just keep in mind, this will have to last us the day."

Rose unleashed a dreary sigh as the tears welled in her eyes.

"What's wrong?" asked Tag, holding the flask out to her. "I didn't say you couldn't have any water; just drink a little bit. Go on! Take it."

"Don't cry, m'lady," pleaded Cankles, as she began to sob. "You can have my share, if it pleases you."

"It is not that," whimpered Rose, as hot tears tumbled down her dirt-smudged cheeks.

"Then what is it?" asked Tag, sitting down next to her.

"This… all of this," wept Rose, her arms wrapping around her legs as she unleashed another great sob. Resting her forehead on bended knees, she tried to hide the tears of defeat and humiliation from Tag and Cankles.

"*This?*" repeated Tag, stooping to peer into her face.

"We are in the middle of this God forsaken land. We are looking for a Sorcerer we might never find, and he may not even have the dream-stone I'm looking for. Plus, I am exhausted, hungry and thirsty."

"And that's it?" asked Tag.

"Because of my greed and stupidity, I almost got us killed," admitted Rose.

"But if you didn't have the egg, I'm sure that dragon would have been our end," said Cankles.

"But if I had just left that egg behind in the first place, like Tag said, that mace-tailed dragon would have never bothered us."

Tag was momentarily taken aback. It was rare for the Princess to admit to any of her shortcomings, but the trauma of the encounter shook her to the very core.

"Look here, we all make mistakes," said Tag.

"Ones that nearly get us killed?" asked Rose, despair and disappointment in her voice.

"Well, maybe not quite, but the point is, we all make mistakes. The important thing is to take responsibility for them. And you did."

"And that is a good thing?"

"It's a very good thing," praised Tag, nodding in approval. "I'm most impressed."

"You are?"

"Of course!"

"Still, this is bad... so very bad," whimpered Rose, as she blinked away the tears.

"What is so very bad?" probed Tag.

"I am covered in dragon pooh!" cried Rose, as another wave of tears streamed down her face. "It cannot get any worse than this."

Before Cankles could say she was wrong, Tag quickly raised a hand for silence.

"If it's any comfort to you, I've never met a girl who looked better in dragon dung than you do," praised Tag, putting a comforting arm around her shoulders. "I don't know many who can pull off this look better than you can."

Rose peered up, a small smile curling her lips.

"See, now it's even better," said Tag, smiling back at the Princess as his arm gave her shoulders a reassuring squeeze.

"You are just saying that," said Rose, her cheeks flushing with embarrassment as her eyes moistened with tears.

"No, I'm not," insisted Tag. "Especially this smudge of dung right here on your chin. It just completes the look perfectly."

His hand lifted her chin so the pad of his thumb could gently wipe away the dirt that now mingled with her tears.

"Aaah!" sighed Cankles, staring dreamily at the young couple as he fished about in his pockets for a kerchief. "A tender moment."

Tag and Rose glanced at Cankles, and then at each other. Instantly, Rose leaned away from Tag's body. Just as quickly, he withdrew his arm. This was followed by awkward silence.

"Here you go, m'lady," said Cankles, offering her a well-used rag that doubled as a kerchief. "To blot away those tears."

"Thank you, but no," responded Rose, shrinking away from the soiled, tattered cloth presented to her.

"Very well," said Cankles, tucking the kerchief away. "Just ignore me. You two can resume gettin' cozy. Carry on!"

"*Cozy?*" gasped Rose and Tag, speaking in unison.

"It's not what you think," insisted Tag.

"Not at all," assured Rose.

"Right…" snorted Cankles, giving them a knowing smile.

"What are you insinuating?" asked Tag.

"What is there to insinuate when it is all so very obvious," answered Cankles, giving his comrades a wink of his eye.

"You are speaking in riddles," dismissed Rose. "I have no idea what you are talking about."

"If you want to pretend nothing happened, I'm willin' to play along," offered Cankles. "Just carry on. I'll just turn a blind eye, if that's what you wish."

"Get cozy?" groaned Tag, rolling his eyes in frustration and denial.

"With *him?*" gasped Rose, pointing an accusing finger at her comrade. "He stinks!"

"You stink even more than I do," insisted Tag, sliding away from her side as Rose did the same.

"Actually, I smell even worse than the two of you combined," decided Cankles. "I think I soiled my trousers when that damned dragon dropped out of the sky. Almost scared me to death, it did!"

Instead of continuing to bicker as Cankles thought they would, Tag and Rose broke into a fit of laughter, fighting to subdue their giggles upon hearing this man's candid admission.

"What?" asked Cankles, plucking at the back of his trousers that clung to his backside.

"Never mind," said Tag, grinning broadly. "We are just too tired to fight anymore."

"Thank God for that!" declared Cankles. "Then it's safe for me to leave you two alone while I freshen up."

"By all means!" urged Tag, shooing him off. "Just do not stray too far away."

"And please don't bring back any dragons with you," added Rose.

16
The Devil's Tears

As the sun travelled westward, moving steadily across the sky, the Elves in their company took turns keeping watch as the others slept. This sleep was interrupted only for a midday meal, and disrupted by the occasional, distant roars of battling dragons. These cries were punctuated by the intermittent rumble and quake of the surrounding volcanoes that shuddered as they vented to release building, internal pressure.

So, while Rose and Cankles dozed, Tag put his waking hours to good use. He took the opportunity to hone his swordsmanship, practicing what Halen Ironwood taught him against the four Elves who were more than willing to test his skills.

Under the canopy of the trees to shield them from the eyes of the resident dragon they had yet to encounter, as well as the Sorcerer and his minions should they be lurking about, Tag and his opponents used care to keep the clatter of sword against sword to a minimum. They did so by wrapping their blades in sheaths of cloth to cushion and muffle the blows as they practiced. However, it was Tag's footwork that woke his comrades.

Though the Elves were light on their feet, gracefully maneuvering to and fro to parry and counter Tag's attack, the mortal's heavier steps betrayed his every move. The snapping and crackling of twigs and dried leaves underfoot eventually caused his comrades to rouse from their sleep.

"Are you still at it?" groaned Rose, sitting up as Cankles stirred, coming awake as he suddenly snorted and gasped during mid-snore.

"I couldn't sleep, so I thought I'd be better off practicing what Captain Ironwood shared with me."

"You should at least try to get some more sleep," urged Rose.

"I tried, but what little I had was plagued by a bad dream," admitted Tag.

"A nightmare like the others?" asked Cankles, as he rubbed the sleep from his eyes.

"I don't remember," answered Tag, recalling how he woke up in a cold sweat with only a sliver of a memory involving his father's sword. "I thought my time would be better spent training than to be accosted by more dreams I don't understand or I fail to remember."

"Are you not tired?" questioned Rose, stretching as she yawned.

"No. Why?"

"Because we have a long journey before us in these dreaded lands," reminded Rose. "I need you to keep your wits about you, in case we encounter the Sorcerer or a dragon."

"No need to fret, Princess. I am now better prepared for whatever fate tosses our way."

"You better be," warned Rose, shaking a stern finger in his direction. "If I get killed, mark my words; you are *sooo* dead!"

Tag stared with raised eyebrows at the Princess, and then he began to snicker. "You will never appreciate just how odd that sounded."

"The point being, if I die and it is your fault, I will kill you," threatened Rose.

Tag, Cankles and the Elves in their company began to laugh in response.

"That was even better, m'lady!" praised Cankles. "If you weren't already a princess, you'd make for an excellent court jester."

"Bite your tongue!" snapped Rose, as she bundled up her bedroll. "Just keep in mind; I will hold you both responsible for keeping me safe as we journey on."

"Your concerns and threats have been duly noted," teased Tag, attempting to wipe the grin from his face.

"Good!" grunted Rose. "So, do we leave soon?"

"Soon enough," answered the senior Elf. "The sun advances. Eat now and we will be on our way."

"Even though it is still light?" asked Cankles.

"With the approach of twilight, we will make our way, taking advantage of the cover these trees provide us until we reach the pool fed by the waterfall," explained the Elf. "Once it is safe, we will replenish our flasks and begin our search under the cover of night."

"Makes sense to me," said Cankles, rummaging through his pack to share some food with his comrades.

"But where do we even begin searching for Dragonite's lair?" asked Rose.

"We check every crack, crevasse and cave that fiend can squeeze into. We search every tunnel leading into a cavern, until we find him," answered Tag. "It's as simple as that."

"There must be a better way," sighed Rose.

"We can narrow it down by avoiding the caves already occupied by dragons using them as a hibernaculum," offered Tag.

"Oh, definitely avoid those hibernating dragons," agreed Cankles.

"Well, obviously," grumbled Rose. "Lady Agly did warn us we should avoid an encounter with dragons, at all cost."

"And what else did she say?" probed Tag.

"Why are you asking me?" responded Rose. "It is your job to listen and remember what is being said; it is my job to look good while only pretending to listen."

"Seriously," scolded Tag. "Surely you recall what she said about finding what you most desire."

"What I desire most at this very moment is to be at home, safe in Pepperton Palace and preparing for my grand birthday gala."

"That won't happen until this quest is done... now think, Princess," urged Tag.

"That girl did say something about water and fire, or walking through fire with water to get what I desire," answered Rose; thinking back on their encounter with the seer of the future.

"No, I think the young lady said something about dowsin' fire with water or maybe it was water turnin' into fire," said Cankles, as he pondered this mystery.

"Hey... I think I remember," said Tag, his eyes squeezing shut as he racked his brain.

"Go on, what did she say?" asked Rose.

"I think she said, '*when water turns to fire and you pass through unscathed, you shall seek what you desire, if you follow the way*'," responded Tag.

"*Gibberish!* I do not speak gibberish. Translate for me," ordered Rose; turning to Cankles as she mulled over Tag's words.

"This is gibberish I don't understand," responded her jester, scratching his head in thought. "Sounds like a riddle to me."

"I'm sure that's what Lady Agly said to us," insisted Tag.

"That may be so, but it makes no sense," grumbled Rose. "Since when does water turn to fire or vice versa?"

"Unscathed, you say? Well, I'm not the smartest person in the world, but I've always known fire to burn," added Cankles. "You can't tell me otherwise."

"I think you're right, my friend. I agree with you that it was a riddle of sorts," said Tag.

"That is probably so, Master Yairet, for the only thing that sounds remotely similiar to this whole water-to-fire business is the Devil's Tears," stated the senior Elf in their company.

"The name alone is rather ominous," commented Cankles. "Tell us more."

"It is a waterfall that is not great in volume, but cascades from an incredible height."

"Where is it? Is it far from here?" queried Tag.

"Not far at all, young sir. In fact, it is the waterfall that feeds the pool where we will be replenishing our flasks."

"What luck!" declared Tag, his eyes gleaming with newfound hope.

"What does all this mean?" asked Rose, frowning in bewilderment. "I fail to understand this whole water to fire thing you are speaking of. It makes no sense."

"I have not seen it with mine own eyes, but I have heard tales of old regarding the Devil's Tears," responded the Elf, as his comrades nodded in confirmation.

"Go on! Tell us more," urged Cankles, leaning forward as he listened intently.

"It is said, for only four consecutive days of the year, when the conditions are perfect and the sun hangs in the sky just so, if you are lucky, you will catch a glimpse."

"A glimpse of what?" asked Cankles.

"It is only during this golden moment, as the sun prepares to set, the water turns to fire," informed the Elf.

"No… How can that be?" gasped Cankles, his eyes wide in wonder and bewilderment.

"Sounds like strange devilry to me," decided Rose, shaking her head in trepidation. "Hence, the foreboding name to begin with."

"Can this be possible?" questioned Tag.

"I suppose anything is possible," responded the Elf. "It is a rare phenomenon seen by a rarer few, as these lands are hardly inviting, if you get my meaning?"

"So you have not seen the water transforming into fire?" asked Tag, seeking confirmation.

"I have not, but others have. As I said, if the conditions are not perfect, you will not be witness to this spectacle."

"And you are sure it is this same waterfall we are heading to?" asked Rose.

"I am positive, for it is the only one to the north that cascades from the height of a great cliff and is affected by the sun in such a manner," ascertained the Elf.

"But what time of the year does this take place?" asked Cankles. "For if it is so, it must be a breathtakin' sight to behold."

"From all the legends I have heard, it is a breathtaking spectacle indeed," assured the Elf. "Tales from the days of yore say it occurs mid to late spring, but only for these four days and only if the conditions are perfect and the run-off from melting snow is sufficient."

"So if this is the place, and if my guess is correct, the seer of the future was trying to tell us that the entrance to Dragonite's lair is hidden somewhere behind this veil of water," decided Tag.

"If it is true, and this water is somehow able to transform into *fire*, there is a chance we are that much closer to finding the Sorcerer," determined Rose.

"Let us hope," agreed Tag.

"If you give any credence to what this seer predicted, I would say that is exactly the case," said the Elf. "Think on it! It is a perfect way to conceal the mouth of his lair from unwanted eyes."

"But how do we advance?" asked Rose, her gaze turning to the granite formation towering above the trees. "The cliff wall from where the water cascades is sheer – a vertical drop."

"I've been told there is a path," revealed the Elf. "It is narrow and treacherous, even for one as surefooted as I am, but it can be climbed. Once we reach the top of this cliff, we can be lowered down alongside the waterfall to see what we can see."

"And we plan to do this in the suffocating darkness of night?" gasped Rose.

The Elf glanced up through the tree canopy. "The skies are clear. Even before the sun hides its face, the air shall cool substantially. It promises to be a chilly night if the clouds do not materialize to insulate the earth."

"So we will be on the move, climbing before darkness falls?" asked Cankles.

"That shall depend," said the Elf.

"On what?" questioned Rose.

"If this is indeed the firefall of legend," answered the Elf.

"I am willing to chance that it is," decided Tag.

"So we leave now?" queried Cankles.

"We eat first, and then we shall move on, for you do not know when you will have the chance again," replied the Elf.

"In an hour or two, dusk will settle," said Tag. "At the very least, we shall move into position; ready to advance when the conditions allow it."

"So we shall bide our time for now," said Cankles.

"The Elf is correct. There is no way of knowing when we shall have a chance to eat again," responded Rose, motioning Cankles to pass her the pack containing food. "We eat now."

"Yes, I suppose there is no point in meeting our destiny on an empty stomach," decided Cankles, nodding in agreement.

Sharing an austere supper, mortals and Elves spoke in hushed tones as they passed the time.

"Say, we do not even know your names," said Cankles, turning to the senior Elf and the men in his company.

"At this time, our names are not relevant," responded the Elf. "What is important is to keep you three alive so this quest can meet a successful end."

"I suppose… Mind you, have you ever noticed in tales and legends of old, whenever the creator of these stories couldn't be bothered to name certain characters, those were the ones that became the casualties of war or met up with some ghastly end?" noted Cankles.

"Say, you are right," agreed Rose. "I have noticed just that in many of the books I have read and the plays I have seen."

"Good gracious! Quickly sir, what is your name?" asked Cankles, hoping to circumvent a possible curse.

"I am Denatheen-Aralur Brookstone, son of Durasell, brother to Lady Valara the wife of Lord Rainus Silverthorn."

"Oh my! That is a lot to remember," gasped Cankles, realizing his minimal capacity to recall such complex names was going to be his, or in this case, the Elf's undoing.

"Indeed, but worry not, for our names our irrelevant at this moment," stated the Elf. "We must remain focused on the task at hand."

"Absolutely," said Cankles, cursing himself inwardly for having such a feeble memory.

"You are correct, Denturcleen," said Rose, nodding in agreement.

"That is not my name," grunted the Elf, as he stared with raised eyebrows at the Princess.

"No matter! You are right. We should stay focused," stated Rose, knowing full well her worst bad habit was incorrectly recalling the names of others. Unless she was regularly exposed to the name and the person attached to the moniker, along with constant reminders of proper pronunciation, she was a lost cause.

"For now, we will rest while we sup," stated Tag, "and then we shall advance to the waterfall."

"If our luck holds, perhaps it is the firefall the fortune-teller spoke of," said Cankles, his words, optimistic.

"With a name like the Devil's Tears, we can only hope," sighed Rose, tearing off a chunk of stale bread before handing the shrinking loaf to Tag.

Using stealth, they ventured on, creeping along to make as little noise as possible. Even though the forest canopy sheltered them, their presence could be revealed if they were not careful. As mortals and Elves advanced, they encountered little in the way of wildlife in this patch of forest.

The small herds of deer that survived here only did so by a combination of sheer luck and by dashing off at the first sign of danger, or remaining motionless until it passed. To make the desperate dash across the open expanse to dwell in the relative safety of the Dimbolt Forest had proven fatal for those that had tried it, so the remaining, scattered herds learned to live in constant fear of the dragons inhabiting this region.

As Rose and the men in her company advanced, the stand of trees gradually thinned out to open into a small clearing. Here, the clean, fresh water cascaded down over the sheer rockface, splashing loudly to gather in a small, but deep pool. Crowns of lush, green ferns and tussocks of sedge surrounded it. The coursing water was loud enough to dampen the distant sounds of battling dragons as well as the rumbling of volcanoes erupting to the north.

Glancing about for signs of danger, the senior Elf motioned for his comrades to proceed, once he knew it was safe to do so. "Quickly, replenish your flasks."

Darting to the water's edge, Tag and Cankles worked with haste, filling the containers as the Elves kept watch.

"Wait... we haven't yet encountered the large dragon that supposedly lives here," whispered Cankles. His eyes were wide with fear at the thought of meeting up with such a huge beast, one of such size it could easily make a meal of them in a single swallow. "What if it comes and finds us wanderin' through its domain? And what if it's as big as Master Elf said..."

Cankles' face twisted with horror as his imagination began to run amok.

"Are you trying to scare me?" asked Rose, her words spoken in a hushed tone while she nervously glanced about as Cankles' words began to sink in.

"We have avoided the resident dragon thus far," reminded Tag.

"If we are careful, there is a possibility we will avoid the beast altogether."

"There is a chance it has moved on to expand its territory," offered the senior Elf, listening above the crashing water to hear dragons battling far off in the distant mountains. "There is also a possibility the creature has met its demise."

"I like that option the best," decided Cankles, handing a full flask to Tag. He pushed the cork stopper into the mouth of the container before slinging the strap over his shoulder.

"Are you ready, Princess?" asked Tag, wiping his hands dry on his trousers.

"Does it matter if I'm not?" whined Rose, dreading the next leg of the trek.

"Better to move now before we lose all light," suggested Tag.

As the sun rested on the pinnacle of a distant mountain far to the west, it set the errant clouds snagged on its peak ablaze in crimson. Golden sheets of light burned through these gossamer wisps, spreading across the lands in one final, defiant attempt to hold night at bay.

"Sweet mother-of-pearl!" gasped Cankles. His eyes opened wide in wonder as he pointed to the waterfall. "Look at that! The Devil's Tears indeed!"

As the sky deepened and the sun gradually slipped behind the mountain, the golden sheen of light cast its magic. Snow that had gathered on the heights of this cliff to melt in the warmth of the sun now coursed over the ledge, sending plumes of fine mist into the air. With the sun's waning light angling just so on the horizon; the refraction of light caused these droplets to transform into swirling vapours of gold as the cascading water turned a brilliant amber/orange in colour, like liquid fire.

As the last sliver of golden light retreated, the sun cast the water into a deeper shade of orange/red. It rushed over the cliff to spill and splash over the granite face like glowing, molten lava.

"Truly a spectacle to behold," marvelled the senior Elf, gazing at the firefall that poured into the deep pool.

Rose was mesmerized, gasping in amazement. "Oh, my! I never thought such a thing was possible. The water truly does look just like liquid fire."

"This is what Lady Agly must have been referring to," determined Tag, taking in this rare, but natural phenomenon. "Water turning into fire… to pass through unscathed."

"Thank goodness for that," stated Cankles, admiring the glory and beauty of one of nature's greatest mysteries. "It'll be much safer passing through water than flames, that's for sure."

"Shall we commence?" asked the Elf.

"How?" Rose wondered aloud as she glanced over to what she could only determine were the remnants of a crumbling trail ascending to the top of the cliff. "Up that?"

"Apparently so," answered Tag, after scrutinizing their surroundings.

With the setting of the sun, the lands were eerily quiet once more. Aside from the sporadic venting of distant volcanoes to the north, the resident dragons of this vast expanse of wasteland had settled down for the night, seeking shelter from the impending cold that was sure to follow with the rise of the moon.

"No point in waiting," decided Tag. "I believe we'll be safe for now."

"How do we even begin?" asked Rose, staring up to the top of the cliff.

"We start at the bottom, and then we work our way up, one step at a time," answered Denatheen, the senior Elf in their party. "That is the most logical thing to do."

"We plan to *climb* this cliff? In the darkness of night?" gasped the Princess, scrutinizing the sheer face as fear began to creep into her heart. "All the way to the top?"

"I'm not liking this idea, but it's better than in the light of day when dragons can fly up there and pick us off, one by one, for an easy snack," reminded Cankles.

"It will be a full moon on this eve," reminded Tag. "I'm confident we will have sufficient light to move by and the temperature will drop enough to prevent any dragon from wanting to leave the warmth of its shelter."

"That is so. As for the quality of light, my men and I will definitely have adequate light on this eve," assured Denatheen.

"Good for you, but for those of us without magic Elf-eyes, can we light a torch to show the way?" asked Rose.

"Why don't we just announce to the Sorcerer that we're coming, while we're at it?" scolded Tag.

"I will be your guide; show you the way," offered Denatheen, as he motioned for his mortal comrades to follow. "What you do not see, I will. Trust in me and I shall lead you through the darkness."

"Can I take your hand?" asked Rose, tentative as ever.

"If it gives you some peace of mind, of course," answered Denatheen. "I promise to keep you safe."

"I suppose we should move on then," decided the Princess, her eyes struggling to adjust to the ever-dimming light.

"Remember, we are in no rush," said Cankles. "Better to be safe than sorry, I always say."

"As long as we get up there before the coming of the sun, I'm good with that," said Tag, waving Rose on to follow Denatheen. "The last thing we need is to be attacked by dragons just as we reached the top."

"We cannot have that," agreed Rose, taking the Elf's hand as they proceeded with the gruelling trek.

"As we get higher, do not look down," ordered Denatheen. "Keep your back against the cliff wall. Side-step as the trail narrows and whatever happens, do not look down."

"Good advice," acknowledged Rose, as she nodded in under-standing. "And if I should slip?"

"Do *not* slip," cautioned the Elf, his words matter-of-fact.

With a deep breath, Rose began the ascent, following close behind Denatheen as he guided the party along.

The higher they travelled, the darker the sky became. A dusting of brilliant, white stars sparkled against a cobalt sky as the moon rose, following their progress.

With this steadily growing darkness, the only comfort Rose found was that with this deepening sky, it made it harder to see the ground shrinking far below them.

"So we journey all the way to the top? We cannot just search for the mouth of the Sorcerer's Lair along the way in case it is *next to*, not actually hidden behind, the waterfall?" whispered Rose, keeping her voice down so it would not echo off the granite face of the cliff.

"Yes," answered the Elf. "When we reach the top, we shall use ropes to lower one of my men down first to find an opening to a cave, if one does indeed exist."

"I should be the one to go down first," said Tag.

"Your intentions are noble, Master Yairet," praised Denatheen, "but it is a matter of efficiency and experience."

"How so?" asked Rose. "All your men are taller and bigger than Tag. It would make more sense to send him down first."

"Looks can be deceiving, Princess. Though what you say is true, we are much lighter than the young master, at least by a stone or two. It is an Elf thing, if you get my meaning?"

"I suppose you are right. Tag is much more *dense* than the average Elf, and in more ways than one," teased Rose, as she inched her way along.

"Har, har!" scoffed Tag. "Less talking; more walking, please!"

"Yes," agreed Cankles, using the back of his hand to blot away the beads of perspiration from his forehead. "We best focus on the task at hand."

"If we keep this pace, we should reach the top before the moon is at its height," said the Elf, maneuvering easily in the darkness as the three mortals scuttled along. They were reduced to side-stepping all the way, stopping each time the edge of the trail crumbled, disintegrating under their footfalls as they journeyed on, ever higher.

"Just a few more steps," said the Elf, spying the sharp contrast of cliff silhouetted against the night sky.

"Thank goodness for that," gasped Rose, still refusing to release the Elf's hand as he guided her along.

One by one, mortal and Elf gathered on the top of this sheer cliff. Taking a moment to catch their breath, they gazed out, staring across the expanse. Under the fractured light of the moon shining through the odd patches of clouds floating across the sky, the lands looked eerily dismal and strangely barren. The only thing standing out against the terrain were the glowing, red-hot veins of lava oozing down several of the mountains to the north.

"That was close," gasped Rose, sighing with relief. "I am surprised we survived the trek."

"It was tough, but it wasn't that bad," responded Tag, passing the water flask to the Princess.

"Are you mad? It was tough *and* bad!" exclaimed Rose. "It was bloody dangerous, too."

"Well, you know what they say if you're not living on the edge?" said Tag.

"You're taking up too much room?" offered Cankles.

Tag merely shook his head, giving his friend a sympathetic pat on the shoulder.

"Now what?" asked Rose, peering nervously over the ledge where the melted snow rushed over the cliff.

Turning to the shortest, lightest member of his company, Denatheen pointed at the most junior Elf standing at attention. "We will lower him down first. He will take a look; see if he can spot a possible opening behind this waterfall."

Tying three lengths of rope to form one long, single line, they set to work. Securing a rope around this Elf's waist, they carefully lowered him over the edge as Rose, Tag and Cankles looked on.

With hand signals, this Elf motioned for Tag to let his comrades know to release more line, dropping him further down the face of the cliff.

"I hope you have lots of rope," whispered Rose, losing sight of the Elf in the darkness and the plumes of mist rising from the splashing waters.

"I don't know how he can see in this darkness," said Cankles, glancing up to see another billowy wisp of cloud pass before the moon's face to diminish its glow. "The moon is stingy with its light on this eve."

"I'm confident he will fare just fine," assured Tag, squinting to see as he was only able to detect the Elf whenever he moved against the darkness.

The rope suddenly went slack, only to come alive as the Elf below gave the line three hard tugs.

"He found the cave!" announced Denatheen, as he pulled the rope in hand-over-fist.

"I pray the good man did not fall," whispered Cankles.

"Fear not, my friend. I am confident my man would only signal as he had, if he met with success. It is highly unlikely he was signaling that the rope had unravelled and he was about to meet an untimely demise."

"He's right, Cankles," reassured Tag, wrapping the end of the rope around his waist. "In fact, I'll go next; prove to you and the Princess that it's safe to proceed."

"Are you sure, young master?" asked Cankles.

"Quite sure," answered Tag, giving the knot a good yank to make certain it was secure.

"Remember, lean back and keep your knees slightly bent," instructed the Elf, checking the knot to make certain it was not about to untie at the most inopportune moment.

"I'll do that," said Tag. He nodded in understanding as the Elves took up the rope. Just as he maneuvered to the very edge, Cankles rushed over, throwing his arms around the young man.

"Do be careful, my friend," urged Cankles, hugging Tag as though it could very well be the last time.

"I will," promised Tag.

"Take no unnecessary risks," cautioned Cankles, looking into his friend's eyes to make sure Tag had his complete understanding.

"Of course. Now retreat before you go over with me."

Cankles inched away, giving his friend room to safely back over the ledge.

"Tag!" called Rose, as she rushed to his side.

"What now?"

Rose stood before him, gazing into his eyes with genuine concern as her arms awkwardly lurched about, as though wanting to hug Tag, but having no idea just how to do this.

"What is it?" Tag asked once again, staring with suspicious eyes at the Princess.

His uninviting tone caused her arms to fall limp by her side.

"Go on, we don't have all night. What's on your mind?" asked Tag, urging her to speak now.

In response, Rose balled her fist, suddenly punching Tag's arm as she snapped, "You better not do something stupid and get yourself killed!"

Tag rubbed his smarting arm as he grumbled: "I have no intentions of doing that."

"Good!" responded Rose, taking a step away from the edge of the cliff.

"I'll meet you down there," said Tag. Grasping the rope in his hands, he leaned back as the Elves eased him over the cliff.

Slipping down into the darkness, the sounds of earth and rocks coming loose and crumbling under Tag's feet went unnoticed, drowned out by the splashing of the water coursing over the cliff. The evening breeze suddenly became noticeably colder as the droplets of water clinging to his clothes and skin chilled him.

Tag's heart thundered, pounding in his chest to resonate clear through his body. He swore his hands were probably so slick with sweat that if the mist swirling around him wasn't soaking the fibres of this rope he clung to, then his perspiration surely was.

Though he didn't dangle from the end of this tether for long, it felt like an eternity. His steady descent came to an abrupt stop as a voice called to him through the veil of water streaming down.

"Here! Over here!" called the Elf. "Swing toward my voice. I will catch you."

Tag began to rock back and forth like a pendulum, swinging toward the Elf waiting on a hidden ledge.

His breath caught in the back of his throat as Tag burst through the sheet of ice water, his eyes squeezing shut with the shock of the cold. He felt a hand seize him by the wrist, pulling him in toward solid ground.

"You are safe, but come away from the edge before I untie this rope," ordered the Elf, tugging at the tether that secured the mortal.

"This is it?" asked Tag, using the damp sleeve of his shirt to wipe the water from his eyes and face.

"This opening leads into a tunnel. Torches burn, so it is safe to assume this is the Sorcerer's present lair, for there is none in my mind mad enough to want to inhabit such a place."

"Did you go far?"

"No, I thought it better to wait for you and the others."

"Good idea," praised Tag, giving the rope three sharp tugs. He watched as it disappeared through the waterfall.

"Who is next?" asked Denatheen, as he retrieved the last of the rope.

"He is," said Rose, as she volunteered Cankles.

"I am?"

"Yes! Age before beauty; I always say," responded Rose.

Cankles gulped as he peered over the edge of the cliff, his eyes searching for the ground below that was swallowed up by the darkness.

"If you insist," said Cankles, taking a deep breath to calm his racing heart.

"Oh, I do," replied the Princess, watching as the Elf she was sure was named Denturcleen secured the end of the rope around the mortal's narrow waist.

"Re- remember," stammered a nervous Cankles, "don't let g-go."

"Fear not, good sir, we will keep you safe," promised the Elf, as he tugged on the knot to make certain it was secure. "This will only come undone when you are ready to untie it."

"Wonderful! So it's a magical Elven rope?" hoped Cankles.

"No, just a well tied square-knot," replied Denatheen.

"Better than a *slip*-knot on this occasion, I suppose," sighed Cankles, hoping a pun and a deep breath would help to calm his pounding heart and quaking hands.

"If Tag can do this, then so can you," assured Rose.

"Will you be sayin' this when it's your turn to go over this cliff?" asked Cankles.

"If it helps, then absolutely!"

"If you are frightened of heights, just resist the urge to look down," reminded Denatheen, as he and his men took up the slack rope.

The three Elves proceeded to back up, measuring out their steps to replicate the length it required to lower the first two down. This way, instead of releasing the rope, hand-over-fist, a little at a time in a herky-jerky motion, they merely walked toward the edge of the cliff, smoothly and easily lowering their subject to the desired depth.

"Don't look down," repeated Cankles, closing his eyes to say a silent prayer.

"Lean back, brace your feet against the cliff wall, then simply *walk* down," instructed Denatheen. "We will do the work to lower you safely."

"Sounds easy enough," said Cankles, but more to convince himself it was so.

"You can do it," encouraged Rose. "Just do as Master Elf said and you will be down in no time."

"I hope you're right."

"I have to be, otherwise, I will have no reason to risk going over myself," said Rose.

"Well, I trust you, m'lady," decided Cankles. "So I best get this over with."

"Yes, and quickly, for we do not want to be caught out here with the coming of the sun," reminded Rose.

Cankles unclenched one hand, but only long enough to signal to the Elves he was ready to go.

"*Do not* wind the rope around your hands," cautioned Denatheen. "You may not get them free in time."

"In time for what?"

"To circumvent a tragedy," answered the Elf.

"I see," gulped Cankles, repositioning his hands of the rope.

"Ready?" asked Denatheen.

"Don't rightly think it matters, but I'm as ready as I'll ever be."

Cankles' breath caught in the back of his throat as he took that first, tentative step that saw him teetering out against the lip of the cliff. With a nod of his head, as the Elves walked towards him, he gradually disappeared from their sight as they eased him down.

Sensing he was safe in their hands, Cankles cautiously inched his way along, following in Tag's footsteps. The farther he ventured with no incident, the more his confidence grew. Instead of moving gingerly, his steps became wider and heavier as his death grip on the rope lessened.

"Not bad at all," decided Cankles, speaking aloud even though none could hear his words. "Much easier than I had first thought."

Cankles' foot suddenly hit a slip of granite that broke away. He shrieked in fright; his cry drowned out by the water thundering over the cliff. When Cankles finally forced his eyes open, he realized he was now dangling upside down, spinning like a spider caught in a stiff breeze.

"Hey! Over here!" shouted Tag, seeing the blur of a shadow through the curtain of rushing waters. "Follow my voice! Swing toward me."

Cankles breathed a sigh of relief, albeit from this new position. His descent had come to an end and the promise of solid ground beneath his feet was merely one shout away. Like an over-sized inchworm dangling from a strand of silk, Cankles began rocking his body to and fro, swinging closer and closer to the waterfall, getting wetter with each frantic attempt.

Finally, his last energetic swing forced him through the sheet of water. He gasped at its icy embrace, snorting and choking as the downward flow sent water up his nostrils and into his gaping mouth.

Sputtering and coughing, the rising tide of panic was suddenly quelled by the firm grasp of Tag and the Elf's hands. They seized Cankles by his legs, pulling him in to safety as they up-righted the man.

"That was a unique way of climbing down," noted the Elf, untying the knot as Tag steadied his friend.

"Believe me, it was not intentional," admitted Cankles, the blood draining from his flushed cheeks now that he was standing on his feet.

"No matter, at least you are here now, and in one piece," responded Tag, nodding in approval.

"Thank goodness for that!" exclaimed Cankles, watching as the end of the tether disappeared through the waterfall.

"You are next, Princess," said Denatheen, pulling up on the rope to secure its end around her waist.

"Are you sure you would not rather leave me here?" asked Rose. "I think you need someone to watch this tether; make sure it remains secure so everybody can get back out of there when the quest is done."

"No need for concern, Princess. I will go last, securing this rope to that rock, thereby anchoring it so we can climb out safely," explained the Elf, pointing to a jagged piece of granite protruding from the ground.

"I do not mind keeping watch," offered Rose.

"I suppose we can use a watchful eye in case the resident dragon should appear," said Denatheen. "You can use the longbow and arrows gifted to you by Lord Silverthorn to fend off an attack, but only after you launch a flaming arrow into the night sky."

Rose gave the Elf a blank stare.

"Remember? The arrow that must be set ablaze?" reminded Denatheen. "It is how we are to tell the others we have located the Sorcerer's hiding place."

"Flaming arrow? I have no flaming arrow! And this is hardly the place to start a fire to make one."

"All we need is this," said Denatheen, pulling out a small ceramic jar that was hidden somewhere in his Elven cloak. Removing the loose fitting lid, he released a wisp of smoke into the air while one of his comrades wrapped a strip of cloth around the steel bodkin tipping an arrow.

"What is it?" asked Rose, fanning the pungent fumes from the air.

"Dried horse dung."

"*Horse dung?* What is it with you and pooh?" grumbled Rose, as she frowned in disgust.

"Unlike dragon dung, horse excrement is more grass than anything else. When dried, it is perfect to keep an ember smoldering until it can be fed with tinder and re-ignited into a full flame worthy of a campfire."

"But there is no tinder," argued the Princess. "Everything up here is wet or covered with snow."

"That is why we will use this," said Denatheen, pulling a small vial from the folds of his cloak.

"What else are you hiding in there? Your manservant?" questioned Rose; amazed by what this Elf kept concealed on his person.

"If need be, but at this moment, Halen leads a battalion to the west and I usually carry only what we need to survive on such a quest," replied Denatheen, uncapping the vial. "We will soak the rag wrapped around the arrow's bodkin with this highly flammable liquid. All it will take is a single ember to set the oil ablaze and keep it burning as the arrow takes to the sky for all to see."

"Oh my, you have a solution for everything," muttered Rose, annoyed but amazed at the same time, as she watched the Elf set the glowing ember to the oil-soaked cloth.

"I try my best," responded the Elf.

The orange spark jumped to life. In a *'whoosh'*, it engulfed the arrow in flames. Denatheen calmly launched the projectile skyward, a trail of amber light blazing behind it as the arrow streaked to the heavens.

"So, Princess, do you still wish to stay here, alone; to warn us should the dragon appear?" asked the Elf, as he prepared to secure the rope around one of his comrades.

"Come to think of it, it is my duty to help my friends through the quest," decided Rose, dreading a confrontation with the beast should it appear while she was here, on her own.

"A wise decision, Princess Rose," praised Denatheen, as he proceeded to wrap the tether around her waist. "And remember –"

"Yes, yes! I know. Lean back. Do not look down. Do not wind this rope around my hands, and so on and so forth."

"It seems trivial to you, but I do not want to be held responsible if your carelessness gets you killed, Princess."

"I will heed your advice," conceded Rose, giving the knot one final tug to make sure it was properly secured.

"Just pretend you are walking backwards on a vertical floor," suggested Denatheen, attempting to downplay the danger. "And whatever happens, *do not* panic. We will keep you safe."

"Do not panic," repeated Rose. These words were rote as she steeled her nerves for this task.

"Understand?"

She merely nodded at the Elf as she inched closer to the edge of the cliff.

"Remember, three tugs on this rope once you are safely delivered, and then we shall retrieve the line to begin our descent."

Leaning back against her tether, Rose eased herself over the ledge, her feet shuffling along as she made her way. Gradually lowered down, the Elves eventually disappeared from her sight.

Turning back was no longer an option.

Rose kept her gaze fixed straight ahead, not wishing to see what was below or how far she had come down thus far.

"Keep walking. Just keep walking," Rose whispered under her breath as she ventured down, praying for no missteps.

Rose gasped as a tremor rippled through the cliff wall. It vibrated through her feet to strike a chord in her frightened heart.

Glancing up, she saw nothing untoward, only the odd stone and bits of earth coming loose from where the rope bit into the edge of the cliff as the Elves lowered her down.

Again, the cliff wall trembled beneath Rose's feet. It was enough to shake loose the rocks and pebbles above, showering her with debris. Instinctively, she ducked her head to shield her eyes. Rose gasped in surprise. She spied shadows moving against the darkness cast by this cliff. Unhampered by the steepness of this sheer wall, these strange figures scrambled toward her.

Rose screamed in fright as her eyes focused on not one, but seven dragons racing in for the kill. Though smaller than the mace-tailed dragon she had first encountered, these ones were leaner, meaner and desperately hungry for an easy meal.

They were unlike any dragon species known to exist, at least in her mind and limited knowledge. Instead of wings, a membrane of skin stretched from wrist to ankle. These dragons were designed for gliding, not for true flight. Webbing between the toes, as well as a flattened head and body helped to capture and distribute air over a wide surface to slow these creatures' descent should they be forced to leap from great heights.

Each toe was armed with a stout, curved claw. The pads of their toes were covered with tiny barbules that allowed these creatures to cling to vertical surfaces so they could climb with relative ease. The only thing that slowed their ascent was their nasty, belligerent behaviour as they snapped and clawed at each other in their race to feed first.

"Don't panic! Don't panic!" squealed Rose, holding onto her tether with one hand as she used the other to arm herself with the longbow she had thrown over her shoulder for the climb down.

Frantically tugging on the rope, instead of pulling the Princess up and away from the danger rushing toward her, the Elves continued to lower her down, oblivious to the menacing peril coming her way. With the sounds of splashing water and the wind racing up the cliff wall, her screams were effectively drowned out.

Realizing help was not forthcoming; Rose did the only thing she could. Taking the longbow firmly into her hand, she was prepared to prod, poke and beat off any dragon coming within biting distance to her.

Her eyes opened wide in terror as these threatening shadows climbed and clawed their way ever closer. The light of the moon reflected against the orbs of their red eyes that shone with ravenous hunger. Their snarls and growls became louder, as did the gnashing of their teeth.

"*No! Stay away!*" screamed Rose, the tip of the longbow lashing out to smack the closest dragon on its sensitive snout.

The panic rose in her heart, filling her with utter fear. She now knew how a trapped fox must feel like when a pack of hounds close in for the kill. As one dragon backed down, another bold lizard lunged, snapping at her feet as she dangled helplessly, dropping ever closer into this frenzied mob.

Rose screamed as one of the lizards scrambled over top of the others. Clamping its mouth onto the rope just inches above her head, the creature's teeth grabbed hold. Twisting its head about, it attempted to gnaw through the tether.

"What the?" gasped Denatheen, as he and his men lurched forward, pulled by a powerful yank on the rope. "What was that?"

Knowing it was not the three-tug signal they agreed on to relay a message the Princess had found safe footing with the others, the Elf acting as the anchor quickly tied the end of the rope to the rocky outcrop before joining his comrades at the edge of the cliff.

"Quickly! Arm your bows!" ordered Denatheen. He leaned over to take aim at the dragon sawing through the rope as Rose desperately fought to beat off the other creatures.

Through the rushing, opaque waters, Tag, Cankles and the Elf could see a blur of frenetic movement as the Princess wildly thrashed about while the dragons skittered along the cliff wall. All seven jockeyed for position, attempting to snap at her while trying to avoid contact with the icy waters.

"She's in trouble!" gasped Tag.

"Bloody hell!" cried Cankles, staring through the waterfall. "They'll kill her!"

Without a rope at their disposal, yanking his cloak free of its clasp, Tag shouted at Cankles and the Elf, "Take this! Hold on!"

As they gripped one end, Tag grabbed the other. Holding his breath, he leaned out over the ledge to appear through the waterfall.

"Look out!" hollered Rose.

Tag ducked as the tip of her longbow swung about, narrowly missing him to strike a dragon in its eye just as it was about to seize him by the head.

"Take my hand," ordered Tag, straining to grab her by the skirt of her frock to bring her within his reach.

Just as she stretched out, Tag pulled away. His balled fist struck one of the dragons on its snout as it made a lunge for his hand. Soaked with water, the cloak seemed to stretch as he leaned out while the others held on. Each time their hands almost touched, the dragon gnawing at the rope sent Rose spinning out of his reach.

Tag leaned out, standing on the very lip of the crumbling ledge, frantically struggling to grab her.

He gasped as Rose screamed. The frayed rope snapped under her weight. As she fell from his grasp, Tag went down, his body slipping back through the waterfall to slam hard against the ledge. He fought to hold on as Cankles and the Elf pulled him to safety.

"I lost her!" cried Tag. "She's gone."

17
A Meeting of Great Mimes

The wind rushed around her, stealing away Rose's terrified screams as she plummeted to her death. Twisting through the air, she clawed at it, as though she'd chance upon an invisible hold; anything to stop this fall.

Above her, the dragon that had sawed through the rope pushed off against the cliff. The membrane of skin between each wrist and ankle was spread wide as the creature glided down in pursuit, hoping to feast before the others could join in. By raising and angling the crest of spines along its back and the connecting skin in between, like a sail on a ship the lizard maneuvered about, following its prey. Just as it headed straight for her, a blur of a shadow dove down through the night sky. The dragon bellowed in pain as a pair of sharp talons ripped through its dorsal spines, tearing into its back to send it spiralling in an uncontrolled freefall.

Rose screamed, watching as the wounded dragon plunged downward. Frantically, she struggled to swim through the air so the creature would not come crashing down upon her. In her panicking mind she thought by some miracle, if she survived impacting the ground, the irony of being squashed to death by this falling dragon was just too much.

Just as she twisted about, seeing the earth below rushing toward her at a frightening speed, Rose squeezed her eyes shut. Fleeting images of her young life flashed through her mind. Just as the turbulent air swirled around her, Rose's senses were jarred as she landed hard, but it was not upon the unforgiving earth. The night air rushing around her suddenly felt like a gentle breeze blowing against her face. Freed from the terrifying pull of gravity, she sensed she was now travelling upward, feeling the undulating movement of powerful muscles working to thrust a pair of wings skyward. Beneath her hands, Rose could feel a thick hide of tough scales.

She gasped, opening her eyes as her ride suddenly banked, veering away from a boulder jutting from the cliff wall. Rose's scream of fright snagged in the back of her throat upon realizing she had landed between the wings of a mace-tailed dragon – her dragon!

"Oh, no!" hollered Tag, hearing the scraping of sharp claws scrambling up the cliff. "Those bloody creatures are on the move!"

"They are after my friends!" cried the Elf. Grasping Cankles' hand, he leaned out beyond the waterfall. He spied upon the six remaining creatures racing up the cliff like giant geckos on the hunt for food.

Cankles pulled the Elf back through the pummelling waters.

"The rope!" shouted Tag. "We can use the rope to climb back up to help them."

"It is not there," responded the Elf. "And even if we did, we would not get to them in time. Those creatures move swiftly, unlike any dragon I have ever seen."

"What do we do?" asked Cankles, his eyes wide in horror as a silhouette of an Elf came and went, passing by the curtain of water. His frightened scream echoed behind him as he plunged to his death.

"There is nothing we can do," said the Elf, speaking with utmost certainty. "Not now. We are trapped."

"Why, oh why, did I not take the time or have the smarts to remember all your names?" lamented Cankles, his hands smacking his forehead in frustration. "This never would've happened if I had, and now they are all doomed because of me!"

"Steady on, Ayden. I have lost one friend. I do not intend to lose another," stated Denatheen, dropping the end of the rope to draw his sword as the dragons breached the top of the cliff.

With nowhere to run, he gave his orders as the dragons encircled them, "Stand your ground, Ayden! Back to back, there is a chance we can keep them at bay, if not outright kill them."

"Yes, sir!" answered Ayden, as he, too, dropped his bow to take up his sword.

"Their scales are hard; not even our arrows can penetrate them," warned Denatheen, as he watched the dorsal spines and connecting membrane along the creatures' backs rise like sails as a similar frill around the head flared out to make these lizards appear much larger and more imposing.

"What are we to do?"

"Strike their eyes! Blind them!" ordered Denatheen. "If one should open its mouth, ram your blade into it. Pierce the roof of its maw to stab its brain."

Like a pack of starving wolves closing in for the kill, the dragons attacked. The Elves battled back, desperately slashing, hacking and stabbing with their swords as the ravenous creatures snapped and snarled, lunging at their intended prey.

Outnumbered and overwhelmed, the Elves waged a brave battle, fighting back with every ounce of strength that remained.

Ayden cried out in pain as his forearm snagged against a dragon's fang as it fell over dead. His blade pierced through the roof of its mouth to stab at its small brain, but he was unable to retract his arm in time. The tip of the dragon's tooth tore through raiment, slicing into skin and flesh.

As the smell of the Elf's blood permeated the air, the five remaining dragons suddenly stopped their attack. Forked tongues flickered, tasting these tantalizing particles wafting about. All fiery red eyes stared in Ayden's direction as the Elf gulped, "Oh, no…"

"To a glorious death, my friend!" bellowed Denatheen, as he brandished his sword. "We shall meet it covered in blood to mark this battle!"

"A little late for me," whispered Ayden, clutching his bloodied arm against his chest.

Before Denatheen could shout a defiant, *come and get me*, the dragons, now in a frenzy driven by bloodlust, attacked without mercy.

Denatheen fell against Ayden, landing hard over top of him as the biggest of the dragons stomped down, a scaly foot pressing on the Elf's chest. Just as the creature moved in to snap down on his head, Denatheen roared at the top of his lungs into the dragon's face.

All five reptiles froze in their tracks. Hissing, they backed away from the Elves, retreating to the edge of the cliff.

Denatheen pulled his comrade onto his feet as he hoisted his sword once more. Shaking his weapon at the cowering dragons, he shouted in triumph, "Be gone all of you, for this is not the night we die!"

"Thank goodness it is over," sighed Ayden, relieved for this sudden turn of good luck as one by one, each dragon pitched its body over the edge, gliding off into the night to become one with the darkness.

"Indeed!" said Denatheen, stooping to reclaim his friend's sword from the ground.

Picking up the weapon, the reflection of the moon shining in a puddle of melting snow quivered, rippling only to glow smoothly upon the glass-like surface. Suddenly, the moon's reflection distorted again, wavering like a pebble had been tossed to break the calm surface of a pond.

Then he felt it.

Beneath his bended knee Denatheen felt the tremors rising through the ground as something of gargantuan size hammered the earth. Just as Ayden pulled on his shoulder, the Elf glanced up. His eyes filled with horror as a dragon, the monster they knew resided here, but had yet to bear witness to, suddenly appeared before them.

"RUN!" hollered Denatheen.

The Elves sprinted with all their might as a fiery ball of heat and flames gushed from the dragon's mouth. As though sharing the same thought, Ayden and Denatheen seized the frayed end of the rope. Holding on for dear life, they dove over the edge of the cliff, plunging into the dark abyss.

"Are you sure this is the way?" whispered Cankles, as he tiptoed behind the Elf.

"It is the *only* way."

"Perhaps we should wait for the others?" suggested Cankles, glancing over his shoulder at Tag, as he took up the rear.

"There is no point in doing that," responded Tag.

"Why not?"

"We have no way of knowing if Denatheen launched a flaming arrow to announce our find to the others," explained the Elf.

"But if he did, perhaps help is on the way," said Cankles. "There is a possibility they are comin' to our aid, even as we speak."

"Our friend is right, Cankles. It is best we continue on," urged Tag. He gathered his courage, stifling his emotions as he wiped away the tears mingling with the water dripping from his hair. "We are trapped. We have no choice but to go on from here."

"Well, if that be the case, then what is your name, Master Elf?" questioned Cankles.

"Pardon me?" The Elf stopped in his tracks to address the mortal.

"Your name… What is it? If I wish to prevent you from meetin' the same end as your nameless friends, I will go no further until I know your name and learn it well."

"If you must know, it is Roen-Aldus Riverstone."

"Ronald-us Riverston?"

"No, Roen-Al-dus Ri-ver-*stone*," enunciated the Elf.

"Roan-Albus?"

"Almost, but not quite."

"Can I just call you Ron?" asked Cankles. "Take no offense, but it's much easier on my ol' mind, if you get my drift?"

"Ron will do. Now quickly, there is no telling how far we must travel to find the Sorcerer."

As they followed the Elf through the gloom toward the unsteady light of the torches burning farther down the tunnel, an uneasy feeling gripped Tag's heart. He listened above the echoes of their footsteps and the pounding of his heart, straining to hear over the sounds of the water cascading down at the mouth of this tunnel. It was at this very moment he swore he heard something odd.

"Tag... Where are you?" This whisper of a voice, barely audible, echoed behind him.

"Did you hear that?" asked Tag, cupping a hand to his ear. "It sounded like the Princess."

"What are you speaking of?" asked Roen. "You said she fell to her death."

"I know what I saw. There's no way anyone can survive a fall like that, but I swear on my life, I heard her calling to me," responded Tag, glancing nervously over his shoulder into the darkness.

"It could be nothing more than your conscience," suggested Roen, thinking Tag was traumatized by the events of this night. "Perhaps guilt is playing havoc with your mind."

"I feel absolutely terrible about what happened, but I don't feel guilty," denied Tag.

"Princess Rose did swear that she'd come after us if she died," reminded Cankles, gulping to force down the lump catching in the back of his throat. "Maybe she's calling to us from the great *you-know-where.*"

"I tried to save her. I really did," insisted Tag. He pushed against the rising tide of guilt filling his heart; that gnawing sensation in the back of his mind that if he had only been a bit faster; if he had only been able to stretch out a little further; she would be here now.

"It was probably nothing more than the echoing of our own voices," dismissed Roen.

"Or the echo of a ghost callin' to us," whispered Cankles, his eyes growing wide with fear.

"Oh hush! It's not a ghost," scolded Tag, dismissing these words. "I was probably just hearing things."

"Like a *ghost*," whispered Cankles.

Tag scowled at his friend, motioning him to follow Roen.

As they ventured on, the flames of the torches lining the way twisted about, at the mercy of the draft rushing through the tunnel.

"Tag... Cankles... Where are you?" The same whisper of a voice chased them through the tunnel.

Tag froze, as did the others as a chill ran through their veins.

"Bloody hell!" whispered Cankles. "I've lost more of my mind than I thought possible. I heard the Princess, too."

"Did I not tell you so?" said Tag, motioning Cankles not to panic as he tried to make sense of this.

"I do not believe in ghosts," stated the Elf, speaking with conviction.

"It could be nothing more than echoes from the past," reasoned Tag. "Perhaps it is merely her voice, that final scream, resonating through these chambers and coming back to us."

"Or it's her ghost comin' back to haunt us," gulped Cankles, his eyes nervously darting about for signs of the paranormal.

"Hush!" ordered Roen, motioning for the mortals to cease their chatter. "I hear something coming."

"Where?" asked Tag, drawing his sword from its scabbard.

"Behind you," whispered the Elf, nocking an arrow onto his bow as his keen eyes stared, piercing through the shadows.

All three listened, straining to hear above the sounds of the distant waterfall and their madly beating hearts.

The Elf pressed a finger to his lips, motioning for silence, and then he pointed down the tunnel they had just come from as he whispered, "Something comes our way."

Pressing his back to the wall of the tunnel, Tag hid in the shadows, sword poised in his hands as Cankles scampered behind the Elf, taking cover from potential danger.

The sounds of loose rocks and pebbles crunching underfoot echoed through the tunnel.

The Elf raised his bow, the arrow aiming into the darkness, waiting for the most opportune moment to let the deadly projectile fly.

Tag's breath snagged in the back of his throat. His eyes stared ahead, narrowing as they focused on a shadow moving within the shadows.

"Ready?" whispered the Elf, drawing back on his bow.

Tag nodded, gripping his sword, but holding it close to his body so the light from the torch would not shine off the silver blade to give away their position.

"Aim..." whispered Roen.

"You dolts!" A hostile voice sounded through the tunnel. "How dare you abandon me?"

"Princess?" gasped Tag, lowering his sword. "Is that you?"

"Who do you think it is? The Sorcerer?" grumbled the agitated voice as a shadowy figure moved closer.

"Should I shoot?" asked the Elf, bow still at the ready.

"Not just yet, I recognize that cynical tone," stated Tag, sheathing his sword. "It's Princess Rose."

"Princess?" gasped Cankles. He rushed past Tag and the Elf to greet her, scooping her up in his arms to hug her. "Oh, joy! Thank goodness! You're alive."

"Of course I am, no thanks to you and Tag!"

Just as Tag was about to hug her in relief and greeting; Rose's fist angrily punched his arm.

"Hey... what was that for?" Tag rubbed the smarting point of impact. "Why do you keep hitting me?"

"You deserved it!"

"But I didn't do anything," argued Tag.

"Tell me about it!" snapped the Princess, shaking off the pain in her throbbing hand.

"Are you blaming me for what happened to you?" gasped Tag, his eyes rolling in frustration. "It's not as though I called on those dragons to attack you."

"You might as well have rung the dinner bell; letting me fall and all!"

"I tried to save you!"

"Try harder next time!" grunted Rose.

"Hey, how did you get here?" asked Cankles, stepping between Tag and Rose. "You fell. We thought we had lost you forever."

"Indeed I fell, but my salvation came in the form of a dragon; a mace-tailed dragon to be exact. Swooping in from the sky, I landed on its back. The creature saved me, delivering me to the mouth of this tunnel."

"Incredible," gasped Cankles. "I suppose the dragon was repaying a debt when you spared it from the Elves' arrows."

"Or perhaps the beast wants revenge, knowing that the Sorcerer stole her egg and you were the one to return it," offered Tag.

"No... I believe the creature knew I was royalty and that my life is of great value."

"How is that even possible?" rebuked Tag.

"Why not? I thought it was pretty impossible to survive the fall, but here I am now." Her shoulders rolled in a shrug of indifference, dismissing his doubtful tone.

"She does have a point, young master," said Cankles, nodding in agreement.

"Whatever the case, let us be grateful that some of us survived and pray for those who lost their lives on this night," whispered the Elf. "Now, we must move on."

"Quite correct, Ron," agreed Cankles, motioning him to lead the way.

"Ron?" repeated the Princess, glancing over at the Elf whom merely shrugged in response.

"It's a long story, but his name is actually Roen-Aldus," explained Tag, motioning for her to proceed.

"Ron, it is," responded Rose, knowing she'd have as much luck in remembering how to pronounce this Elven name as Cankles would.

"Keep up," ordered Tag, waving her on to follow the others.

"Where are we going?" whispered Rose.

"We believe this is the Sorcerer's Lair," explained Tag. "We're going to hunt that fiend down."

Glancing about their gloomy surroundings, Rose said, "By the style of the décor gracing this hole in the ground, it must be Dragonite's hideaway."

"There is no décor to speak of; only rocks, cobwebs, dust and torches," responded Tag.

"Exactly! It screams of that demented soul," declared the Princess, wrinkling her nose in disgust.

"Hush! Keep your voices down," whispered Roen. "We have no way of knowing if the Sorcerer or his minions are skulking about near to us."

Making their way down the tunnel, Roen led the way with the flames of the torch lighting the path before them.

The mortals lifted their feet, gingerly setting them down to minimize the amount of noise they made to emulate the Elf's silent footfalls. The only sound was the loud, incessant dripping of water echoing through this tunnel.

Rose then muffled a scream, her hand slapping over her mouth so only a small squeak squeezed out between her fingers.

"Bloody hell, Princess!" Tag scolded her in a hushed tone. "What's wrong now?"

"S-something crawled over m-my foot," she whispered, her voice quivering in fear.

Roen held the torch toward the Princess. Its light revealed a small rat sniffing the toe of her shoe. Rose's eyes widened in horror as her hands flew up to her mouth once again to stifle more screams.

Tag merely shooed away the rat. Grabbing Rose by the arm, he guided the hyperventilating Princess down the tunnel.

"Filthy beast!" cursed Rose, shaking a fist at the rodent as it scampered off.

"Stop with the dramatics, will you?" ordered Tag. "It was just a harmless, little rat."

"I know, but how dare it touch me? I am a princess! Something as lowly as that vermin should not even look at me with those beady little eyes," commented Rose. Inhaling long and slow, her breathing returned to normal.

"It was just a rat, m'lady. It's not like it could kill you," reasoned Cankles.

"It could have scared me to death," insisted Rose.

"You've encountered a mace-tailed dragon; eluded those giant cliff-crawling lizards and even survived a great fall, but it's a wee rat that's capable of scaring you to death?" grunted Tag, rolling his eyes in frustration. "You *are* an odd one!"

"I am not odd," argued Rose. "I am complicated; obviously, much too complex for you to understand."

"We should just keep movin' on," urged Cankles. Hoping to nip this argument in the bud, he motioned for Tag and Rose to follow the Elf.

Their journey came to a sudden stop. Before them, the passage branched off into three tunnels.

The Elf continued on, not even taking the time to deliberate on which path to proceed on.

"How do we know if we are going in the right direction?" asked Rose, her voice in a whisper.

"No light. No light. Light," answered Tag, pointing to the two dark tunnels, and then to the torches burning along the length of the tunnel they ventured down.

"Oh… I suppose that makes sense," decided the Princess, following close behind Cankles as Tag took up the rear.

"Of course it does, and we shall carry on until we find the Sorcerer or the dreamstone, whichever comes first," explained Tag.

"At least it is not as cold and damp in here," decided Rose, using her longbow as a walking stick as she journeyed on.

"Let's just hope it does not keep gettin' warmer," said Cankles.

"Why? I prefer toasty warm any day over cold and damp," responded the Princess.

"Cause if it keeps gettin' hotter, it can only mean we're headin' straight into the bowels of Hell," explained Cankles, dreading the possibilities as he followed behind the Elf.

Roen removed another torch from its wall mount as he discarded the old one and its dwindling flames. Raising it forth to light the way, the Elf stared down the length of the tunnel that dissolved into a stifling blackness.

"I am *not* liking this," whispered Rose, pulling a tangled cobweb from her hair, "not in the least."

"None of us do," responded Tag, his tone hushed. "But we must forge on."

Roen suddenly stopped, holding the torch before him.

Cankles gasped as the flames of the torch swelled, its light glowing steadily, only to be lost in the light cast by molten pools of lava sputtering and roiling on the floor of a massive chamber.

"Welcome to Hell," announced the Elf, as he glanced about.

"No wonder it's gettin' hotter," noted Cankles, his worried eyes taking in the fiery, oozing magma that churned up from the earth.

"Do we continue on?" asked Rose.

"I see an exit from this chamber," said Roen, pointing with the torch across to the opposite wall of this large cave.

As they crept forward, using stealth so their footfalls would not echo to betray their presence, the Elf and the mortals in his company stopped in their tracks. They were overcome the by strangest sensation; not so much threatening as it was annoying.

Roen's hand slipped down, unsheathing his sword as he whispered to his comrades, "We are being followed."

Tag quickly and silently drew his weapon. He nodded in understanding to the Elf as Rose discreetly nocked an arrow onto her bow.

"Ready?" whispered Roen.

His comrades nodded in response.

"Now!"

They spun about to confront the Sorcerer. Instead, standing just paces behind them, four mimes had been following their every step, mimicking their every move.

The tallest, thinnest mime even mouthed the word *'now'* as he assumed the same defensive posture as Roen.

"Oh my!" gasped Cankles, watching in fascination as another mime copied his every move, even releasing his club when Cankles fumbled, nervously dropping his dagger.

"Mimes!" muttered Rose. This word curdled with malice as she glared at the four men. "I *hate* mimes!"

"Be gone!" snarled Tag, his sword poised in his hands as he took a threatening step toward them.

Instead of running, the one mimicking Tag's every move stepped forward, too. His face adopted the same angry scowl as he held his staff like a sword.

"It is like looking into a bizarre mirror of sorts," noted Cankles, watching his mime double tossing back the hair falling into his eyes just as he did.

"I am insulted! That mime looks nothing like me," grumbled Rose, her arrow aching to be unleashed.

The mime standing across from her held his staff before him as though he, too, had an arrow ready to unleash. He even batted his eyelashes at Rose as he mouthed the words she spoke.

"In my kingdom, death is the punishment exacted on those considered a public nuisance," sniffed Rose. "And you are annoying me to no end!"

"What now?" asked Roen, his sword still poised to attack. "I feel a bit odd about taking them on. There is a moral dilemma to contend with, being that they are performers, not true soldiers."

"They are *poor* performers; this alone is reason enough to do away with them," responded Rose.

"We certainly can't let them just walk away," decided Tag. "They'll probably head straight to the Sorcerer and warn him of our coming."

"We cannot have that," agreed Roen.

"But we cannot simply kill them! That would be like… murder," argued Cankles.

"Oh, but it is fine for *them* to kill *us*?" questioned Rose, her arrow still poised at the man standing across from her, mimicking her every move, right down to the trembling of her hands and the nervous twitching of her brows.

"As a matter of principle, we have swords and a bow, those four have… sticks," reasoned Cankles.

"Sticks?" snapped Rose, her voice quivering with agitation. "Harmless enough until it pokes you in the eye!"

"A poke in the eye won't kill you, but a sword most certainly can," said Tag, lowering his weapon as the thought of fighting an opponent so unevenly matched lost its appeal. "There will be no honour in such an undertaking."

"I agree with that, but much is at stake here," reminded Roen. "We cannot chance them returning to Dragonite with news that we are on his trail and closing in."

"So, *you* will do away with them?" asked Rose, looking to the Elf and Tag for a resolution.

"What do you mean by that?" asked Tag, as he stared at her armed bow. "You're the one who looks ready for action."

"It is for show, to keep those miscreants at bay," explained the Princess. "It is *your* job to do the killing."

"Not like this," grumbled Tag, watching as the man copying his every move wagged a condescending finger in the face of the mime pretending to be the Princess, just as he did to her.

"If they are doing nothing more than mimicking our every move, why not let them do so," said Cankles. "No harm done."

"Yes, let them follow us so if that dragon should show its ugly face, we can feed those idiot mimes to the beast to keep it distracted," offered Rose, her tone cynical.

"There's a plan!" said Tag.

"Really?" gasped Rose.

"No!" snapped Tag, his eyes rolling in frustration twice over as his mime double did the same.

"A word in private," suggested the Elf, motioning for the mortals to come together for a discussion.

Rose watched through narrowed, suspicious eyes as the four mimes huddled together, pretending they were having a private conversation, too.

"Oh, look!" said Cankles, watching their foes in action. "A meetin' of great mimes! Get it? Great mimes, instead of minds."

"We get it, we just don't know what to do with it," grunted Tag, giving his head a dismal shake.

"Yes, and I may have to reconsider your appointment as court jester," responded Rose. "That was not funny at all."

"Never mind, it's just the pressure of this whole quest catchin' up on me," said Cankles, wanting nothing more than to change the subject now that his position was in jeopardy. "So, what say you, Ron?"

"I say we take them on."

"To what extent?" asked Tag.

"Yes, I want to know, too, as I refuse to touch any one of them," added Rose, her pert nose wrinkling in disgust.

"We use only enough force to capture and contain them," explained Roen. "How is that?"

"No mime killing?" ascertained Cankles.

"No killing of mimes, whether they perform poorly, or not," confirmed the Elf.

"Unless they ask for it," insisted Rose.

"I'm good with this," agreed Tag, speaking in a whisper. "I will use my sword to incapacitate, than to kill."

"Hold on here," said Rose. "We are outnumbered."

"Outnumbered?" grunted Tag, frowning in confusion. "There are four of them and four of us."

"I'm no genius, but that sounds like we're pretty evenly matched, Princess," decided Cankles, holding up four fingers on each hand.

"Are you both dolts? I am a damsel, one of whom will most certainly be in distress, if made to manhandle one of those mimes. Surely, you do not expect me to wrestle one of those idiots into submission?"

"Might be entertainin' to watch," said Cankles, thinking on the thrill of the Princess brawling with one of these performers.

"Not in my world," grumbled Rose. "I tell you what though. I will permit *you* to wrestle my mime for me, and I shall stand by, longbow at the ready should things get out of hand."

"How hard could it be?" said Tag. "After all, it's not as though we can't anticipate what they're next move will be when they seem to copy everything we do."

"I think we should exploit that," suggested Roen.

"Good idea," praised Tag, nodding in approval. "Ready, my friends?"

"Never am, but no matter," answered Cankles.

They leapt into action, turning on the mimes.

Taken by surprise, their unlikely foes quickly hopped into place, mimicking Rose and her comrades as they made their stand.

"Now!" hollered Tag, racing toward the mime brandishing a staff like it, too, was a sword.

As Roen and Cankles confronted their opponents, Rose was faced with the mime standing before her, staff poised in his hands as he mimicked the Princess aiming an arrow.

Instead of clashing like the others, these two merely circled around each other. Though Rose had the clear advantage, armed with a genuine longbow and arrow, her mime brazenly copied her every move with his pretend weapon.

"Stop it! Stop or I shall unleash my wrath upon you!" promised Rose, drawing back on her arrow. "Then you will be sorry!"

In mimely fashion, her opponent mouthed her every word, adopting the identical stance.

"I swear I am an excellent aim! I will skewer your heart upon this arrow if you do not surrender," insisted Rose, stepping back as her foe suddenly broke with protocol, stepping toward her.

The situation turned ugly. Sensing she was not actually intent on using her weapon, the mime lunged forward, batting the nocked arrow from her fingertips as he grabbed the longbow by the stave.

"Hey! Let go! You were supposed to mimic my every move!"

snapped Rose, seizing the bow by its sinewy string to prevent the mime from using this weapon against her.

He dug his heels in, refusing to let go while the Princess held on, pulling with all her might.

Rose winced in pain as the string felt as though it would cut clean through her fingers with the growing tension. With no choice, she released her hold. Before the mime even realized what happened, the bow snapped to life. The wooden stave struck him smack-dab on his forehead to render him unconscious as Rose scrambled onto her feet.

"Serves you right!" grunted Rose, snatching up her bow as she kicked dirt at the mime's leg.

As Roen and Tag battled their foes sword against staff, Cankles was waging a losing battle against his club-wielding opponent. It was only in hindsight did he wish he had not sheathed his dagger in an effort to fight fairly. Now, with the mime on his back, clinging to him like a rabid, oversized monkey, Cankles could do nothing more than spin in circles, trying to throw his enemy off.

The spinning, aside from making them both dizzy, prevented the mime from using the club with any real power as he struggled to hold on.

Cankles stumbled, tripping over his feet. Both hit the ground, their minds numbed by the dizzying revolutions, but the mime still clung to Cankles. Raising his club to smash in the back of Cankles' head, the first blow missed as the mime's vision continued to blur, reel and spin as he attempted to focus.

Raising his club to strike again, this time, the mime knew he would not miss, adjusting his aim just so.

"Do not make me do this!" growled Rose; the steel bodkin of her arrow pricked the skin on the mime's neck. "Get off! Stand down!"

The mime dropped his club in surrender. Sliding off Cankles' back, he staggered onto his unsteady feet, swaying to and fro before the Princess.

"Do not move!" ordered Rose.

Instead of listening, the mime proceeded to back away. Before he could escape in a full out sprint, Tag hollered: "Shoot him, Princess! Don't let him get away!"

In an absolute panic, the arrow flew from Rose's bow. Rather than flying straight and true to pierce the mime's heart, the projectile arced up. As it came down, the bodkin punctured through skin and flesh, forcing its way between bones before biting into the dirt.

For a lingering moment, the mime stood in stunned disbelief, staring at the arrow pinning his left foot to the ground. It was not until the blood seeped through that he responded.

Rather than opening his mouth to unleash one of those mimely, silent screams she expected, every word of profanity imaginable, real or made up poured from the mime's mouth. They spewed forth, almost indiscernible, as the man screamed and swore simultaneously.

As Tag's sword sliced through his foe's staff so now all that remained was in the mime's grip, he shouted at Rose.

"Shut him up! Before he let's the whole world know we're here," ordered Tag, ducking as the mime threw what was left of his staff at him.

Just as Rose nocked another arrow onto her bow, Cankles dashed up to the mime, cracking him on the head with his own club as he muttered, "We've heard an earful from you! Now, hush!"

The wounded mime crumpled to the cave floor, joining Rose's first victim in an unnatural sleep.

The keen edge of Roen's sword bit into the last, dwindling section of his mime's staff as the desperate man hurled it at the Elf, turning to flee with Tag's embattled foe.

As they dashed off, Roen merely flicked his wrist forward, the force and momentum was enough to send the section of staff sticking to his blade to fly forward, clipping the mime on the back of his legs.

Stumbling from the impact, the mime tripped, falling against his comrade. Both tumbled head-over-heels, coming to a skidding stop at the edge of a bubbling pool of lava.

"Hurry!" shouted Tag. "They must not get away!"

As he and Roen took after them, Rose hollered as she pointed to the unconscious mimes, "What about these two?"

"Leave them!" ordered Tag, waving to her and Cankles to follow. "They won't be going anywhere anytime soon!"

In a mad scramble, the mimes leapt up onto their feet, dashing to the opening Roen had pointed out earlier.

"Hey, what happened to your precise aim?" wondered Tag, as he sprinted after the mimes.

"I was precise. The arrow went exactly where I wanted it to go," hollered Rose, struggling to keep up with him.

"You were aiming for his foot?" gasped Tag, shooting a confused glance over his shoulder at the Princess.

"Of course! Fighting is all very new to me. For now, I prefer to make maiming my business, than to outright kill for the time being."

"I suggest using that bow as it was intended to be used," said Tag. "You may not be so lucky the next time."

"Enough chatter! Quickly, now!" said Roen, as he charged past Tag in pursuit of the mimes. Racing through the dark tunnel, the Elf's eyes could see the mimes ducking into a huge chamber that was aglow in red from molten lava. He watched as the mimes' dash became a series of hop, skips and jumps. As Roen raced into the chamber, he came to a sudden stop, teetering on the edge of an abyss. Earth and rocks crumbled beneath his feet as the ground beneath him dissolved, falling away into a great chasm. Below, a river of lava churned, roiling and bubbling, waiting to incinerate anything that falls in.

"Phew!" gasped Roen.

Relieved he had stopped in time, the Elf regained his balance, only to scream in fright. Cankles ploughed into him, bouncing off Roen to fall against Tag and Rose as they raced into the chamber.

"Nooo!" cried Cankles, watching as Roen fell, disappearing from his sight as his scream of fright echoed through the chamber.

"Oh, no!" gasped Tag, pulling back on his friend to keep him from going over, too.

"If I only learned to say his name properly," lamented Cankles. "He might be alive now."

"He is alive!" said Rose, daring to peer over the edge.

There stood the Elf, balanced on a narrow ledge some twenty feet below.

"Ron! You live!" gasped Cankles, clambering to the edge to gaze down upon the Elf. "Thank goodness for that!"

"Thank goodness, indeed!" agreed Roen.

"We'll get you out!" promised Tag. "We'll find a way."

"I will be fine for now. Go on! After those two before they warn the Sorcerer!" ordered Roen, waving them on.

"We cannot just leave you down there," argued Rose.

"Come back for me later," urged Roen. "I will be fine for now. Go, before it is too late!"

Tag watched as the mimes made their way across the chasm, hopping from a series of pillars rising from the river of lava below. Like a series of cobblestones, the flattened tops of these formations created a natural land bridge to the other side.

"Come with me!" ordered Tag, motioning for Cankles and Rose to follow.

They froze, watching in horror as the mime leading the way cried out. In his mad dash, he realized too late he had leapt onto the top of the wrong pillar. By some dark magic, a stalactite situated directly overhead came crashing down, crushing the mime and demolishing the column he stood on.

Man and debris were quickly swallowed up by the churning lava below.

"Hurry!" shouted Tag, watching as the remaining mime neared the other side of the chasm.

Balanced on one of the smallest pillars, the mime turned about, thumbing his nose at his foes as his tongue protruded from his mouth in a derisive display. Leaping on the largest column nearest to him, the mime mouthed the words: *Bugger!*

In an instant, another stalactite came crashing down. The man was dead before his body hit the molten lava, vanishing with the debris from the fallen stalactite and the demolished pillar.

"Come on," urged Tag, inching toward the ledge where the first in a series of columns protruded from the lava.

"You cannot be serious!" gasped Rose, her eyes wide in terror.

"This can end badly for us," gulped Cankles, trembling in fear as he watched the dead body burst into flames before sinking from view.

"It can be done! Look how far those mimes got," said Tag.

"Yes, before they both *died*," added Rose, her tone incredulous as she gave Tag her best *are-you-crazy* stare.

Tag glanced up to the roof of this monsterous cavern. Spying on the calcareous protrusions hanging from the ceiling, it became obvious many of the stalactites, especially the largest ones, were situated directly above some of the biggest pillars forming this cobblestone of a land bridge.

"So they *almost* made it," corrected Tag. "The point is; I believe it can be done."

"Well, I don't want to sound pessimistic, but I don't want us *almost* making it either," said Cankles. "It can be bad for our health, if you get my meaning?"

"I know, but we can do it," insisted Tag.

"Maybe in your dreams," countered Rose.

"It is so, Princess!" shouted Roen. "From where I stand, it appears that the most stable columns are the smallest. By some strange magic, it seems that the largest, safest looking ones are the pillars that are collapsing, destroyed by the falling stalactites."

"Take no offense, Ron, but I think your tumble addled your brain," Rose hollered down at the Elf. "What you said makes no sense! How can the smallest, narrowest ones be the safest to cross on?"

"Roen, is correct, Princess," said Tag. "The Sorcerer uses magic to protect the way. All those unfamiliar with this crossing will instinctively want to move forward using the most obvious pillars that look the most stable."

"I suppose that makes sense," said Cankles.

"Think on it," urged Tag. "If you want intruders that are hunting you down to meet an early demise, this would work. Obviously, any person in his right mind will take what he perceives to be the safest route. And if you give any credence to Lady Agly's predictions, this is not the way we'd meet our end – by falling into a river of lava."

"Say… you're right!" exclaimed Cankles, nodding in agreement. "We're supposed to get eaten by a dragon."

"Maybe she was wrong?" said Rose, thinking back on the fortune-teller's words.

"Why are you doubting her now when all along you had come to dread everything Agly said, holding her accountable to her every word?" groaned Tag, his hand slapping his forehead in frustration.

"I believe we can do this," decided Cankles, "for if Lady Agly's prediction holds true, we shall meet up with a dragon, if we do meet an untimely death in this place."

"We will not meet up with a dragon, and if we do, it will not be our end," stated Tag. "We can do this!"

"Do you truly believe this to be so?" asked Rose, staring across the chasm to the other side.

"I have no doubt, it'll just be a matter of selecting our steps wisely," answered Tag.

"But how will we know for sure?" questioned the Princess.

"If I'm correct, by some strange enchantment, the surface of these pillars seems to be sensitive to pressure. Step on the wrong one and… well, you know what happens."

"So how can we be sure?" asked Cankles.

"I know! We can tie a rope around your waist, and you can jump from one pillar to the next," offered Rose. "If you land on the wrong one, before you fall to your death or get crushed by one of those falling stalactites, Tag and I will pull you to safety."

"No offense to you, Princess, but I'm really not likin' the sounds of that idea."

"Cankles is right, Princess. If he falls, there's a chance he'll take us down with him, being that he's heavier than you," said Tag.

Rose's eyes opened wide in dismay. "Well, you are not suggesting I be the one to venture forth with nothing more than a rope to spare me a torturous death!"

"You are the lightest," reasoned Tag. "If you fall, you aren't likely to plunge to your death."

"I am not liking the sounds of 'aren't likely' when you should be saying you can guarantee my safety," scolded Rose.

"That's what I mean to say; you'll be safe. Cankles and I will swear on my father's sword that you will be safe," promised Tag.

Rose pondered these words for a moment. "On your father's sword, eh? Well, knowing how important that thing is to you, I believe your word is good."

"It is," vowed Tag, removing his cloak to shred it into long strips. Together, the three braided the strips, tying them together to create a tether.

"You have given me an idea," shouted Roen, removing his cloak to create a rope of his own.

"I think you should wait," hollered Tag. "We'll come back for you."

"Not that I lack confidence in you or your friends, and even though this ledge feels stable enough, the heat rising from the lava below is becoming uncomfortably hot," responded Roen. "If I can find a way to extricate myself from this situation, then I will."

"I hardly think your cloak will make a rope long enough to see you out from there," said Tag.

"I must try."

"Here!" shouted Cankles. "You can use my cloak. It's gettin' a little too warm in here for me anyway."

"Are you sure?" asked Roen, glancing up to Cankles as he leaned over to drop his cloak down to him.

Before Roen could instruct Cankles to wrap the material around a rock so it'd drop straight down, he tossed it over the ledge. The warm air rising up from the molten lava caught the cloak like the sail on a ship, causing it to unfurl. An updraft snagged the material, blowing it just out of Roen's reach as it floated down, burning to cinder on the lava.

"*Oops!*" groaned Cankles, his hand smacking his forehead in frustration. "Didn't see that comin'."

"Catch," said Rose. She wadded up her cloak around a fist-sized rock to weigh it down. Hovering directly above the Elf, she dropped it down into Roen's waiting hands.

"Thank you, Princess," called Roen, as he set to work. "If fate and luck conspires in my favour, I will be out of here and on my way to joining you and your comrades before the end."

"Don't say *the end*," whimpered Cankles, watching as Tag tugged on the makeshift rope, testing to make sure the knots would hold.

"You do not trust my knots?" asked Rose, as she offered to help.

"Need I remind you what happened the last time you offered to tie a knot?" asked Tag.

This fleeting memory was like an unwelcomed slap of reality. She recalled how the knot she used to fasten a climbing rope onto her bedpost unravelled as they crossed over to her dresser when they used the dreamstone to shrink to the size of a ladybug.

"Never mind. Test away," urged Rose.

"This should hold," assured Tag, as he tied one end around her waist, "it's as strong as any conventional rope."

"And you will not let me fall?" asked Rose, searching Tag's eyes for the truth.

"I cannot promise you that," admitted Tag.

"*What?*" gasped Rose.

"I can only promise that I will not let you fall to your death," vowed Tag. "You have my word on that."

"Then I will hold you to your promise."

"No worries, Princess," assured Cankles, winding one end of the tether around his hands. "We have no desire of havin' you comin' back to kill us, if we should fail you."

Rose stared with raised eyebrows at Cankles, and then recalled how she had once threatened them should she meet an untimely demise.

"Yes, you would not want that," agreed Rose, forcing herself to smile at him.

"Ready?" asked Tag, giving the knot around her waist one final tug.

"No... but I will do what I must." She answered in a small voice. "So, I jump from pillar to pillar and pray it does not crumble as I land on it?"

"Use this," offered Tag, handing to Rose her longbow. "Use the tip to test the pillars before stepping on them."

"Good idea!" praised Rose, eagerly taking up the weapon.

"Let's go, then," said Tag, gently prompting her on.

"Remember, Princess Rose, I suspect it is the safest looking ones that are cursed with dark magic," warned Roen, watching as she inched her way to the first cluster of pillars.

For the longest moment, Rose stared at the flat surfaces, each looking like paving stones floating on a sea of red. Using the tip of the bow, she gave the first one in the cluster of three a hard poke. She held her breath, waiting to see what would happen.

Not even a pebble fell from this pillar.

"Do you think it is safe?" questioned Rose.

"Take my hand," instructed Tag, winding the rope around the other as he steadied the Princess. "If that pillar gives away, I'll pull you back onto solid ground."

Rose held onto Tag's hand, squeezing it so hard he could feel the blood draining from it, as the bones in his fingers painfully ground against each other under her grip.

The tip of her toes gingerly pressed against the hard, flat surface.

"Easy does it, Princess," urged Cankles, offering words of

encouragement. "Don't worry, we have you."

The top of the pillar, its surface only large enough for one person to stand on at a time remained stable as she rested her full weight upon it. She breathed a sigh of relief.

This rocky formation was not moving, nor did a stalactite come crashing down on her. Slowly, she released her hold on Tag's hand as she inspected the next two pillars for her consideration.

"They look of equal size to me," assessed Rose. Both were large enough for two people to stand on, if both stood shoulder to shoulder, but one was only slightly smaller to the trained eye.

"Test them both, then," suggested Tag, shaking the pain from his aching hand before taking up her tether.

Rose used the tip of her longbow to prod the nearer of the two, only to scream in fright. She teetered to and fro as this pillar crumbled under the pressure of her longbow as a long, narrow stalactite crashed down from on high.

"Steady on, Princess!" shouted Tag, gripping the rope in case she lost her balance.

Rose drew a deep breath, composing herself as she used the bow to poke the slightly smaller pillar. To her relief, it seemed sound. Taking another tentative step, she placed her foot onto the stony surface.

Tag moved onto the one vacated by Rose as he warned Cankles, "Remember, step only on the ones the Princess stepped on. Follow in our footsteps."

"Will do," acknowledged Cankles. He was willing, but not eager, to take that first step. "I have no intention of strayin' from them."

Their advance was painstakingly slow, but Tag dare not coax Rose to move faster than she was willing to go. One mistake and they could all meet a fiery demise.

Halfway through this ordeal, bolstered by her growing confidence, Rose moved on at a slow, but steady pace.

"I can do this," said Rose, prodding the next pillar. At this point, she barely flinched as it collapsed under the weight of the falling stalactite. Knowing the Elf's observation held true gave her the courage to venture on. Unfazed, the Princess turned to the next rock formation waiting to be tested for stability. "It is really not that bad."

"Glad you think so, but remain focused on the task at hand," urged Tag. "This is no time to get cocky."

"I am not being cocky," insisted Rose. "Boys are cocky. A lady of refined breeding like me is confident… determined."

"And you'll be *dead* if you let your mind stray," scolded Tag. "Now concentrate, before you jinx us."

"Very well, we are in no need of jinxing," agreed Rose, giving the next pillar a stiff poke before proceeding.

As she advanced, Tag and Cankles moved on accordingly. Where Rose's dainty feet easily fit on the top the smallest surface, her comrades wavered about, arms out for balance as they struggled to keep from toppling over.

"Almost there," announced Rose, sighing in relief as only three pillars separated them from solid ground. Just as Roen had predicted, the largest pillars, the ones that were large enough for two or three to stand on at a time were the ones to prove most deadly, destroyed under the crushing weight of massive stalactites crashing down from above.

Testing the largest of the three remaining columns, it stood firm against the tip of her longbow.

Again, all three advanced, successfully hopping onto their respective pillar. As the next one was smaller and the last, smaller still, without testing its stability, Rose moved on.

"Just one more," announced Rose.

Before Tag could tell her to forego testing this one and to make a great leap to the other side, Rose hopped straight onto the pillar.

She screamed in fright as the last formation suddenly dropped, crumbling under her foot as a stalactite fell, heading straight down to impale Rose through the top of her head.

Tag immediately dropped. Sitting on the pillar, his legs wrapping around the column, he leaned back. Yanking hard on Rose's tether, he pulled her out of the way of the falling debris.

Rose screamed long and loud, continuing to scream long after the cascading rocks and crumbling pillar sank into the lava below.

When she finally opened her eyes, she shrieked in fright again as the rope around the narrow of her waist suddenly tightened as it slipped up, resting just beneath her ribcage.

"I've got you, Princess!" hollered Tag, waiting for her to stop struggling before hoisting her up. "Whatever you do, don't start flailing around."

With the rope clenched in his hands, Tag leaned forward. Raising his forearms, he blotted away the beads of sweat before they rolled down to sting his eyes. Drawing in a deep breath, he steeled his nerves for the next step.

Tag pulled his legs up, folding them beneath him. Adjusting his grip on the tether, with calculated steps, he carefully found his footing, standing up ever-so slowly as Cankles took up the slack, pulling the rope in. With knees slightly bent to lower his centre of gravity, Tag was now forced to use his upper body strength to hoist Rose to safety.

Like a rag doll hanging from the end of a rope, the Princess dangled helplessly. She fought back her tears and the rising tide of panic waiting to overwhelm her.

"Just a little more!" grunted Tag, heaving on the rope as the frayed strips of braided cloth bit into his hands.

As he lifted her to the top of the pillar, Rose scrambled, her arms wrapping around one of Tag's legs as she knelt on this small, but solid piece of ground.

Tag was sure the blood from her nails sinking into his flesh was about to rise through his trousers, seeping through the punctures created by her talons.

As Cankles drew in more of the slack line, Tag let go of the rope. He steadied Rose as he lifted her onto her trembling legs. They are standing toe-to-toe, huddled against each other on this column.

"You're safe now," whispered Tag.

Rose threw her arms around his chest as she began to weep in relief and fear.

Tag held her tight in his arms, comforting her. He knew to order the Princess to stop blubbering would only cause her to cry all the more.

"There, there! I told you I'd keep you from falling to your death," whispered Tag, using a soothing voice to calm her down as she trembled in his arms.

Rose shuddered as she unleashed a gasping sob, the hot tears streaming down her dirt smudged cheeks. Burying her face in his chest, her hysteria subsided. The feeling of solid ground underfoot and the safe embrace of Tag's arms holding her close restored calm to her shattered soul.

"That's better," sighed Tag, relieved the panic that had ensued was now but a memory.

In response, Rose thumped her forehead against his chest. Her balled fists angrily pummelled Tag in retribution.

"Hey!" snapped Tag, pulling her in against his body to diffuse these blows. "Stop it, before we both fall!"

"Please calm down, Princess!" pleaded Cankles. He wiped away the sweat trickling from his forehead as he wavered to and fro, regaining his balance while still clinging to Rose's tether.

"Get a hold of yourself!" ordered Tag, his words, stern. "We must still clear this gap to reach safety."

Rose suddenly froze in his arms, peering down to see the river of lava flowing in unrelenting procession, glowing red hot as it churned and roiled beneath them.

Her eyes squeezed shut. Swallowing the lump catching in the back of her throat, Rose fought to compose herself.

"Are you ready?"

"I can't do it," whimpered the Princess.

"Yes, you can," insisted Tag. "Look how far you've come. You can do this. It's just one more jump."

"I can't." Rose began to shake at the very thought of this task.

"Look at me, Princess," ordered Tag, lifting her chin to gaze upon her face. "Look me in the eyes!"

"I can't do it."

"Yes, you can and you will!" ordered Tag. "Now, look at me!"

Rose blinked back her tears as she forced herself to stare up into Tag's eyes.

"One more jump and we'll be there, on the other side," encouraged Tag. "You can do it."

"No…" sobbed Rose, teetering on the verge of breaking down into hysterical tears once more. "It's too far."

"So it's a little farther than the others, but it can be done. All we need to do is time it just so, that way, when we jump over there, Cankles can land on this pillar without falling to his death."

"Are you trying to scare me even more?" gasped Rose, as she clutched onto Tag.

"No, I'm telling you what we must to do to leave this place behind us."

"I do not like what you are telling me!"

"Please, Princess, I really don't want to be stranded here," pleaded Cankles. "There's no tellin' if these pillars will collapse if we're standin' on them for too long."

"We cannot stay here. We must move on," urged Tag.

"But I'm scared," whimpered Rose, clinging to him for dear life as she stared over to the safety of the ledge. "I cannot do it on my own."

"I'll jump with you. I'll go at the same time."

"You will?" Rose stared into his eyes for the truth.

"Knight's honour," vowed Tag. "We'll jump at the same time - together."

Rose glanced over at Cankles as he wobbled about, fighting to keep his balance. She then glanced over to the other side where the promise of solid ground beckoned her.

"What say you, Princess?" asked Tag. "Are you ready?"

Rose merely nodded in response.

"On the count of three," said Tag. His eyes stared ahead as his right arm wrapped around her waist, making sure she would leap when he did.

"Wait! We jump on *three* or you count to three, and then we jump?"

asked Rose, wanting to be positive of his instructions.

"We *jump* on three," replied Tag, speaking with all certainty as he glanced over at his comrade teetering on the pillar behind them. "We jump on three, Cankles."

"Don't like it, but I'll do it!" shouted Cankles, as he steeled his nerves.

Before Rose could question his instructions once more, Tag counted down: "One... Two... *THREE!*"

18

Into the Dragon's Keep

Launching off from the pillar, Tag and Rose jumped, pushing off with all their might, but that split-second hesitation as the Princess made her leap worked against them.

In desperation, Tag pushed her, thrusting Rose to safety, but in doing so, he lost momentum, falling short. As the Princess landed on solid ground, Tag groaned in pain as he fell, landing hard against the ledge. His legs dangled over the river of lava churning below as the edge of this chasm began to crumble from the impact and his weight.

Screaming in fright, Rose dove forward. She snagged him by the back of his vest, holding on to Tag as his fingers clawed at the dirt and rocks disintegrating under his touch as his feet frantically scrambled to find a toehold on something, anything.

"Hold on!" cried Cankles. He rushed on, leaping from one pillar to the next, his own safety not even entering his mind as he hurried on to rescue Tag.

Propelled by the adrenaline coursing through his veins and the panic rampaging through his heart, Cankles practically flew across the gap, landing with ease on the other side.

He leaned over to pull Tag up by his wrist, but under a shower of debris, Tag lost his hold on the crumbling ledge. Slipping down, he was jerked free of Rose's grip. As he fell from their reach, above her horrified scream, Tag heard Cankles shout, *"Catch!"*

With all the rocks, pebbles and dirt cascading down with him, it was by some strange miracle that Tag was able to seize the end of the rope.

"Hold on and lean back, Princess," ordered Cankles, grabbing the tether that was still tied around Rose's waist as he braced for that powerful tug that would signify Tag's sudden stop.

Rose did as she was told, digging her heels in as Cankles prepared to assume the brunt of the weight.

Tag's freefall came to an abrupt, but painful stop. His arms felt as though they'd be wrenched from their sockets as his hands latched onto the rope Cankles threw down to him.

With a sharp *'twang'* the line snapped taut. Tag dangled from the end of this tether, hovering over this giant cauldron of lava.

Cankles breathed a great sigh of relief; thankful they were able to spare their friend a horrible death.

"Pull!" ordered Cankles, motioning for Rose to walk backwards to help hoist their comrade to safety. As Tag appeared over the edge of the cliff, scrambling to haul himself onto solid ground, Cankles rushed forward, pulling him up the rest of the way just as the knot around Rose's waist came undone.

"I'm safe!" announced Tag.

"And not a moment too soon," said Rose, staring at the frayed bit of rope falling away from her.

"See? Did I not say that together, we're a great team?" asked Cankles, nodding in approval to Rose.

"That, you did, my friend," sighed Tag, crawling on his hands and knees to get away from the edge of this chasm. Flopping onto his back in utter exhaustion, he gasped for his breath as Rose threw her self on him. She wrapped her arms around Tag in relief; grateful he had survived. They both groaned in pain as Cankles joined in, gleefully tossing his body atop of them.

"Get off me!" snapped Rose, jabbing Cankles' bony ribcage with her elbow. "You are both mad!"

"Actually, m'lady, you're the one who sounds mad," responded Cankles, grimacing under her scathing tone.

"And you!" snarled Rose, a balled fist slamming into Tag's chest in frustration and angry retribution. "How dare you? First you almost get me killed, and then you almost do yourself in! We could have died."

Instead of agreeing or apologizing, Tag began to laugh long and hard, his arms wrapping around his aching ribs as he chortled in mirth.

The same wave of relief washed over Cankles, as he, too, began to laugh.

"You are an idiot!" cursed Rose, pointing first at Cankles, and then at Tag. "And you are a *crazy* idiot! How dare you laugh?"

"What's wrong with laughing?" grunted Tag, as he chortled.

"Has your brain been addled by your fall? Danger and disaster does not equal good times," scolded Rose. "We almost died a horrible death!"

"But we didn't," reminded Tag. He slowly sat up, only to be assaulted by a torrent of angry, balled fists pummelling his chest as Rose wailed on him in resentment and frustration.

"Stop it!" hollered Tag, seizing Rose by her wrists. He ceased his chuckling when he saw the hot tears spilling from her eyes as she unleashed a geyser of emotions on him.

"It's one of those *ugly* cries," gulped Cankles, awashed in fear and guilt as the Princess lost all control. "We're in real trouble now!"

"You stupid, reckless fool!" sobbed Rose, her quivering fists fighting against Tag's grip as she crumpled to her knees, weeping before him. "You could have died."

Tag now realized what she was trying to say. He wrapped his arms around her, holding Rose tight as her tears left a trail of sadness on his shoulder.

"I'm sorry," whispered Tag. "I'm truly sorry. I'll be more careful next time."

Rose then erupted like a volcano. "You bloody well better be! Or I swear; I *will* kill you!"

In embarrassment and frustration, she lashed out once more. Her balled fists slammed into Tag's chest, bowling him over as she leapt onto her feet.

Hastily wiping away her tears, Rose snatched up her longbow.

"Hello! Down here!" This voice wafted up, rising over the sounds of the belching, churning lava.

"Ron!" shouted Cankles. "We must not forget about our Elf friend."

"Is everyone safe?" hollered Roen. He feared Tag had survived the fall, but was about to meet his demise by Rose's hands.

"Other than a terrific scare, and getting a bit beat up, we're none the worse for wear," called Tag, waving at the Elf to show they had made it to the other side.

"Now that the mimes are of no concern, we can come back for you," offered Rose. "I will send Tag and Cankles over to help you up."

"It is quite all right, Princess. I urge you to go on. I am afraid all the commotion was enough to alert Dragonite of your coming," said Roen. "Time is of the essence! Go forth before that devious soul can set other trap for you. I will make my own way out, and if not, I shall just wait for your return."

"If you succeed in finding your way from that ledge, let it be known the smallest of the pillars that remain standing are all safe for your crossing now," assured Tag, watching as the Elf worked to knot the end of his newly braided rope to one of his arrows.

"I pray you are correct, my friend," hollered the Elf. "Make haste! Do not allow the Sorcerer to foil your attempt to reclaim the dreamstone."

"We'll be back for you, if you can't get back up on your own," promised Cankles. "Just sit tight where you are."

"If I cannot leave this spot, it is not as though I can go anywhere but down," reminded Roen.

"Exactly! So sit tight," called Cankles.

"Just be careful," warned the Elf. "Mark my words; if these pillars were bewitched by dark magic, there is no telling what else the Sorcerer has in store for you."

"Worry not, Ron," said the Princess. "I hardly think it can be any worse than what we had just endured."

"Be careful nonetheless. Now, go!"

"This way," ordered Tag, pointing down the darkened tunnel. "Follow me."

Tag removed one of the two burning torches mounted at the entrance of the narrow passage. Holding it before him, the light of the flame illuminated the way.

"Cankles, take to the rear. Princess, stay behind me," whispered Tag, as he stared into the tunnel.

"Are you sure this is the way?" asked Rose.

"There was a reason why that very last pillar, the small one you assumed was safe to step on, collapsed," answered Tag. "The way is set so any intruder wishing to steal away into the Sorcerer's Lair will meet his demise. We would be wise to keep our wits about us."

"I suppose that makes sense," decided Rose.

"With an obstacle like the one we just survived, I'm sure the rest of the way is safe," assumed Cankles. "The old coot probably thinks anyone able to pass through the Devil's Tears to encounter that river of lava would surely meet their demise trying to cross over."

"I pray you are right, but do not let your guard down," cautioned Tag, as he unsheathed his sword.

With the flame of the torch to light the way, the three comrades ventured on, creeping throught the tunnel.

"Unless my eyes and mind are playing tricks on me, I get the feeling this passage is becoming wider and higher as we advance," whispered Cankles, glancing about nervously.

"It is no trick, my friend," said Tag. "It has been gradually growing in size."

Just as they neared a bend in this subterranean passage, Rose whispered, "Do you hear that?"

Cankles and Tag stopped in their tracks. Both listened intently for what the Princess heard.

Whoosh...whoosh...whoosh... This sound whispered through the tunnel.

"What is that noise?" gasped Cankles. Cupping a hand to his ear, he cocked his head to listen.

"Hush," ordered Tag, straining to hear this sound echoing from the darkness before him.

Whoosh... whoosh... whoosh...

"It does not grow louder, nor does it fade away," noted Rose.

"Then that's a good thing," decided Cankles, nodding judiciously.

"What makes you say that?" asked Tag, glancing over at his nervous comrade.

"It means it's not comin' at us," answered Cankles, "and that, to me, is a very good thing."

"But what can it be?" asked Rose, as she frowned in bewilderment.

"We shall find out soon enough," said Tag, holding the torch before him to light the way.

As they rounded the bend, the noise became louder as the tunnel continued to expand in size.

Whoosh... whoosh... whoosh...

The noise was steady and unrelenting as it sounded through the passage.

"Oh, I'm not likin' this, not in the least," whispered Cankles. "It's gettin' louder."

"That's only because we're getting nearer to it, whatever *it* is," explained Tag, his eyes squinting to pierce through the darkness before them where the torch's light had yet to reach.

"Call me crazy, but it sounds like one of those torture devices," said Rose, her words matter-of-fact.

"Say again," responded Tag, glancing in confusion over his shoulder at the Princess.

"You know the one? The huge, curved blade that swings back and forth like a big pendulum; the one that slowly lowers, each swipe of the blade cutting deeper and deeper into the victim's flesh, until it hacks through bones and innards," explained Rose.

The colour drained from Cankles' grimacing face as he absorbed her disturbing words.

Whoosh... whoosh... whoosh...

As though something was slicing through the air, the sound was unrelenting as it echoed toward them.

"Methinks the Princess is right," gulped Cankles.

"Let's not jump to any conclusions just yet," urged Tag. "It could be absolutely nothing."

"Since when did *nothing* ever sound like *something* so very menacing?" grumbled Rose.

Tag motioned for them to follow as he pressed on, the wavering light of the torch pushing back the darkness.

And there it was.

Whoosh... whoosh... whoosh...

Cankles stared in wide-eyed horror as he squeaked, "It absolutely looks like *something* to me – something pretty darn deadly."

Blocking their path was a huge, curved blade. Just as Rose had described, it swung like a great pendulum. Suspended to a wooden arm that swayed to and fro, even rusted, the weight and momentum of the swinging blade would still be enough to do severe damage, if not outright kill a human being getting in its way.

"Hmph... and just what did I say?" grunted Rose, staring with raised eyebrows at Tag.

"Well, it's now even more obvious we're on the right trail," decided Tag.

"The young master is right. You don't go puttin' up one of these killing machines unless you wanted to prevent anything or anyone from advancin' any further," added Cankles.

Tag stared at the swinging blade, noting its timing and rhythm as well as a safe point of passage where the cutting edge would not do any damage. At a single glance, it was clear this narrow gap would only prove safe if one was as slender and small as a starving cat forced to crawl through on its belly.

"We can do this," declared Tag, watching the blade swing by.

"Crawl through there?" gasped Rose, pointing at the gap. "I am tinier than you and I know for a fact I cannot fit through without coming out the other side half the person I am now!"

"Not through there," corrected Tag, as he pointed straight ahead. "I mean through here. We can do it."

"You said that the last time with those bewitched pillars that almost got us killed!" groaned Rose.

"But we weren't killed. We survived," reminded Tag. "Remember, if we were to meet our end, according to Agly, it'd be by the bite of a dragon, not the bite of a blade such as this."

"Oh, lovely!" muttered Rose, rolling her eyes in frustration. "So you want to survive this, only to run smack-dab into destiny; meeting your end roasted medium-rare and in the maw of a hungry dragon?"

"You know it does not have to end that way," insisted Tag. "We know of the dragon. It does not yet know of us. We will keep it that way."

"Well, unless your flesh can hold up against the swing of that blade and your bones can resist snapping under its bite, just how do we pass this death trap in one piece?" asked Rose. "As far as I can tell, we can neither go under, over, nor around this contraption."

"We pass *through* it," said Tag.

"*What?*" Rose and Cankles gasped simultaneously.

"How hard can it be?" asked Tag, "Look at it. Study its rhythm as it swings. Just as it passes this point, you can slip by before the blade swings back again. It'll be like playing jump rope. Timing it just so, you can duck in without getting hit by the rope as it swings around."

"Easy for you to say! However, I do not partake in games played by commoners," grunted the Princess.

"Trust me," insisted Tag. "It's easy."

"There is a big difference between getting whipped by a swinging rope than sliced by a deadly blade," snipped Rose.

"But the principle is the same," insisted Tag.

For a long moment, all three stood before this death-dealing pendulum, their eyes rocking to and fro, following its hypnotizing motion as they timed its arc.

"It'll be far easier than crossing the river of lava," assured Tag. "If you want, I'll go first."

"Are you sure?" asked Rose.

"Of course! I'll go first; show you how it's done." His words grew in confidence as he timed the blade's movements.

Standing as close as he could without getting knicked by the rusted blade, Tag waited. Just as it came down, swinging past him, Tag slipped by.

"See? Easy!" announced Tag. He turned to face his friends only to see their eyes open wide as they gasped in horror.

Tag was overcome by a sensation of dread as the flat stone he stood on suddenly sank down. This pressure plate triggered a series of blades to drop, swinging into action; each one moving faster than the one before it so if a human body did pass through this obstacle, it'd come out the other side looking like coarsely minced meat.

"Wasn't expecting this," groaned Tag. He glanced over his shoulder to spy on the blade of the next weapon as it sliced through the air directly behind him. In the wake of its movement, skimming dangerously close by his body, strands of hair blew across his eyes.

"Now what?" asked Rose. "For if you think I am going to follow you through there now, you can think again."

"Of course it's impossible to pass through now," said Tag. Timing it just so, he slipped by the first blade to join his comrades.

"Perhaps there is another way to move forward," suggested Cankles. "Maybe there's another tunnel that will deliver us to the same place, but in a safer manner."

"Even if there were, do you not think that the Sorcerer has set up other deadly obstacles to hamper our movement?" asked Tag, staring through the row of swinging blades.

The first one continued its steady, unhurried pace, but each one behind it rocked to and fro progressively faster. The last blade was moving the fastest, swinging so quickly Tag was certain only a foot or a hand would make it through to leave an unrecognizable, mutilated body on the other side.

"There must be a way to stop it," determined Tag, staring up as the mechanism that allowed these blades to swing continuously. The slower the swing, the larger the cogs. Each set became progressively smaller, allowing for faster, tighter movement.

"Yes, like crashin' through it with a batterin' ram," offered Cankles, "if we had one."

"How do you stop something powered by dark magic?" asked Rose, looking on with dread.

"It may be powered by magic, but this contraption is still made of metal and wood," answered Tag, examining the components that allowed this maiming machine to move with such deadly precision. "If it can be made, it can also be broken."

"You want to *break* it?" asked Cankles.

"If that's the only way to stop it, then yes! We need to break this thing," decided Tag.

"And just how do we do that?" asked Rose. "Because if you think you can hoist me up there and have me do something silly like jam a rock in between those cogs, you have another thing coming."

Tag's eyes lit up as a smile spread across his face.

"Oh, no! I know that crazy look!" gasped Rose, shaking her head in dismay. "You have an idea and I already know I will not like it."

"Hear me out!" urged Tag. "It will involve you *and* jamming those cogs, but you will not have to be lifted or made to climb up there."

"So you say! Just how am I supposed stop those cogs, then?"

"Your longbow and those arrows Lord Silverthorn gifted to you," answered Tag, pointing to the quiver hanging from her hip. "The steel bodkin will effectively jam it, if you aim the tip of the arrow between the teeth of those two cogs."

"Do you truly think that will work?" asked Cankles.

"We can only try," said Tag, "and hope for the best."

"That is all that is required of me?" asked Rose, staring suspiciously at the young man.

"Yes! We take them out of commission one at a time," replied Tag. "Can you do that?"

"With an aim like mine? Of course I can!" Rose pulled an arrow from the quiver.

"Are you sure?" asked Cankles.

"As easy as picking off sleeping grouse from a low-hanging branch," assured the Princess, giving him a wink of her eye.

"Good! Then you won't miss," said Tag, pointing up to where the teeth of the two cogs meshed together. "Aim right in there."

Rose nocked the arrow onto her longbow. Drawing it, her eyes fixed on the small target above. As she exhaled, she let the string slip from her fingertips. The arrow flew in an unerring line, the bodkin striking the teeth of the cog. The arrow's shaft shattered on impact, but the steel tip remained snagged between the teeth where the two cogs fit together to move the wooden arm swinging the giant blade.

With an ear-piercing squeal and the crunching of metal against metal, the rusty cogs ground to a halt. The weapon, like a great battleaxe locked in perpetual motion, suddenly ceased its back and forth movement. The shaft the blade was attached to no longer swung like a menacing pendulum, instead, it trembled with building tension, the dark magic that set it into motion working against the jammed cogs.

"Brilliant!" praised Tag, as he waved her on. "Now quickly! Proceed to the next."

Slipping by this stilled blade, Rose took quick, precise aim. The arrow hit its mark, the steel bodkin becoming lodged between the teeth of the cogs to disable this blade. Like the first, it quivered with energy as the unleashed tension started to build.

"Five more to go!" said Tag, motioning the Princess to proceed to the next moving target. With only enough space between the blades to fit one slim person at a time, Tag and Cankles followed behind her.

As they reached the last swinging blade, the fastest of all, Rose took aim. With the cogs moving so quickly the first arrow was deflected, the projectile flying off to become embedded in the wall.

"Again, Princess!" ordered Tag. He could hear the ominous creak of bending wood and the sharp grinding of the metal teeth of the cogs as the Sorcerer's magic worked to set the blades back into motion.

"This is *not* good!" gasped Cankles, his hand touching one of the wooden shafts to feel it trembling with mounting tension. It quivered like the stave of a bow pulled to its limits, fighting to unleash its weapon.

"What do you mean?" asked Rose, glancing over her shoulder to see the look of dread on Cankles' face as the row of disabled blades struggled to be free.

"I don't think it's gonna hold," replied Cankles.

"Hurry, Princess," urged Tag. "Forget about those other ones! You must stop *this* blade.

Again, Rose took aim, but once more, the tip of the bodkin was deflected by the moving piece of metal.

"Try again," ordered Tag, as the first blade she had immobilized creaked, moaning as though in agony as it fought to swing back to life, further crushing the mangled bodkin caught between the cogs.

"I *am* trying!" snapped Rose, the longbow trembling in her hands as her confidence began to dissolve with the first two failed attempts.

"No pressure," said Cankles. "Just hurry! Something bad is going to happen. I can feel it."

Rose gasped, rolling her eyes in frustration. She tried to regain her focus and composure, fixing her sight on the cogs.

Fighting to steady her quaking hands, Rose took aim, letting the arrow fly. They ducked their heads, closing their eyes as the bodkin ricocheted off one of the cog's teeth while the shaft of the projectile shattered, sending splinters of wood flying.

"I can't do it!" cried Rose, her fingertips now stinging from the bite of the sinewy string.

Tag was in no mood to cajole or force the Princess to do what was becoming obviously impossible for her. He knew the creaks, groans and the grinding of metal and wood were becoming louder; more urgent as the blades fought to be free. He was forced to act.

Before Cankles could sputter a panicked, "What do we do?" Tag shoved the torch into his hand as he grabbed one of Rose's arrows.

Holding it by the very end, Tag jumped as high and as hard as he could. With adrenaline rushing through his veins to propel him upward, he rammed in the steel tip of the arrow. The bodkin snagged onto a cog's tooth, feeding it into the mechanism. With a grinding crunch, the blade lurched to a stop, quivering with growing tension as the seven blades, all stressed by varying degrees of pressure, waited to explode into action.

"Hurry!" shouted Tag. Pushing Rose to safety, he rushed behind her. *"MOVE, NOW!"*

Just as Cankles slipped by the last blade, he panicked. A loud *'snap'* sounded behind him. Cankles shoved Tag through in his mad dash to be away from this death trap.

Tag stumbled, tripping over Rose as she fell. All three hit the ground as the building pressure caused the central rod passing through each wooden shaft supporting a blade twisted, heaving as it buckled under incredible stress.

Tag leaned over, shielding Rose with his body as fragments of fractured metal and chunks of wood exploded from the pressure. The blades, now broken free of the main support, resumed their movement. Biting into the stony walls of this narrow passage, it was a testament of their deadly power.

"Is everybody safe?" asked Cankles, struggling to stand on his quaking legs as he picked up the torch before flying debris could smother the flame.

"Thank goodness, we survived," gasped Tag, sitting up as Rose continued to tremble in fear, the colour slow to return to her face. "We're all fine!"

"Oooh… She's not lookin' fine to me," noted Cankles, seeing the tears well up in Rose's eyes.

Fearing her wrath, Tag leapt back, away from the impending fury of small fists waiting to pummel his chest again.

"Go on! Say it," whimpered Rose, wiping away the shame as her cheeks burned with disgrace.

"Say what?" asked Tag, staring with bewilderment at the Princess as she fought against another wave of tears.

"That I failed! That I couldn't hit the target when our lives depended on it!"

"What are you talking about?" gasped Tag.

"You want to mock me; tell me what a failure I am. Go on! I know it's true."

Tag smiled, dropping to his knees before her. "You *are* crazy. You do know that don't you?"

Rose's eyes narrowed in suspicious. "And you are angry with me. Just say it! Get it over with!"

Cankles backed away from the pair, sensing a volley of angry words were being readied to lob.

"You did great," praised Tag, his words sincere.

"Stop mocking me!" snapped Rose, wiping the tears from her eyes. "I failed. I did great at failing miserably."

Tag offered her an understanding smile, squeezing her hand before she could ball it into a fist to accost him. "Six out of seven is pretty damned good in my way of thinking."

"It is?"

"Did you try your best?" asked Tag.

"Yes."

"Then that's all any of us, you included, can ask for."

"You're not mad at me?"

"You tried your best and I'd say that alone is great, Princess, especially considering the fix we were in," praised Tag, patting her hand in comfort.

"You speak the truth?" gasped Rose, searching his eyes.

"I swear, on my father's good name, you did very well. I certainly couldn't have done what you did with a longbow."

"You are only trying to make me feel better about how I failed," whined Rose, fishing about for more praise.

"If I wasn't so afraid of falling onto one of those swinging blades to jam the arrow into the cogs as I did with the last one, we probably would have gotten through faster."

"No... we would have died," said Rose, her words spoken with certainty. "Up until that last one, I was much faster dispensing the arrows than you would have been. If anything, you just got lucky with that last one, jamming it in the way you did."

"Oh, really?" grunted Tag.

"Brilliant!" interjected Cankles, hoping to nip this argument in the bud. "Between the two of you, we survived! Good job! Now let's move on to the next deadly obstacle awaitin' us. Hippity-hop! Let's get to it."

"So you are not mad at me?" asked Rose.

"No... not this time. Not unless you want me to be."

For a split second, Tag cowered, thinking he was about to be the recipient of another one of her punches. Instead, the Princess threw her arms around him in a grateful hug.

Tag was momentarily taken aback.

When Rose realized he was not reciprocating with a hug of his own, she immediately let go.

A moment of awkward silence followed as Rose's face burned with embarrassment. Not knowing how else to respond, Tag punched the Princess lightly on her arm.

"Owww!" groaned Rose. "What was that for?"

"I don't know... you seem to like punching me. I thought you'd like it, too."

Tag stepped back, thinking she was going to retaliate; winding up to punch him to the moon, if she could, but instead, Rose began to giggle.

Tag and Cankles exchanged confused glances.

"I really don't understand you," admitted Tag, as he shook his head in bewilderment.

"I know," said Rose. "I am a very complex, young lady."

"That, you are," agreed Tag, pulling the Princess onto her feet.

"So, we're good?" hoped Cankles. "Cause I really can't handle any more bickerin' right now. I'm too traumatized at this moment."

"Considering everything we've endured, I'd say we're doing better than good," stated Tag.

"We're ready to move on, then?" asked Cankles.

"There is no point in lingering," decided Rose, brushing the dust from her hands. "We should leave now."

"Take no offense, but did you get knocked on your noddle?" questioned Tag, as he rubbed the back of his head.

"Why?"

"Because you've never been in a rush to venture on before," answered Tag. "Why so eager now?"

"We have come this far, defying the odds. If that loopy fortune-teller is correct about the dragon, then we have nothing to fear," explained Rose.

"I'm sorry, but if I encountered a dragon down here, I'd be doin' a whole lot of fearin'," admitted Cankles.

"But that is just it! We are underground, *waaaay* underground. If there is a dragon lurking about down here, it will have to be small," reasoned the Princess, as she glanced about their cramped surroundings. "Small enough that Tag can keep us safe with his sword, if need be."

"A dragon, no matter how big or small, should be avoided, however, I'm glad you have that kind of faith in me," said Tag.

"In *you?* I was speaking of your silver sword," teased Rose. "You spend so much time honing the blade I am surprised it has not cut through that whetstone you sharpen it on!"

"Nice," grunted Tag, offering her a feigned smile. "If that is the case, should I just hand my father's sword over to you, so you can do battle with a dragon, should it show up?"

"That is quite all right, if anything, you make for a great shield," responded Rose, grabbing Tag by the arm to turn him toward the dark unknown.

"Thank you. I am overwhelmed by your confidence," muttered Tag, his tone sarcastic as he accepted the torch from Cankles.

"Good, just do not let it go to your head," urged Rose, giving him a nudge to advance.

"This way," said Tag, waving them on to follow. "Maybe you're right about a small dragon, Princess. The tunnel continues to narrow."

"I am so sure, I will bet your life I am correct," said Rose, speaking with conviction.

"Then soldier on, m'lady," suggested Cankles. "It's best to keep up with the young master."

As they journeyed on, the passage continued to shrink, forcing them to stoop to avoid banging their heads along the ever-lowering ceiling.

"I hope we're not reduced to crawling like animals," grumbled Rose, her back now aching from maintaining this posture as she followed behind Tag.

"That might not be such a bad thing, m'lady," responded Cankles.

"How so?"

"If what you said about the small surroundings will mean an equally small dragon, then that could only mean the beast Lady Agly warned us of would have to be no bigger than a large dog or a small bear to move in and out of the Sorcerer's lair."

"Oh! I like your way of thinking," praised Rose.

"Hush! Keep your voices down and keep moving," ordered Tag. "We must get out of this tunnel before this torch burns out."

Just as Tag spoke these words, as though jinxing their trek, a great draft suddenly whispered through the tunnel, swirling around them. The dwindling flame died.

For the longest moment, the trio stood there, immobilized by the pitch black that swallowed them up.

"I cannot see a thing," whispered Rose.

"Neither can I," said Cankles. "What do we do now?"

"There is nothing we can do, but move on as best we can," answered Tag. Using the tip of the torch to probe in front of him, he used the other hand to grope along the tunnel wall.

"In this darkness? It is blacker than black!" gasped Rose, the panic rising in her heart. "I cannot even see my hands before my eyes."

"That's because it's dark," reminded Cankles.

"No! You don't say?" snapped the Princess, her agitated voice growing higher in pitch to match her stress level.

"This is no time to panic," said Tag, his voice trying to remain calm for the benefit of the others.

"Bloody hell! I'd say now is a good a time as any," responded Cankles, as he bumped his head against the invisible ceiling.

"We can do this," assured Tag. "Just stay close so we don't get separated."

"But we cannot even see where we are going? Suppose you go down one tunnel, and we diverge on another?"

"Keep to the left, Princess," instructed Tag. "Use your left hand to follow the length of the tunnel, that way you won't stray if this passage should branch off."

"Makes perfect sense to me," responded Cankles, extending his right hand to feel his way.

Groping about to feel which one Cankles was using, just as she thought, her comrade had employed the wrong one.

"Use your *other* left hand," grunted Rose.

"Good idea, m'lady," said Cankles. Switching from his right, he felt the hard, stony wall beneath his fingertips.

"Before we lost our light, I noticed this tunnel curved to the left," warned Tag. "Just follow my voice and keep moving. And please, Princess, I know this situation is not good, but please, don't start crying now, for it's not going to help any of us."

"*Not good* is the understatement of the century! And who said I was going to cry?" snapped Rose, as she contemplated punching Tag on his arm, if she could only see where he was standing.

"You seem to be doing a lot of it lately, especially during this particular quest," reminded Tag.

"So I am a little emotional. This is not exactly what I had bargained for," complained Rose. "Nonetheless, I will make the best of a bad situation."

"That's what I want to hear," praised Tag. "Let's journey on."

With one hand extended in front to prevent him from walking into a wall, the left hand kept him on course. Tag guided them on, moving gingerly with every step.

"Watch your head," cautioned Tag, his scalp grazing a rock protruding from the ceiling as he followed the bend. "There's a rock hanging down."

"Where?" asked Cankles, staring into the blackness.

"Over here," whispered Tag.

"I can't see," said Cankles.

"About three paces ahead of you, just as you round the corner," instructed Tag.

"What corner?" asked Cankles.

"You'll know it when you feel it," said Tag. "Just keep moving."

"Ouch! Found the rock," announced Cankles, rubbing his sore head.

"Just be careful," warned Rose. "There are probably more obstacles ahead of us."

Probing the floor with the toes of his boots, Tag shuffled along to make sure the way was safe. He stopped as the feeling of solid ground disappeared beneath his feet. Yanking his foot back onto the firm earth, he warned the others. "Watch out – "

Tag gasped in surprise as Rose bumped into him. For that split second, his breath snagged in the back of his throat. It was like taking that final step off a flight of stairs; that split-second when one is suspended in midair after suddenly realizing that solid ground was still at least one more step away.

She screamed in fright as Tag suddenly fell.

"Oh no!" cried Cankles. Scrambling on his hands and knees to feel his way in this consuming darkness, his head bumped into the back of Rose's knees as his hand recoiled in fear, feeling nothing as the ground dropped away from his touch.

"Bloody hell!" cried Cankles. "He's gone! Tag's gone!"

"I'm right here!"

"What?" gasped the Princess. "I thought you fell to your death into a great, black abyss."

"So did I," Tag sighed with relief. "The ground dips; drops a hand span or so, but I'm fine."

"Thank goodness for that!" exclaimed Cankles. "You gave us quite the scare."

"I gave myself quite the scare," admitted Tag, feeling his way forward on all fours. "Just be careful. It's not a big fall, but it's enough to twist an ankle if you're not careful."

"So you are not hurt?" asked Rose. Groping about in the darkness, she stumbled into the dip, landing on Tag's legs as he moaned in pain.

"I am now," groaned Tag, as the point of her elbow dug into his calf. "Get off!"

"Sorry," said Rose, wincing in pain as Cankles' hand poked her in the back of the head as he felt about for his comrades.

"Sorry, too, young master," apologized Cankles.

"That was me you poked, not Tag," grumbled Rose.

"Then I'm sorry to you, too, m'lady. Meant no harm."

Tag stood up, steadying himself against the tunnel wall as Rose blindly felt her way up his body to stand, only to have him leap away from her groping hands.

"Watch it!" snapped Tag.

"Sorry!" Rose apologized. "I can't see."

"None of us can," reminded Cankles, his hand feeling for the ground that dropped away under Tag's feet.

"Follow me," instructed Tag. "Just make sure you use your feet to feel the ground before you take a step."

"Like you just did?" teased Rose.

"I was. I even stopped in time," explained Tag. "You were the one to bump into me, pushing me in."

"I say we focus on the task at hand," urged Cankles. "I don't know how much more of this utter darkness I can handle."

"Good plan," said Rose. "Tag, lead the way."

"Fine, but do be careful of where you tread," cautioned Tag, moving on through the narrow passage.

"This is what they must mean by the blind leading the blind," commented Cankles, feeling his way along as he gingerly stepped behind the Princess.

"Salvation!" gasped Tag, seeing a faint, erratic glow at the end of the tunnel. "I see light up ahead."

"Salvation is but an illusion, if it is the Sorcerer bearing the light," whispered Rose.

Tag contained his excitement as he drew his sword. Whispering, he ordered Rose and Cankles to keep their voices down in case they were heading straight into Dragonite's lair.

As the narrow tunnel came to an end, it opened into a massive chamber; the biggest they had ever seen. They slowly stood upright, stretching their weary backs. No torches lined the walls of this chamber. The only light came from the pools where molten lava churned and roiled, rising up from the core of the earth.

The temperature rising from these natural cauldrons turned any moisture trapped in this cavern into a muggy, humid crypt.

The trio glanced up, staring at the great stalactites hanging from the ceiling. Beads of water dripping down from these calcareous formations hardened on the cave floor to give rise to pillars, some so large the stalactite and stalagmite fused together to form a single column. Wherever these drops of water missed solid ground to land in a vat of molten lava, the moisture evaporated on contact, hissing as steam escaping this fiery quagmire.

To their left, the cave floor dropped away, overlooking a river of lava that sputtered and spewed. To the right, a solid rock wall that looked as though it had been rubbed smooth over the ages greeted their eyes.

"Look! We must be near to the Sorcerer's lair," whispered Rose, pointing to the back of the chamber. "Behind that massive boulder is a large tunnel. I can see torches burning on either side of the entrance."

Before the Princess could rush ahead, Tag seized her by the arm. "Wait! That's no boulder."

Rose and Cankles froze in their tracks, staring at what Tag saw.

Their eyes opened wide in horror as the massive lump expanded, only to contract as it breathed in deeply, snorting loudly as it exhaled.

"This is not Dragonite's lair," whispered Tag, as they ducked behind a stalagmite to hide. "We are in the dragon's keep."

The gargantuan lizard slept soundly at the entrance, using its sheer size to guard the way. Its legs suddenly twitched, as if the beast was giving chase in its dream, much like a dog would dream of chasing down a rabbit. Just as abruptly, these frantic movements ceased as a gurgling noise rumbled from its throat, as though the creature was snoring, if dragons did indeed snore.

"The Sorcerer is usin' that beast to guard his lair?" gulped Cankles, looking on with certain dread as his eyes measured the dragon's length, height and girth.

"It would appear so," said Tag, motioning for Cankles to lower his voice.

"The Sorcerer means to keep the dreamstone away from us," whispered Rose. "Of course he would go to extremes to guard his prized possession."

"Well, such is our fate. So much for meeting up with a small dragon in tight places," sighed Cankles. "The Sorcerer must have used magic to get that huge beast in here."

"Or it could be something as simple as keeping a young dragon trapped down here for a very long time, until it grew too large to move through the labyrinth of tunnels to see the light of day again," offered Tag.

"I suppose," responded Cankle, staring in fright and awe at the sleeping behemoth.

"But still, that creature must get out to eat from time to time," said Rose.

"No need for that, when food is delivered," whispered Tag, pointing to a scattering of shattered bones littering the cave floor.

"Those aren't human bones, are they?" gulped Cankles, using the toe of his boot to poke a broken femur long denuded of flesh. By the light emitted by the pools of lava that pocked the floor of this chamber, he spied upon teeth marks gnawed onto a thighbone.

"What difference does it make at this point," responded Tag. "We must focus on getting from here to over there, without rousing that sleeping beastie."

"And how do we do that?" questioned Rose, watching the dragon's ribcage swell as it inhaled, only to shrink as it slowly released the spent air from its lungs.

"Very carefully and quietly," replied Tag, his eyes scanning the chamber for the best possible route. On one side, the cave floor dropped off into a flowing river of lava. On the other side, a solid wall of rock would prevent their escape, if the dragon should corner them.

"I know that much," whispered Rose. "But what happens if that creature wakes while we are on the move?"

Tag huddled with Cankles and Rose as he shared some advice. "The worst thing to do is to panic. If you run and the dragon sees you running, it'll chase you down. My father told me their vision is not acute."

"There is nothing cute about them, at all," gulped Cankles, glancing over his shoulder to spy on the sleeping giant.

"Tag means to say, their vision is not good," explained Rose.

"Yes, a blur of movement means food on the hoof, trying to escape," continued Tag. "If anything, dragons, like deer and horses, have a blind spot. If you stand directly in front of them, so close that you can touch its snout, you'll be safely out of its field of vision."

"And what are we supposed to do if that creature wakes up?" asked Cankles.

"Nothing," advised Tag. "Do not move a muscle. Do not even breathe."

"So… if we do not move, the dragon will not be able to detect us," surmised Rose.

"According to my father, yes."

"Your father is dead," reminded Rose.

"True, but he wasn't killed by a dragon, so take some comfort in knowing that."

"But suppose it smells us?" questioned Cankles, lifting his limb to take a whiff of his armpit.

"It reeks of brimstone down here," responded Tag. "If that dragon can still smell at all, I'm sure its senses have been dulled by the stink."

"Well, with what we've been through, we probably smell as bad as this brimstone," decided the Princess. "Even with my refined senses, I am embarrassed to admit I am getting used to how badly you two smell."

"All kidding aside – " said Tag, only to have Rose cut off his sentence.

"Who said I was speaking in jest?"

"You aren't?" questioned Tag.

"No, I am not," answered Rose. "And right now, it could be a very good thing. There is a chance we shall just blend into the dragon's surroundings than to stand out like fresh game waiting to be slaughtered and eaten."

"Then I am glad I'm so stinky right now," admitted Cankles, as he blotted away the grime and sweat from his forehead.

"Shall we move on?" asked Tag.

"So, you have a plan then?" asked Rose.

"Yes, step lightly; do not speak; and if the dragon should wake, do not run," instructed Tag.

"Sounds easy enough," said Rose.

"Easy is good. I like easy," whispered Cankles.

"As long as the dragon does not wake up, we'll be fine," promised Tag, motioning for his friends to follow him. "Once we get around that beast, ducking into that passage, we'll be safe. It's much too small for the dragon to pass through.

Pressing a finger to his lips, he motioned for silence as he used the fingers on his other hand to gesture that they will have to tiptoe through the chamber, and then around the dragon to access the lair it was guarding.

With cautious, measured steps, the intrepid trio ventured on, taking care not to accidently step on the scattering of dry, brittle bones littering the floor. The churning of bubbling lava as they crept closer toward the sleeping dragon effectively squelched the sounds of their movements. Each time the earth vented its gases, they froze in their tracks, pretending to be one of the stalagmites protruding from the cave floor as the great reptile's ears twitched with life, but its eyes remained closed as these ambient sounds lulled it back to sleep.

Glancing up, Tag knew it had to be well into morning now. He spied seams of light seeping through the domed ceiling, shining like veins of silver in a dark mine. It was apparent they were in the center of a volcano, under the cinder bowl, and the cracks overhead allowed heat to escape, as well as any internal pressure that would force this mountain to explode if it was allowed to build.

Creeping their way to the passage blocked by the dragon's body, Tag motioned for Rose and Cankles to stay put as he ducked around one side, and then the other, to see if there was space wide enough to squeeze by the beast to access the passage to the Sorcerer's lair. The creature remained curled in a tight ball like a napping cat; scaly tail tucked under its chin; leathery wings folded over its back as it slept.

Around the dragon's neck, a tight-fitting metal collar and a heavy, rusted chain kept the beast tethered to the wall in case it had any thoughts of bursting through the ceiling of this chamber to escape to freedom. By the way the collar bit into the dragon's scaly neck, Tag could tell the creature had been held down here for years. The bones of its ribcage protruded through its armour-clad skin as evidence its captor rarely fed the beast.

It was obvious the Sorcerer was of the mindset that the hungrier the dragon was, the more attentive it would be; guarding his lair and devouring any person, man or Elf, stumbling upon this place.

Instead, the dragon slept, reserving its energy to devour and digest its next meal. And sleep was its only respite from this miserable existence. Dreaming its dragon dreams, the creature soared high above the clouds as it soaked in the warmth of the brilliant, noonday sun.

To the right of the entrance to Dragonite's lair, there was a narrow gap, only wide enough for them to pass through one at a time. If they sidestepped while pressing their backs to the cave, they'd be able to just squeeze by.

Tag motioned to the others, gesturing that he'd go first and for Rose and Cankles to wait until he was sure it'd be safe for them to join him.

With his back plied against the stony wall, Tag held his breath. Sidestepping past the dragon's rump, he steadied the sword's scabbard to make sure it did not rattle or bump against the reptile's scales. Once inside the entrance to the lair, Tag removed one of the burning torches. Creeping up behind the sleeping dragon, he used the flaming torch, signaling to his friends to advance.

As much as Rose detested coming this close to the scaly hide, the Princess was more frightened the dragon would wake up just as she was sneaking by.

Angling her body while pressing her back against the cave wall, she gasped, freezing in her tracks as Cankles' foot accidentally kicked a human skull to send it rattling and bouncing across the cave floor. For a split-second, Cankles, too, froze. His breath caught in the back of his throat and then he suddenly scrambled, dashing after the rolling bone. Before he could seize it, the skull came to a stop, but only after bumping against the dragon's snout.

The reptile's eyes flashed open. Black, snake-like pupils floating on orbs of red stared, unblinking as though seeing straight through this human. A great puff of spent air gushed from its nostrils as it sniffed at the skull while Cankles stood there, paralyzed in fear. A disappointed growl rumbled from its throat as hopes of a tasty morsel vanished. With a disgruntled snort, the dragon picked up the skull, crushing it between its fangs.

Unleashing a dreary sigh, the creature lowered its head, tucking tail under chin. The third eyelid, this translucent, nictitating membrane, slid obliquely across these fiery orbs as the heavy lids closed once more.

Cankles breathed a sigh of relief as the dragon drifted off to sleep. Rose quickly ducked into the passage to join Tag as he used the torch, signaling Cankles to move now.

With his heart still pounding madly, Cankles rushed on with quick, silent steps. He skirted around the beast, pressing his back against the cave wall to avoid even touching the dragon as he squeezed through the gap.

Tag motioned for Rose and Cankles to follow him. Pointing to the length of chain that kept the dragon shackled to mouth of the tunnel, he gestured for his comrades to carefully step over this rusted tether, ducking into the passage, they slipped away from potential danger.

"We did it!" whispered Rose, trying to contain her excitement. "No death by dragon!"

"Yes!" exclaimed Cankles, his fist pumping the air in victory. "Tag was right! We were able to change our destiny."

"Didn't I tell you we could use Lady Agly's predictions to our advantage," said Tag. He nodded in approval as he glanced back to see the dragon remained fast asleep, oblivious to their passing. "As we survived this encounter, we can survive anything."

"Then how about this?" An angry voice snarled from darkness before them as a great bolt of energy flew in their direction.

19
Trapped

Rose screamed in fright.

The blur of light flew overhead, narrowly missing her as Tag yanked her to the ground while Cankles dove behind a boulder for cover.

This powerful magic lit up the passageway, deflecting off the dragon's scaly rump. Like a bolt of lightning, it exploded against the cave wall in a shower of sparks to send dirt and rocks flying in all directions as the dragon, startled awake by this stinging assault, bellowed in rage.

"Why are you here?" growled Dragonite. The staff trembled in his grip as the obsidian crystal mounted atop glowed, waiting to be discharged again.

"We're here for the dreamstone," answered Tag, as he boldly brandished his sword.

"Never mind the dreamstone! Why are you here, when you should all be *dead?*" responded the Sorcerer. "It is not exactly a merry, little romp to get to my lair, and deliberately so!"

"Did you honestly think a few measly obstacles would stop us?" grunted Rose, daring to defy him.

"Yes! Yes, I did, Princess," sputtered a thoroughly incensed Sorcerer. "If anything, I thought your servants would have abandoned you, and this quest by now, than to endure such misery and the potential of a painful death just to help you."

"They are *not* my servants," snapped Rose. "They are my *friends.* And friends do not abandon friends!"

"They do if they're *dead,*" grunted Dragonite, turning the tip of the black crystal on Tag, and then Cankles. "So, Princess, if you wish to live, and you want your friends to go unharmed, then come with me. I have *something* that belongs to you."

"Oh, stop it with all that *I'm-trying-to-be-mysterious* rubbish," scolded Rose. "I know that *something* is the dreamstone."

"Shut it, you royal snip!" growled the Sorcerer, the black crystal throbbing with light once more. "If you do not come with me, I will be more than happy to feed your friends to a ravenous dragon."

Tag raised his sword, pulling Rose behind him to shield her. "I will die before she is made to go with you!"

"Oh, blah, blah, blah!" mocked Dragonite, turning his crystal on them. "Spoken like a true knight. That was exactly what I was hoping for!"

"If you discharge your magic to strike us down, we will both die," warned Tag.

Dragonite lowered the tip of the staff. The light glowing within was not even at half-strength compared to the first discharge.

"You are only partially right," snarled the Sorcerer, aiming his weapon again. "You will die and the Princess will receive a violent jolt, of which she will survive, only to wish she had died along with you when I am done with her."

Just as Dragonite took aim, Cankles popped up from the boulder he was hiding behind. He lobbed a rock at his foe. Instead of striking the Sorcerer on his head to render him unconscious or on his hands to disarm him of the magical staff, Cankles missed. The rock landed on Dragonite's foot.

The Sorcerer yelped in pain, hopping about on one foot as the power from the black crystal shot forth. As Rose ducked behind Tag, he used the broad edge of the silvery blade to deflect this magic. Though not as powerful as the first, the impact still knocked him onto his back. The bolt of blue energy ricocheted off the sword, forcing all to duck or take cover before it was sent flying off. It struck the dragon's nose as the beast wedged its snout into the opening of this tunnel. In response, the dragon recoiled, bellowing in surprise as it shook off the pain.

Before Dragonite could unleash another bolt of energy, Tag leapt onto his feet. Charging at the Sorcerer, he shouted at Cankles to deliver the Princess to safety.

In a mad scramble, Cankles seized Rose by her hand. Armed with nothing more than his dagger, he pulled her along, racing to escape. As they neared the mouth of the dragon's keep, the beast suddenly reappeared. That sinister black pupil floating on a fiery red orb stared hungrily at them as the Princess shrieked in fright. Tripping as she leapt back, she pulled Cankles down with her.

Spying the promise of fresh meat, the dragon was determined to feed. Too large to fit into the passage, the reptile was like a giant cat, thrusting its paw through a mouse hole in hopes of snagging its prey.

As one of the dragon's clawed talons blindly groped about, in frustration, it came smashing down toward them. Rose and Cankles rolled in the opposite direction to avoid becoming smears on the cave floor. As this paw withdrew, the other rushed in, slamming down. Rose rolled away, crashing into Cankles just he stood up. Knocked off his feet, Cankles' dagger flew from his hand as he hit the ground.

Stretching, he strained to reach the handle of his weapon. Cankles shrieked in horror. His eyes squeezed shut under the wake of displaced air as a great, scaly paw came crashing down on him.

The dragon roared in pain as Rose dove in, ramming Cankles' dagger into the pad of the monster's foot as it came down.

The Sorcerer snarled in anger, hearing his dragon inflicted with pain dealt by someone other than him. "Damn you, mortals!"

As Tag lunged with his sword, the Sorcerer pivoted, blocking the blow with the tip of his staff. Without hesitation, Tag countered. The blade slashed so close to Dragonite's ribcage, had he any meat on his bones, Tag would have sliced through flesh rather than just tear through the Sorcerer's robe.

Moving with confidence, Tag used everything Halen Ironwood had taught him, putting his entire weight, rather than just his arm, behind his sword.

"You've improved," grunted Dragonite, raising his staff up to block Tag's weapon, as the blade came down to cleave his head.

"And you have not!" snapped Tag, his foot coming up to slam the Sorcerer in his bony chest.

Dragonite gasped in pain, somersaulting over until he came to a skidding stop against the cave wall. Like a crumpled scarecrow, the Sorcerer lay there, moaning in pain.

As Tag rushed in, the keen edge of his sword thirsting for blood, Dragonite countered. As the end of his staff deflected the tip of Tag's sword, the other end flew up. The sharp edge of the black crystal slashed the mortal high on his left cheek.

Tag reeled from the blow, staggering back as he winced in pain. The salty beads of sweat trickling from his forehead stung as it mingled with the hot blood coursing from this wound.

"I did not say you were any good," scoffed Dragonite, rising up to meet his adversary once more. "I only said you had *improved*, and not by much!"

Ignoring the pain and these mocking words, Tag attacked the Sorcerer. Each slash and lunge of his sword failed to connect with his scrawny foe.

The Sorcerer parried and countered each blow as though gifted with unearthly skills; supernatural powers that made him unusually spry and strong for an old, leathery wisp of a man.

As Dragonite lashed out at Tag, aiming to striking his right cheek so it would match the left, the boy ducked, stepping in to drive his left elbow into the Sorcerer's ribcage.

Dragonite folded with the blow; the wind knocked from his lungs as he staggered back.

Tag rushed in, sword poised to cut his foe down. Just then, an eerie glow swelled from the obsidian crystal as the Sorcerer uttered words from an ancient, forbidden tongue.

Tag's sword swung out to strike Dragonite down. Instead, it was like hitting against an invisible shield. The blade reverberated with the impact, jarring the boy to his bones.

As the Sorcerer recited an incantation, the black crystal continued to swell with light.

"*Run!*" hollered Cankles, waving Tag on to retreat with the Princess as the walls and floor of the cave began to quake. "He's gonna blow!"

Sprinting toward the entrance of the dragon's keep, the trio was forced to dive over the heavy chain as it was suddenly yanked taut across the entrance of this tunnel as the behemoth struggled to pluck out Cankles' dagger that was embedded in the pad of its foot.

The dragon snorted with pleasure as three mortals somersaulted, landing in front of him. As they fell on their backs, an invisible wave and a brilliant flash of light exploded from the Sorcerer's crystal.

The nictitating membrane stretched across the dragon's eyes, shielding it from the percussion of this magic, as well as the dazzling light. For this brief moment, the creature was blinded by its third eyelid.

"Scatter, then freeze!" ordered Tag, hoping to confuse the dragon. Pushing Rose toward the tunnel from whence they came so she could escape, Cankles dashed to the far wall of the cave while Tag made a sprint to the opposite side set aglow with the light from the river of lava.

As the three dashed off in different directions, it was as though the beast didn't know which one to hunt down first. As it glanced from Cankles to Rose, and then Tag, the Princess was the most frenetic in her mad dash to freedom. Like a dog excited by the thrill of the chase, the emaciated dragon was fast on its feet. Unencumbered by its weight had it been properly fed, instead of a slow, lumbering gait, this creature moved with alarming speed.

Rose screamed in panic, the earth trembling beneath her feet as the beast pursued her. Just as she tripped, Cankles raced forward, hurling a rock. He struck the beast on the side of its scaly head.

As though this assault was an invitation to dinner, the dragon veered to the left, chasing after Cankles.

With gangly limbs a-flailing he sprinted off as fast as he could. Sweat ran down his face as panic filled his heart. Heading for the cave wall, there'd be no escape this time as the dragon neared, cornering Cankles like he was nothing more than a trapped animal.

"Freeze!" hollered Tag. "Don't move!"

Cankles threw himself against the cave wall, hoping his dirty raiment would allow him to blend into this stony backdrop. He held his breath, fighting the tremors of his body as he quaked in fear, struggling to quiet his racing heart.

This sudden lack of movement served to confuse the dragon. With a disgruntled snort, it turned its head toward Rose once more. Her legs were a blur of movement as she ran, knowing her life depended on it. This flurry of activity was irresistible to the dragon. Like a deranged dog, it charged after the Princess. Drained by the stifling heat and this burst of energy, Rose's breathing became ragged. Exhausted, she stumbled.

Just as the dragon lunged to snap down on her, another rock bounced off its snout.

Tag whistled loudly, hurling an even bigger rock to strike the dragon on the side of its head.

"Get me! Come after me!" shouted Tag, banging his sword against a stalagmite to draw the beast away from the Princess.

More than this mortal's frantic movements or desperate shouts, the scent of fresh blood seeping from the gash on his face proved tantalizing. Inhaling as a forked tongue flickered from its mouth, the sharp scent of blood mingling in the air served to whet the creature's appetite.

With a hungry roar, the dragon gave chase.

Tag raced off in the opposite direction to lure the creature away from Rose. Thinking that the stalagmites would form an obstacle to slow the dragon down, he glanced behind as the beast moved, undaunted. As the metal chain tethering the dragon to the cave wall was yanked taut, the tops of these stony formations, exploded; sheared off by the force.

Tag was trapped. There was no escape.

Glancing down over the edge from where he stood, it was a sheer drop into the burning lava. From here, to the right and the left, the flowing lava had eroded the cliff, undercutting it so these sections jutted out over the molten river of death.

Below him, a narrow ledge could provide a safe perch away from the dragon's reach and its fiery breath, but it was only wide enough if he were able to stay balanced on the tips of his toes, while clinging to the jagged cliff wall.

The lanky dragon followed its nose, sniffing out the delectable scent of blood in the air as Tag tried to back away.

Cocking its head to one side, the black pupil of each eye dilated, and then narrowed, allowing the reptile to focus in on its prey.

Tag stood his ground, his father's sword gripped tightly in his hands as he braced for the dragon to attack. If he timed it just so, there was a slim chance he'd be able to rush in as the dragon recoiled, pulling its head back to fill its lungs to capacity before attempting to incinerate him. If Tag were lucky, he'd be able to plunge the blade of his sword between the ventral plates of scales to pierce its heart.

Instead of pulling back to fill its lungs, the dragon attacked Tag, its yellowed teeth gnashing as it snapped at him. As a forked tongue darted from its mouth to taste the scent of human blood, Tag attacked. He struck the only part not protected by scales as thick and tough as a knight's shield.

Slicing through the dragon's tongue, the sword's edge was so razor-sharp the reptile didn't even feel the cut of the blade at first. The smell of blood, even its own, and the movement of the disembodied tongue as it writhed about on the ground before it, drove the dragon mad with the need to feed.

To Tag's astonishment, the dragon snapped up its bloodied tongue, cannibalizing itself as it devoured what it could only see as a source of food.

Gulping down this piece of meat, the dragon's remaining length of tongue flickered out, splattering Tag with blood.

Steeling his nerves, he braced for another attack while searching for a possible escape route. For a fleeting instant, Tag considered dashing straight toward the dragon, ducking under its belly, but with the speed this creature moved, the possibility of being trampled underfoot was even greater than the hope of escape.

Just as the dragon took another step closer, forcing its prey to the very brink of the ledge, a rock landed in its gaping mouth.

Spitting out this inedible object, the creature's massive head swivelled in Rose's direction as she threw another rock to draw its attention away from Tag. Instead, her pesky attempt went ignored as the draw of Tag's blood was too great.

"Here! Over here, you stupid beast!" hollered Rose, as she nocked an arrow onto the bow. She let the projectile fly, hitting its mark, only to see it deflect off the scaly armour. The arrow sliced through the air, striking the ceiling of the cave. Dirt, cinder and rocks fell to reveal a patch of blue sky from the world above.

"The eyes, aim for its eyes!" shoutedTag. "Blind the dragon!"

With an unerring aim, Rose unleashed three arrows, one after the other. Each one met its mark, sinking deep into the dragon's left eye.

The shaft of each projectile protruding from this bloodied orb snapped as the nictitating membrane slid over the wounded eye. Undetered, the dragon was determined to feed, the scent of fresh food too irresistible to ignore.

"It's my blood!" warned Tag, as he used his forearm to blot away the hot crimson streaming from his cheek. "It's drawn to the scent of my blood."

Realizing her bid to down the dragon with her arrows was as futile as Tag's efforts to be rid of the blood flowing from his wound; Rose did the only thing that came to mind.

Taking the steel bodkin of the arrow, she lanced the palm of her hand. Tearing off the sleeve of her frock, Rose blotted the blood onto the fabric.

"Hey, beastie! Over here!" shouted Rose. She frantically waved the bloodstained cloth about like it was a flag of surrender.

Fixated on the meal standing before it, and blinded in its left eye so it couldn't see the female mortal flapping about, the dragon lowered its snout. With mouth agape to snatch Tag up between the rows of jagged teeth, the creature's head suddenly recoiled, bellowing in pain as Tag stabbed at the exposed gum where an abscessed tooth wasted away in decay. The touch of cold steel against inflamed nerves in the tooth socket sent a shock of pain coursing through the beast.

Tag hopped back as yellow pus from the infected gum gushed out like a giant, popped boil. He gagged on the foul stench wafting forth while the dragon's body rattled, its coat of scales clattering like loose armour as it shook off this pain.

It was at this very moment the dragon's right eye caught a glimpse of the frantic Princess as she waved the bloodied fabric about to draw its attention.

"Come on, you stupid beast!" hollered Rose. "Follow me!"

If she was fast enough, she'd be able to duck back into the narrow tunnel. Safe from harm's way, she would be able to tease and distract the dragon so Cankles and Tag could deal with the Sorcerer, and the business of reclaiming the dreamstone.

Rose summoned her courage, rushing in closer when the creature showed only tepid interest. She was unaware the missing segment of tongue hampered the dragon's ability to smell, but only now did she understand this behemoth could see from only its right eye.

Working her way behind Tag onto the ledge protruding over the lava, Rose waved her bloodied banner for the dragon to see as she shouted, "Over here, you scaly beast! Come and get me!" Tag glanced behind, shocked to see the Princess frantically jumping about, waving her arms to draw the dragon away from him.

"Get back!" Just as he shouted these words, the earth beneath her feet heaved, crumbling away to collapse into the churning lava below.

Rose shrieked, screaming in terror as she made a leap for solid ground. She fell short. Her fingers clawed at the earth to find a firm handhold. Dangling over the ledge, she glanced down to see the bloodstained sleeve land on the roiling river of molten lava. Instantly, it ignited. Reduced to ashes from the intense heat, all traces of fabric disappeared beneath the bubbling ooze.

Just as the earth beneath her fingers dissolved under her weight, Rose screamed in fright, and then in pain, as Tag lunged forward, snagging her by the wrist before she fell from his reach.

With the dragon straining against the heavy links of iron, from where Tag hung over the ledge, he was out of the creature's reach, but just barely.

"Stop flailing about!" shouted Tag, as she dragged him further over the edge.

"Don't let go, Tag!"

"I won't, but we'll both go over if you don't stop!"

Rose squeezed her eyes shut, her tears evaporating with the heat radiating from below as she fought to calm her frayed nerves.

"Use your other hand," ordered Tag, as he drove the pommel of his sword into the earth to anchor him against the downward pull. "Grab my wrist!"

"I – I can't," stammered Rose, her trembling hand straining as she struggled to reach up to him.

"Try! You must try!"

Rose's right arm ached, throbbing with excruciating pain from bearing her weight as she dangled in Tag's grip. Drawing a deep breath, as she exhaled, she lunged upward, her left hand seizing his wrist.

"You'll have to pull me up!" shouted Rose. "There is nothing for me to climb on."

Pushing against the hilt of his sword, the pommel bit into the ground. It offered Tag some leverage as he inched his body back onto the ledge. Ignoring the snapping of the dragon's teeth and the rattling of chain as it fought to reach him; Tag struggled to pull Rose to safety.

"I can't do it!" cried Rose, her strength waning as she fought to hold onto Tag's wrist. "You must let go of the sword!"

Just as her left hand lost its grip, Tag released his weapon. Seizing her with his now free hand, he watched the silver blade flash before his eyes. In a glint, reflecting the seams of light seeping throught the ceiling, the sword disappeared over the edge.

"I've got you, Princess!"

"Don't let go!"

"I won't," promised Tag, as he leaned back, pulling her to safety.

Rose scrambled, standing on her quaking legs as Tag stood between her and the snapping jaws of the dragon as it fought against its iron tether to devour them.

"Back away," instructed Tag. "If we stay along this wall, we'll be out of the dragon's reach."

"Fire!" bellowed Dragonite, as he appeared from the settling dust at the entrance of the keep. "Incinerate them!"

Though away from the creature's grasp, they were now trapped. The dragon's fiery breath would burn them alive. With no shield to protect them, Tag braced himself for the worst, pushing Rose behind him.

As the dragon reared up, its head recoiling as it filled its lungs with air, the large ventral scales spread apart to expose the vulnerable skin beneath it. This was the most opportune time to strike, to drive the blade of his sword deep into the dragon's heart. But now, when he needed his father's sword the most, it was lost to the river of lava.

Shielding Rose behind him, Tag's eyes squeezed shut, expecting a torrent of fire as the dragon exhaled. Instead, a gush of rank air blasted into his face, as blood from the dragon's wounded tongue and pus oozing from its abscessed tooth splattered across his chest and startled face.

Being so malnourished, the gases created from the slow fermentation of meat in its gut failed to manifest on an empty stomach.

"Run!" hollered Tag, grabbing Rose by her hand.

"You useless beast!" cursed Dragonite, watching as the reptile snapped and snarled, straining against the chain that kept its prey just out of reach. Pulling the metal pin on the last link that kept the creature shackled in place, the Sorcerer raged, *"Kill them all!"*

Before Tag could lead Rose to safety, the dragon rushed at them. The Princess shrieked in horror as the creature was set loose, rampaging toward them. Tag pushed her against the cave wall as he yanked his dagger free of its holster. It would be no match against the dragon, but he was not about to go down without a fight.

If anything, by sacrificing his life, he was sure it'd be enough time for Rose to flee to safety.

As the dragon lunged at him, the creature gagged as it jerked to a sudden stop. Choking on its collar that already bit into its neck, the chain was stretched tight.

"Run!" hollered Cankles, as he stomped down on the end of the tether. The metal links became snagged between rocky outcrops protruding from the cave floor, effectively pinning the dragon in place.

"Go, Princess!" shouted Tag, pushing her toward the tunnel as he dashed back to the cliff where the river of lava had swallowed up his sword.

The ground beneath his feet quaked, trembling with the percussion of the dragon's footfalls as it gave chase, bellowing in pain and frustration as it charged after Tag.

"Come on! Come and get me, you overgrown lizard!" jeered Tag, taunting the dragon to catch him.

In no need of encouragement, the dragon scurried toward him. As Tag neared the cliff, he slowly backed away from the creature as it prepared to pounce on him. Standing on the very edge, the lava bubbled, hissing as earth and rocks crumbled under Tag's heels to land in the molten quagmire below.

Cocking its head to stare through the undamaged right eye at its prey, the dragon suddenly lunged at Tag.

With impeccable timing, he ducked, leaping from the ledge. He threw his body on to solid ground as the dragon came crashing down. Rock and earth gave way under the creature's weight. Before it could spread its tattered wings to take flight, the lava belched and churned, sucking the screaming beast down.

Tag ducked just as Cankles kicked the last link of chain free of the rocks, sending the metal tether whipping toward him as the dragon was swallowed up by the lava. An ear-piercing bellow of agony was stifled by magma filling its mouth.

"Thank goodness, it's over," sighed Tag, watching as the dragon vanished from sight.

"You fool! It has only just begun!" growled Dragonite.

As the dust settled, Tag spied upon the Sorcerer. Pressing the jagged edge of the obsidian to Cankles' throat, he dared Tag to attack him. "If you want this man to live, it will not be without sacrifice."

"Then I shall willingly sacrifice my life for his," offered Tag, his hands raised in surrender as he crept forward.

"You are brave, but stupid!" cursed the Sorcerer. Yanking back on a fistful of hair, he pulled back on Cankles' head so the chords of his neck were stretched taut. "Your life means as much to me as his does."

"He wants *me*, Tag," said the Princess, as she stepped out of the shadows of the tunnel.

"Usually, she is the stupid one, but for once, the Princess is correct!" snapped Dragonite, motioning Rose to step forward.

"What do you want with her?" asked Tag.

"I want her as my wife," revealed Dragonite, his words matter-of-fact. "When she ascends to the throne of Fleetwood, I will be her king, and together, we shall rule. And I will reinstate the art of mime into every royal courtyard from here, to Axalon and beyond! Mwa-ha-ha!"

"Surely you jest!" gasped Rose, grimacing in disgust at the mere thought of this union, not to mention the reinstatement of mimes.

"Yes, I do," grunted Dragonite. "You are not my type, but if my original plan should fail, I suppose I can force myself to wed the likes of you, if it means getting what I want in the end."

"I would rather gouge out my eyes with a rusty spoon, than marry a foul toad like you!"

The Sorcerer reached into the folds of his robe, his hand fishing about.

Rose jumped with a start as a metal spoon clanged against the rock at her feet as he cackled, "Prove it!"

"Let him go!" ordered Tag, his dagger poised in his hand to throw, as Dragonite backed toward his lair, the black crystal glowing brighter.

"Even if you were faster than the powers emitted by my crystal, do you truly believe your aim is so precise you will kill me and not your friend, if you should throw it?"

"Oooh! No offense, young master," groaned Cankles, wincing as the sharp edge of the obsidian pricked his skin, "but perhaps if you gave that dagger to the Princess to throw instead, that'd be better."

"Shut it!" snarled Dragonite, pressing the crystal hard against his prisoner's throat.

"It doesn't have to end this way," said Tag, lowering his dagger.

"How right you are! It will end with the Princess coming with me, and you and your friend trapped in this volcano until you waste away and die or it erupts, in which case, you will die anyway."

"So… you promise to release him, both of them, if I go with you?" questioned Rose.

"It is a time-limited offer that ends in… ten seconds," snapped Dragonite. "So what will it be, Princess?"

"Ten seconds is not much time to think about it," complained Rose.

"Exactly! Now, think fast. What will it be? Will you come with me and allow your friends their freedom, or shall I kill this one now?"

"Don't do it, m'lady," urged Cankles. "Flee while you can!"

In agitation, Dragonite smacked his hostage on the head as he snarled, "Quiet! The Princess is thinking!"

"I will go with you," decided Rose.

"You will?" gasped the Sorcerer, frowning in surprise.

"I will," agreed Rose.

"But Princess – " Tag's sentence was cut short as she motioned for silence.

"I will go, only because I know with all certainty Tagius Yairet will search you out. He will scour the farthest corners of these lands to hunt you down, and to set me free," declared Rose.

"An idle threat!" dismissed Dragonite, sneering in contempt.

"It is no threat. Consider it fair warning," responded Rose, as she lay down her bow and quiver of arrows. "Tag will save me, and he will most certainly kill you."

Just as Rose stepped toward the Sorcerer, the whine of an arrow sounded in her ear.

Dragonite gasped in surprise as the tip of the arrow bit into the staff he held against Cankles.

"Release him!" ordered Denatheen. He nocked an arrow as another Elf alongside Roen, took aim, pointing their weapons at the Sorcerer. "Free him or the next arrow will go straight through your eye."

Pulling Cankles in front of his body to use as a human shield, Dragonite backed into the gloom of his lair, taking his hostage with him.

"Now!" shouted Tag, as he and the Elves raced toward the darkness. "After the Sorcerer!"

As they rushed into the passageway, a flash of white light and an invisible shockwave knocked them off their feet. Denatheen seized Tag, pulling him away as the tunnel came crashing down.

As the dust cleared, all could see the way was destroyed; the mouth of the lair, sealed.

"This is my fault," gulped Tag. He fell to his knees as he stared in disbelief at the mountain of rubble blocking their path.

"No, if you want someone to blame, then blame me... and that magic crystal," confessed Rose. "This is my fault."

"It is a waste of time and energy to find blame when it can be better spent finding your friend, and a way out of this place," reminded Denatheen, fanning the dust from the air.

"The wise Elf speaks the truth. So what are you going to do about it?" asked Rose, plopping down next to Tag.

"What can I do? I failed."

"How can you say that, Tag?" gasped Rose. "I would never have gotten even half way on my own! We only got this far because of you."

"And because of me, the Sorcerer has the dreamstone *and* our friend," lamented Tag.

"And that is exactly why we must get them back. We will do it together, because, like Cankles said, we are a team."

"I can't... I can't fail again."

"You only fail when you give up," argued Rose, pulling on Tag's arm to make him stand up and rise to the challenge. "That is what you have always told me."

"I can't do this anymore," said Tag, admitting defeat as he pulled free of her grasp.

"Yes, you can!" insisted Rose. "And I can really use a hero about now."

"That, I am not." He was too ashamed to look into her eyes.

"Maybe not at this very minute, but we can work on it."

"What's that supposed to mean?" grumbled Tag, frowning in confusion.

"We are not defined by that one moment when greatness is thrust upon us. Instead, we are defined by all the little things leading up to it."

"And who told you this?"

"You did, Tagius Oliver Yairet."

"I did?"

"You said your father often told you there are times when we are forced to make decisions that turn out in our favour, so we look the part of the hero, but when you consider a man whose every thought, word and action steers them on this course, all these things combined give indication of one's true character."

"This is not the time for a lecture," grunted Tag.

"I agree! But I sense it is time for you to show your true character," stated Rose. "This is no time for self-pity. You are a knight of Fleetwood; rise up and meet this challenge!"

"You think I can do it?"

"I *believe* in you! Of all the people I know in this world, I believe you can do this," assured Rose.

"You do?" Tag searched her eyes for the truth.

"Yes, with all my heart. And so does our friend. As long as Cankles lives, he will believe we will be coming for him. He knows you will never abandon him to Dragonite's mercy, for there will be none."

Tag drew a long breath as he gathered his courage and steeled his resolve. "Then let us not keep him waiting, Princess. We'll find a way to free him and get that dreamstone back."

"Absolutely! We are far from done," declared Rose, "and this quest is far from over."

Tag nodded in agreement, hoisting her up on her feet.

And though Rose spoke with conviction, pleased that Tag was ready to resume this mission, in her heart, she could not. This time, the Princess knew she was the one struggling with self-doubt. If Tag falters again, how was she to summon her courage and continue on without him?

YA Fantasy Series
(in reading order)

The Dream Merchant Saga: Book One,
The Magic Crystal

The Dream Merchant Saga: Book Two,
The Silver Sword

The Dream Merchant Saga: Book Three,
The Crack'd Shield (Available October 2012)

Adult Fantasy Series
(in reading order)

Imago Chronicles: Book One, A Warrior's Tale
Imago Chronicles: Book Two, Tales from the West
Imago Chronicles: Book Three, Tales from the East
Imago Chronicles: Book Four, The Tears of God
Imago Chronicles: Book Five, Destiny's End
Imago Chronicles: Book Six, The Spell Binder
Imago Chronicles: Book Seven, The Broken Covenant
Imago Prophecy (Prequel to Imago Chronicles series)
Imago Legacy (Sequel to Imago Prophecy)

About the Author

*L.T. Suzuki is a fantasy novelist, script-writer and
a practitioner and instructor of the martial arts system,
Bujinkan Budo Taijutsu; a system incorporating
six traditional samurai schools and
three schools of ninjutsu.*

*For more information, please check out L.T. Suzuki's
official website at: **http://web.me.com/imagobooks***